**"I heard you found a toy, Chuck.
A stuffed toy. That true?"**

Chuck pulled it from under his arm. It *was* a bear, smudged with a dark stain. A ribbon was tied around its neck, and what looked like a note.

"Give me the bear, Chuck. I need to see it." Chuck handed it to her. The stain was sticky and the note . . . Dani knees went weak.

Mitch came to her side. He read the note, holding Dani's elbow as if to steady her. "Where did you find this?" he demanded.

Chuck pointed to the alley. A heap of old wooden planks sat on the cement. Chuck pointed down.

Dani shot the flashlight at the ground. Mud and puddles. Then she realized. It wasn't mud on the bear: It was blood. But there'd been too much rain. Even if Chuck had picked up the bear from a puddle of blood, the storms had washed it away and—

"Dani."

Mitch took her wrist, guiding the flashlight to the side of the building. Dani followed the halo of light to the planks. Her stomach turned over.

That was blood . . .

PRAISE FOR
ONE SCREAM AWAY

"Kate Brady has made her mark with a taut, masterful debut of chilling suspense that grabs you by the throat and heart and won't let go. Riveting storytelling packed with unexpected twists and unforgettable characters. Prepare to stay up all night, then sleep with the lights on."

—*I*

New Yo

"Terrific...Fans of tense cat-and-mouse confrontations will want to read this tale."
—*Midwest Book Reviews*

"Gritty and harrowing! You won't be able to put it down."
—BRENDA NOVAK,
New York Times **bestselling author**

"[P]ulls the reader in from the first page...compelling... dark twists and turns."
—SuspenseRomanceWriters.com

"Kate Brady's debut novel is everything romantic suspense should be...Remarkable characters, pitch-perfect pacing, and a memorable villain make *One Scream Away* a standout book."
—ALLISON BRENNAN,
New York Times **bestselling author**

"Intriguing...the author hooked me... many twists and turns and each new discovery adds a sense of urgency to the story...the pages were flying."
—LikesBooks.com

"A wonderful debut author...gripping romantic suspense...I read all night with my heart in my throat... fast-paced and scary."

—DearAuthor.com

"A nail-biting story...a powerful novel full of terrifying details and chilling revelations...edge-of-your-seat intensity."

—CoffeeTimeRomance.com

"*One Scream Away* has it all: rich, multilayered characterizations; a harrowing, serpentine plot; and a diabolical and cunning villain...the sexual tension absolutely smolders...Kate Brady brings a fresh and incredibly skilled voice to the romantic suspense genre and is on the fast track to the top."

—BookLoons.com

"A suspenseful romantic thriller. It also reads like a good police procedural...The suspense is chilling, with page-turning action. The dialogue is snappy, with just enough romance."

—MyShelf.com

Also by Kate Brady

One Scream Away

LAST
TO DIE

KATE BRADY

FOREVER

NEW YORK   BOSTON

This book is a work of fiction. Names, characters, places, and incidents are the product of the author's imagination or are used fictitiously. Any resemblance to actual events, locales, or persons, living or dead, is coincidental.

Book design by Giorgetta Bell McRee
Cover design by Diane Luger
Cover illustration by Dale Fiorello

Forever
Hachette Book Group
237 Park Avenue
New York, NY 10017
Visit our website at www.HachetteBookGroup.com.

Forever is an imprint of Grand Central Publishing.
The Forever name and logo is a trademark of Hachette Book Group, Inc.

Printed in the United States of America

First Printing: September 2010

10 9 8 7 6 5 4 3 2 1

For Brady and the kids, of course.

ACKNOWLEDGMENTS

To Celia Johnson, my wonderful editor, whose patience and kindness are apparently without limits.

To Jenny Bent, my tireless agent, whose supportive nature is surpassed only by her wisdom in All Things Literary.

To Carol, Elaine, and Emily, for you-know-what. Over and over again.

To Chris Dockery, Ph.D., for his willingness to share attributes of nitric acid and other fascinating forensic facts. And for saying, when asked what nitric acid would do to photography paper: "I don't know, but it sounds like a good thing to find out some afternoon when I'm bored in the lab."

To the Delaware County Cultural Arts Center (Ohio), better known as the Arts Castle, of which my childhood memories served as the model for the Sheridan Foundation's physical features.

To Emerson Choir personnel, who accept my split personality without complaint, who nourish me in ways beyond the musical, and who want to be in a book...Does this page count?

CHAPTER
1

Camden Park, Lancaster, Maryland
Sunday, October 3, 7:50 p.m.

WHOOPS AND GIGGLES, the scent of Belgian waffles in the air, the screech of balloons being bullied into bubble-eared poodles. The sidewalks teemed with mothers pushing overstuffed strollers and fathers talking into Bluetooth earpieces, while preschool children orbited their parents like forgotten moons—lagging behind, straying from the paths, lured from arm's reach by the colorful remnants of popped poodles on the ground or the call of a snow cone vendor. Bait, if you were a child molester or kidnapper. Easy pickings.

The killer was neither. Children were of no interest; they committed no crimes. Their mothers did. Heinous, unspeakable crimes they thought would go unpunished.

Wrong.

One such woman was about to learn that. Young, with dark flowing hair and porcelain cheeks, she lurked behind a magician's kiosk, aiming her cheap little camera at the

Kinney family—Robert and Alana and their two-year-old son, Austin. For the past hour, she had secretly trailed the Kinneys through the carnival, snapping photo after photo of the child. Yes, two years after the fact, her conscience had apparently kicked in.

Too little, bitch. Too late.

Oblivious to her own shadow, the woman hunched deeper into her denim jacket and followed the Kinneys into the parking lot, keeping to the outer row of cars then edging into the woods to sneak more photos of little Austin. Fool. She was making things easy, tucked out of sight with her righteous ambition and her camera. The killer cut between cars and closed in, face lowered though there was little chance of being recognized: boots, cap, beard. Loose nylon jacket with big square pockets. Trusty shears inside.

Easy, now. Watch, wait for the right moment. The Kinneys headed for the far corner of the parking lot, Austin's legs straddling his father's neck, his little face stuck in a blue cloud of cotton candy. Robert Kinney pushed a button in his hand and a black Mercedes bleeped to life, and the woman who was about to die skirted behind a row of huge rhododendrons. The killer straightened, adrenaline surging. She was only fifteen feet away. Distracted, out of sight, unsuspecting.

Now.

The killer came in fast, from behind, shears aiming for that slender throat like a missile. The woman must have heard; she whirled and opened her mouth to scream, but the blades sank into her larynx and the sound came out *Unkh*. Her knees buckled and she dropped, the shears plunging in and out, in and out, time dragging each thrust into the slow motion of a dream. *The cheek, don't leave the cheek.* The shears pulled out and smashed higher against her face, the smooth flesh turning to pulp, blood spraying onto the killer's lips, tasting like copper.

Fifteen seconds, maybe twenty—Stop now, before she's gone. It's important that she live long enough to understand what's happening. Quit, stand up. Breathe.

The killer straightened, lungs heaving, and wiped spittle onto the jacket's sleeve. The woman lay wide-eyed on the ground, her knees pulling in like an accordion losing air. A gurgle bubbled from her throat and her heart kept at it for another few seconds, then that beautiful moment of dawning came to her eyes.

She knew. In that final, glorious second, the women always understood. *Take it*, her dying eyes said.

Yes, now, take it. For Kristina. To bring her back.

The killer knelt, gathered a handful of blood-slick hair, and sawed at it with the shears until the hank came free. One step closer to retribution.

A car horn blasted, picking up time again. Shit, get going—there's still so much to do. Call Fulton; tonight, he would earn his pay. Even back here in the woods, if left, the woman's body would eventually be found. There was no time for that sort of complication. Only a week until the meeting with Kristina.

So, pocket the shears and the hair. And take the camera—for God's sake, don't leave the camera. Shot after shot of Austin Kinney.

The killer looked down, satisfaction pulsing in every vein, then pulled out an embossed card and opened it. The clock was ticking, but this was important: Keep the records straight. On the right side of the card, a scrawled promise: *Next Sunday, Kristina, 7:00 p.m.* On the left, written in a different hand, a list of six names. Smears of brownish-red marked through the first three.

The killer bent, touched a finger to the dead woman's cheek, then placed the glistening red ink on the fourth name and dragged a bloody line across it. Woman Number Four, done. Only two more to go.

Now, to tie up the loose ends the dead woman had unraveled. The killer gave a final glance to the body and walked away, keeping to the woods and digging out a pre-paid cell phone. Fulton answered on the first ring. "Are you with Russell Sanders?"

Fulton yawned. "He's been in his apartment all evening."

"What's he doing?"

"How the hell should I know? He's alone, spent some time in the kitchen."

Okay. So at least Sanders wasn't out talking to the police. Maybe the dead woman hadn't told him yet that she'd found Austin Kinney. Still, she had consulted with Sanders, that much was certain. Probably planned to run right over to him with the camera full of pictures tonight. Reason enough to make sure he didn't go digging around trying to uncover secrets, or worse, calling his buddy Mitch Sheridan.

"You want me to take him?" Fulton. He was getting antsy. "He's pacing. Looks like he might be on the phone."

Calling police? The dead woman? Mitch? Sanders had to be stopped.

"Yes. Take him now."

The bandages reeked, the tang of infection wrinkling Mitch Sheridan's nostrils even from several feet away. An aging Kurd crouched still as a heron, robes pooling around his ankles and grenade launcher propped against his one good shoulder. The sun pulled ripples of heat from the sand, while in the distance, row upon row of tents sagged against their poles, like soldiers too weary to stand.

K-chhr, k-chhr.

The camera's shutter whirred. Mitch zoomed in with the Leica. Not too small; keep the stump of the man's right shoulder in the frame, the bandages filthy and oozing. Don't ask his name—that was a cardinal rule. Don't think about the pain or wonder how it happened. Just get the pictures, tell the story.

K-chhr.

"Your turn," Mitch said, standing and tucking his Leica into the case hanging around his neck. The kid stepped in, about ten years old, and aimed a second camera just as Mitch had done. Mitch had met him soon after arriving at the refugee camp, found him digging through a trash pile with a mongrel dog. The kid was fascinated by the camera and after a few days, Mitch let him try his hand with an extra Canon. He was good, had a good eye.

Mitch started to bend down but noticed the sentry rise from his crouch. The old eyes crinkled into the sunrise, his body quivering like a live wire. "Firoke," *he whispered.*

Mitch frowned. Firoke, firoke. *He should know that word, but couldn't place it. Not until a sound started in the distance.*

Thwp-thwp-thwp-thwp...

Jesus, firoke. *Helicopter, in Sořani.*

Mitch's heart lurched. "Come on," *he said, grabbing the boy's hand. He had to get to shelter. The sentry shouted into a radio, frantic, the sound of the chopper growing louder. A hundred yards ahead, the camp erupted. Men grabbing weapons, women racing about, crying for their children.*

Thwp-thwp-thwp...

"Faster," Mitch shouted, his hand a vise grip on the kid's. The chopper swooped in, a giant bee, and the boy stumbled, kicking up sand. Mitch hauled him to his feet. "Run," he said, but the rotors hacked up his voice and threw it to the sky where the chopper stopped in midair. The doors slid open. Rivers of terror poured down.

Bombs. Explosions. Gunfire.

Mitch kept running, crouching over the boy and covering his head, geysers of sand exploding in every direction. Fifty yards from shelter, forty. Keep go—

His legs went out from under him; the kid screamed. Mitch humped halfway up, spitting sand. Don't let go. Whatever you do, don't let go of the kid. But his legs gave out and pain seared his limbs. The kid yelled at him, tugging on his hand.

Let him go, *Mitch thought.* He can get to shelter. *But his fingers squeezed tighter, while sand and debris and hot spatters of blood rained against his face like tiny darts. He tried to crawl, but it was as if the desert had turned to quicksand. He couldn't drag his legs beneath him.*

"Come," the boy cried, and Mitch knew he had to do it. Let go.

He cursed and opened his hand. "Run," he yelled, and the boy took off. Mitch watched, sand blurring his vision, and the boy dashed toward the shelter of the camp, closer, clos—

The sky went white.

"Noo!" Mitch screamed, the ground rattling. The boy jumped, thrown into the air. He looked like a rag doll, limp and helpless, hurtled through a silent sky, complete

*with pigtails and ribbons, ice cream in his hand. What?
Mitch shook his head; it made no sense. But it wasn't the
boy now, it was Mitch's little sister, Aubrey, who'd twisted
from his hand and run into the street.* Don't let go. *But he
had. Mitch called out, the battle coming back to his ears
again, and from high above, the chopper began to bleep,
like a dump truck backing up.* Bleep-bleep—

Mitch jerked. His eyes popped open and he jolted
upright, heart slamming into his rib cage.

The dream again. He cursed, letting the sound of his
voice scatter the nightmare, like dust from an old blanket shaken in the wind. He rubbed a hand over his face
and found it damp with perspiration, his breaths coming short. For Christ's sake, he thought he'd gotten past
this. He'd put his sister's tragic impulse from mind two
decades ago, and this wasn't Iraq. He was in Switzerland
now—he had been for six months. In a hospital for two,
fighting for his life, then at rehab learning to walk again,
then to this bungalow with its comfortable furnishings,
state-of-the-art physical therapy equipment, breathtaking
view of the Alps. The perks of wealth. No choppers here,
no bombs or photographs of a kid he didn't save. Just the
incessant *bleep-bleep* from a nightstand a foot away.

The satellite phone.

He reached to the nightstand. Only one person would be
calling him on the sat phone: Russell Sanders. Damn him.

Mitch picked it up, grunted.

"Mitch, are you there? Can you hear me?"

He flipped on a lamp and dropped his head against the
phone. It was the size of a brick, like the walkie-talkies
he and his brother used to play with as kids, crawling
around in the web of drainpipes at Sedalia Park, dodging

goose shit as they emerged from any one of a half dozen culverts on the bank of the lake. Except that what used to be static at fifty yards now allowed conversation halfway around the world. He cleared his throat. "I can hear you," he said.

"Christ, I was afraid you wouldn't answer."

"I'm not coming home, Russ. Get off my back. I told you, I'm done."

"You don't mean that. You need to show the pictures, tell the stories. You need it like you need to breathe."

"Like hell I do." Mitch dragged his legs over the bed, forced himself to sit up. There was a time he believed his photographs made a difference, but the attack on the camp at Ar Rutbah had only proved it was never enough. No matter what he did, the bleeding didn't stop. Somewhere in the world, the choppers still came, famines still raged, diseases still killed. Little boys got blown to the sky.

"Damn it, Mitch, this exhibition matters more than the others."

"Sure. It's the one where famous photographer and humanitarian J. M. Sheridan let a kid get blown to bits. Big money for shots of that, I'm sure."

"That's not what I mean."

"You want to do the Ar Rutbah show? Do it without me. You're lucky you even have those pictures. It wasn't my choice to send them." No, some well-meaning hospital staffer had gone through Mitch's things, given them to his brother Neil sometime during Mitch's unconscious phase. Neil, in turn, had sent them on to Russ. Mitch had never even seen most of them. Not that he wanted to.

"Mitch, this is important." Russ paused. "If something happens, promise me you'll do this show."

"If something happens?" The hairs on the back of Mitch's neck stood up. "What are you talking about?"

"I'm in trouble, Mitch. It's about the Foundation. You need to come home. Mount the show."

"Oh, please…" But Russell's tone of voice made Mitch stop. It wasn't like Russ to try to manipulate him. "Look, I don't know—"

"What?" Russ said, but his voice seemed aimed away from the phone. Mitch heard a thump.

"Russell?"

"No." Something scraped in Mitch's ear, then Russ again. "*Unh.*"

"Russ, what's happening?"

Another sound, some shuffling. Maybe a piece of furniture dragging across the floor. "Russ, what's going on?"

"*Mitch.*"

Mitch stood, wide awake now, his left leg screaming at him. He gripped the phone tighter. "Russ."

More scrapes and scuffs, another voice. A man. Panic trickled in. Mitch listened, straining to interpret sounds that were happening on the other damn side of the planet, then, as suddenly as the commotion had started, silence streamed over the satellite phone. No more voices, no more scuffle.

"Russell."

But all Mitch could hear was the thundering in his chest. The connection was dead.

CHAPTER
2

A STORM ROLLED THROUGH Dani Cole's dreams. Thunder mingling with gunshots, until a cell phone chimed in and yanked her from sleep. A nose nuzzled her chin.

"Ick," she muttered. "Get off."

The forty-five-pound pit bull on her chest didn't move. Dani pushed at the muzzle with one hand and groped for the phone with the other. "What?"

Chief Gibson.

"Wake up," he said. Gibson wasn't a man to waste words on pleasantries, at least not to Dani. She rolled upright, shoving Runt to the other cushion of the sofa. Two weeks since she'd slept in her bedroom. The thunder and gunshots were worse in there.

"What's going on?" she asked.

"We have a murder at Camden Park," Gibson said. "You're on it."

She must still be asleep. He wasn't making sense. "You mean, I'm back?" she said. "No more administrative duty?"

"You're back," Gibson said, but he sounded unhappy about it. "Tifton caught the body. He said he needs you to look at it."

Dani stood, alert now. Tifton? They'd been partnered back in their patrol days, but moved through the ranks separately. Getting back on a case was great. Doing it with Tift was even better.

But not with Internal Affairs watching her every move. Dani tamped back a thump of anger and padded to the living room window. "Hold on," she said. She stuck two fingers through the blinds and scissored them open. Sure enough, a gray sedan squatted against the curb, less than a block away.

She dropped the blinds. "So if I'm working again, get IA off me," she said into the phone.

Gibson hedged. "I'm not the one who ordered it."

"But you can call them off. For two weeks, I haven't been able to pee without those bastards breathing down my back. I'm not sneaking around making any deals with Ty Craig and you know it. Call them off." She paused, frustration burning her cheeks. "I'm not my father, Chief."

But Dave Gibson had never believed that. Dani knew he was just waiting for her to cross the same lines her father had crossed before he'd gotten fired, before he spent the rest of his pathetic life as an ex-cop and a two-bit thug for Ty Craig. In spite of Dani's record in the department, Gibson still gave her the kind of look you'd give something crawling under the kitchen counter.

She held out. "Am I working or not?"

He cursed. "I'll handle IA. You get over to Camden Park."

Twenty minutes later, twisting her hair up into a quick ponytail, Dani watched the sedan pull away from the curb and a small weight lifted from her shoulders. She rolled through the gates at Camden Park a little before seven-thirty. A uniform waved her onto a television-perfect crime scene: yellow ribbon strung around the perimeter of a parking lot and disappearing into the woods, half a dozen black-and-whites parked at various angles, a couple of gray Chevrolets belonging to investigators. An ambulance sat square to the curb, the back open and two EMTs sitting on the bumper swapping tales—no one to save. Members of the media were roped off at a respectable distance, as if distance mattered with the kinds of magnifying lenses they used, and a handful of detectives in coats and loosened ties stood in the parking lot.

Reginald Tifton was one. He spoke with two of the uniforms, pointing in an arc behind them. Dani walked up as the officers jogged off in the direction Tifton had pointed.

"About time, Nails," he said using her departmental nickname. He dropped from the curb and met her in an empty parking slot. He was a big man of forty-five, black, going for wife number three, with a bowling-ball head perched directly on wide shoulders—no neck. He spoke like a Yale graduate, except when he decided to turn on the street charm and make a suspect believe he was from the hood. He was actually from the old-money area of Cheshire Hills, and secretly, Dani suspected he *had* gone to Yale. "Your beauty routine hold you up this morning?"

"Screw you," she said. Too early for creativity.

Tifton's eyes homed in on hers. "I haven't seen you since your dad's funeral. You hanging in there?"

Something tugged in her chest. Not heartache—her relationship with her father certainly hadn't merited that. Must be heartburn from the coffee. "You mean, do I enjoy pushing papers and doing mandatory grief counseling? Sure." She looked around the scene. "What do we have?"

Tifton knew when to back off. He jerked his chin toward the bushes. "Guy trolling the woods with a metal detector found a dead woman. Stabbed sometime during the clownfest this weekend."

"Why did you call me?" she asked, starting toward the site of the body.

"Thought you might know something on this one the rest of us don't."

"Why?"

"The vic was one of your charity cases."

Dani stopped, the words hitting like ice water. Someone she knew? A knot climbed to her throat and she picked up her pace. Tifton jogged after her.

"Nails, hold on. It's ugly back there. It's—"

The feet came into view and Dani hesitated, slowing as she approached the body. The left side of the face was battered beyond recognition, but it was a woman with dark hair, her knees in a fetal position as if she'd pulled herself in while dying. Her throat had been slashed—hacked, rather—and the dark puddle beneath her crawled with flies. Even in the open air, the smell of death hung over her: dried blood and waste and stale flesh.

Dani stepped around to look at the face, caught a glimpse of the flesh peeking between blouse lapels. Her gaze snagged on a tiny rosebud tattoo.

"Aw, no," she said, shock pushing her back. She turned away. "No, no, no."

Tifton said, "It's her, right? Rosie?"

The backs of Dani's eyeballs prickled and she braced her hands on her knees, squeezing her eyes closed to keep the tears from coming. After a moment, she looked again at what was left of the face and forced her lungs to function. "Rose McNamara."

"Okay," Tifton said, then called to another investigator over Dani's back: "I was right, Carter, it's Rose McNamara. She hooked for Ty Craig out of Readi—"

"No," Dani said. "She hasn't been hooking for a couple of years. She moved away, called me about a month ago to tell me she was back." Dani turned from the body, looking at Tifton. "She wasn't tricking anymore—not for Craig, not for anybody. She had a job at the Big Lots on Grimby Street. She was paying rent on her own apartment and trying to mend fences with her family. She was *making* it."

Grief came in a flood, but Dani conquered it and took a deep breath, forcing herself back to work. Don't think about who the victim was, just do the job. Pretend she's a stranger and focus on finding the sonofabitch who would do something like this.

She pushed up her chin and walked the perimeter of the body, taking in the details. The victim's eyes were open, sunken, her throat stabbed into a mishmash of blood and torn tissue. The right side of her face was untouched—turned to the ground, probably—and the fingers of her right hand were open, hollow, as if she'd been holding something. Her limbs were stiff with rigor. She was fully clothed, and her hair—

"What the hell?" Dani crouched down to get a better look.

"Someone took a chunk," the ME said.

Dani was shocked. "Here? You mean postmortem?"

"Postmortem, I can't say. Here? I can say. He probably used the same object to cut the hair he used to stab her throat."

"Object. What kind of object?"

"Long blade of some sort. Narrow, single-edged."

"Like a hunting knife, or bowie?" Dani's father had used one during hunting season, to slit the throats of his kills and hang the carcasses to bleed. Dani still remembered the smell in the yard: sharp, coppery.

"Could be. Or boning knife," the ME said. "You know, like chefs use."

Dani inched around the body, trying to feel the killer—hunter or chef?—then sank in a crouch next to Rosie's face. Tifton bent down beside her.

"So, what's the theory?"

Monster, Dani thought. "I don't have a theory." But an image reeled through her mind: some maniac decorating his bedposts with women's hair.

"Come on, you're the one with that degree in psychology. What does Freud say about knives and hair?"

She started to snap at him then remembered it was Tifton. He wasn't ridiculing the degree; he was serious. She shook her head. "Freud's specialty was penises. I don't know what he said about hair." She stood up, took a deep breath. "But whatever's going on here, it's not anonymous. You don't get this kind of overkill for nothing. It's personal. Sexual, maybe."

"So she knew him, or he knew her. That might explain why she came back here in the woods with him."

"Got some footprints here," a CSI guy said. "Boots, probably."

"Boo-yah," Tifton said. Prints were good.

The crime scene guy started taking the print and the dance got under way, the steps rehearsed three or four hundred times a year in big cities like Philly and Baltimore, a few dozen times a year in bedroom communities like Lancaster. Techies, uniforms, and detectives—all donning booties and gloves—went about their jobs: studying the body, canvassing for witnesses, searching the woods and parking lot and collecting items that would ultimately prove there had been a carnival.

Dani hung with Tifton until reporters cornered her into updates for the noon news reports. She was careful not to give away much, careful to make sure the department came across concerned: "Police are doing everything possible to protect innocent citizens like our victim..." And, in case the murderer watched the news, she threw in some firecracker words: *stupid, freak, monster.* If this was more than a random act—and the hacked hair meant *something*—maybe the killer would take up the gauntlet.

Two hours into it, the ME gave a shout: "We're ready to flip her."

Dani shut down the interviews and went back to where the ME and one of his assistants flanked Rosie. A techie started to bag her phone and Dani said, "Let me have it." Wearing fresh latex gloves, she took it, then forced herself to watch while Rosie's body was ceremoniously flipped.

Nothing. No new wounds on her back side. No murder weapon beneath her. No clues dropped on the ground by her murderer, at least not those visible to the naked eye.

She walked to the parking lot with Rosie's phone, bent over the hood of Tifton's car, and pressed Power. Copied down numbers from recent calls, incoming calls, missed calls, then handed off the phone to a crime scene specialist and took out her own. She dialed the precinct. Spelled each name and number to a desk officer.

Fifteen minutes later, the guy called back and recited the names and addresses of people matching the numbers from Rosie's phone. Dani recognized a few of them—Rosie's sister, her landlord, her mom. No one identifiable as a boyfriend or lover. No one unusual at all, at least not that Dani could tell, until the last name on the list. *Russell Sanders.* For half a second, the name didn't register, then she saw the rest of the tagline: *JMS Foundation.*

Her belly flopped. She remembered a Russell Sanders. She'd never met him, but she'd heard about him—one summer eighteen years ago. A summer she'd worked hard to forget.

She glanced around, illogically making sure no one else noticed the secret flutter in her belly, then checked the time of the call: Sunday, 8:07 p.m.—the last call made from Rosie's phone. There were two other calls to the same number from earlier in the weekend.

"Careful, your brow is gonna stay that way." Tifton had stepped over to her, pressing his thumb into the frown line above her nose.

She brushed his hand away, using her own phone to dial that last number. She had to be sure.

Voice mail picked up. *"You've reached Russell Sanders, managing director at the JM Sheridan Foundation for Photography Art. Please leave a message..."*

Oh, God, she was right. Sheridan.

She took a deep breath, trying to wash the name from her mind and concentrate on what the call meant for Rosie. She turned to Tift. "What would a hooker-turned-Big-Lots-cashier have to do with an upscale art-photography guild?" Tifton didn't understand. "The last call Rosie made was to Russell Sanders."

"Who's Russell Sanders?"

"The director of the J. M. Sheridan foundation."

"Open eyes, open hearts. *That* Sheridan?"

Like there was another. Despite every effort, a memory unraveled: Local boy turned photojournalist extraordinaire. Rich, handsome do-gooder and champion of every underdog. Once, he'd tried to be Dani's champion.

For that, she'd broken his nose.

Jesus, get a grip. She'd put memories of Mitch Sheridan away years ago, along with any futile regrets or silly pipe dreams. "Yeah," she said to Tifton, "that one."

"Pretty posh circle of friends for a hooker."

"I told you, she wasn't hooking anymore." But he was right. What would connect Rosie McNamara to a social paragon like Russell Sanders?

"Looks like we're done here," Tifton said, pointing. A county van pulled away, the coroner's wagon behind it. The crime scene unit was packing it in. "We need to get to Rosie's next of kin."

A finger of sadness touched Dani's chest. She'd met Rosie's mother and sister—a couple of years ago when Rosie was still in trouble. They were hurting then because of their estrangement. Dani could only imagine how much worse it would be now. "I'll go talk to them as soon as the ME's office makes it official."

"Meanwhile, let's go see if we can catch this Sanders dude. He's the last person Rosie talked to and a piece that doesn't fit."

"Sure," Dani said, trying not to react. Relax. Russell Sanders wouldn't know her, and the Foundation's namesake, James Mitchell Sheridan, was—as always—

overseas. The only thing to think about now was finding Rosie's killer.

Dani drove from the park, got stuck in the wrong lane, and did a U-turn across a bed of flowers in the median. Tifton laid on the horn behind her—he liked flowers—but she ignored him and headed toward Franklin Avenue, putting the Sheridan Foundation out of her mind and filling it with Rosie instead. Two years ago, Dani had interviewed her in a case. In the first ten seconds, Dani's heart had gone out to her. Other cops looked at her and saw a street bust for their record. Dani looked at her and saw a kid who was...lost. Sixteen years old, with the pale, blank expression of someone who didn't understand how she'd gotten there. Dani had cornered a couple of other hookers and learned that Rosie had disappeared from the streets for a few months, and when she came back, she wasn't quite right. Dani also learned that her pimp was Ty Craig.

That's when it got personal. It shouldn't have, but it did. Ty Craig was an upper-class, fancy-ass criminal whose interests in the underworld—high-end hookers and high-interest loans—were fronted by a legitimate chain of jewelry stores and real-estate interests. Lancaster's own version of a mob boss. He protected himself with significant contributions to the right politicians and well-placed community service, and he stayed above the law by keeping a cop or two in his pocket.

Like Dani's father.

Shame prickled her skin and she cursed. She hadn't been foolish enough to take on Craig, but neither would she send sixteen-year-old Rosie McNamara back to him. So Dani had brought in Keller Brooks, a psychologist at a teen help center. Keller was one of the good ones, and eventually, Rosie came around. When she called Dani four weeks ago, she'd come back home to be close to her family, had done her GED and found a job, an apartment. She was doing great.

Until some freak hacked her up at a carnival. Took a hank of her hair.

Ty Craig? He didn't like to lose employees, but above all, Craig was a business tycoon. Personal rage wasn't his style, especially two years after the fact. Russell Sanders? That would be too easy. Still, he was a strange person to be the last call Rosie made. That alone merited a chat with him.

Dani was a block from the photography foundation when her phone rang. Tifton. "Turn around," he said. "The squad sergeant just called."

"Why?"

"Russell Sanders's son is at the precinct filing a missing persons report. Sanders disappeared."

CHAPTER
3

DANI BANGED THROUGH the double glass doors of Homicide in front of Tifton, then stopped to let a uniform fill them in.

"Brad Harper says his father hasn't been around since early last night," the cop said.

"Harper?" Tifton asked. "Why don't they have the same name?"

"Harper is his mother's name. He was fourteen or fifteen when he first met his dad. Harper was a bigwig corporate lawyer for a while, then left the big bucks to do pro bono work at the Foundation for his dad. He and Sanders share the house next door to the museum."

"Does he look good for anything to you?" Dani asked.

"He's not all broken up about his dad being gone, if that's what you mean." The cop shrugged. "Then again, there's not really anything that looks like foul play."

Except that his dad was the last person Rosie called, Dani thought.

They went down the hall to an interview room, an eight-by-eight cement square equipped with a table, three wooden chairs, and a video camera. Tifton paused to straighten his tie. This wasn't the crowd to play thug.

"Mr. Harper," he said, entering and offering a hand. "I'm Detective Reginald Tifton and this is Sergeant Dani Cole. We'll be looking into your father's whereabouts."

Harper stood. He was a slender man, an inch or two shy of six feet, wearing a pin-striped suit and burgundy tie with paisley whorls. His face was sleek, not unattractive, but his features were sharp and his eyes could have belonged to a gerbil. Or a lawyer.

"Tell us why you're worried," Tifton said.

"We're premiering an exhibition at the Foundation this Saturday night," Harper said. "This morning, my father was supposed to meet with the setup crew but didn't show."

"He couldn't have forgotten?" Dani asked.

"It's the most hyped exhibit in years. The *New York Times*, *People* magazine, *Photography in Review*, and a dozen other reviewers are expected at Friday's preview. These are the pictures of a camp that was attacked, where Mitch almost died."

"Mitch..." Tifton prompted, and Dani found her throat going dry. She'd heard about the attack, held her breath and searched the Internet for updates for weeks afterward.

"James Mitchell Sheridan," Harper said, a little chill in his voice. "He's the Foundation's namesake. The photographer of the exhibition. He's been an asshole about it, but Dad called him last night in Switzerland, around eight-thirty our time, and Mitch heard some noises then the line disconnected. He called me right afterward, convinced something happened to him."

"Like what?" Dani asked.

"He doesn't know. He says he heard bumps, and Dad saying he was in trouble and 'No,' and then he was gone."

"What did you do after Sheridan's call?"

"I was in Philadelphia. I called Dad, but there was no answer. But he'd mentioned that he was meeting someone last night—a woman. So at the time, I didn't think anything about it."

Dani straightened. "Who was he meeting? And where?"

"I don't know."

"Could her name have been Rose McNamara?"

Harper opened his mouth then did a classic double take. "Who?" he asked, but his eyes slid left. Rosie's name had rung a bell.

Dani felt a throb. "You know her." Not a question.

"No, no." He changed gears. "Look, my father doesn't do much confiding in me. If you want to know what women he knows, talk to Mitch."

"In Switzerland?" Tifton asked. He hadn't missed Harper's sudden interest in shifting their scrutiny to a man half a world away.

"He's on his way home. His plane's due at BWI this afternoon."

"What?" Dani's pulse skittered. Tifton frowned and she reined in her shock. "I mean, I didn't hear you. Did you say Sheridan's coming here?"

Harper nodded.

Oh, God.

"What do you mean, he's being an asshole?" Tifton asked. "He and your dad don't get along?"

"They get along. Mitch just doesn't want to do the show. Or any more shows. Says he's retiring his camera."

Dani blinked. Mitch, without a camera?

Tifton said, "I understand you and your dad live together. Can you let us look around?"

"No," Harper said. "I mean, yes, you can look around, but we don't live together. The Foundation owns the house next to headquarters. The first two floors are split into our two apartments, and the third floor is another one. My father and I just share an entrance hall."

"Who lives on the third floor?" Dani asked. "Someone who may have seen him?"

"It's empty. We use it for guests, clinicians, VIPs. Sometimes Mitch stays there."

Dani tried not to think about that. "Did your father happen to mention where he was going to meet the woman? A restaurant, an apartment…"

"No."

"A park, maybe?"

"I told you, I don't know." Harper stood, frowning. He was finished. Didn't like talking about the woman, Dani thought. She started to open the door for him, then cocked her head. "Do you or your father hunt?"

Harper frowned at her. "No. Why?"

"What about cook?" she asked.

He was confused. "Dad cooks. He's quite the chef, in fact."

"Huh," she said, and stepped from the door. Harper left and Dani waited until he was down the hall before turning to Tifton. "I think we ought to go see what kind of knives Russell Sanders keeps handy."

The shears hung on a hook over a worktable, old and dull, with rust eating tiny notches in the blades. They'd always had the rust. Even twenty years ago when they'd hung from a hook on the side of a kitchen cupboard—a constant warning—the rust had been there. Mother had called them antique, but they weren't. They were just old. So old and rusty they hurt, the blades tugging and ripping at hair.

Shorter, Mother would say, hacking at handfuls almost too short to grasp. Spittle sprayed from her mouth, her teeth clenched in rage as she sawed away. *You know better. Keep it short…*

The killer chilled with the memories and flipped on a small space heater. The room was cool, a third-story dormer designed as storage not a work space, and if anyone chose to climb the steep, narrow staircase to get here, that's what they'd see: boxes of long-forgotten Christmas decorations, a couple of outcast lamps, a few pieces of exiled furniture.

Go deeper, though, past the dusty collection of life's excesses, and the true purpose of the dormer was revealed: six easels standing in an arc, each displaying a photo of one woman on the list. Four of the portraits, now including Rose McNamara's, bore faces sizzled and burned. Two were yet unscathed.

But not for long. *Sunday.* It was finally happening— after all these years and heartbreak almost too intense to endure—retribution was at hand. Absolution.

So, get busy. The wig was time-consuming, though a labor of love…Hook, poke through, twist, hook, poke through, twist, over and over again, one thin strand at a time until sometimes it seemed there was no feeling left in the fingers. The work went faster now than it had with the first couple of women—practice makes perfect— but it would still take hours to get Rosie's dark tresses woven in.

The hair was ready now, washed free of the blood,

conditioned, and dried. The comb slid through the strands with barely a catch, an overhead light reflecting off the dark tail. Beautiful locks. Not permed or damaged, and not too short, either. Short hair was a nightmare. So much waste.

But Rosie's would be ideal.

The killer hit a button on a small TV and settled onto a work stool. Pulled out the hackle with its five hundred thin nails and began slapping the black tail of hair onto it. Slap and pull, slap and pull, letting the weak strands break away, combing through the rest until every strand was straight and not a tangle remained. The TV anchor droned through the noon news in the background. So far, there'd been no mention of McNamara—not last night, not today. So far, her sudden absence from the world hadn't drawn any attention after all.

Still, let the news play, just in case. And slip the tail of Rosie's hair between the holding cards. Ready. Bring the wig block close and decide on placement...A swatch of Rosie's dark length, right along the cheek? Or would it be more beautiful to spread it out, working it into the shades of red and gold and light brown so the differences in color weren't so pronounced? What would Kristina like?

"...*a carnival at a park over the weekend.*"

The anchor's voice slipped in.

"*The woman, whose name is not yet being released, was brutally stabbed in the throat...*"

What? Rosie's hair dropped to the table. On the TV screen, a camera panned a parking lot filled with emergency workers. It cut to a group of detectives and then pulled back from the scene and scanned the parking lot along the woods.

No, it couldn't be. But it was. That was Camden Park.

Body? Panic bubbled up, tainted with fury. *Body.* How?

Fulton. Damn him.

He answered the phone right away, defending himself from the get-go.

"I couldn't get to her," he said. The *bastard.* "I went there after I picked up Sanders and found a bunch of vendors and performers and shit. You didn't tell me you were sending me into a fucking carnival."

"You could've gone back later."

"I did. But they were breaking down the rides and cleaning up. A guy noticed my truck, talked to me. I couldn't hang around."

Rage seeped in, like an icicle dripping poison. So, so close—and now Fulton might have risked everything. *Sonofabitch.*

But he couldn't be cut loose. He knew where the bodies were buried—literally. He'd put them there. And Fulton's type wasn't easy to find. A misdiagnosed schizophrenic who was really a sociopath, Fulton had been born without that quirk of chemistry that allowed for emotion. There were no therapies or medications for men like him; modern psychiatry hadn't yet learned how to manufacture a conscience.

He also had reason not to risk being discovered. The next time Ron Fulton went behind bars, he'd never come out again.

A reminder worth repeating: "I could ruin you."

"You're not that self-destructive," Fulton answered, a thread of arrogance woven in. "You knew this girl had a family. You knew there would be police this time."

"I thought she'd be reported missing, not found dead at a crime scene a forensics team could tear apart."

"What will they find?"

What *would* they find? Nothing. A footprint or two, which would lead them no further than a man with size eleven feet, wearing boots. Rosie's own hair and blood. No camera. No connection.

"Nothing. They won't find anything."

"Then relax," Fulton said. "They'll probably find out she'd been talking to Sanders, but we both know he's a dead end. No pun intended."

"I just don't want another situation like Jill Donnelly."

In the dormer, Jill Donnelly's eyes seemed to glow from her easel. A tall, stringy redhead, after years of estrangement, she'd made a call to her family the very day she died. They went to police, but with no body and no reason to suspect foul play, nothing had come of it. Hookers come and go: Jill Donnelly, they concluded, was just another who'd gone.

Still, it had been too close. The fact that anyone had noticed Jill's absence at all had served as a wake-up call.

"It's not like they'll find Donnelly," Fulton said, "or any of the others. Thanks to me."

All right, breathe. Fulton was a necessary evil, and there was nothing to be done now. And all the more reason to hurry, mark the last two off the list before the discovery of McNamara's body kicked over too many stones. "I'll need you tonight."

Fulton chuckled. "I'm impressed."

"Fuck you. Don't mess it up this time. Take this body to Virginia, to the mine shafts."

"I know where the mine shafts are. Where will you leave her?"

"Near the old railroad depot, north of Reading. You know it?"

"I know it. A helluva lot better choice than a fucking carnival."

They hung up, the television still rolling, the anchor gleefully returning with a segment called "More Details."

It was bullshit and more bullshit, just the news team creating hype. The camera followed a body bag on a gurney, interviewed bystanders and carnival officials and police, but they clearly had no leads, no ideas.

So relax. Fulton was right, there was nothing to worry about.

A detective's face filled the screen giving an interview, a name appearing at the bottom in capital letters: SGT. DANI COLE, LCPD. Something familiar about her. Cole. Who was she? She spoke with the reporter:

"...what kind of monster would do something like this...doing everything we can..."

The memory kicked in. Cole. This was in Rose McNamara's file. This was the bitch-cop who'd cozied up to Rose McNamara two years ago. Arrested her then cut her loose and pulled her off the streets.

"...working to protect other young women like the victim, who appears to be innocent of any wrongdoing..."

Innocent. Wild, sharp-edged fury cut through surprise. Rose McNamara, innocent?

The word turned hot, rage swelling like a cancer. Sergeant Dani Fucking Cole, defending Rose McNamara—for a second time—saying she couldn't imagine what kind of monster would do this to an innocent woman...

The news went on to the next story, but Dani Cole's face stuck in mind, like a tick. Stupid, arrogant, misguided.

Promising to punish the wrongdoer and avenge an *innocent* girl.

I think not, Detective Cole. You've done enough in Rose McNamara's life. There'll be no avenging her now, nor stopping the rest from dying. You say you can't imagine what kind of monster would do this?

Hold on, bitch. I'll show you.

CHAPTER
4

Rosie's mother had a touch of the Irish in her—pale skin, dark hair, a little lilt in her speech. She was built lean and strong, an outdoorsy woman in her forties. Had a temper lurking beneath her grief.

"She came back thinkin' everything was fine," Mary McNamara said, her voice breaking. "Like she'd not already sent her father to his grave for worryin' about her. And now—"

"Momma, stop." Rosie's older sister, Janet. She was as fair as Rosie had been dark, as plain as Rosie had been striking. She juggled an infant on her hip. Two years ago when Dani had looked them up, Janet told her that Rosie was dead to them, a shame to the family. Today, she looked stricken.

Dani turned to her. "When Rosie called me a few weeks ago, she said you two were back on good terms."

"We were working on it," Janet said, cupping her hand over the baby's head and doing the continuous bounce that mothers do. "She wanted to be with her nephew, Kyle." She touched her cheek to the baby—Kyle—and a tear slid down her face into his baby-fine curls. "She was good with him."

"God forgive her," Mary McNamara muttered, crossing herself.

Maybe, Dani thought, but she wasn't sure Rosie's mother
would. Dani tried to be sensitive but found herself more
sympathetic to Rosie than her family. She'd pulled herself
off the streets and out of Ty Craig's stable. Had come back
to get to know her nephew and make amends with her family, and been greeted with a cool reception at best. So much
for the unconditional love and support of a parent.

Dani set her feelings aside and pushed through the
routine: Who had Rosie been seeing? Was there a man
in her life? What was her mood the last time they spoke?
Mary McNamara confirmed what Dani already knew—
there were no more men, pimps, or drugs. Rosie had
gotten her life together. Now she was just trying to earn
back a place in her family.

Janet helped with lists: Rosie's coworkers, friends,
favorite haunts. Russell Sanders? The name didn't ring
any bells for them.

Thirty minutes into the interview, the calls started
coming. Family, friends, neighbors. A funeral home. Dani
watched Mary and Janet trying to field the calls, everyone
offering condolences but making things worse. Question
after question, and each one catapulted Dani back to her
own hell, just two weeks ago: When do you want to hold
the service, Ms. Cole? Cremation or burial? Is there any
special music your father would have wanted? Where
shall flowers be sent?

I don't know, she thought, her chest squeezing. *He
wasn't supposed to die yet...*

She smothered the thought and left Mary McNamara
with her remaining daughter and grandson, then called
and found Tifton at the Foundation with Brad Harper.

Ten minutes later, with no sign of IA's gray sedan on her tail, she cruised past an enormous stone structure that resembled a castle. A sign tucked into a bed of red bushes and yellow pansies proclaimed it the JMS FOUNDATION FOR PHOTOGRAPHY ART.

Dani slowed to look at it, not for the first time. This was Mitch's legacy, his vehicle for trying to fix the misery of the world, for doing overseas what he hadn't been able to do in his own home. With his rugged good looks and hometown roots, Mitch Sheridan was a local hero. Revealer of injustices and fixer of world tragedies.

Whirlwind summer lover.

Forget it, Dani told herself. *He* probably had.

She rolled on down the street. The castle itself shared the block with a few other huge Victorian homes: a private residence, an interior decorating business, a law office. The one next door must be the one shared by Russ Sanders and Brad Harper.

She got out of her car, found an officer posted at the front of the castle. "Detective Tifton?" she asked.

The guy pointed. "Next door, in the apartment building with Brad Harper."

"Thanks."

Dani walked halfway down the block and entered the lobby of the apartment building. It held an elevator and stairwell straight ahead, and two apartments—one to the right and another to the left. The door to the right was slightly ajar: Sanders's place.

She went in, allowed herself to be awed by the size and splendor for ten seconds, then heard Tift's voice upstairs. She found him in a hallway with Brad Harper, one hand on a doorknob.

"Hey," Tifton said. "I talked to the employees next

door. No one's seen Sanders. And everything downstairs looks normal." He meant: *no bloody knife in the kitchen.*

Dani nodded. "What's this?" she asked, pointing to the room he was about to enter.

"Mr. Harper agreed to let us look around. This is his dad's bedroom."

Dad's bedroom. The thought nearly knocked Dani back a step, but she nudged past Harper and Tifton and entered the room in spite of it. Everything about Sanders's bedroom appeared normal. There was no body sprawled between the bed and the dresser, no smudges on the wall, no bloodstains creeping through the fibers of the bedspread or thunder vibrating the floors...

"As I told you," Harper said, following them into the room, "I came in here and looked around right after Mitch called me. I didn't see anything unusual."

The bedroom had the earmarks of comfort: an Oriental rug over polished cherry floors, classic furniture, a king-size bed with the comforter yanked partway down and decorative pillows strewn on the floor beside. A newspaper, its sections pulled out and restacked with sports on top, lay on a blanket chest at the foot of the bed. A jacket had been tossed on the back of a desk chair and a wallet and spare change sat on the surface

"You didn't consider it unusual that he left his wallet here?" Dani asked Harper.

He flinched, and his eyes darted to the desk. "I didn't notice."

Huh. Dani went to the newspaper: Sunday, October 3. "When does the maid come in?" Clearly, there was one.

"Once a week, on Fridays. She works at the Foundation building next door two nights a week. On Fridays, she comes over here and does our apartments."

It fit. On Fridays, the pillows would all be lined up across the head of the bed, the wrinkles tugged from the comforter and jacket hung in the closet. Anything lying out now had been left since the maid's last visit.

Tifton strolled into the master bath, came out, and headed for the walk-in closet. Dani went to the bed and lifted the comforter. The sheets were rumpled but bright clean—no signs that Sanders had a girlfriend. Harper tensed but didn't say anything: Calling off a search now would be hard to explain.

She moved to the nightstand. A roll of half-gone Tums, a pair of reading glasses, the rest of the sports section. A phone and blank notepad and pen—one of those wood-and-gold pens that probably cost a hundred bucks. Dani flipped on the light on the nightstand, and it was only when the wash of warm yellow hit the notepad that her pulse kicked up.

"Tift," she called, torn between a rush of adrenaline and a wave of sadness. This was going to turn out to be the sonofabitch who butchered Rosie. Mitch Sheridan's dearest friend.

Tifton came out of the closet. Dani held up the notepad, then peeled back the top page and let the light shine through. The indentation of two words appeared.

"Does that say what I think it says?" Tifton asked.

"Do you think it says, 'Camden Park'?"

He nodded, scratching his head. "Guess we better call an Evidence Response Team. And pick up Sheridan. We're gonna need to hear about that phone call he got in Switzerland."

Dani-Fucking-Mother-Teresa-Cole of the LCPD stepped out of Russ Sanders's house, unaware of the eyes that followed her. They had picked her up at the police station after the noon news and followed her to Rosie's mother's house, and now, two hours later, they watched through a Canon 360 from a Saab parked a block away. A magnifying lens picked up the details: dark slacks and a blazer, a light knit shirt underneath. When she moved, the flare of her blazer revealed a police shield on her belt, a gun at her waist. She was slender and leggy, a little long in the torso—probably five-six or -seven. Her hair was the color of black coffee and pulled behind her head in a plain rubber band. Nothing fancy, but good genes had made her one of the lucky ones: high cheekbones and pale eyes, a tomboy who was nonetheless innately feminine, who would turn a man's head without even trying.

And, she was wired. Her hands were balled into fists, her movements agitated. When she stepped onto the front porch she let the screen door go, hitting the big cop as he came through behind her. The two of them talked for a moment. About Rose McNamara and Russ Sanders, no doubt. About monsters. "What kind of monster would do this to an innocent woman?" Cole had asked.

Look this way, Detective. Snap. Snap. Look behind the camera and you'll see. Snap.

Cole's partner held out his fist. They each pulled something from his hand then Cole put her hands on her hips. She said something that was probably obscene, wagging a finger at him until he took her by the shoulders and gave her a gentle shove. She dropped down the stairs and headed for her car.

That's it. The camera came down. Cole was off and running, angry about something. Anxious to avenge Rose McNamara, no doubt.

Stupid bitch. Won't she be surprised when she learns

that tonight, while she's out there trying to find Rosie's killer, another one just like her is going to die? Number Five, Alicia Woodruff. Everything was ready. Fulton was ready. No mistakes this time.

The dashboard clock moved: 3:42. Alicia, given her chosen profession, would just be getting going for the evening.

Plenty of time to deliver a message to Sergeant Cole first. Make sure she understands.

Dani drew the short straw—toothpick, rather—and got drafted to meet Sheridan at the airport. Nerves fraying, she pulled away from the Foundation, took a deep breath, and ordered herself to buck up. For God's sake, eighteen years had gone by and a man like Mitch Sheridan had probably filled every one of them with a different woman. Dani was just one of many.

Besides, this was business.

Halfway to the airport, she called her next-door neighbor. "Becky, hey. It's Dani. Say, could Seth get Runt for a while? I can't get home yet."

"Sure," Becky said. She was a forty-something single mom with a twelve-year-old son who was Runt's favorite person. Not that Runt was particular; Dani had always marveled at that. The bait dog for countless fighters-in-training, by the time Dani came across her, her canine teeth had been yanked out by the trainers and both ears ripped off in the ring. She bore numerous scars of a dog that had spent her entire life getting beat up, yet she was infinitely sweet and docile.

Go figure.

"I'll send him over," Becky said. "You wanna come get her when you get home?"

"Nah, I'll probably be late. Just have Seth put her back in the house when he's had enough slobbery kisses."

Becky chuckled. "Will do."

Dani hung up. She turned her flashers on and pushed through traffic to BWI, bullied her way to the curb outside baggage claim, and used her shield to get through security to Concourse E. The flight was just arriving at a British Airways gate, no one yet off the plane.

She stood across the aisle against the far wall, letting curiosity about Sheridan momentarily run its course. Would she recognize him? Of course she would. Like anyone in Lancaster, she'd seen his publicity photo: a shot capturing his height and breadth and the classic hard edge, with a perennial three-day beard and light blue eyes brooding beneath dark brows. In most photographs, the crook of a once-broken nose could be seen, but Dani had chosen to believe that was just the camera angle—a savvy publicist going for a rugged air. Fans no doubt chalked up the bent nose to rough living.

Dani knew better, shifting with the memory . . . A hard-muscled eighteen-year-old, with compassion she'd never known, ardor she'd never fathomed, and a burning need to fix what was wrong in the world. With *her*.

Only she'd been too afraid to let him that close. So she'd elbowed him away instead. Literally.

She cursed, realized her arms were clutched around her midriff, and dropped them. Relax. Even if he did recognize her, a summer fling when you're just out of high school isn't something a man hangs on to for two decades. Dani certainly hadn't: She was long past it. That swirling in her gut right now was from a demanding day with too much coffee and no food, that's all.

She paced a few steps, then stopped when an airline attendant propped the gate's door wide. People began streaming through—parents with sleeping children, an elderly couple, a couple of businessmen hurrying to catch their connections. Dani held her breath and a moment later, in a sea of moving humanity, Mitch Sheridan appeared.

Her mouth went dry, an illogical spread of goose bumps rising on her skin. Dani watched him stride into the terminal. He towered a few inches taller than most other passengers, but there, the resemblance to the handsome publicity shot ended. His hair stuck out, his cheeks were drawn, his eyes hooded and bloodshot. Worry had chiseled lines into his face—crow's-feet at the corners of his eyes and deep grooves bracketing his mouth, darkened by a few days of beard. He wore faded jeans and a ragged polo shirt, and he looked rangy and long-boned, leaner than she'd expected. His gait was stiff. Hours on a plane? By her calculations, he'd been traveling for the past nineteen hours, seven of which were lost in the time change. Or maybe the stiff limbs were the legacy of the attack at a refugee camp a few months ago, the one Brad Harper had referred to.

He walked with a cell phone to his ear, coming within five feet. Dani blinked: The aristocratic nose had a decided crook to it. Well, shit. It wasn't just a trick of the camera angle.

He walked right past her.

Dani kicked into gear and followed. *Mit—Mister Sherid—* Suddenly, she didn't know what to call him.

"Sheridan," she said, and he snapped the cell phone closed. "I need to talk to you."

"I can't right now," he said, not stopping.

She pulled her shield from her belt and came around to cut him off. "You have to."

He glanced at the police ID and opened his mouth, then stopped cold. His eyes locked on hers. "Jesus Christ," he said.

CHAPTER
5

A CURRENT OF ELECTRICITY skimmed Mitch's flesh. The woman in front of him shifted from foot to foot.

"It's me, uhm, Dani Cole," she said. "I'm with the police de—"

"I know," Mitch cut in. He couldn't believe it. Her voice rang a touch lower, her face had aged gently, but there was no question who she was. Slender and dark-haired, a dainty chin jutting out as if expecting a fight, dark-lashed eyes that were colorless, like rain. He caught his heart picking up speed and warned it to slow down, to remember. Don't be an idiot.

That bit of wise counsel didn't keep him from glancing at her left hand. No rings. Something deep inside relaxed a little. "You became a cop. I heard."

"Like father, like daughter, huh?"

Mitch winced at the insult, but couldn't bring himself to offer anything in the way of comfort. No matter how bad things were with her father, she didn't want solace from Mitch, he remembered that well. *Damn you, go away. You can't fix this. Go somewhere you can make a difference . . .*

Mitch shook it off, forced himself to remember why he was here. Why she was here. "Did Brad talk to you? Did you find Russell?"

"We're looking for him."

"Fuck." He tipped back his head. "What the hell happened?"

"I'm supposed to take you to the station so you can tell us about the last phone conversation you had. Sanders's son says you think something happened to him."

"Something did. I heard it, damn it. He called me, and I thought it was about photos for this weekend's exhibition." He touched his chest, expecting to find his camera, but there was nothing there. He'd get used to it. "But it wasn't about the pictures. He said he was in trouble."

"Come with me. You can tell us about it."

"I need to go to headquarters—Foundation, not police. I can tell you about the phone call on the way, but I want to get in Russ's apartment."

"You can't do that right now. Police are there, looking around."

A sliver of alarm slipped in. "What for?"

"Come to the station. My partner and I can catch you up there."

"Catch me up here," he snapped. She turned, but Mitch caught her arm and every fiber of her body turned to steel. Her eyes took on the look of a trapped animal and in a heartbeat, eighteen years slipped away. *Déjà vu.*

Mitch loosened his fingers. "What do you know about Russ?" he asked.

She took a half step back. "Almost nothing, except that you can't get into his apartment yet." She sighed. "Just trust me."

The words left a scrape. "Where have I heard that before?"

She flinched and Mitch cursed himself. Nearly two decades had passed. He couldn't believe how thin-skinned he suddenly felt.

Dani headed down the causeway and Mitch lengthened his stride to catch up, accompanied her through the airport and outside to a county Chevy parked outside baggage claim. She bleeped the locks and he tossed his carry-on into the back. Dani started to fold into the driver's seat but stopped with one leg in the car.

She pulled her leg back out and a second later, Mitch saw what she did: an envelope under the wiper blade.

The look on her face lifted Mitch's hackles. "What is it?" he asked over the top of the car.

"I don't know." She shut her own door, pulled a piece of paper from the envelope, and unfolded it. Gasped.

"Dani?" Mitch started around the nose of her car. "What the hell—"

"God," she said, staggering back against the car. The fear in her voice caught Mitch in the gut. He reached for her, but something fell from the fold of the page and Dani nearly dove at the ground to pick it up. She stuffed it back in the envelope, teetering on crouched limbs. Mitch took her by both arms, pulling her to her feet. She was trembling.

"What is it?" he asked.

"Let go, let go." She wrenched away and Mitch cursed, watching as she spun in a circle and scanned three hundred and sixty degrees, her breaths shallow, her cheeks the color of rice paper. She spotted a security guard and beelined to him.

"I'm a cop," she said to the guard, and pointed to the shield on her belt. She was hyped, her voice unsteady. Whatever had fallen from that envelope had knocked her for a loop. "Someone left a note on the Chevy parked right there. Did you see who?"

The guard looked at her like she was nuts. "About a hundred people walk by here every two minutes, lady."

She pulled something from a small notebook in her blazer pocket—it looked like a snapshot. "This man?"

The guard looked, shrugged. "Who could tell?"

"Where are the cameras?"

He pointed and Dani looked, followed the angle of the lenses to her car, and said, "*Shit.*" She stepped away to dial her cell phone. Mitch heard her ask for a Detective Tip-something, but he couldn't make out the rest. He hung back.

A couple of minutes later, she signaled toward the car. Her color was back.

"So, you're all right?" Mitch asked. He fell into step beside her. "For a minute there, I thought you might pass out."

She gave him a look that could only be interpreted to mean *Bite me*, and a surge of relief pulsed through Mitch's limbs. Her anger, he could deal with; fear was something else again. He'd spent enough years letting that haunt him.

She pocketed the mysterious envelope and slid into the driver's seat, sticking the snapshot into a little spiral-bound notebook and setting it on the console. She nosed into traffic, adrenaline still steaming from her skin, fingers flexing and fisting on the steering wheel.

"Who is he?" Mitch asked.

She blinked. "Who?"

"The guy you're looking for, who scared the shit out of you back there with that envelope."

"I'm not scared, I'm pissed."

Okay. But her bravado only served to prick his temper. He picked up the notebook from the console.

"Hey, put that down."

"Is this him?" he asked, unfolding the picture.

She swerved trying to snatch the page, but he held it from her reach and she had no choice but to focus on driving. He opened the page and stared.

Russ.

His gut clenched. He looked at Dani. "What the hell is going on?"

"I told you we were looking for him."

"And you think he just left some fucking note on your windshield?"

She tried to backpedal. "It might've been someone else."

"Bullshit. You didn't show *someone else's* picture to that security guard. You showed Russ's. Why? What was in the note?"

"I'm not at liberty to—"

"Like hell you're not. This is *me*, damn it," Mitch shot, then remembered that didn't mean squat to Dani. She hadn't confided in him at seventeen and apparently wasn't going to now. She took a ramp from the highway and Mitch looked back at the picture in his hand, tried to piece together what little he knew. Police were in Russell's apartment, looking for him, and Dani was running around with a photograph of him. When it hit Mitch, he stared. "Jesus, you think he's done something."

She pulled to a stop at a light, saying nothing. Mitch cursed. "Damn it, Dani." He took her arm. "Talk to me."

"That's the third time in twenty minutes you've grabbed me," she said, her body turning to stone. "I'd think you would have learned better. Let go."

The memory of trying to hold her eighteen years ago rose like a third presence between them. *Let go of me, I don't want you here*, her limbs flailing at him. But Mitch was older now, harder. He didn't let go so easily anymore. "Gonna break my nose?" he asked, and the look on her face brought a throb of triumph. "I'm not trying to pry into your life. This is about *my* life, about Russ. Just tell me why the police are looking for Russ."

She turned to him, her eyes like steel. "Because a woman got hacked up last night. Your buddy Sanders might have done it."

CHAPTER
6

IT WAS INCONCEIVABLE. Mitch paced a tiny room at the police station trying to wrap his brain around it. An ex-hooker, only eighteen years old, stabbed in the throat. A phone call to Russ, and an incriminating note on his nightstand. Brad's confirmation that his dad had been planning to meet a lady Sunday night and Russell's subsequent disappearance.

And near the time of the murder, the phone call to Mitch. *I'm in trouble, Mitch.*

"Tell us again, Mr. Sheridan," said a big, bald detective. The badge clipped to his lapel said his name was Tifton. He was the lead investigator on the woman's murder case, and thus in the search for her murderer: Russ.

Impossible. Russ could never hurt anyone. Russ was a good man. He was the part of Mitch's life that meant something. When Mitch had been flailing around in the world, a teenager whose family had literally fallen apart in his hands, Russell offered redemption. Gave Mitch a way to feel again, then a way to take those feelings and make a difference in the world. *Shoot the pictures, Mitch, tell the stories. You need this...*

"No," Mitch said. "I'm finished." He shot a glare at Dani. She'd known Russ, at least through Mitch. She should know better than to believe he could kill anyone. "Unless you want to charge me with something, I'm finished here."

Tifton held up a hand. "You can't even consider the possibility that there might have been something in Sanders's life that you don't know about, something shady?"

"You're not talking about something *shady*, Detective, you're talking about murder. For more than twenty years, Russ has been my partner, friend, mentor, the father I lost when I was sixteen years old." He looked at Dani, remembering the pillow talk of young love, divulging his soul to her about his dad and Russ, and thinking that sharing was mutual. It wasn't. "No," he said, pulling his brain back on track, "I can't consider the possibility that Russ is a murderer."

Dani shifted, her arms crossed over her breasts. She was all cop. She hadn't let on to her partner that she and Mitch had a history. "You mentioned he was like a father. Seems to me I remember reading that he treated you more like a son than he did his own kid. Is Brad Harper at odds with his dad?"

Mitch slipped a shard of ice into his voice. "Do you do your reading in the grocery store checkout line, Sergeant?"

"Hey," Tifton warned, but there was a knock on the door and he went into the hall.

Dani skewered him with a glare. "I'm trying to keep this professional."

"But it isn't. I know it's in your nature to expect the worst of people, but you know about Russell. You know how he took me under his wing after my dad died and you know when he learned he had a son, he took him in. What you might not know is that later, he paid Brad's way through college and law school, then when Brad's career went south in corporate law, he created a position for him at the Foundation."

"What I remember is that you never much liked Brad."

"I still don't. He's an ungrateful tight-ass who owes his father everything but never once gave a thought to thanking him."

She shrugged, but her eyes went dead. "Sometimes people don't show gratitude the way you think they will, do they?"

Mitch stiffened. "I never asked for your gratitude. All I wanted was a little trust."

"I didn't mean yo—" she began, but snapped her mouth closed. For a heartbeat, he wanted to push her, find out what the last eighteen years had been like after the night she'd turned him away. Find out if she'd ever wished she could do it all over again and this time, let him help her.

Then sanity leaked back in. He blew out a breath. He hadn't come home to rekindle any flames; he wasn't here to shoot pictures or tell a story or try to fix anything. He was here to find Russ.

Tifton stuck his head in, crooked a finger to Dani. She stepped out and shut the door, but Mitch caught it before it closed all the way. Listened.

"Fisherman snagged a body in the Monocacy River, a few miles south of Highland Bridge," Tifton said, his voice low. "Description's not great, but it could be Sanders."

Mitch's gut clenched. No. God, *no*...

"Ah, man," Dani said. "We gotta get over there."

"I'll go spring Sheridan," Tifton said, but before he came back in, Mitch swung the door wide.

"I'm coming with you."

Alicia Woodruff opened the cardboard box she kept tucked beneath the mattress: nothing. The last rock was gone, and her john early this morning had gone through her last bag of weed. She dug into the toe of her shoe, counted what was left of her money: a hundred and eighteen dollars. Not much. One finger of cheap heroin would eat that up, or a few lines of coke. Barely enough to keep her buzzed through another night, and she'd learned years ago that in this business, nights were easier with a buzz.

Alicia was nineteen. She was a hooker, a user, and an occasional crook. And a mother.

Well, no—the mother thing wasn't quite right. She'd had a baby eight months ago but gave her up for adoption. She guessed that simply giving birth didn't make her a mother, though that's all *her* mom had ever done to qualify. Still, Alicia hadn't spent two minutes with the baby before the doctor carried her away. And a couple of days later, with five thousand dollars in her bag from someone known only as "the broker," Alicia had returned to the shabby warehouse-apartment she shared with five other girls and spent the next few weeks throwing money around. Pretty much managed to forget all about the kid.

Until a couple of months ago, when the reminders started popping up. The first had freaked her out, even half-tripped-out on heroin. She'd staggered back to her room after a long night on her back and found a pink helium balloon tied to the doorknob. A couple of weeks later, a *Congratulations on Your New Arrival* card

appeared in the crack of the door, then a baby bottle. And
just last week, a pair of crocheted booties showed up in
a little box.

Someone was messing with her mind, trying to make
her feel bad. But it wasn't going to work. The broker had
sent Alicia pictures of where her baby was going. A big-
ass mansion in Connecticut. Rich parents. Private pool.
Helluva lot better than living in this shit.

So, screw whoever was sending her stuff. Screw 'em.
The kid was better off.

She crammed her toes into the shoe on top of the
bills and stuffed a box of cigarettes into a big vinyl bag.
Looked at the clock: still time. She could get out there
now, dope up for the night, and get back to the streets to
meet some tricks. Earn enough to do it all over again.

She headed out the door but froze when she stepped
into the hallway.

A teddy bear.

Alicia's heart stumbled, and she looked down the hall.
No one. She reached down and picked it up, looking at
the note tied around its neck.

RR DEPOT, 8:30. IT'S ABOUT YOUR DAUGHTER.

Oh, God. For a second she couldn't breathe, then
read it two more times. She couldn't believe it. Damn it,
besides the girls here, who even knew she'd had a baby?
And who among them knew it had been a girl? Alicia
had gone to stay at the broker's beach house when she
was barely five months along and hadn't talked about it.
Not to anyone.

Was this about the money she'd been paid? Was the
baby all right? For one awful second, a knot tightened

in her belly. Her baby. Her little girl. But someone else's now.

She closed her eyes, pulling her jacket tighter around her. She didn't want to go to the railroad depot. That place creeped her out.

But she would. *It's about your daughter.*

There was no way cops would let a civilian—who had been close to the possible victim—come along and look at a body dragged out of a river. But there wasn't much Dani could do to prevent it, either. Lancaster was Mitch's home turf; he knew where Highland Bridge was, knew the access areas south of it, and apparently jumped a cab and arrived at the location not long after Dani and Tift. Uniforms kept him back, along with a few other folks who'd gotten wind of a story-in-the-making, but from down on the riverbank she could see his dark head outside the perimeter, his long legs carrying him around the yellow ribbon as he tried to get a view. Now and then he exchanged words—angry ones—with an officer whose job it was to keep people back and occasionally, Dani caught him rubbing a big hand over his face. Eventually, he disappeared.

Good, Dani thought. She wouldn't wish this on anybody.

A body that's been submerged is a gruesome thing. A recovery team had already pulled it out and laid it on the bank—bloated, pale, and sporting a number of small head injuries.

"Dead when he went in?" Dani asked the medical examiner. He was the same narrow man who had been on the scene at the park with Rosie, making notes in a spiral. Long day.

"Don't know yet," he muttered. "Bodies float face-down with the head drooping. Blood gathers there. Wounds from hitting the bottom or from bumping rocks and tree trunks can bleed postmortem."

Shit. Tifton strode over and she caught him up: "Gonna have to wait for the autopsy to see what shape he was in when he went into the water, and then we still may not know."

The ME looked up from his notebook, smug. "Of course, the bullet hole on the other side of his head might be something."

Dani's eyes widened. "Bullet hole?"

She cursed at the ME and they walked back to the body. One of the gloved guys rolled it to the side so they could see.

"Not too big and no exit wound," Tifton said. "Twenty-two, probably."

Dani barely heard: The sight rolled over her like a freight train—a small black hole in the middle of short gray hair, just above the ear.

Dad.

She tried to swallow, but the gorge in her throat swelled into full-fledged nausea. She muttered something to Tifton and dashed down into a ravine, bent over and retched the near-nothing in her stomach. She dropped to her knees, gagging, holding herself until the image of her father began to fade and she could see straight again.

God, she thought, her breaths coming in gusts. *Stop it. You're stronger than that.*

"Nails?"

Tifton. Oh, hell.

"I'm coming," she called. "I thought I saw someone over here, but I was wrong. I'll be there in a minute."

His steps retreated, and Dani pulled a pack of gum from her pocket and chewed the mint out of it. A minute later, she tossed it into some bushes and stood, brushing herself off. She took a deep breath and scanned the handful of people gathered beyond the police line tape. Mitch appeared to be gone. She didn't know where he was or what he was doing, but the last thing they wanted in this investigation was a civilian with notoriety and an emotional stake in the case, sticking his broken nose where it didn't belong. The last thing *she* wanted was to have Mitch around, touching her or steadying her or studying her, seeing things he wasn't supposed to see.

She started back to the bank, skimming the horizon. A distant figure stopped her cold. Tall, standing on a dock ten yards out over the water. His arms were up, elbows out, and Dani's heart gave a lurch.

It was Mitch, with a camera. Aimed directly at her.

CHAPTER
7

MITCH HAD ARRIVED at the riverbank an inch behind
the police, then prowled the yellow crime scene
tape with a prayer on his lips. *Not Russ, not Russ*, he
chanted. But he couldn't see. He moved thirty yards
around the perimeter, and couldn't tell from there, either.
Too many trees, too many people, and soon it would be
dark. There was a body—that much he knew. It looked
fatter than Russ, but he wasn't sure...

Not Russ, not Russ.

The idea hit him when he squinted, trying to make out the
scene: his camera. His best one was in his bag—he'd planned
to give it to Russ and let *him* finish changing the whole
damned world. But now, it sat in his carry-on bag where the
cab had dropped him off. Mitch jogged back to where he'd
dropped it, hesitated, then pulled it out and attached the
lens, the pieces moving in his hands like extensions of his
limbs. For a while after the attack, he'd felt naked without
it; now it hung like a ball and chain around his neck.

But this wasn't about shooting images or telling stories. It wasn't about fixing anything. This was just about
being able to see.

He started along the river—an upscale neighborhood of riverfront properties. Nearly every one had a dock and a small boat, and it took only a few minutes. The owners of the third property recognized him, let him use their dock. Mitch put the camera up, the scope bringing the riverbank scene almost into his lap.

Too many people—people bending over the body and the face to the side, away from Mitch. It could have been Russ, he couldn't tell from the clothes. Hell, he didn't know Russ's clothes; he hadn't seen him in nine or ten months.

He zoomed back a little, taking in more of the scene. Dani, Tifton, a bunch of others. A thin man with a pocket protector and glasses spoke to them, and suddenly Dani and Tifton walked back toward the body. Move, move. Get out of the way. They squatted down and a third man bent and shifted the body, but there were too many people around to see.

Then Dani popped up and hurried away, and Mitch followed her with the camera. She didn't stop until she dropped down into a gully, out of sight of the others. There, she bent over, her slender spine heaving with convulsions.

She was throwing up. Tears on her cheek.

Mitch lowered the camera, his heart rusting as he tamped down the impulse to soothe her. He'd learned long ago that the last thing Dani wanted was for someone—him—to see any vulnerability. For a minute he couldn't help but wonder where they would be today if she hadn't been so self-protective, if he hadn't been so eager to go someplace he could make a difference. Had Dani been more open and Mitch been more dogged, what might have happened between them?

Forget it. Whatever was eating at her, she sure as hell wouldn't share it with him. Besides, he hadn't come home to get tangled up in emotions. He'd come home to help Russell.

Wise intentions fled when Dani stood and brushed off her slacks. Mitch went back to the camera, watching as she did a quick survey of her surroundings. He held still, knowing she might turn his way and catch him intruding, oddly unwilling to stop looking even when she did. Fury chased across her face. She whirled away and hiked back to the riverbank.

Mitch cursed, adjusted his lens, and followed with his camera. People still milled, but there were fewer around the body now, and he zoomed in on it. He had to wait thirty more seconds until someone bending over moved out of the way, and when they did, the dead man's face had been turned toward Mitch.

He dropped the camera, staggering backward. *Ah, God, no.*

An hour later, herded behind the police tape, Mitch still couldn't believe it. Russell, dead. *I'm in trouble, Mitch...I need you.*

A lot of damn good he'd done.

"Mr. Sheridan."

It was Detective Tifton, coming up the bank in the wash of floodlights. Dani trailed one step behind him.

"There was no ID, but it looks like the picture we have of Mr. Sanders," he said. "We've called Mr. Harper. Maybe he can identify the watch or ring—"

"It's Russ."

Tifton gave him a skeptical look.

"This lens magnifies thirty-two times, Detective,"

Mitch said, touching the heavy camera around his neck. "It's Russ."

"Okay, then," Tifton said.

Mitch looked at Dani. "How did he die?"

"We won't know until an autop—"

"Damn it, how did he die?"

She looked down. "There appears to be a gunshot wound to the head."

He closed his eyes. "He didn't kill himself. He didn't stab a woman in the throat and he didn't shoot himself in the head."

"We'll figure it out," Dani said. "Let us do our jobs."

"How?" Mitch glared at her. "By writing it off as a murder-suicide? That's convenient."

"Did I say we wrote it off as a murder-suicide?" she shot back. "Sanders was already dead when someone put that note on my windshield."

Mitch blinked. Christ, she was right. At the time, he hadn't known about Rose McNamara's death, so he hadn't yet put it all together. But for some reason, Dani believed the note on her car was from McNamara's murderer.

"Listen," Tifton said, "we'll push the autopsies, go talk to people around both victims. There's some reason Rose McNamara and Russell Sanders are connected."

"There's the obvious," Dani said, and Mitch looked at her.

"You think he was banging her. For God's sake, he was sixty-two years old."

"Did he like women?"

"Yes. But he only *loved* one: Brad's mother. Any others over the years were just...company."

"And you're sure he never hired anyone, just for company?"

"Russell didn't have to pay for sex," he said. "Besides, what he said to me didn't sound personal. It was about the Foundation."

A shout went up from down on the bank, two men heaving Russ's bagged body onto a canvas stretcher. A couple of other people stuck their hands in handles on the sides and they climbed up the bank, taking Russ to the black coroner's wagon along the road.

Mitch watched, and a wall of grief hit. He stepped forward and one of the recovery workers looked at Tifton, who nodded and signaled to set down the stretcher. A man peeled down the zipper and Russ's bloated white face came into view.

"Mr. Sheridan?" Tifton said quietly a few moments later. "They need to go."

Mitch stepped back and they loaded the body into the back of the coroner's wagon. The engine turned over and the wagon pulled away, dragging fuzzy red taillights into the distance.

Russ was gone.

"I called you a cab," Tifton said.

A cab. Time to go.

Mitch started toward the street, his hand cradling the camera around his neck. Halfway there, he passed Dani. She glanced at the camera, pain flaring in her eyes like the blue and red strobes throbbing in the night. Suddenly, she looked seventeen again—standing outside her run-down little house, exposed and frightened, red and blue lights flashing, her father shouting and little brother crying. Officer Artie Cole railed against the fellow cops who held him by each arm, and Dani lashed out at Mitch: for coming, for having his camera, for seeing what she'd so scrupulously hidden. She'd turned away and when Mitch reached for her, she'd flailed and fought as if he were a stranger rather than the man she'd claimed to love. Busted up his nose with her elbow.

Go away, she wailed. *I told you never to come here...I don't want you here...*

Now, Mitch saw that same fear in her eyes—the knowledge that while looking at her through his camera tonight, he'd seen more than she was willing to show him, and the clear expectation that he couldn't be trusted with that knowledge.

Some things never changed.

Mitch pushed a button on his camera, ejected the memory card and walked over to her, holding up the tiny device between the tips of two fingers. She frowned, not quite recoiling, and he reached out and tucked it into the pocket of her blazer.

"I'm going," he said. "But take a look at this when you get a chance. It might surprise you."

It was always surprising how readily the girls came. A few taunts with the baby gifts, a few tugs at their conscience or their curiosity or their greed, and they were easy pickings. They could be lured to any given killing ground: An alley behind a strip club. A forest behind some Little League field. A narrow strip of gravel off a seldom-traveled county road.

The exception, of course, was Rosie—she'd been trouble from the beginning. Dani Cole's doing.

Alicia wouldn't be, though. She wasn't smart, she wasn't driven. No one had pulled her off the streets and put her back in touch with her family. She'd had no Mother Teresa cop looking out for her.

She was as good as dead.

Fulton was right: The railroad depot was remote and dark, a good choice for her killing. A ramshackle building a couple of miles north of Reading, it had once been the site of a grisly hanging. The incident was shrouded with a mystical flare—it had even been featured on TV on one of those shows about haunted houses and supernatural events. Since then, the depot was a lonely place. A few drug deals went down there each month, and a couple of drunk teenagers crept in now and then on a dare. Otherwise, it was pretty much forsaken. Even the cops patrolled a wide berth around it.

But Alicia would come. Except for Rosie, they always did. Lambs to slaughter.

Footsteps. The thin drumbeat of high heels on concrete. Hooker-shoes.

She was here.

The shears came to life, the cold steel of the loops warming in hand. Alicia's heels clicked on the broken pavement, slowing as she drew near like the sharp tocks of a dying clock. Her bright blond hair splashed into the darkness and in her hand, she carried the bear.

The shears came out. Easy pickings.

CHAPTER
8

M ITCH LEFT THE RIVERBANK at eight-thirty and went looking for Brad. Surely, he'd know something. As the Foundation's lead attorney, he had a finger in pretty much every slice of the pie. He also had a love-hate relationship with his dad. Mitch was about ninety percent sure the love was stronger than the hate. Ten percent not.

The cab rolled onto Franklin Avenue in front of Foundation headquarters. The building—a stone castle built in 1854—had been a private residence for one of Lancaster's prominent families when Mitch was growing up. It had been Russ's idea to buy the place and turn it into a venue for Mitch's work, and a few years later Mitch bought the huge Victorian home next door, as well. Now, the JMS Foundation had grown from Mitch's first feature exhibition to benefit an AIDS-ravaged village in Tanzania to the far-reaching efforts of an overseas adoption service, famine relief, postwar aid, and government lobbying. Domestically, it offered scholarships and workshops to train young photographers, and sometimes mounted premiere exhibitions of new artists. All Russ's doing.

Grief climbed on top of Mitch. He was almost thirty-seven years old and felt like a sixteen-year-old boy again watching his father die in his arms, not knowing how to go on without him. Not knowing how to forgive himself for letting him die.

He paid the driver, poured out of the taxi, and dragged to the apartment building next to the main offices. Before he got there, the door opened, the interior light silhouetting two figures.

"Mitch, is that you?"

It took a second, then the voice rang a bell. The silhouette of the second, smaller figure sank in an instant later.

"Marshall," Mitch said, meeting them on the steps. A motion-sensor light came on and they shook hands. Marshall and Mia Kettering. Marshall was the president of the Foundation board, a well-known psychiatrist much envied for his money, his position, and his wife. Twenty-five years his junior, Mia was the classic trophy wife, a volunteer at several charities and an amateur photographer in her own right. A drop-dead beauty.

"Mitch," she said. "I hate that we're seeing you under these conditions."

"Christ, that's the truth," Marshall said. "But I'm glad you're home."

"Brad called you?"

"Yes, right after the police notified him about Russell," Marshall said. "We came by to see him, but he isn't here."

"He's not at the police station, either, or answering his phone," Mia said.

Mitch shook his head. "I haven't heard from him."

Marshall stroked his beard with his fingers. He was a medium-size man, with a slight paunch, given to wearing tweed. Mitch had always pictured him sitting in his study with a pipe, reading the *Iliad* for pleasure.

He didn't look so relaxed now.

"We're calling the board together first thing in the morning," Marshall said. "I hate to turn to business at a time like this, but this weekend's exhibition has been hyped for months and wasn't quite finished." He looked at Mitch. "Russ kept hoping—"

"I know." Mitch closed his eyes, saw Russ's body going into the hearse. *This one matters more...Promise me, if something happens...*

Damn you, Russell.

He looked at Marshall. "Was there anything off about Russell lately? Did you see anything going on?"

"I hadn't seen him for about a week, but no," Marshall said. "From what Brad told me, you were the first to hear anything."

Mia gave Mitch's hand a squeeze. "He loved you, Mitch. More than anything."

"Well, I can't argue *that*."

They all turned toward the new voice. Brad, at the foot of the stone walkway.

Mitch stepped toward him. Whatever their differences, the man had just lost his father. "Jesus, Brad, I'm sorry."

Brad swayed on the steps. He wore a lightweight jacket, his shoulders a little crooked, one hand stuffed deep inside a pocket. His hair, classically short, stuck up as though he'd raked his hand through it.

He was drunk.

"So, you're back: Mister Fucking Save-the-World," Brad said. His relationship with Mitch wasn't love-hate. It was pretty much just hate.

"Hey, I just wanted to talk to you," Mitch said.

"Talk? You mean, a heart-to-heart, like we do so often?" He laughed and looked at Marshall and Mia. "Isn't that sweet?"

"This won't help anybody, Brad," Mia said.

Brad teetered, his arms flailing wide. "What *will* help?" He turned to Marshall. "Hey, come to think of it, Marsh, you've got the goods, a man in your profession. How about a little Demerol, some OxyContin. C'mon, Doc, fork over the painkillers, some OCs or maybe a little perco—"

"That's enough," Mitch snapped. Marshall's face had gone tight and Mia gasped, looking downright shocked. Mitch snared Brad's shirt collar and hauled him up the last few stairs. "Let's go inside."

"There's a board meeting in the morning, Brad," Marshall called to his back. Mia was herding him away. "I trust you'll pull yourself together for it."

"Sure," Brad threw over his shoulder. "Gotta get everyone together and figure out how to cover Dad's affair with Rose McNamara. Save his name, his"—he made a Shakespearean gesture that encompassed the whole block—"precious Foundation."

"What?" Marshall spun back around. Even in the dim light, Mitch could see the alarm on his face.

"Don't worry about him," Mitch said.

"No, no, I'm not. But, wait. What did you just say?" Marshall pressed.

Brad spoke with relish. "They say Dad murdered a girl."

"They don't know that," Mitch growled. He looked at Marsh, whose expression had gone to stone. Christ, if this got out…

But there was nothing he could do to stop it. It *would*

get out. Russell would be linked to Rose McNamara's murder.

"What are you talking about?" Marshall pressed. He glanced down at his arm, where Mia's nails seemed to be biting into his sleeve.

"There was a girl murdered at Camden Park last night," Mitch said. "But they don't know who killed her."

"They think it was Dad," Brad whispered.

"They don't," Mitch snapped.

Marshall didn't look convinced. "Did you say McNamara?"

Brad put his palms to the sky. "Who knew my father had a thing for teenage hook—"

"Shut the fuck up," Mitch said, shoving him against the wall. Directly under the light of a sconce now, his pupils were aimless and cold, like the eyes of a lizard.

Ninety percent slipped to eighty. *If something happens . . .*

"Dear God," Marshall said, "it can't be true."

"It's not true, Marshall. Brad's full of shit. I'll fill you in later."

"Come on," Mia said, tugging at her husband's arm, "this is between them." She finally got Marshall's legs moving and when they were out of earshot, Mitch snarled at Brad.

"For Christ's sake, watch what you say."

"They've got evidence. From Dad's bedroom."

"It doesn't matter. McNamara's killer was still alive this afternoon and your father wasn't." He gave Brad a shake. "Who was she?"

"How would I know?" He was incensed. "Rose McNamara was a hooker. Why would I know about some stupid hooker?"

"Did Russ know her? Man, you gotta tell me what was going on."

Brad lifted his brows. "You want to know what's been going on? Here? Here, in your own organization? The one with *your* name on it?"

Mitch fisted his hands. The sarcasm wasn't unfounded, and it cut. For all that Mitch's photography and money had founded the organization, for all that his name was on the letterhead, he'd been as distant from the day-to-day operations as anyone could be. Mitch didn't like coming to Lancaster—too many failures here. "I want to know what happened to your father," he ground out. "Don't you?"

"He died. That's what happened." Brad lurched away, heading for the front door of the apartment lobby. Apprehension knotted in Mitch's gut. He didn't think the police had released Rose McNamara's name yet.

"Wait," he said, stopping Brad. "How do you know the dead woman's name?"

Brad's shoulders straightened. "They asked me about her, to see if she was the woman Dad was meeting last night. Then I heard about the girl's body. I put two and two together." He held up his fingers, a taunt. "Got five."

He slid inside and Mitch closed his eyes on a hope. Even so, eighty percent dropped to seventy.

Marshall drove with a stone in his chest, Mia sitting silently in the passenger seat. He felt as if he'd been hit by a ball-peen hammer, right between the eyes. Russell. The Foundation.

Rose McNamara.

His knuckles tightened on the steering wheel and he turned past Sedalia Lake and followed a finger of water into their neighborhood, edging along a strip of mansions with soft gold lights and four-car garages, expansive lawns with wrought-iron gates. This was the life he'd made for Mia; the life she deserved after the pain she'd endured. He glanced across the seat in the darkness, her silhouette like an artist's sculpture—the high cheekbones and full lips, lush hair that, though recently cut to just shoulder-length, still flowed like thick silk around her face. Mia made a man simply *yearn*. He'd known the moment he met her he would do anything to possess and care for her.

Even if it meant sharing her.

He swallowed a smack of bitterness in his throat. Sometimes, when she came in late, he could smell the sex on her. His physical impotence hadn't mattered to her when she was young—victims of abuse commonly show little interest in sex and he knew she regarded him as safe. Marshall was both man enough and psychiatrist enough to know that would change someday; he even claimed partial responsibility for her transformation, having seen her through the years of emotional healing from her childhood. No, he would never begrudge Mia the happiness she deserved. But sometimes he thought the sharing would kill him.

Now, that would be the least of his worries. When Mia learned what had happened . . . Dear God, he couldn't bear to think about it.

He pulled up the long cobblestone drive to his house but didn't pop the garage door. Instead, he pulled to the front door and Mia looked at him.

"You aren't coming?" she asked.

"When Brad called, I was still elbow-deep in paperwork, love. I have to get back to the office. Will you be all right for a few hours?"

She gave his hand a squeeze. "A few." She added a pretty pout and Marshall couldn't help but thread his fingers into her hair, combing through the thick auburn mane along one of the light highlights. He kissed her with everything he had. Three months ago, he thought he'd lost her—she'd suddenly come to an emotional edge that was almost beyond his grasp. But finally, he'd been able to bring her the happiness he'd always promised.

But now, if the rumors about Russ and Rose McNamara were true, all was lost. He couldn't let that happen.

He watched until she was safely inside, then closed his eyes and drew a shuddering breath. It was happening: The one thing Mia had dreamed of all her life was falling apart, and the truth would destroy her.

And him.

So, she couldn't know. No one could. Marshall would do anything to make sure.

CHAPTER
9

Eight fifty-five p.m. Dani refused to acknowledge the roiling in her stomach, followed Russell Sanders's body to the morgue, and forced herself to stop at the coroner's office. Rosie's autopsy was finished.

"I expected you or Tifton a couple hours ago," said Kelly Lang, one of the assistant medical examiners. She was five-foot-nothing, with a gold hoop through her eyebrow and spikes of black dye in inch-long blond hair. Dani found her to be illogically cheerful.

"We had a missing person connected to Rose McNamara's murder," Dani said. "We just pulled him out of the Monocacy River."

"Is he the rich dude?" Kelly asked, glancing at the new gurney.

"Rich dude?"

"We got a call from the chief to make sure a new floater gets done tonight. Only time we get calls like that is for rich dudes."

Of course. "He was kind of a bigwig, I guess." Dani tried to ignore the fact that Rosie's toe was sticking out between them, tagged. Under the sheet, she'd be naked, cold, sliced open and hollowed out, then reassembled like a 3-D puzzle.

"Freeling will do him," Kelly said. "He'll be here in a few minutes." She handed Dani a clipboard. "McNamara's autopsy. News flash: She was stabbed to death. Between six and twelve last night."

"With what?"

"Well, now that part is interesting. The wounds were fat. Not wide, like the wide flat of a knife, but *fat*. Twice as fat on one edge than the other, and some in mirror-image pairs." She showed Dani with two fingers.

"Scissors?" Dani was shocked.

"That's what it looks like. I sent part of her hair upstairs." She got on an intercom and summoned a guy named Clinton—the same technician who'd been given the note containing the hair—then summarized the findings about Rosie: "Five stab wounds to the throat, done by a right-hander. The first one was probably aimed to keep her quiet. The second went through the carotid, and the others—they were just for fun. She would have bled to death in two minutes."

Dani's stomach turned. "What about her face?"

"Bashed with the flat of the blades."

"Why?" Dani asked, but she already knew. Rage like that came from one of two things: vengeance or sex. "No rape?"

Kelly shook her head; since Rosie had been found fully clothed, it hadn't seemed likely.

"Maybe she looked like someone he knew," Kelly suggested.

"Maybe he was trying to ruin her identity." Clinton walked in, adding his two cents. He was a freckled redhead with rectangular wire-frame glasses, skinny as a pole. "I consulted on a case like that once: The killer didn't want her to be *her* anymore."

"Huh," Dani said, but it didn't feel right. The damage was too controlled, too localized to be an identity-wipe. No wounds on the right side. "Maybe he was trying to scar her."

"She was already scarred," Kelly said.

"What?"

"A long time ago—I mean, like when she was a kid." Kelly pulled back the blue sheet covering Rosie's face. Dani's throat hitched, but she forced herself to look. "She's had surgery," Kelly said, "more than once."

She pulled on a glove and fingered what was left of Rosie's hair. "Right here," she said, separating the hair to expose the scalp. "And here. And if you look really close, you can see lines along the hairline, sort of like she had a face-lift. And skin grafts on the scalp."

Dani frowned. Had the killer known that?

Clinton handed her a piece of paper. "Here's the report on the note from your windshield," he said. "The hair belongs to Rose McNamara. It was cut with a dull pair of scissors. A little rusty."

"Any prints?"

"No. And no saliva on the envelope, either. NOT INNOCENT. That's the only thing that was ever written on the page, done in block letters written with a black Sharpie—the kind everybody has in their kitchen junk drawer. The person who wrote it could be male or female, of virtually any age, but is definitely right-handed. Standard twenty-pound white paper, Georgia-Pacific."

Dani felt like a balloon slowly leaking air. "Nothing there then." She turned back to Kelly. "How did he do the hair?"

Kelly started to lift the sheet again.

"Just pretend," Dani said.

"Okay." On top of the sheet, Kelly used her left fist to mimic grabbing Rosie's hair. On the left side of her head, above the ear. "It looks like a fistful. Probably grabbed like this, and came in with the scissors in the right hand like this."

Clinton put in: "He sawed at it. The scissors aren't sharp. Like my grandma's old kitchen shears."

Dani thought about that, and came up with nothing. "Blood?"

"Not on the hair that was in the note. It had been washed. Conditioned, too."

Dani's brain stalled. Washed and conditioned? "With what?" she asked, a spark of hope flaring.

"Can't tell that. At least not yet. We'll do some tests."

So for now, there was nothing more. Dani's hopes deflated even further and Kelly pointed to her desk. "You can read over there. *I* have a date tonight."

She took off her lab coat and primped at a small mirror while Dani settled at the desk. She hated the smell of this place—formaldehyde and human waste and sometimes rotten flesh, all beneath a sickening layer of Hibiscus Breeze air freshener Kelly kept plugged in beside her desk. Dani breathed through her mouth and opened the file: Rosie had turned eighteen just three months ago. Discounting whatever childhood surgeries she'd had, all systems were healthy. No venereal diseases or cancers or drugs or alcohol in her system. No breast implants. No weird scars. No nipple rings or tattoos besides the tiny rosebud above her left breast.

But there was one thing. Dani was shocked. She frowned, read it again, then caught Kelly just as she headed out the door. "Hey, are you sure about this?"

"What?"

"Rosie had a baby?"

"Yup," Kelly said. "You can always tell if the uterus has been through birth."

"Any idea when?"

"Sure, I can tell you that right after I figure out who was on the grassy knoll." She sighed. "Not too recent. Probably at least a couple years ago."

Kelly left and Dani closed the file. Rosie had never said anything about a baby. Of course, she'd never said anything about having had surgeries as a child, either. For all that Dani had taken a liking to her, she hadn't really known Rosie McNamara very well. Dani had just helped out a girl headed down a bad path, that's all.

Not that it mattered. She was dead now.

Russell Sanders? Despite Mitch's sentiment, Sanders was involved somehow. But he sure as hell hadn't put the note on Dani's windshield. Of course, that didn't mean he hadn't killed Rosie. Maybe someone else was in it, too. Maybe, instead of asking Harper about his dad's chef's knives, she should go back and ask about a fetish for scissors or long hair—

She rubbed her hands over her arms, feeling as if something were crawling on her. She scrawled a note to Freeling—*Call when you're ready to break Sanders open*—then left the building and phoned Rosie's mother from the front stoop. A neighbor answered and said she'd taken a sedative. Dani asked to speak with Rosie's sister.

"Oh, come on, she's in trying to put the baby down. Can't you people leave them alone for a little while? Just give them tonight, please."

Dani hung up, feeling cruel.

She decided to take a break and go home for a little

while. Get something to eat, pet Runt, and unwind for ten minutes. Then come back and end the day with another autopsy.

What a life.

She started across the street to the precinct parking lot and slid her hands into her pockets. Felt the memory card Mitch had stuck there.

Take a look at this when you get a chance...

A ribbon of anger knotted in Dani's belly. Damn him for intruding. Damn him for always seeming to know things she tried to keep private, for being where he didn't belong.

It might surprise you...

She changed her mind and veered back inside the building. Homicide was almost empty. She went to the desk she'd been using for this case, fingered the tiny card, then took a deep breath and stuck it into the computer. "Okay, Mitch," she said beneath her breath. "Surprise me."

CHAPTER
10

T HE SHEARS SMELLED of blood, the odor of cold wet copper. The scent of death filled the car. Soothed the soul.

Alicia was finished. A streak of blood through her name and a clump of bright yellow hair in hand. It was curly, might be hard to work with, but the color would be a nice change. The last two girls had been so dark.

Fulton called: no problem with the body this time. And now, there was only one more girl to go. Plenty of time to finish the wig for Sunday's visit with Kristina.

If Dani Cole didn't get in the way. It certainly didn't seem that she'd taken the first note to heart.

The Saab rolled onto West Ashe Street. Four-fourteen, four-fourteen...Finding Cole's address hadn't been hard. It wasn't listed in the free White Pages, but for the right price, anything could be found. Birth dates, previous residences, criminal records. A little time and money, and *Bingo*.

Four-fourteen West Ashe Street. There it was—a cozy Cape Cod with a big front porch and black shutters. Go on past, park a few blocks away. Brisk night; a little walk would feel fine.

Shears, envelope of yellow hair—into the pockets. And screwdriver. Just hope for no alarm system, no nosy neighbors.

The windows of Cole's house were dark. Could be a car in the garage already—have to peek—but more likely, Sergeant Cole wasn't home yet. She had two bodies on her hands, after all. One was a shame: Russell Sanders. He wasn't on the list; he'd just been an unfortunate necessity. Rosie had brought him too close to uncovering the baby brokerage. And Rosie, well...She'd earned her fate two years ago when she sold her baby like a fucking sack of flour.

Innocent? That's what you think, Sergeant Dani Cole. You have to understand.

A sound—a door opening. Whoa, slow down. Did it come from Sergeant Cole's house? No, the neighbor's.

Stay back, duck into the bushes, some big-ass azaleas. Stay put and hide. Watch.

A dog—a boxer or pit bull, maybe, it was too dark to tell—bounded down the front steps of the neighbor's house. A boy came out after. Soft and a little pudgy, he jingled a set of keys in his hand, chomping on a snack while the dog did its business, then took its good old time sniffing every last blade of grass in two yards. Finally, the boy whistled.

"C'mon, Runt, you gotta go home."

They started toward Cole's back gate. Toward the azaleas.

Oh, no. Don't move. Too close, too close. How dare they interfere, how dare this stupid kid get in the way. Stupid, *stupid* dog and fucking kid...

The shears warmed in hand, fingers curling into the handles. The kid sauntered nearer, the dog almost at his heels. The boy took another bite of whatever he was eating, then tossed a scrap to the ground and kept coming. Ten steps away, coming closer, closer.

Pull out the shears, slowly, slowly. Ready. Don't move.

The dog stopped when the food hit the ground. Chomped it down, chewing while it trotted past the bushes. It didn't bother sniffing the hedge. Didn't catch wind of an intruder, the smell of the blood on the blade, like wet pennies...

They both passed the azaleas. Too close, but okay now. Breathe, let go of the shears. They're gone, both of them, at least for a moment.

The boy got to Cole's back gate and went through, and a minute later came out again, sans dog. He passed by the hedge and went home.

Safe.

But now a new problem: Dani Cole had a dog. Friendly enough to that boy, but you never knew.

Time to think, regroup. Leave the note for Cole on the front door or in her mailbox? No, that would lack impact.

Okay. Stand up, stroll away. Wait a little while. Let the neighbors get to sleep then come back, more prepared. There was always a chance Cole would come home in the meantime, but that was a chance worth taking.

Dogs could be dealt with. So could Dani Cole.

Dani stared at the computer screen on the desk. *Zero images*, it said. Nothing. The memory card Mitch had given her was empty. He hadn't collected pictures of her getting sick, crying. He hadn't studied her like an insect under a microscope.

Her spine softened and she closed her eyes.

You might be surprised.

Okay. A little.

"Well, push it, will you?" Tifton's voice snapped her back. He walked in, talking on his cell phone. "The governor knows this guy. Everyone's on our butts already to solve it yesterday." He hung up and looked at Dani. "Search team just brought up a handgun along the riverbank. Smith & Wesson M41."

"That's a .22. You think it's the one that shot Sanders?"

"If we're lucky. They'll have to dig the bullet out of him to know for sure, but I'm about to run the serial number, find out who it's registered to." He sat down at a computer. "You talk to the ME?"

Dani told him about Rosie, the surgery scars, the preliminary forensics on the note and hair from the airport, the baby. Tifton clasped his hands behind his head, a crease in his brow.

"Where's the baby?"

"I don't know. I just called her family, but they're in no shape to talk right now. I'll hit them tomorrow." She shook her head. "What bothers me most is that the hair in that note was all cleaned up. No blood, no rust from the scissors that cut it. That speaks of something beyond impulsive rage or vengeance. There's some sort of plan here."

"Like what?"

"What am I, psychic? I'm just saying if the killer is only trying to taunt the police with the hair, then why clean it up? The one thing freakier than getting a dead woman's hair on my windshield would have been getting *bloody* hair."

"So the killer's got some use for it, or maybe gets a hard-on stroking women's hair. Maybe he wants to be a woman and is collecting it to we—"

"Eew," Dani said. She shivered.

Tifton typed in the gun's serial number and turned the computer screen toward Dani so she could see. "If there were no prints on the envelope, then whoever left it wore gloves," he said, watching the numbers run. "There were no cameras at the airport aimed right at your car, but there were some nearby on the strip. They're looking through tapes now. Gloves ought to narrow the scope."

"He could've pulled on gloves once he passed the cameras. *If* he passed them. The most logical thing is: He drove up, stuck the note on my windshield, and drove away. Wearing gloves, maybe even a disguise. Even if we have a shot of him walking by the cameras, we'll never know it without seeing him stop at my car."

"Well, aren't you a bundle of optimism?" Tift said. The computer program came to a stop and he leaned forward to read. "Whaddya know? Russell Sanders owns a Smith & Wesson M41. We're gonna find out he was killed by his own gun."

Dani's heart stuttered. *Your father was killed by your own service weapon...*

"Nails. You hear me?"

"I heard you. So the guy popped himself in the head. It's the new fad, it's going around."

"Aw, Christ, Dani."

Her phone rang: Freeling.

"Autopsy?" Tifton asked when she disconnected.

She nodded. "He says he'll start in half an hour—has some paperwork to do first." She glanced at the computer screen: *Zero images.*

She stood, ejected the memory card. "I'll meet you there. There's something I have to do first."

CHAPTER
11

M ITCH WAITED UNTIL Brad got inside his apartment, then went up to the guest apartment and changed shirts, moving around, heavy-footed. When he was sure Brad had heard him upstairs, he softened his steps and left the apartment via a back staircase. For six months, he'd avoided the Ar Rutbah photos, unable to face portraits of people who no longer existed. But he couldn't avoid it any longer. He had to see what Russ had been referring to.

Promise me you'll do the show, Mitch…You need this…

It was just like Russell to believe that. To think that earning aid for the people who had survived the attack would somehow give Mitch a way to heal his own guilt for letting go of the boy. It was the same hope Russ had clung to since Mitch was sixteen years old and had let go of his little sister Aubrey's hand when she darted into the street. Their father ran after her, mindless of the approaching car, and bled to death in Mitch's arms. Mitch spent the next twenty years trying to make up for it. Without Russell, his efforts would have remained paltry, at best.

He took the stairs all the way belowground. The cellars of both buildings were connected by a tunnel that had been put in just after the second building was constructed in the 1890s. Several people had access to the tunnel and cellars, but only a couple could get into the castle itself.

He used his keycard to open the exterior door of the castle's cellar and turned on a light. It looked like a cellar but didn't have the smell or feel of one. It was as spotless as the galleries upstairs and climate-controlled, containing the artwork from fifteen years of Mitch's exhibitions, equipment for matting, framing, and displaying the pieces, and the outdated files that every business collected.

He climbed the stairs leading up to the enormous lobby of the Foundation castle—marble floors, gilt-trimmed pictures, plush furniture. The lobby suited the museum aspect of the Foundation, while behind it sat a warren of hallways and cubicles where modest-income employees did the work of spinning photos into gold. This exhibition would be held on the second story, in what used to be ballrooms and dining halls, with a number of smaller parlors used to house various groupings of images.

Mitch took the second set of stairs slowly, his limbs moving like clay. He punched in a pass code to the first gallery, opened the door, and hit the general room lights. He didn't bother with the carefully placed par cans and Fresnels mounted in the ceiling. He didn't need to check lighting and shadows and angles yet. He just needed to see the content.

And there it was, staring at him from wall mountings and easels. A lump lodged in his throat. *Damn you, Russell, I don't need this.*

But he did.

He walked around slowly, his breath hitching at the very first shot: a woman in long, flowing garb, bending over the mangled face of a girl. The girl couldn't have been more than twelve or thirteen—raped by insurgents who had left her to die.

He bit back the taste of bile and moved on.

A mass grave—a shot that might have come from one of Hitler's concentration camps, but for the fact that no one had even dug a ditch in the sand. He remembered the stench of rotting flesh in the air.

Keep going.

The old man, stump from one shoulder, grenade launcher against the other. Eyes crinkled to the horizon. *Firoke...*

Then, a picture of the boy. Twelve or thirteen years old, smiling into the camera with a white-patched mongrel at his side. He'd called the dog "*Kûçik*"—dog, in Sořani. Apparently the kid wasn't big on names, either.

Mitch's heart grew thick in his throat. Christ, he'd never wanted to see these shots. He wanted to be finished trying to change the world.

But Russ was gone now. There was no one else to tell the boy's story, or that of the others. Only Mitch could finish this show. *Promise me...This one matters more than the others.*

Mitch closed his eyes. Damn you, Russell. But he knew he had to do it.

Okay, Russ. One more show.

He pulled himself together and circled the display again, this time forcing himself to look with the eyes of a critic rather than the soul of a participant. One entire alcove had been left empty—for the shots Mitch hadn't sent yet. He looked at the space and counted how many he'd need, then turned on the display lights and went back through the exhibition, one picture at a time. He stopped at the dog and boy.

The matting was sloppy. Mitch frowned. Russ was a freak about clean mat cuts, yet this one was overcut in all three layers. He spared a thought to wonder how it had gotten past both Russell and the curator, then took it from its easel and propped it against the wall. He'd have to recut it before the sh—

A sound came from his pocket. He stepped into the hallway where the people of Ar Rutbah weren't looking at him. "Yeah," he said into the phone.

"It's me. Dani."

Her voice stroked him like a hand. Mitch shifted, leaning back against the doorframe. He'd had plenty of alliances with women over the years, a couple of them serious. But Dani had always been there. Sometimes, on that rare occasion he allowed himself to consider it, he'd wondered if she was the reason none of the others had stuck.

"Where are you?" he asked.

"On my way over. I want to talk to you."

His blood warmed a degree, and picked up speed. "What's it about?"

She hesitated. "I have something for you. Do you mind?"

His heart thumped like a damned teenager's. "Park out front. I'll come down and get you."

At a little after nine o'clock, Dani parked the Chevy across the street from the Foundation's apartment building, paused, and might have pulled away again had a shadow not emerged from behind the building. She started, touching her gun. Then the size and shape of the shadow registered, the long, slightly uneven strides. Mitch.

"Shit," she muttered. So much for changing her mind. No chickening out now.

She walked across the street and met him on the sidewalk. "You didn't have to come down," she said.

"I said I would."

And that was that. Said was as good as done—Dani remembered that about him. *I don't want you here*, she'd said, and it would have never crossed Mitch's mind that what she said to his face and what she longed for in the dead of night could be two different things. There were no layers of camouflage with a man like him: just raw truth. It was what made his photography so gut-wrenching.

"Come on," he said, nodding to the front stairs. "There's an elevator in the lobby."

"No." Dani's caution bells clanged. Being alone with him would only bring back memories she couldn't afford to have. Tender, eager hands, skillful lips. "I can only stay a minute. They're about to start on—" She started to say, "Sanders's autopsy," but caught herself.

He guessed anyway; gravity pulled at his features. The streetlamps cast his face in hard planes and angles, his Adam's apple bobbing in the dark shadow under his chin. The scent of bar soap touched Dani's nostrils and she realized he'd changed his clothes: jeans and a new shirt, wrinkled from the carry-on bag. She, on the other hand, wore the same clothes she'd had on when they found Rosie's body this morning. For a minute she wondered how they smelled, then cursed herself for caring.

"So, what have you decided?" he asked, out of the blue.

"Excuse me?"

"About me. That I'm a bastard planning to exploit your secret weakness in my next exhibit, or that I'm a man who happened to catch you at a bad moment?"

"Oh, that." Dani's cheeks prickled with heat. "I wanted to give this back to you." She dug the memory card from her pocket, held it out to him. He took it, his fingers brushing hers, and a frisson of electricity rippled over her skin. Like the first time he'd touched her, on a dark street like this, handing her his phone number over the dented front fender of his Barracuda.

"Thank you," she said, "for the pict—I mean, for not taking—I mean—"

"I know what you mean."

"Okay." Well, then. Must be time to go. "I'll see you in the morning," she said, turning.

"You haven't changed," he said, and Dani stopped. She looked up at him.

"What do you mean?"

"You're still expecting people to disappoint you, you still expect the worst from them. But you're wrong about Russell. He couldn't have hurt anybody."

"So you keep saying."

"You're also wrong about me." His gaze locked on hers. "You can trust me, Dani. You could have trusted me twenty years ago, too."

She felt as if he'd stripped her open, baring her soul. "I didn't come here to rehash—"

"Then why did you come?" He stepped closer and his mere proximity sent a wisp of sensation straight to her belly. Jesus, eighteen years and she was no more composed now than she'd been when she met him...Seventeen, driving past curfew and with no license. She'd run him into a ditch, messed up the front bumper of his car. All he'd had to do that night was make one phone call and she'd have been busted, but instead, he'd recognized that she was in trouble, chatted and flirted, asked her to meet him at a movie later that week. He buffed the dent from the bumper himself and never told another soul that she was responsible.

Dani was smitten; she couldn't remember anyone ever putting her well-being first before, couldn't remember anyone touching her with tenderness or looking at her as if she were beautiful. Sparks flew, and for the next two months, they'd gone on the whirlwind ride of first love.

Until one night he showed up at her house and found out what she really was.

She shifted. Mitch was still waiting for an answer. "I just wanted to be sure you got that memory card back," she said, "that's all."

"Liar," he said, his voice like chipped glass. "Another recurring theme."

Shame prickled her cheeks, but took a turn toward anger. "I'm finished her—"

"Wait." Mitch drew his hand down her arm, catching her hand.

"You're holding me again," she said, but he wasn't really. He was barely touching her. And it was warm and strong and tender and, God help her, she didn't want him to let go.

"You never told me what you decided."

"About what?" she asked.

"Me." He lifted up the memory card. "Asshole or helluva guy?"

She looked at him, standing there with his road-weary ambition, timeworn good looks, and off-kilter nose. Even more handsome now than when he'd been a clean-shaven, perfect-featured young man. Even more seductive.

She stopped herself, before she turned stupid. She'd managed all these years without him; no need to get weak-kneed now.

Dani pulled back, stepping toward the street. "Jury's still out," she said. "I'll let you know."

CHAPTER
12

EARLIER IN THE EVENING, when the boy and the dog were out, Cole's street had been mostly dark. Now, it was close to midnight and almost pitch-black. Only a few pinpoints of light shone up and down the street. At one house down the block from the Cape Cod, an upstairs window flickered blue and gray, as if the owner might be propped up in bed watching Letterman. At another, the pale glow of a candle or night-light showed through sheer curtains and a chimney puffed wisps of smoke into the night. Otherwise, everyone had turned in for the night. Sergeant Cole? Her house had been totally still. Two passes now, and nothing had moved.

The Saab sat almost a mile away in a half-constructed cul-de-sac—a graveyard of poured foundations and partially framed homes, their growth stunted when the housing market tanked. It made for a long walk, but if anything happened, there was a better chance of escaping on foot back to the car than trying to get the Saab out of Cole's neighborhood unnoticed.

Third pass: nothing going on at Cole's house.

Time to go.

Up the driveway, sauntering, hands in pockets. Don't hurry—a midnight stroll. Hat low, collar high. The gloves, tape, and screwdriver in the left pocket, shears in the right. The dog's midnight snack swung from one wrist in a plastic grocery bag.

Around the back, peek into the garage window. Empty. So, Sergeant Cole was still trying to solve Rose McNamara's murder. Your tax dollars at work...

The kid returning the dog had locked the door—too much to hope that he hadn't, but worth a try. It took ten seconds to choose the best window: in the back, just past the garage, above a row of spindly bushes poking from a bed of stone. The stone was good. Less chance of leaving viable footprints.

Now, be quick. You never know when that dumb dog will start barking or some neighborhood insomniac will look out his window.

The window was easy: several lengths of tape over the glass so the shatter wouldn't make noise, then a few taps of a screwdriver tip right up against the frame. It was an older house, with older windows—none of that tempered, triple-paned stuff.

Tap-tap. Wait. Dog?

Nothing.

Tap. Tap-tap.

The glass cracked. With the jab of an elbow the rest came out, the shards hanging together by the tape. Still no dog, but with the glass gone, a faint whine from inside could be heard. Quick, get in before someone sees or hears. Have the meat ready.

The room was almost totally dark. Slow now, step carefully. Don't want to trip on something.

But there was nothing there. It was empty, totally. No

furniture. Not even any carpet or flooring, as if it had been stripped bare for remodeling.

The whine came again, then a scratching sound. Shit, the door was closed, and the hound was trying to get in the room. Okay, get the meat, let him sniff it under the door. Make sure he has his mind on the food when you turn the doorknob.

It worked like a dream. The dog trotted in—a faint wash of light from the hallway following. It cocked its head and, tongue dangling, wagged its stump tail like a hula dancer welcoming a guest.

Stupid hound. The dog sank onto the bare wood floor and dug into the meat as if it hadn't eaten in a week. Not steak, anyway. Hell, the tablets of OxyContin pressed into the center of the steak—enough to down a grown man—probably hadn't even been necessary. A waste of expensive drugs.

Still, it would be good to have the dog quiet, behind a closed door. One less thing to think about.

Now, leave the dog eating, shut the door. Dani Cole might be working now, but it was late, even for a murder case. Sooner or later, she'd come home.

So get busy. This time, make sure she gets the message.

It was almost midnight when Freeling dropped the bullet from Sanders's head into a pan. It clanked like a tin bell.

"Pretty messed up," he said, handing the pan to Dani.

She winced. Twenty-twos didn't hold up well when they went through something hard, like skull. Nine millimeter bullets, on the other hand—she knew this first-hand—could take out the whole back of a man's head and lodge in Sheetrock without losing their shape.

She smothered the thought. "Bag it," she said to Freeling. "I'm gonna take it over to Ballistics before it gets any later, see if they can run it."

"Don't you want to see if the bullet was what killed him?" he asked.

"Even if he died of a heart attack, I wanna know who shot him." She turned to Tifton. "You staying?"

"At least 'til he gets to the lungs." Find out if Sanders had been breathing when he hit the water.

"Okay. Call me when you know something." Exhaustion dragged at her limbs. "After Ballistics, I'm going home."

Tifton followed her to the door. "Drop back by here when you're ready to leave. I'll walk you out, make sure there aren't any weird notes under your windshield."

A chill raced across Dani's skin. She was tough, but she wasn't stupid. "Sure," she said.

By the time Ballistics had a feel for the bullet, Tifton had had enough fun for one day and took off with Dani. He followed her to a diner that served all-night breakfasts, and over mounds of scrambled eggs and hash browns, they ticked off everything they'd amassed from the day's investigation, adding the forensics highlights: Sanders's own gun had fired the bullet into his head; he was still breathing when he hit the water. Time of death was Sunday night or early Saturday morning, and yes, the wound was consistent with suicide, though the river had washed away any nitrates that might have been found on his hand. Remnants of fingerprints on the gun were thought to belong to Sanders.

Dani threw a tip on the table. Tift followed her to her house and they circled the block. Nothing. No one skulking around in the bushes, no one parked a block away waiting for her, no notes on her front door. One light was on in the back hallway, but that was the one Seth would have turned on when he brought Runt home.

She popped her garage door and reached out the car window to wave at Tifton. "I'm good, thanks."

He waved back and left, and Dani pulled into the garage, entering her house through a small mudroom. She whistled for Runt, started to call out to her dad, and caught herself. Jeez, he hadn't lived with her all that long and he'd been dead for two weeks, and still the impulse to call out to him surfaced, along with little memories and vignettes of conversations during those last few months...

Hey, Dad, Mike Schnell caught a bullet in the ass cheek today...

He'd chuckled at that one. *Running away, was he? Mike Schnell always was a yellow-bellied hen...*

Hey, Dad, I got promoted to detective. Going to Homicide...

Snort. *Homicide. Buncha pansy-asses at desks...*

Screw him. Conversation wasn't the way to her father's heart. If she'd wanted camaraderie, she should've taken him to gamble on a dogfight or signed on as one of Ty Craig's goons.

She dropped her blazer and purse on a chair in the living room, and reached for a lamp on the end table. "Runt?"

That was weird. She turned the lamp switch, glanced around the room, and nearly retched.

Her couch was slashed. So were the cushions. The chair and rug.

Her heart took a dip and she slid out her gun. *Stay*

calm, she reminded herself, but her pulse kicked into high. She started walking, looking around. The curtains and a canvas 3-D picture above the sofa were cut. Throw pillows.

"Runt?"

A pang of fear tugged. She extended her gun in both outstretched hands, glancing at the front door. The dead bolt was still locked—the intruder hadn't come in that way. She rotated, a slow sweep with her pistol. Nothing. She backed up against the wall and slid toward the kitchen, counting off: *one, two, three*—she rounded the doorway. Clear. Checked the pantry closet, the biggest floor cupboards. No one.

Down the hall to a bathroom and guest room. Moving fast, she checked every closet and beneath the spare bed then came back out and headed down the hall. She paused outside her dad's bedroom, her pulse throbbing in her throat. That door hadn't been opened in two weeks. Not since she'd been dead asleep one night and a crack of thunder had yanked her from bed.

No, not thunder. A gunshot. Her own gun.

She cursed. This wasn't the time to think about it.

She flattened her back against the wall, elbows at a right angle with the gun pointed skyward. Do it. Go in, check his room. Sweat beaded up on her brow and she tried to listen, but all she could hear was the sound of her own breathing.

She blew out a breath and hurried past the door. She did the upstairs, eyeing her dad's bedroom door from the loft as she moved, and conducted the same routine with the spare room and bath upstairs. Closets, under the desk, behind the drapes. Nothing.

Runt?

She inched back down the stairs. The only room left was Dad's. There was no one here, she told herself, but of course, she couldn't be sure of that without going into that last room.

Do it. For God's sake, grow up.

She kicked the door open and stepped inside, trembling behind the gun. "Come on," she yelled to the nobody who was there. Then hit the light switch on the wall.

Oh, God.

Nausea wrenched through her belly, and she stared at the lump on the floor that was Runt. She bent and started to pick her up, then stopped, realizing a chill had raced over her skin.

Dani looked up. The window was open.

"No," she ground out, and lunged. She shoved aside the dangling shards of glass and peered into the darkness. She couldn't see. Damn it. She ran back across the room and turned off the light then tried again, her eyes taking a few seconds to adjust, her lungs refusing to expand. Two houses away, a shadow ducked behind a garage.

Dani lifted both arms straight out the window, her Glock aimed at the shadow. "Police," she yelled. "Freeze!"

CHAPTER
13

*P*OLICE. *FREEZE.*
  And the reptilian brain responded: *Run.*

Duck down, left. Keep going. Shit, that had been too close. If the sergeant had come in the empty room first rather than last, there would have been no getting out. Even now, the bitch was coming out the window. But it was dark and she wouldn't be able to see. She wouldn't fire, not in a neighborhood.

Run.

Across an alley, behind a hedge, around the corner of a stucco house. Front or back? The backyards were dark, but some would have fences. In front was pale light, pooling in the street from occasional streetlights and windows.

"Stop. Police," the sergeant called again.

Both front and back. Go to the front and cross the street, then duck to the backs of those houses on the other side.

And keep going. No, don't wonder what you stepped on, don't wonder how far the sergeant is behind you. Just think about what's in front.

A fence. Damn it, this yard was fenced, and littered with a sandbox and playset in the back, a little light coming from solar lanterns stuck in the flower beds. Risk it? Yes. If Cole is giving chase on foot, she'll avoid fences and streetlights, thinking that's what any good prowler would do. She'd seek out hiding places instead.

Go. Across the yard, climb over the fence on the other side. Damn boots. They were too loose, made it hard to run.

From the next yard, Cole's voice could still be heard. Not too close, but coming, heaving with exertion...

"Freeze. Police..."

"Freeze!" Dani shouted, but the shadow had darted left and disappeared. She clambered through the window, holding on to the gun and trying to keep her eyes on the figure. Coming out, her pant leg caught on the glass and she yanked the leg through, feeling the glass slice through the fabric into her calf. She landed on a box elder, got her feet beneath her, and sprinted through Becky's yard. Groping for her phone.

"Stop. Police," she called again, but she didn't know where to aim her voice anymore. The prowler had headed around the Wilsons' garage. Dani ran the same direction, fumbling with the phone to catch Tifton.

"Come back," she huffed when he answered. "Eleven-seven on foot. Headed toward Berkeley and Ashe."

"Jes—"

That's all she heard, but for the squeal of Tifton's tires and his engine revving. She stopped at the corner of the Wilsons' house and pinned her back against the rough stucco, straining to listen around the corner. Nothing. Her left leg was wet—bleeding—and she looked down but couldn't see in the dark. She bent the knee: It still worked.

She drew a deep breath, counted off in her head, and rounded the edge of the house, gun straight ahead, eyes peeled for movement. A couple of streetlamps threw light on the pavement and parked cars, but looking at the areas off the street, behind houses and garages, was like looking through a thick black scrim.

"Damn it," she whispered. She weighed her options; the streetlights were an issue, but in the backs there were fences. No way to go far without climbing them, alerting dogs. A least a couple were high privacy fences.

So, go for the street. Dani scooted around a hydrangea, ducked down, and a sound stopped her. Something moved, right in front of this house.

She came out, pointing the gun. "Freeze," she shouted. A light came on at the same instant she said it, and the trembling figure of Harold Wilson stood with his hands vibrating beside his shoulders. His wife flattened against the door.

"Ah, jeez," Dani said, dropping her gun.

"We just heard s-something, that's all," Wilson said, throwing his voice into the darkness.

"It's okay, Mr. Wilson. Police." She tried to sound calm, but that had been too close. Jesus, she'd drawn on her neighbor. "Go inside and lock the door. Leave the porch light on."

The Wilsons piled inside, and Dani let out a breath, muttering something between a prayer and a curse. *Sonofabitch almost made me shoot Hal Wilson.* She scanned the street, teeth grinding with fury. *Where are you, you bastard, where?*

She looked up and down the street: Which way? A siren

whined, coming from the east—Berkeley Street—so she went west and hoped Tifton would cover behind her. Farther out, another siren scored the air: Backup coming.

Go. A hundred yards out, Dani slowed, started checking between houses, under cars, behind trash cans, anywhere a person running might try to hide. She'd gone six blocks and cut across to backtrack on another street when she phoned Tift again.

"I lost him," she said, breathing hard. Her leg was gushing, the pain now reaching consciousness. "Set up a perimeter."

"They're rolling, twelve blocks out," Tifton said. "You got any gear?"

Gear. Vest, night-vision goggles, flashlight. "No. Just my gun."

"I'm in front of your house now. Where the hell are you?"

"I ran down Greer. I'm about six blocks west. You gotta get those units around the outside of—"

The shadow moved, a hundred feet away, in front of a garage. Dani dropped the phone and drew. "Police. Freeze." She fired a round and the figure ran, a little awkward. Wounded? Dani went after him, shouting, the encounter with Wilson making her too afraid to take another shot. She gained on the prowler and out of nowhere, a pair of headlights popped over a hill and caught him in silhouette—hat, square jacket, boots. Dani ran in the columns of light from the vehicle, watching the suspect's gait, and a thought pinged in the back of her mind, but there was no time to look at it. The driver of the oncoming car made a sharp left turn—to Dani's right—throwing the street in darkness again. Decision again: left or right.

The car's taillights winked to her right; near pitch-blackness to her left. Going for the blackness, Dani whirled left, then, like fingernails on a chalkboard, tires squealed behind her. She spun. The car swerved, the left wheels bumping up over a curb. The red eyes of the tail-lights went vertical, then a tremendous crash filled the night.

Dani stared. Oh, Jesus. No, no. She ran for the crash site, sirens wailing behind her, Tifton's car fishtailing to a stop. Tifton adjusted the angle of his headlights, aiming them at the crash, and jumped out and followed Dani. The car had crashed onto a parked car. It stood on its side, a small flame fanning up in the undercarriage.

"Ten seventy-eight, ten seventy-eight," Dani heard Tifton shouting into his phone. Another unit pulled up in front of the crash site, more headlights shining on the smoking metal. A uniform came with a fire extin-guisher, killed the blaze in ten seconds, and Dani started to climb up the wreckage, trying to see the driver inside. The hood was covered with chemical foam from the fire extinguisher and her foot slipped—

"Here, let me, let me," a guy was saying. "You're hurt…"

She backed off, ran into Tifton, who pulled her back. The street was beginning to swarm with emergency vehicles. An accident took precedence over the net they'd been called in for.

The prowler who'd caused it was gone.

A man was being helped out the driver's-side window. Bloody and shaken, he sputtered: "Get my wife, get my wife. She's still in there…"

A barrage of cops was already on it. For the next fifteen minutes, Dani watched in horror, hovering near the driver, needing to hear his story the minute he could speak. His name was Frank Gardner and paramedics pulled him out of sight of the work being done on his car, started fluids and first aid, and when Dani thought he was coherent, she walked over to him and crouched down.

"What happened, Mr. Gardner?" she asked. "How did you lose control of the car?"

He answered exactly the way she'd known he would.

"Someone ran across the street... I swerved to miss him..."

Mrs. Gardner didn't look good, but there was nothing for Dani to do. She sought out Tifton. For the first time— the scene now under floodlights—he noticed her leg.

"You're bleeding," he said. "Jesus, Nails, you're bleeding bad."

"And my house is fucked and the sonofabitch killed my dog," she said, her voice quaking with rage.

"What?" Tifton was flabbergasted.

"I'm going home."

"Hold on." He shook his head, not understanding, but signaled to a paramedic to come over.

"I'm going home."

"Fine, Nails, I'll take you. But I wanna see the leg first."

She pulled up her pant leg, twisting toward the light. The paramedic crouched down and eyed it. "You're cut," he said brilliantly. "Gonna need some stitches."

"Later," Dani said, and Tifton added: "Patch it for now."

He drove her home, even though it was only a few blocks. With the night settling down now, Dani noticed the slice in her leg. It felt like a row of bee stings, the paramedic's gauze like a fist. If she took her pant leg in hand and squeezed, it would probably crunch with dried blood.

But she could move okay. Outside, she went to the back window first, showing Tift the taped glass where she'd been cut, then popped the garage door opener and walked him through what she'd seen. Everything trashed. Runt in Dad's room, on the bare wood floor.

Dani bent down, touching her. She was warm, breathing. Oh, God, she wasn't dead.

Dani's pulse started going again. She looked around. There was a stain on the bare planks of the floor. Not blood, it just looked greasy, like the wood had been licked.

"Runt, you stupid chowhound," Dani said. She scooped up the dog and turned, then stopped when Tifton said, "Dani."

The look on his face said it all. She followed his eyes.

An envelope. Runt had been lying on it.

No. God, no.

Tifton picked it up with a handkerchief, pinching the edges open. Dani didn't want to look. She knew what she was going to find inside and the thought churned her stomach. She knew it would be another reminder that Rosie was dead.

She swallowed, braced herself for the sick memento, and peered into the envelope. Staggered backward.

"God," she said, and the dark tones of Tifton's face went pale. She hiked the dog higher in her arms, just trying to hang on.

It was another lock of hair. But not Rosie's. Blond, this time. Bleached, with a curl to it.

Another one dead? A bleached blonde with curls. Dani could hardly think.

"What does it say?" Dani asked, her voice quavering.

Tifton angled his head, trying to read the block letters. "'Stop protecting them,'" he said. He looked at her and repeated. "'Stop protecting them.'" Worry came to his eyes. "You're in trouble, Dani. This asshole's talking to you."

She couldn't think about it right now. "I have to go," she said, Runt's weight like a sack of grain. "There's a twenty-four-hour vet on Dunn Parkway. Can you call the ERT to process the house?"

Shaken, Tifton glanced at Runt. "Yeah, go. Then go to the hospital and get your leg sewn up. I'll take care of things here."

She limped to the garage, Tifton holding doors for her, and when he opened the car door the image of the accident rose up. "Call me about Mrs. Gardner, okay?" she said. "Soon as you hear."

"You got it."

But they'd both seen accidents like that one before. There was a reason the front passenger position was known as the "death seat." Frank Gardner might have become a widower tonight.

CHAPTER
14

Tuesday, October 5, 7:12 a.m.

MORNING ARRIVED IN ODORS: oily coffee, micro-wave noodles, sweaty vinyl against Dani's nose. She moved, nearly rolled off a couch, and caught herself with one hand against the linoleum. Opened her eyes. Chief Dave Gibson stood across the break room, holding a sludgy coffeepot.

The night came back in fragments: Sheridan. Prowler. Vet. Hospital.

Gibson said, "I didn't mean to wake you."

"Bullshit." Dani pushed upright. "You might as well have come in with a skillet and a metal spoon."

He set down the carafe and leaned against the counter, propping his hands on his hips. He wore a crisp white shirt with a perfectly starched collar, his cuffs neatly fastened. He looked down his nose at her.

"Whose hair was it?" Dani asked. "Besides an innocent woman in a car, who else did the motherfucker kill?"

"The woman in the car isn't dead, she's hanging on.

And we don't know whose hair it was. But it does look like the same guy. The cuts on the blond hair were made the same way as McNamara's, only this time the hair isn't clean. The slashes in your furniture have traces of blood, too. Same blood that's on the hair."

A chill raced over Dani's skin.

"They're working the evidence. The blood on the window is probably all yours, but they went all over your house."

"Well, why not?" she said, with the bite of sarcasm. It was the second time in two weeks her house had been invaded by police. The first time was in the middle of a stormy night, when a gunshot had jerked her awake. The second time, some freak had come in and walked into every room, slashed every major thing she owned, and left hair in an envelope. Poisoned her dog.

She looked at her phone: no messages. The vet said Runt ate something—meat—with some sort of narcotic in it. Her blood work had been sent to the police lab to find out what. He'd also said the first twelve hours were critical: If Runt hung on that long, there would be a better chance she'd last through the next twelve, and the next. Dani did some quick math. It had been between seven and eight hours, given what time Seth had brought Runt home. *Hold on, baby.*

She stood, wincing at the stretch of stitches in her leg—she'd forgotten that—and picked up the clothes she'd grabbed from her closet. "I'm gonna get a shower then hit the streets with Tifton. There's a blond girl lying in a ditch somewhere with her throat cut and her hair hacked off."

"Hold on, Sergeant. We've got it covered."

Dani didn't understand.

"Vice and patrol units are out there asking about

blondes who may have disappeared. I've got someone bringing in Ty Craig for questioning about the years Rose McNamara worked for him. Tifton is hitting the JMS Foundation first thing this morning. Sanders and Sheridan—these are big names. Sanders sure as hell didn't do anything at your house last night, but we need to know if he had an accomplice, how he's wrapped up in a murder."

"Two murders," Dani corrected.

"One." Gibson showed an emphatic finger. "There's no evidence of anoth—"

"Bullshit." But she knew that until they actually found a body missing a curly hank of blond hair, the second murder was speculative fiction. "We've gotta find the body," she said. "That's the only thing that will tell us what this bastard is up to next. I'll check missing persons reports. And we need to work up a description of the prowler... He's not huge, kinda lanky. Dark-faced, like maybe with a beard. And his running was a little awkward—"

"We got all that last night," Gibson said, then looked straight at Dani. "And *we* doesn't include you anymore."

A splinter of uncertainty slid beneath Dani's skin. "I don't understand," she said. But a moment later, her flesh tightened. She did understand. "You can't," she said, her voice like a knife blade.

"You're off, Dani," Gibson said. "You're too close and there's too much shit surrounding—"

"I didn't do anything wrong. I discharged my weapon into the side of a garage. No one but the suspect was—"

"It isn't about discharging a weapon. That will be investigated—it always is—but no one thinks you did anything wrong last night."

Besides chasing the prowler in front of a car... Dani

refused to let that thought take root. It wasn't her fault the Gardners' car had crashed. It wasn't.

"Then why?" she grated out, but in the back of her mind, she knew. She *knew*. "Goddamn it. It's because of Ty Craig." Her teeth ground. "I haven't gone near him. I'm clean as a fucking whistle, and you know it."

"But you can't *stay* clean and do this investigation. This thing's gonna take you right into your father's circle, and IA will be watching the whole way."

"Why?"

"I told you, I don't know. They're laying off for now, but you go climbing around Rose McNamara's old pimp, her old haunts—"

"Then why did you send me on the case?"

"I wish I hadn't. I didn't know the ID of the vic at the time. I just knew Tifton asked for you."

Her fists closed, trembling with rage—at the chief, at Ty Craig, at her father. No telling how many times Artie Cole had looked the other way or tampered with evidence in his short career as a cop, all for a payoff from Craig. And no telling how many times he'd handled dirty deals for Craig after he'd been fired from the LCPD, in his much longer career as a criminal.

And ten hours after his death, Craig had come to Dani. *The apple doesn't fall too far from the tree*, he'd proposed, and tried to railroad her into taking her dad's place. *Tit for tat. You keep me and mine outta jail, and I pad your wallet.*

"I told Craig to fuck off," she said, hands fisting.

"Maybe. But you're smart enough to know the score. You're fruit of the poison tree, Sergeant *Cole*. There's no getting away from your name. The best thing you can do is stay clear of this investigation. Protect your reputation."

"You mean protect *your* reputation, and the department's."

He shrugged, silent.

"People will want to know why I'm not working, right after I was reassigned. What do I tell Tifton?"

"Tell him there's an asshole following you to airports, breaking into your house, leaving threats. The next time this guy contacts you, it might be more than your leg gets cut up. Makes sense to tuck you away awhile."

She quailed at that, then scoffed. "That's your story and you're sticking to it, huh?"

He rocked back on his heels an inch. "I'm not trying to scare you."

"You're not scaring me. You're pissing me off. Christ, Chief, you can't pull me from this case."

"I already did." He handed her two pieces of paper. "Personal leave form—it's filled out, just needs your signature. And the other is the receipt for your room at the Radisson down the street. Go stay there a few days, keep away from your house. It's on the county."

She glared at the pages like they might burn her and Gibson started out the door.

"Do you want to tell Tifton or do I need to?" he asked.

Dani's jaw went rigid. "I will."

"Tell him to come by at noon and brief Rollins. He's wrapping up the Winston thing this morning and then taking your place on this murder."

Rollins. A dick.

She waited until Chief Gibson left then threw the papers to the ground. At least she had until noon.

Lie low.

Fat chance.

CHAPTER
15

M ITCH JERKED when the doorbell rang.
"Sheridan." A man's voice, and the bell rang
again. "Mr. Sheridan?"

"Hold on," he called out. He pushed back in the chair,
and a mountain of ledgers beneath his arms slid across
the desk and collapsed into a pile. Slices of sunlight
slanted through the blinds and threw strips across the
whole mess.

Morning.

He strode through the huge living room, realized he'd
taken off his shirt sometime during the night, and tugged a
new one from his suitcase. "Coming," he called, and opened
the door on Tifton. And Dani. Her eyes fluttered down his
chest—over the tangle of scars there. Mitch felt her gaze like
the touch of a feather. And her shock.

"Sorry," he said, and shrugged the shirt over his head.
It wasn't pretty.

"You got a few minutes?" Tifton asked. "We've been
next door, talking to employees."

Mitch stepped back and they came in, Dani wearing
gray slacks with a low-slung belt and navy blazer that

flared at the hips. Her hair was stuffed into a barrette at the back of her head—a few tendrils having fallen free and dancing at her throat. She wore no makeup, but for a sheen of gloss on her lips and maybe a few swipes of mascara. She looked worn down, but even more beautiful than he remembered.

"You look terrible," he said.

She grunted. "Thanks."

She followed Tifton to the living area, her steps a little stiff, as if her leg had fallen asleep. Mitch turned a chair around for her.

"I'm fine." She waved away the offer and did a double take on Mitch's hands. "Jeez," she said. "Whose lights did you punch out?"

Mitch flexed his fingers. His knuckles were scraped and swollen. "A wall. Turns out these are lath and plaster, not drywall."

Tifton stifled a smile that Mitch knew meant *been there, done that*, and took a seat on the sofa. Mitch perched on the arm of a wide leather chair; Dani remained standing, stretching her left heel now and then.

"Okay," Tifton said, "here's the story. You're familiar with Highland Bridge, Mr. Sheridan?"

"Mitch," he corrected. "And yes. It's a favorite spot for jumpers. But Russ didn't jump. He was shot."

"He was shot with a .22, at point-blank range. We found the gun late last night. It belonged to him."

Mitch had been afraid of that. They were going to write this off as a suicide. "That doesn't mean he's the one who fired it."

"The wound to his head is consistent with suicide. If he was standing at the edge of the bridge when he did it, he fired with his right hand…"

Tifton shot a glance to Dani, whose face, Mitch noticed, was the color of limestone. She shifted, as if uneasy with the scrutiny.

"The best we can tell," Tifton said, "is that it probably happened sometime Sunday night."

"How do they know he went in from the bridge?" Mitch asked, dragging his gaze from Dani. She really didn't look good. "His body was found three miles away."

"The wounds are consistent with that sort of fall, and with the speed of the current and wind and where the body washed up…" They'd accounted for those variables. Mitch closed his eyes and Tifton went on. "We've got uniforms canvassing the banks this morning and knocking on all the doors in the area, trying to find someone who might have seen something, but it looks pretty clear that—"

"Was he alive?"

"Excuse me?"

"Was he alive when he hit the water?"

Dani's gaze hit the floor and Tifton swallowed. "Yes," he said. "The ME found water in his lungs."

A piece of Mitch's soul turned to dust. He'd heard details of drownings before. A terrible way to die. He stood, pacing a couple of steps. "How did he get there? His car is here. If he went to the bridge to throw himself off, how did he get there?"

"Bus. Taxi. There are ways."

"Why? And don't try to tell me it's because he'd just killed Rose McNamara."

"Easy," Dani chimed in. "Sanders isn't looking so great for McNamara anymore."

"She's right," Tifton said, "but we can't ignore the

phone calls from Rosie or the evidence we found in his apartment. Somehow, Sanders is connected to this. The note on the nightstand was his handwriting."

Mitch glared. "And it said *Camden Park*, not *Murder Rose McNamara*. There was a lot going on at the park this weekend. Maybe he was there for some other reason. Maybe someone set him up."

"Besides you and the maid," Tifton said, "only one other person has access to Sanders's apartment: Brad Harper. All three of you have alibis. You, for obvious reasons. The maid was at the hospital all Sunday at her mother's bedside. Harper attended a dinner event in Philadelphia Sunday night, and stayed over. That's where he was when you called him after you talked to Sanders."

"You checked that?" Mitch asked.

Dani said, "A hundred people saw him at the dinner; two different night clerks and a security guard say he didn't leave the hotel in the middle of the night. He checked out at nine in the morning, had brunch at the hotel in the midst of thirty other guests, and got back here about noon yesterday. That's when he found out his father hadn't shown for the meeting and came to us."

Mitch closed his eyes. Convenient.

"We need to look through Sanders's files," Tifton said, then added: "Files you apparently moved up here."

Mitch cocked a brow; Tifton's subtext was clear. "I wasn't trying to hide anything."

"Then can we see the files?" Dani asked.

"Down that hall, left. Help yourself."

She did. Tifton started to follow, but Mitch put up a hand, letting her get out of earshot. He spoke under his breath. "Hey, is Dani okay?"

Tifton peered at him. "*Dani?*"

To hell with privacy. "We go back a ways. She's limping. And looks like she hasn't slept in two days."

"The case is getting to her. Rosie was sort of a lost soul, and Nails is a sucker for those."

"She knew her?"

"She helped her out of a bad situation once. And this is her first case since she lost her dad. It's rough."

Whoa. "Her dad died?"

Tifton crossed his arms. "You go back a ways, huh?"

Mitch tightened. Yeah, they went back. But that didn't mean he knew much of anything about her personal life. Not the truth, anyway. All he knew was that the Beaver Cleaver family she'd talked about while lying in his arms had been a lie, and even that he hadn't come by freely. He'd learned it the night he showed up at her house unexpectedly and watched her dad get hauled away by cops, while Dani tried to shield herself and her little brother from their father's rage. The night Mitch had let her push him away. *Let go of me...Leave me alone...*

"We were kids, teenagers," Mitch said. "I know her dad was trouble."

Tifton gave a small shrug. "Things are a little hard on her right now," he said noncommittally. He was finished. Anything further about Dani's private life would have to come from her. "Something a man like you will want to keep in mind."

Mitch arched a brow. "You two got a thing going?"

"Nah. I just figure her dad fucked her up enough for one lifetime." He sharpened his gaze on Mitch. "I wouldn't wanna see another man come along and do it again."

Mitch was starting to like Tifton. He remembered something else. " 'Nails.' What's that about? She uses red nail polish or something?"

Tifton snorted. "Not nails as in fingernails. Nails, as in 'tough as.' They don't grow 'em any tougher."

Mitch thought of her on her knees at the river yesterday. Maybe not as tough as everyone thought. Maybe not as tough as she'd once led him to believe, either.

Dani reappeared, scowling. "You two finished bonding? There's a mountain of paperwork in here."

"We're coming," Tifton said and stepped away from Mitch, holding his eyes an extra pulse. Mitch nodded—message received. Hands off Dani.

Good advice. Even though he wasn't going to take it.

CHAPTER
16

DANI DIDN'T HAVE TIME to spare. She wanted in Sanders's files. She might not have access to the streets just now, but she had access to Russell Sanders, at least until Tift found out about her change of status.

He was gonna be *pissed*.

She'd taken the moment alone in Mitch's apartment to look around, leaving the two men to their dog-sniffing. Straight down the hall was an impressive bedroom—the bedcovers untouched—and to the right was a bathroom approximately the size of Dani's backyard. To the left, one hell of a mess: a huge office filled with papers and file folders and boxes, some still stacked on a dolly. One wall looked as if it had been hit by mortars, or one nasty fit of rage. Mitch was lucky he hadn't broken all the bones in his hands.

Tift ran a finger over one of the dents. "Whoa," he said, turning to Mitch. "Did you feel any better afterward?"

Mitch snorted; Tifton chuckled. Jesus, they *were* bonding.

Tifton's phone rang and he stepped out. Mitch turned that clear blue gaze on Dani and the room seemed to shrink.

She looked away, recalling the unexpected shiver that had passed over her skin when he came to the door, shirtless, his chest scored with scars. She guessed she'd convinced herself that all the hype surrounding the attack at Ar Rutbah was the work of a cagey publicist. The realization that he'd been genuinely wounded injected some shame into her thoughts. For one crazy instant, she'd wanted to reach out and touch the mangled ridges, soothe the pain.

Maybe let him touch her back.

God, stop thinking like that. He'll see. Mitch Sheridan didn't look *at* you, he looked *into* you. And he was doing it again now.

He crossed over to the desk where Dani stood. "You should have told me you just lost your father."

Oh, God. Damn Tifton. "It's neither here nor there."

"Bullshit. I've been there, if you recall."

She recalled. She recalled the nights they'd spent drinking beer in the fastback of Mitch's Barracuda, looking up at the stars through the rear windshield and talking about their families. He spoke of sheer idolatry for his deceased father, worry for his mom and little sister, respect for Russ Sanders. She spoke lies.

"Dani." Mitch's voice intruded, a low rumble from a foot away. His fingers stroked her cheek. "I know how much it hurts."

Dani snapped to. "Sure," she said, unable to suppress the sarcasm. She crossed two fingers and held them up. "Because my dad and I were like this."

Mitch shrank back a little. "What happened after I left? I mean, I know he was scheduled for trial..."

"He went to jail for a few months. Then he got out. Then he went back. In and out. He was a real blessing to society, my dad. Especially to the police department."

"Is that why you became a cop?"

"I became a cop to—" She stopped. To feel clean. To try to redeem herself and the family name. But it had never worked. The fraternal good-old-boys network of police wasn't quick to forgive. Most cops remembered her dad and, like Gibson, considered Dani tainted blood. Few were willing to let her earn her reputation by starting with a clean slate. "I just did," she said.

"Where's your brother?"

Dani softened. Jason was the one thing she'd done right in her life. "Air Force. He's doing his second tour in Afghanistan right now."

"So, after I left, you took care of your brother until he left and your dad until he died." Mitch canted his head, looking straight into her eyes. "Who took care of you?"

Dani flinched. *No one. I pushed away the one person who wanted to.*

The door opened on Tifton pocketing his phone. Dani began to breathe again.

"That was Brad Harper," Tift said. "He's in a panic because he went into his dad's office and found it emptied out." He gestured to the mess around the office and looked at Mitch. "You couldn't have let him know you were bringing Sanders's files up here?"

He shrugged. "I could've," he said, not taking his eyes off Dani.

"Humph," Tift said. "So, the tabloids at the grocery store checkout line were right? You and Brad..."

Mitch finally pulled his gaze away. "I never said Brad and I were buddies. But I always respected him as Russell's son."

"And does that respect go two ways?"

"Ask Brad."

"We did. He told us if his father shared confidences with anyone, it would have been you, not him."

Mitch shook his head. "That could be, but Russell didn't tell me he was having an affair with an eighteen-year-old hooker or that he was planning to kill her and then shoot himself and jump off a bridge."

"Okay, okay," Tifton said. "So lay out the operation of this joint. Who's in charge now?"

Mitch rubbed a hand over his face, as if he had to think about it. "There's a board of directors. Twelve of them."

"Meeting at ten o'clock," Dani said. They'd learned that when talking to employees next door.

"Right." He looked at his watch, prompting Dani to do the same. Nine-twenty.

"And the board will take over the day-to-day management?" Tift asked.

"The board is made up of fund-raising gurus and photography-buff socialites like Marshall Kettering and his wife. You've met them?"

"The distinguished gentleman and the hottie?"

Dani rolled her eyes.

"That's them. They throw balls and sponsor exhibits. Russ and his staff did the real work."

"And you picked him?"

"We picked each other. Russ was a newspaper photographer and family friend. After my dad died, he became my mentor. I struck out to fix the whole damned world, but the only attention my photos drew was from art lovers. The elite started attending my shows and publishers put my photos in big, glossy coffee-table books only the privileged could afford. The people *in* the pictures were still starving or killed by ethnic cleansing or disease." His face grew hard. "I couldn't stop the bleeding."

"Excuse me?" Tifton asked, but Dani's heart sprang a leak. Mitch's father had bled to death in his arms.

So that's why he'd taken off into the world. Doing penance.

"I don't know what you mean," Tifton said.

"I mean," Mitch said, "I got rich and famous but didn't change a goddamn thing. Russ was the one who built the Foundation and made my photos actually mean something. For a while, I almost believed we were doing some good."

"The JMS Foundation website says that your northern Afghan exhibit has been touring museums for two years and raised two million dollars for villages like the one you featured," Tift said. "That sounds like doing good to me."

"Yeah, that's me," Mitch said. "World fucking hero."

A cosmic little sound rang out and all three of them looked at their phones. It was Mitch's. He listened for a second and a crease folded into his brow. When he hung up, he said, "That was Mia Kettering. She's volunteering next door this morning and says there's a woman asking for me."

"Who is it?" Dani asked.

"I don't know. Mia says her name is Janet Milano."

Dani straightened, and both men noticed.

"Nails?" Tifton said. "Who's Janet Milano?"

Dani swallowed. "Rosie McNamara's sister."

CHAPTER
17

Mɪᴛᴄʜ sʜᴏᴡᴇʀᴇᴅ ᴀɴᴅ sʜᴀᴠᴇᴅ in less than ten minutes, pulled on a fresh pair of jeans, and found a long-sleeved dark-stripe shirt in one of the closets. He was pretty sure it belonged to him, left here during one of his rare visits over the years.

He looked in the mirror. Okay. Rose McNamara's sister had been through enough—he didn't want to meet her looking like a terrorist. He needed her cooperation.

Mia Kettering met Mitch at the back entrance of the Foundation, elegantly groomed as usual, her hair smelling of coconut. "I put her in the first conference room," she whispered to Mitch. "That woman scares me. She keeps asking to see a picture of Russ."

Mitch frowned and strode to the front lobby. He lifted a large framed photo of Russ from the wall—a plaque at the bottom of the frame naming him cofounder and managing director of the JMS Foundation—and carried it to the conference room. He placed the portrait on the table.

Janet Milano watched, a plump young woman with her hair pulled back in a bun and mascara smeared beneath her eyes. Without speaking, she walked over and looked down at the portrait.

"So, he's the one," she said after a moment, clutching her arms around her waist. "This is the man they say murdered my sister."

"Who is *they*?" Mitch asked, keeping his voice warm and low.

"TV. The news."

"That's the media, Ms. Milano, not the police."

She gave him a blank look, then recognition sparked. "You're him. You're the one who—"

"I'm Mitch Sheridan. Russell Sanders was like a father to me."

That took her aback. He supposed she expected him to apologize for Russ's actions, to try to distance himself and the Foundation from the horrific rumors about Russ and Rose McNamara.

No way.

He noticed a crumpled photo in her hand. "Is that your sister?"

She looked down, as if she'd forgotten it, and handed it to Mitch. It was a candid shot of two young women, grinning at the camera, cradling a baby together. One was Janet Milano; the other, Rosie.

Jesus, Mitch thought, stricken by how young she looked. What in the world would Russell have to do with a girl like that?

He handed the picture back to her sister. "She was beautiful."

"Yes," she said, and Mitch thought he caught a trace of bitterness in her voice. "Beautiful."

"Ms. Milano, what makes you think Russell knew your sister?"

"I heard them talking on the phone this weekend."

"What?" A lump climbed into Mitch's throat.

"She was at my house, babysitting. She was talking to Sanders when I got home." Her face hardened. "They were arguing."

Mitch was thunderstruck. "What was it about?"

"I don't know. They were making plans— 'Okay.' 'Don't worry, I won't.' 'I'll be there.' Things like that. But Rosie was upset."

"But she didn't say anything about him?"

"She just said it was someone she met at work and she'd explain later."

Mitch felt as if a hammer had just nailed him between the eyes. She met him at work? Rosie had worked at a Big Lots. Mitch didn't know of any Big Lots in this area of town and it wasn't a place Russ would go out of his way to shop.

"How did you know it was Sanders on the phone?" he asked.

"I didn't, then. I only thought about it last night after the police had been asking about him, and scrolled back through the numbers on my phone."

"Did you tell police?"

She nodded. "Yes, this morning."

Mitch's jaw ground. Another strike against Russ.

They spoke for another five minutes, but there was nothing more. Mitch jotted down his number. "Janet, I'm sorry about your sister. If you think of anything else, call me. Please."

She looked at Mitch through watery eyes and scanned the furnishings of the conference room. Her expression was filled with a mixture of resentment and confusion—she probably regarded Mitch as a rich bastard concerned only with the reputation of the organization—but there was nothing he could do about that now. He had to figure out what the hell Russell had been doing with Rose McNamara.

Mitch frowned. Russell *had* known Rose McNamara, and the police knew it. Dani knew it. And true to form, she wasn't telling him everything.

Mitch didn't commonly throw his weight around, but he wasn't above doing it, either. He pulled out his cell phone, dialed the LCPD, and got Chief Dave Gibson. Five minutes later, he hung up, jaw grinding.

Dani had some explaining to do.

Brad watched Mitch leave the Foundation and could nearly taste the hatred on his tongue. The director of the Foundation was dead, implicated in the murder of a hooker. The biggest publicity campaign to date had been launched for the upcoming exhibition and the display wasn't even finished. Sponsors were dropping like flies.

But the board wasn't worried. Why? Because the mighty Mitch Sheridan was home. He'd carry on for Russell, finish the photos for the exhibition, and cajole flagging sponsors not to drop. With Mitch in attendance, the media would make the exhibition into more of a spectacle than ever.

James Mitchell Sheridan: everybody's fucking hero.

Brad kept a lid on his emotions until he got into his office and latched the door, then ripped off his suit coat and cleared part of his desk with one wild sweep of his arm. "Goddamn it," he snarled, teeth clenched. He remembered his pills and picked up the coat, digging into the pocket in a frenzy. A few bennies. That's what he needed: take the edge off. He found them and popped some into his mouth, still muttering, "I hate that fucking bastard..."

"Well, that's ironic, considering you're the one who's a bastard."

Brad spun toward the voice.

Mia. World-class cleavage, fuck-me lips, thick, silky hair tinted with shades of brown and gold and red that probably cost more at the hair salon than Brad earned in a week. Brad remembered his surprise the night she'd cut her trademark long tresses—an act of impulse inspired by some argument with Marshall that had left her hysterical and seeking out Brad. She'd found him—in the act of committing a felony. At first he'd panicked, but to his surprise, he soon learned that the new, short-haired Mia had only traded in her demure persona for one that proved sassy and sexy and hot as hell. She'd just about worn his ass out that night, in ways she never had before. Who knew she'd find sex with a felon such a turn-on?

He glanced past her at his office door. "How did you get in here?"

"I saw your secretary step out and made the most of her absence. You'll have to send her out for something when it's time for me to leave." She nodded to his jacket pocket, now turned inside out. "My husband's supply of those isn't endless, you know. Besides, someone might actually expect you to think this week."

"Fuck you."

She lifted one sultry shoulder. "Maybe. I take it the publicity is a nightmare?"

"We're working on it. Sponsors are the biggest risk right now. People tend to like their charity donations to go to places where the directors aren't sex maniacs and murderers." He shook his head. "Imagine the paragon of virtue that was my dad, fucking a teenage hooker."

"Well, I can tell you that Marshall's more worried than he's letting on. I don't think he slept two hours last night." She shook her head. "What do the police think?"

"They're confused. They know Rose McNamara was talking to Dad and don't know why. But they're digging. Mitch emptied out Dad's office and has them going through his files."

She straightened. "What will they find?"

"Nothing." Brad closed his eyes, waiting for the buzz from the bennies to kick in. Damn it, everything had been going so well. His father's precious, charitable Foundation serving as a black-market baby ring. The satisfaction was almost as sweet as the money.

But now everything was compromised. He just had to hope his father hadn't known enough to leave any red flags for the police.

Mia came over to him. "This might be the time for you to think about hitting the Cayman Islands or something. You have money."

"Not enough. I needed more time, more girls." Brad narrowed his eyes on her, let his gaze drop down her curves. "Why? Are you in the mood for a vacation?"

She ran a long tapered nail down his chest. "I'm a happily married woman," she purred.

Brad scoffed. He enjoyed his time with Mia and respected her as a leading lady of Lancaster's high society. But he didn't trust her as far as he could throw her.

Still, in addition to being a reliable source for medications otherwise difficult to come by, Mia had certain skills that not all women had and a willingness to use them. More than once, usually in that moment before his eyes rolled back into his head in ecstasy, Brad had wondered where she'd honed them, and decided he didn't really want to know.

Just now, she was getting ready to show him some—he could see it in the way her breathing deepened, her lashes dropped to half-mast, her lips parted. She put a little pressure on his chest and backed him up, his hips hitting his desk, his blood surging to where her fingers worked the zipper. Like a rag doll whose purpose she well understood, Mia Kettering dropped to her knees.

Cayman Islands...Maybe. But there was one more girl he had to finish first—Nika Love. She was only a few days from giving birth, and they already knew her baby was a white male. White male newborns were the biggest money in the business, and more than half of that money had already changed hands.

He'd have to talk to Dr. Housley. Rush the birth a little.

He stopped Mia with a hand in her hair, then picked up the phone and dialed Housley.

"Meet me," he ordered when Housley answered. "Yes, damn it, it's important. Five o'clock."

He hung up, blew out a breath, and threaded his fingers through Mia's hair as if it made straps for him to hang on to. He tipped back his head and thought about the Caymans and the money and the head between his hands.

Then he didn't have another thought for a long time.

CHAPTER
18

WHOA."
    Holding a receipt from a mound of papers on the floor, Dani's pulse picked up. She'd started with money—hoping to find that Sanders had paid a medical bill to an obstetrician or taken out chunks of cash for Rosie. Anything that might explain the telephone argument Rosie's sister had thrown into the mix this morning. The fact that Rosie had had a baby and had an unexplained conversation with Sanders didn't necessarily mean the baby was his, but it was the most logical thing they'd thought of so far. If he'd been one of her johns and gotten her pregnant, then maybe when she came back to town, he got scared word would come out.

Dani hadn't found anything like that. But this receipt was interesting.

"What?" Tifton asked, looking up from his own stack.

She walked the receipt across the room. The stitches in her calf tugged. "Big Lots receipt, in the trash from Sanders's office. On Sunday, Russ Sanders bought a bottle of water and a pack of gum at Big Lots. The one on Grimby Street where Rosie worked."

"That's a long way to go for gum. That store is twenty minutes away."

He was right, but Dani didn't like it. "I'll tell you what, Tift: No matter how much evidence we find that Sanders and Rosie were involved, or even that he killed her, it doesn't change that he's dead and someone else is out there now, cutting the hair off women and fucking with my life."

Tift's phone rang and he picked it up, jotted a couple things down as he listened. "Okay," he said into the phone, then frowned. "Why did you call me? Why not Nails?"

Dani turned her back. God, this was it—Tifton would find out she was off the case. Behind her, he went silent, listening to the caller, but she could feel his eyes on her back, sense the tension rising in the room. He remained silent for what seemed like an eternity, then said into the phone, "What? What?" and hit it on the desk. From a foot away, he said into the receiver, "You're breaking up, man," and disconnected. An eternity passed before he looked at Dani and spoke. "Are you *trying* to get me fired?"

Her cheeks prickled. "You didn't know. They can't blame you for not knowing." She lifted her chin. "And you're covered. That thing with the phone just now, that was great. You can't expect me to hide out in a motel room like a coward."

He walked over to her, took the receipt. "What happens tonight when you finally need some sleep?"

"Then I'll go to the Radisson, keep my head down. I won't go home. Today, I'll stay locked in here with the files. Someone has to do it." She glanced around at the sheer magnitude of the task. "You can use me, Tift. I can't go out on the streets right now, but there's something here in all this paper, something that'll tell us what Sanders was up to with Rosie."

"And if I report you instead?"

"Then I'll have to work the case alone." She looked straight into his eyes. "My house, Tift, everything I own. My *dog*."

He cursed, but Dani thought she was good with him. Tifton knew she wouldn't stop trying to find the bastard, and cutting her off from the case would only leave her in the dark and make her a bigger target. Not to mention the fact that she could still be helpful on the case. He'd go along.

"I'm taking this receipt and going to catch up my *new* partner." He started out but turned back to her. "That call, by the way, was about Runt."

Dani's heart stopped.

"She's alive, barely. The vet called the lab with blood work and they compared notes: Hard to tell since no one saw the first few symptoms, but they think they're look-ing at some sort of narcotic painkiller, something that affects the neurological system."

"Narcotic painkiller. Like a prescription drug?"

"Yeah," he said and put up a hand. "But I'll follow up with it. You don't need to go running around snooping in medicine cabinets."

A knot of tears formed in her throat. Some asshole had offered Runt meat to shut her up and keep her docile when that crazy dog would've followed him around the house begging to be petted. "Runt was no threat."

"Pit bull, Dani," Tift said, getting out his car keys. "If I'm going into a house with a pit, I assume the dog needs to be taken out, not cuddled. The intruder didn't know your particular dog was a freak of nature."

He left and Dani went back to the papers, but she couldn't get her mind off Runt. Tifton had a point about pits, but then why hadn't the intruder just killed her? Not wanting neighbors to hear a gunshot, maybe? Still, Runt would have willingly walked right into the killer's hands. It made the invasion of Dani's home feel more like a message than a threat. Maybe even a taunt. Made the hair almost seem like a souvenir of some sort.

The front door opened and Dani straightened. She stood, fingers touching her gun, and peeked down the hall.

Mitch.

He looked like an executive on casual Friday: clean-shaven, combed, wearing a long-sleeved shirt and dark jeans with loafers. Rugged crook to his nose.

He wasn't smiling. "I didn't expect you to still be here," he said. His gaze roamed across her bare shoulders, touched stockinged feet. She'd tossed her blazer over the back of a chair and stuck her shoes underneath. Nothing revealing, yet somehow his eyes seemed to divest her of the rest.

"Lots of paper," Dani replied, walking to a file cabinet in the far corner of the office. Distance seemed a good idea.

"Is your partner around?"

He wanted to talk to Tifton? "He just left."

Mitch nodded, as if he expected as much, then propped his butt on the edge of the desk. A muscle jerked in his cheek. "Why didn't you tell me Rose McNamara had called Russell from her sister's house?"

Of course, Janet had told him. "It's not protocol to share every detail of a case with friends of the victims."

"You mean friends of the *suspects*," he accused.

"Sanders isn't a suspect unless he has an accomplice passing out notes."

"Then why are you still here?"

"Because he's still our best lead to Rosie's murderer."

"And who's your best lead to Russell's murderer?"

Dani turned to face him. "His death was ruled a suicide, you know that. And I might as well go ahead and tell you I found a Big Lots receipt in Sanders's trash from Sunday afternoon—the same Big Lots where Rosie worked."

"Christ."

"Look," she said, "I think I know what you'll say to this, but is it possible your friend got Rosie pregnant?"

He blanched. "She was pregnant?"

"No. But the ME says she'd had a baby, sometime in the last few years—probably when she was still working the streets."

"Jesus, she would've been just a kid. What happened to the baby?"

"We don't know. So, is it possible?"

"As far as I know, Russell knew how to do it."

She glared at him.

"Come on, Dani. Russ never forgave himself for not being there for Brad. If he'd gotten a girl pregnant, he would've been a father to the child."

Dani grunted. "Of course."

He eyed her from his perch on the desk like a scientist studying a new species. "What's it like always being so suspicious?"

"It's my job to be suspicious. I'm working a murder case here."

"Well, now, that's funny." He pushed from the desk and strode casually—too casually—across the room.

"Because I just spoke to a Chief Dave Gibson. That's not what he told me."

Dani went still. Busted.

"What, no comment?" Mitch asked, disturbingly cool. "Gibson says you took a few days off, that you wouldn't be working this case anymore."

She turned around to face him. "Go ahead. Report me."

"Impersonating an officer?" Mitch quipped, but he crossed his arms. He didn't look humored. "Of course, that's what you'd expect me to do."

"I'm just trying to find Rosie's killer," Dani said, emotion rising in her chest. "You didn't see her, damn it, I did. He ruined her. Just when she was finally getting her life together, some sonofabitch hacked her up and came into my—"

She stopped, feeling the anger twist into fear and seeing that Mitch noticed. Don't. Christ, if he knew that her house was destroyed and her dog in a coma and that some murdering bastard had followed her, there'd be no convincing him to keep his distance. She'd be right back where she was eighteen years ago: needing him when she couldn't have him.

Couldn't have him? Her mind stumbled on the thought. When she was seventeen and smitten, she had reason to be afraid of letting him—anyone—in. She had a brother to protect. What was her excuse now?

She shook that off. Eighteen years don't just vanish into thin air when lovers come back together. There were all kinds of good reasons not to fall for him now. Chief among them was that it would hurt like hell when he left.

"I wouldn't have left," Mitch said, and Dani's lungs

stopped working. She risked looking up at him. "A broken nose wasn't enough to have kept me away."

That last night she'd seen him came back in a rush...Her father, drunk and shouting, being taken away in handcuffs; her brother, Jason, crying in fear; Mitch standing there watching the whole, horrific thing, though she'd never even told him where she lived. *Go away, you're not supposed to be here*...He tried to hold her and comfort her and shield her from her father's hurtful words, but she wouldn't let him. She thrashed, trying to break free of his hands and her own lies, terrified that her father was right...*They'll take away Jason...You'll never see him again*...Mitch wouldn't let go and Dani flailed, desperate, her elbow smashing into his nose. He staggered back and held his forearm against his face, gushing blood, still unwilling to leave until those last hateful words she slung his way...*There's someone else, damn it. I don't want you*...

Lies and more lies.

Now, Dani forced herself to answer. "I know you wouldn't have left," she said. "That's why I had to lie."

Mitch closed his eyes. When he opened them again, Dani felt as if they were boring right into her soul. "So there wasn't someone else. Then why?" he asked. "You couldn't think I didn't want you. Why?"

"I was scared, I was a kid." She shoved the file drawer closed, her voice vibrating with emotion. "My mom had been dead for years and my father was a drunk and a gambler and a crook, and was gone more often than he was there—and we thanked our lucky stars for that. For as long as I can remember, I lived in fear someone would find out there was no real parent and take Jason away. Dad always said they would."

"I wouldn't have let anyone hurt you."

"You were eighteen years old. What were you supposed to do?"

"Well, I don't know because you never gave me a chance, did you?" Mitch shot back.

"My dad was being arrested. I didn't know if he'd be back. I only had to last a few months, until I turned eighteen." She paused. "And I didn't know you'd go halfway around the world."

"But you were so sure I'd run out and give away your secrets that you elbowed me in the nose and told me there was someone else. Better alone than hurt, is that it?"

"He's my brother. He was all I had."

"No," Mitch said, his hands gripping her arms. "You had me."

His words were like a slap in the face. *You had me.* Maybe. But to Dani, loving Mitch was a source of worry, not comfort. She'd been hiding her father's alcoholism and gambling and even his beatings for too many years to just stop and hope nothing happened to Jason as a result. "I couldn't risk my little brother being taken," she said. "I couldn't take that chance just because my teenage hormones were becoming active."

"Is that what you called it?" Mitch asked, and Dani noticed the heat of his hands on her arms, not clutching anymore, but stroking. He cocked his head, and one hand lifted to brush his knuckles down her cheek. "Teenage hormones?"

Dani's throat went dry. "What else?"

"Let's see." He bent his head, his lips covering hers, fingers unfurling to cup her cheek and slide into her hair. His other hand followed so that her face was cradled between hands so strong, so warm, so gentle that Dani melted, the play of his lips on hers bringing a tiny sigh of pleasure from her throat. She could feel the tension in his arms, the restraint it cost him to keep the kiss tender, and when he finally lifted his head, her lips felt cool in the air that sneaked back in.

"You're not a teenager anymore," he said. "What do you call it now?"

Dani might have stepped back, but his hands still cupped her cheeks and her brain didn't seem to be functioning. Crazy. She called it crazy. And foolish, and maybe even dangerous. She didn't know how strong her heart was these days. By design, it hadn't had much exercise in the man department. "We shouldn't do this."

"Why not?" His thumbs stroked her cheeks.

"I'm supposed to be working."

"No, you're not. I thought we just established that."

The flame of desire fizzled in the wake of that reminder. Dani stepped back. "Rosie. I can't let it go, Mitch. I don't care what Chief Gibson says."

He blew out a breath and looked at her. "Then I guess I'll have to hire you."

She frowned. "What?"

"To work on the case. Find out who killed Rosie *and* Russell. Your colleagues are going to write his death off as a suicide. I need someone who believes it wasn't, who cares."

"Tifton cares," she said skeptically.

"How many cases does Tifton have on his plate right now?"

"Fifteen, maybe twenty."

"And you?"

Dani felt herself warming to the idea. "As of this morning, I'm sort of...between cases."

The tension in his expression loosened. "So, what do you charge for investigative services?" he asked.

"It's a conflict of interest for a police officer to moonlight as a PI."

Mitch snorted. "Wouldn't want to break any rules, would we?"

"Hey," she protested, but it was a token. Inside, she reeled with relief. He was going to let her stay and work through the files. He was going to help her figure out what Russell and Rosie had going.

He was going to kiss her again.

Lord, she had to stop thinking like that. She looked up to find him studying her, mortified to think he might have read that errant thought on her face. A faint smile shadowed his lips.

"So, is it a deal?" he asked. "No official PI status, no salary. Just the opportunity to hang with me and find Rosie's killer."

Dani tried to contain the surge of excitement that rushed through her veins. It had to be adrenaline, not some other—less admirable—hormone. This wasn't about being with Mitch, it was about finding the bastard who killed Rosie.

Yeah, that was it. The thrill in her belly had nothing to do with Mitch Sheridan.

She stuck out her hand. "Deal."

CHAPTER
19

MARSHALL LEFT HIS OFFICE at four-thirty in the afternoon, drove five miles away and five miles back, then let himself back in. Empty now—it hadn't taken long for everyone to call it a day. He'd often thought that bankers' hours were extensive compared to those of psychiatrists who owned their own practice. Marshall and his partners saw patients only three days a week, started at ten o'clock, took a two-hour lunch, and by four-thirty each day everyone was gone, down to the last office staffer. A cushy life for those who wanted it, but that wasn't why Marshall had chosen it. He was a true scientist. A physician and mental health expert. He was a researcher and student of the human psyche and even after thirty years in the profession, he was still fascinated by all it had to offer.

And, occasionally, shocked. Once in a great, great while, all his skill and knowledge and research weren't enough to turn a life around. Ronald Fulton had been one of those—a court-ordered case and a man utterly without conscience. Fulton could step on his mother as easily as he could step on a bug, and never think twice about the difference.

Mia was the other. Not because she was without a conscience—quite the opposite. Hers had almost destroyed her.

She was good right now—looking forward to the meeting that Marshall promised her on Sunday, behaving as befitting the board president's wife during these trying times at the Foundation. But it wouldn't last. As surely as he knew his own name, Marshall knew she would implode. When she learned the truth, it would kill her.

He unlocked a cabinet in the front office, accessed his office manager's safe for the keys, and went down the hall to where the medicines were stored. The practice wasn't a pharmacy—they didn't keep large stockpiles, but they had a decent stash of the most used prescriptions. Anxiolytics, sedatives, hypnotics, antidepressants, opioids, amphetamines, painkillers. Samples of most were all right there and if he was careful, he could make sure Mia met the crushing news on Sunday in a state that enabled her to handle it.

And after that? His heart hollowed out. Jesus God, he didn't know. He only knew that all her life she had waited for this day, and the last time it didn't happen, she nearly went over the edge of sanity. Hacked off her hair and went almost into a trance-like state. *This* would be worse.

He opened the first cabinet in a daze, grabbed a packet of this and a bottle of that—he'd worry about amounts and combinations later—then stopped. He peered into the cabinet and frowned. Unlocked the second one and found the same thing there, and in the third. Marshall rubbed his beard. He would swear that just yesterday he had signed delivery receipts, that they had just restocked.

He pinched the crease between his brows, forcing

himself to think. Sarah Rittenhouse had been his office manager for years and was the only one with access to the keys. She didn't make mistakes and she didn't leave deliveries of narcotics sitting around the office, unlocked.

Sarah, stealing? Ridiculous.

Marshall put back the pills he'd pulled out—better to find out what's going on. Call his partners, talk to Sarah. Straighten this out so he could be sure to have what he needed for Mia.

Someone taking drugs from the practice was a serious matter, but Mia's welfare came first. Always and forever: Mia came first.

•

Brad waited in the parking lot of a huge movie theater: sixteen screens, all of them busy every afternoon and evening. At this hour of day—late afternoon—the parking lot was fairly empty: matinees winding down and the evening shows not yet in full swing. Still, there were people out and about—teens cutting school, singles, retired couples catching matinee prices. He'd met the good doctor here more than once, each time exchanging cold, hard cash for a baby. They were always careful to park outside the range of security cameras, but they were equally certain nothing about their actions would stand out in someone's memory.

This evening, there was no baby. And Brad was in a hurry. When the police found out Rosie had had a baby once upon a time—and they would—they'd use that as a logical reason for her to have hounded Russell. It wouldn't take long to decide to take a fine comb to the Foundation records, and a hard cold look at OCIN, the branch that handled overseas adoptions.

As well as a handful of illegal domestic ones.

A white BMW swung into the space across from him. Stephen Housley climbed out, shot a cigarette to the pavement, and got into Brad's car. He was a small, lanky man in his fifties, with a smoker's deep wrinkles and cheeks that always looked red and rough. Like he was allergic to his aftershave or something.

Housley was an ob-gyn on staff at Spring Grove Hospital, west of Baltimore. But it was his one-day-a-week stint at a clinic for low-income women that had brought him and Brad Harper together—years ago, when Brad had still been in corporate law. Brad had been screwing a girl in the mailroom. With a fistful of Brad's money, she'd gone to the clinic to get an abortion but chickened out. It was Housley who'd offered a solution: He'd take the baby and pay off the girl. Brad didn't know where the child had gone and didn't care. But whoever got it had apparently paid Housley well.

A few years later, Housley came back. By then, Brad was working at the Foundation, setting up a brand-new wing called Overseas Children in Need—OCIN—that facilitated adoptions. *Remember that little deal we struck? I have a girl at the clinic—a hooker, too late for an abortion…I was thinking, with OCIN and all, you could find a place for the baby. The girl and I take a cut, you get the lion's share, the baby gets a home. A win-win-win situation…*

Housley had delivered five unwanted babies over the next three years and Brad, in turn, handed the infants over to carefully vetted parents who had applied for an overseas adoption through OCIN. They were vetted by OCIN for their suitability as parents. They were vetted by Brad for their willingness to look the other way when it came to legalities. If they could pay the price and keep their mouths shut, they could adopt from within the States, he told them. Not only could they get a newborn rather than an older child, but the process was a lot quicker than going through the legal rigmarole of a foreign adoption and they didn't risk the health and socialization problems rampant with the foreign children. All they had to do was fork over the cash and fudge the kid's age by about six months, call the kid a preemie.

"What's going on?" Housley asked.

Brad pulled out of the parking lot, looping the block as they talked. "You've seen the news? Police are looking at the Foundation, trying to connect my father to Rose McNamara."

"If you've been careful, it won't matter."

"I've been careful. But I want Nika Love finished. Get the baby, induce labor or something. She's far enough along."

"She is, but it doesn't matter."

"Why not?"

"I saw her today at the clinic."

"And?" If something was wrong with the baby, it could ruin everything. This was the expensive white male.

"She's changed her mind. She doesn't want to sell."

Brad's fingers tightened on the steering wheel. "It's too late. The deal is done. The bitch already agreed to everything."

Housley sighed. "Have you ever dealt with pregnant girls, Harper? There's no reasoning with them."

Brad ground out a curse. Christ, he needed this one. He couldn't return any of the money now—not with the cops nosing around. Mostly, he couldn't leave both a young woman and a wealthy couple out there who knew about the brokerage but hadn't actually benefited from it. It was their participation that made them culpable and kept them silent: Buying and selling babies was criminal in every state.

"She has to give up the baby," Brad growled. "Too much money has changed hands. The parents are already at the hotel waiting. Too many people are involved."

"Well, just what the hell do you want to do, Brad? Lock her up until she gives birth? For God's sake, you can't just *take* a baby. The mother has to give him over."

"How much does she want?"

Housley shook his head. "She wants the *kid*. I'm not sure more money will matter to her."

Bullshit. Money mattered to everyone. The rich, the poor. It was always about money. "Where is she?"

"She's staying at the homeless shelter on Bailing Street. Her pimp threw her out four months ago."

Brad wheeled back into the parking lot, swung into a spot two rows from Housley's car. A sprinkling of cool rain had begun to fall, spattering his windshield. The drops seemed to strike his brain, inside his skull, like darts. "I'll take care of it," he said, digging into his pocket. Nothing. Damn it, he thought he had a forty-bar in his pocket to put between him and the rain-darts. There were two left this afternoon. Had he taken them?

Maybe at home. Maybe he'd left them there, in the humidor used for pills.

"What are you going to do?" Housley asked.

"I'm going to go see Nika," Brad said. Spikes in his brain. "Convince her to do what's right."

CHAPTER
20

MITCH HAD HELPED DANI for a few hours then spent the rest of the afternoon salvaging sponsors who'd heard rumors of Russ's transgressions. Phone conferences mostly, but Mitch drove to meet personally with those who were close. He wasn't a boardroom type of guy, but he was smart and had an easygoing charm, and had been places and seen things most people could only imagine. With the exception of Dani, his sincerity was rarely questioned. Sponsors liked the idea that he would be mounting this exhibition himself and would be in attendance. It guaranteed good media coverage.

Enough to counteract the bad media coverage in the meantime? That remained to be seen.

By evening, rain falling, he was back in Lancaster, jet lag and lack of sleep getting to him. He dialed Dani.

"Where are you?" he asked when she picked up.

"The same place I was when you left. Ass-deep in papers."

The image made Mitch smile, though what he saw in his mind probably wasn't accurate. In his mind, her ass was bare. "Have you eaten?" he asked, and she hesitated. "Food. You remember what that is?"

"No. I mean, yes, I know what it is, damn it. No, I haven't eaten." She was flustered—uncomfortable being coddled. At seventeen, she'd been the sole responsible caretaker in her house since she was eight, though Mitch hadn't known it at the time. He was too busy playing that role himself for his grieving mom and sister ever since his dad had died. His brother, Neil, had run off to bash in heads with the FBI, and Mitch, three years younger, had become the man of the house. When he fell for Dani, looking out for her had been a natural thing to do, no matter how odd it felt to her.

Apparently no one had gotten her used to it in the meantime. The notion was both sad and motivating. "I'll be there in twenty minutes."

He swung by a sub shop and picked up sandwiches and chips, then pulled up in front of the Foundation apartment building. The muscles in his left thigh yanked at the bone as he hit the front steps, but he pushed through, anxious to see Dani. He'd called Tifton on the way home, pried a little. Tifton had nothing new to tell him about the case and was too professional to say anything about Dani. "She needed a couple personal days, that's all," he said.

Mitch headed through the main foyer of the apartment building and stopped outside Russ's door: A light was on. The skin on the back of his neck tightened. The police tape was gone, the door unlatched. He set down the bag of food and stepped inside, squelching the ridiculous impulse to call for Russ. Russ wasn't here.

But someone was.

He moved through the living room, down the hall,

peering into the spare bedroom and bath, heading toward the office. Silence lured him in, and there, sitting at Russ's desk with an empty tumbler and mostly empty bottle of scotch, was Brad.

"Jesus, not again," Mitch said, catching the scotch bottle before Brad tipped it with his elbow. "You need to get your shit together, man."

Brad looked at him through dilated pupils. "Mitch, Mitch, Mitch. The beloved son. Only, you weren't even his son."

"You're toast, man," Mitch said, ducking from the stench of alcohol on his breath.

"You knew him longer than I did. 'Uncle Russ,'" Brad slurred. "Don't you think that's funny, that his son grew up without knowing him, and all the while, the Sheridan kids were having Saturday-night card games with him?"

Mitch slung Brad's arm over his shoulders and heaved him up. "Russ didn't know your mom was pregnant with you when she left," Mitch said. "My family didn't have anything to do with that."

"That's what he always claimed, too," Brad slurred. "'I'm sorry, son, I never knew about you until now. Mitch has been like a son to me, but you're my real blood,' he told me. 'I love you.' You know, sometimes I almost believed him."

"Russ did love you."

"Not like you."

Mitch half dragged him through the apartment and across the foyer, aiming for the front entrance to Brad's apartment. Brad wouldn't remember this conversation in the morning, but it didn't matter; they'd had it countless times. *My father loves you and tolerates me*, was Brad's theme.

Brad's knees gave out and Mitch almost lost him. "Give me the key," Mitch said, taking it from Brad's hand. He opened up and pulled Brad inside, dumped him into a chair. He stood for a minute looking down at the man Russ had tried so hard to love, and had trouble coming up with sympathy. Brad was drunk and bitter and vengeful. Sympathy would be a waste of time.

"See ya, Brad."

"He would've helped her."

Mitch stopped. "What?"

"He called you to stop it and they both died." Brad began to chuckle. Little belly-hiccups that sooner or later would bring up the booze. "I think that's what they call *irony*."

"What are you talking about?" Brad didn't answer. Mitch seized his collar and pulled him out of the chair. "Stop what?"

Brad wobbled in his hands, not a bone in his body. His eyes focused for one second—the irises no more than thin lines ringing wide pupils, and he stared at Mitch then turned away. One second later, he came back up—spitting.

Part of it missed, but part of it didn't and Mitch didn't think: He drew back a fist and let it fly. Blood sprayed from Brad's nose. He sank to the floor, taking a stack of papers with him as his arms flailed over the coffee table. Mitch wiped the spittle from his jaw with the back of his hand and pulled back for another strike, heaves of fury filling his lungs. He stopped. Brad was out. He was under a quart of scotch, at the least, and probably something more. Feeling nothing.

Mitch cursed but stepped back, some tiny shred of honor forcing him to let it go rather than finish the fight that still clenched his fists. He grabbed Brad's lapels and propped him against the front of a sofa so he wouldn't choke on his own blood dripping down the nasal passages, then scooped up the papers and slid them back across the table. Blood had spattered across the top sheet—a form on OCIN letterhead—but it hadn't been filled in yet, had no information and no signatures. Nothing to have to redo.

Mitch straightened and started to dial Tifton, then stopped. No, let Dani have this one.

He picked up the food from the hallway and headed upstairs, his heart still going fifty miles an hour. *He would've helped her...He called you to stop it.*

"Dani? It's me," he called out as he entered the apartment.

She was on the floor among stacks of paper. She started to speak then noticed the blood on his shirt. "What happened?"

"I just talked to Brad."

"Talked?" She glanced at his fist and humphed. "Who won?"

"I did, if beating up an unconscious drunk is winning." He told her what Brad had said.

"Thought you could stop what?" she asked.

"I don't know."

She stood—that stiff limp again—and paced. "So Rosie *was* into something." She shook her head and her voice broke a little. "I thought she was good, you know?"

Something in Mitch's chest gave a tug.

"It's not your fault if she didn't stay clean, Dani. You did what you could."

She nodded, but it was an empty gesture; he didn't

think she believed him. "I want to talk to Brad," she said.

"Good luck with that. He's out. I wouldn't be so sure he isn't mixing a little something with his scotch."

"Drugs? You mean, like narcotic painkillers?"

"What? Hell if I know. I only know he won't be any good to talk to for a while."

"Janet, then—Rosie's sister. Maybe she'll know what Brad meant." She ducked back into the office to get her shoes and blazer, came out dialing her phone. "Wait, damn it," she said, lowering the phone. A shadow darkened her eyes. "I can't. I'm not…official."

Mitch set loose a smile. "Well, then. Good thing you have me."

CHAPTER
21

HOOK, POKE THROUGH, TWIST. Hook, poke through, twist.

The needle grabbed each strand of hair from the holding cards, punched into the lace, and a twist of the hand left a tiny knot. Over and over again, a mantra rolling through the mind like a tumbleweed—dry and empty and hollow. Hook, poke through, twist. Hook, poke through, twist. It was a knitter's trick to keep the hands moving without thinking, and without dropping a stitch. This evening, it kept Alicia's hair going quickly, one strand at a time, into the wig.

Which was coming along beautifully. Shoulder-length, the bulk of it was golden brown, a little burnt orange worked in at the nape and blond highlights passing down on either front side. Another layer of gold, from Jill Donnelly, had been woven in at the crown so skillfully it gave the illusion of filtered sunlight, and Rosie's near black strands added depth to the whole thing. Only Alicia's had initially caused a little trouble. Curly and bleached, her hair was damaged by too much peroxide and perm solution, and wouldn't lie smooth. That's when a touch of creativity came into play: a little permanent straightener and the decision to weave it into one solid swatch, rather than throughout the brown. An inch-wide stripe of blond on the side that added a touch of whimsy, youth.

There wasn't enough to do any more than that. It didn't matter, though—it had been worth cutting back on the amount of blond in the wig to pass a lock off to Dani Cole and watch her squirm. Nothing like a little unexpected, anonymous gift to keep a woman on her toes.

And as for the wig, it just meant taking a thicker cut from Nika Love to make up for it.

Nika Love. A pang of worry, there. She wasn't ready, hadn't delivered her baby yet. And it was Tuesday.

Patience. Alicia's hair would take the rest of tonight anyway and Nika was due anytime. Once her baby was in hand and Nika was dispatched to the hell she'd earned, there would be time to finish. Just keep working.

Hook, poke through, twist. Hook, poke through, twist.

Mitch got Janet on the phone while he and Dani finished the subs. "...Sergeant Cole is with me. We'd like to come by and ask you about something..."

Dani shrank. Jesus, she'd be in trouble if they caught her using her title or badge to navigate at this point. With her father's history, there'd be little concern for her motives; she'd simply be another Cole using her position for personal gain. *Thanks, Pop.*

Mitch disconnected and said, "What's the matter? You look like you just bit into something disgusting."

"Nothing," she said in a hurry.

"Bullshit."

"Come on," Dani said. "It's seven-thirty already. I want to hear what Janet has to say."

The rain had stopped, but the air was heavy with the promise of more, clouds like steel wool rolling overhead. They walked around the drive of the apartment building and Mitch pointed to a car.

Dani's jaw dropped.

"No way," she said. It was a Barracuda, 1968, just like she remembered it. Pearl-white body, 340 hemi engine, wide-oval redline Firestones. Fastback seat that reclined in the back.

She remembered *that* best.

She tamped down a shiver that came with the memory and walked around to the hood, dragging a finger along the lines of the body. Mitch had bought this car with lawn-mowing money he'd collected from the time he was fourteen. It was a junker, and he and his dad had rebuilt it all through Mitch's high school years. His dad, and then Russ Sanders. By the time Dani had met him, it was in pristine condition. She'd spent the entire two months of their relationship trying to convince him to let her drive it.

"I can't believe it," she murmured.

"I keep it in storage when I'm gone. It's the only car I've ever owned." He shot her a wink over the hood. "It's good for picking up girls."

A rush of something purely sexual raced through Dani's veins. She barely squelched it and crouched at the front bumper. The light of a streetlamp glowed off the chrome—its surface smooth and glossy and perfect. Mitch had spent the whole next day after they met buffing out the dent where it had kissed a fencepost. "No sign of the accident," Dani said.

"Of course not. Don't you remember what I told you?"

She flushed. "That a man doesn't let a woman mark his car, no matter how sexy she is." He nodded, and Dani couldn't help it. "What about his face?"

Mitch touched the bend in his nose, his eyes serious. "I had to keep something to remember you by."

Her skin shrank into goose bumps. For a timeless moment, their eyes held and she was trapped in the summer of 1992…heat and excitement and security. Escape. She'd never felt so pampered as she had when she was Mitch's girlfriend, so cherished as when she was his lover. Not in the seventeen years before or the eighteen years since.

She smothered the rush of nostalgia and walked around the car. Touched the keys in his hand. "I have a license now," she said, a little tease in her voice. "And special training for high-speed chases."

Mitch laughed, snatching away the keys. "Dream on, sweetheart."

Janet Milano answered the door with a hairbrush in hand, her proper bun now combed out around her shoulders. She looked softer than before, as if her sister's death had started to sink in. Less shock and anger, more bald pain. In her living room, the baby slept in a playpen beside an old brown sofa and a stack of scrapbooks sat on the floor. A worn shoebox spilled more pictures onto the coffee table.

"I was being nostalgic," she said, with a water-eyed shrug.

"I understand," Dani said. She settled into the sofa and Mitch sat down beside her.

"Do you mind?" he asked, reaching for one of the scrapbooks.

Janet shook her head, twisting her hair back behind her head. She sat on the edge of a chair.

"We wanted to ask you a couple more questions," Dani said. "We think there was something going on at the JMS Foundation that Rosie might have been involved in. Or at least known about."

"Like what?" Janet said.

"Something she might have thought Russ Sanders could stop. We were hoping you could tell us."

"I have no idea. Until I looked up his number last night, I didn't know she'd ever spoken with him."

Dani leaned forward, hoping she wasn't about to reveal anything Rosie's sister didn't know. "Were you aware that Rosie had a baby?"

Janet's features closed up. Yes, Dani realized: She knew.

"Is that why you and your mother were unhappy with her?" Dani asked.

"Mother doesn't know," Janet said, her voice urgent. "It was bad enough when she learned Rosie was out there, selling herself like a—" She pulled back. "It would kill our mother to know she'd given away a baby."

It was a plea, but Dani knew better than to promise anything. Murder investigations had a way of unearthing secrets. "We need to know about the baby. It might have something to do with her death."

Janet stood, walked to the playpen, and adjusted her son's blanket. "I didn't know, I mean, not at the time. Later, after Kyle was born—that's when Rosie told me. When she came back."

"When was her baby born?" Mitch asked.

"About two years ago. Right before you met her," she said to Dani.

Dani picked up a couple of the photos Mitch had been looking at. Most were Rosie and Janet as kids. Ballerina costumes for Halloween. Girl Scouts selling cookies. Easter dresses with tie-bonnets.

"Did Rosie ever say what happened to him, or her?" Mitch asked.

"Him. And she gave him up for adoption. But after she met Kyle, she started to regret it. I saw a teddy bear in her apartment once, and a baby bib and a couple other things. I asked her about them and she swore she didn't buy them—that someone had given them to her—but I didn't believe her. I mean, no one knew about the baby. And she started talking about finding him."

"Wanting to get him back?" Mitch asked.

"I don't know if she really thought that," Janet said. "But she wanted to know where he was."

Dani's mind raced. If Rosie had been trying to find her baby—and if Russell Sanders was the father of that baby—it made a pretty good case for his wanting Rosie to disappear.

She glanced at Mitch, who was reading her mind. "Did Rosie ever say who the father was?" he asked.

"She didn't know." She looked down. "She was a prostitute at the time."

Didn't know. Then maybe Sanders had nothing to worry about. Or maybe Rosie was just trying to keep it quiet. Could she have been blackmailing Sanders?

Dani moved some more photos around on the table. A July Fourth lemonade stand. A first dance with a wrist corsage, a pimply faced boy smiling uneasily next to her. Then a few more photos when Rosie was young again. A birthday cake with flowers all over it—eight candles. And a Christmas with new baby dolls, Janet cradling one with a tiny plastic bottle in its mouth, and six- or seven-year-old Rosie looking on with a bandage on her left cheek.

"What happened here?" Dani asked, handing the picture to Janet. The ME's report came to mind.

"Oh, that was after one of her surgeries." Janet's voice went hollow. She dug through the box and came out with a handful of pictures. All of them showed a tiny child with bandages. On some, the entire left side of her face and head were wrapped in gauze. "There were lots of operations when she was young."

A chill touched Dani's neck. "For what?" she asked.

"Fire, when she was a baby. I don't know exactly what happened because my parents adopted her, but she'd been burned when she was about two. She spent all of elementary school having operations." She held up a different photo. "Here she is before, when she first came to live here."

Dani looked, and her breath caught in her throat. "Oh, my God," she said. Rosie's left cheek was mangled, the left side of her scalp almost hairless.

It was as if the killer had been scarring her all over again.

"Dani," Mitch said, and she blinked. "What's the matter?"

She hedged. Neither of them had seen Rosie's body. And she wasn't about to paint the picture in front of Janet. "Nothing," she said. "I never knew, that's all. Did anyone else know? Any childhood friends she was still in contact with?"

"Not that I know of. My dad worked three jobs most of his life to pay for the operations—plastic surgery to remove scars and scalp grafts to regrow hair. She was young enough that it helped. And when she was older, he'd say, 'Look at you now. My perfect Rose.'" She closed her eyes, an ordinary woman if not downright homely, and for a second, Dani wondered if Mr. McNamara had ever said something so sweet to his older daughter.

Okay, stop it. You're a cop, not a shrink. And Rosie's dead.

She set down the picture. "Did you happen to show these to Detective Tifton or anyone else?"

"No," Janet said. "Should I have? I mean, it was years ago."

Dani stood, her mind in tangles. "Thank you, Janet," she said, and she and Mitch started to leave. "Wait," she said at the door. She had to know. "Did Rosie have any friends with curly blond hair? You know, like bleached blond."

"Curly blond?" Janet asked. "I don't know. But she knew a lot of girls from the other side of town. People I don't know. You know what I mean?"

Hookers. The words from the second note came to mind: *Stop protecting them.*

"Yeah," Dani said, with a rock in her chest. "I know exactly what you mean."

Nika Love rushed past hookers and drug dealers dotting the corners of Bailing Street, one hand propped on her lower back. She probably looked like a waddling duck, except that ducks didn't get soaked clean through—water rolled right off their feathers. Nika could have used some feathers right about now: The rain was torrential. She was wetter than a used dishrag and cold to the bone.

Hurry. She dodged a couple of big breaks in the cement, slipped, but caught herself against a brick storefront.

Forced herself to slow down. Falling would be dangerous. She didn't know just how dangerous, but she knew it was bad. The baby was due. Two or three more days at most, Dr. Housley had said, though Nika hoped sooner.

Still, she had to hurry. The shelter closed for the night at ten and once the doors were locked, no one got in.

She hobbled around the corner, hurrying as much as her bulk allowed. She did have another choice. Just tonight, the broker himself had phoned her and made an offer she couldn't help but consider: nice place to stay until the baby is born, Dr. Housley right there for the delivery, and a thick handful of cash when it's over—twice as much as Housley had promised. Mostly, the broker swore there was a good family waiting for the baby. A couple from Vermont, who already had one son and had tried for years to give him a brother. He'd show her pictures of them if she wanted...

Nika shook her head. It didn't matter. She wasn't going to give up this baby. Things were bad right now; no two ways about that. But a couple of her girlfriends from Ty's stable were helping out, and it wouldn't be long now—

"Nika."

She stopped, turned toward the voice, but it was too dark to see. The rain drove in sheets and she flattened back against a storefront, under the eave. Some john, maybe? No, she hadn't hooked in months.

"The broker wants to talk to you."

Nika let out a breath. The broker again. She took a couple of steps toward the voice, squinting against the rain. A man stood with his shoulders hunched deep in a jacket. A truck—the passenger door standing open—sat against the curb.

"Where?" Nika asked. She didn't want to go anywhere in that big truck with that big man.

"Right here, in the truck. He's inside. Hurry up, girl, it's wet out here."

She stepped toward the truck, peering through the darkness and rain to see the broker and then, in one heartbeat, realized no one was there. Too late. Hands grabbed her from behind and pushed her across the seat. Nika screamed, but something covered her mouth—something cold and damp that smelled like Mr. Thompkin's school biology lab, a sweet antiseptic that went into her mouth and up her nose and caught her voice in the cloth. She screamed again, but her voice sounded like it was a mile away, the sounds of the street fading. *Nika. Nika.* Was someone calling her name? She couldn't be sure. She was going under, the rain and thunder beating at the truck, her legs turning to lard.

A second later, her lard limbs gave way and she sank beneath the storm. Blackness.

CHAPTER
22

MORE RAIN HAD ROLLED IN, the sky a starless black sheet that grumbled beneath its breath. Mitch held Janet's front door open for Dani, and she stepped onto the front stoop and hiked her blazer up around her head.

"Stay here," Mitch said. "I'll get the car."

"What for?"

"Because I'm a gentleman? Stay here, damn it."

He bent one arm over his head and jogged into the downpour. When he pulled up, he reached across the front seat to bump the passenger door open. Dani folded in and yanked the door closed.

"Thanks," she muttered.

He stayed in neutral, watching the rain pound the windshield. "You gonna tell me what happened in there? What's this about Rosie's surgeries?"

Dani held her breath. It was an active investigation. She was privy to things the general public wasn't supposed to know. Mitch was a civilian.

And, for the moment, so was she.

"Rosie was stabbed in the throat," she said. "But that's not all. The left side of her face was beaten. And a chunk of hair from the left side of her head was cut off. Seeing those pictures...it just made me think—"

"Jesus Christ." Mitch went totally still. A minute later he rubbed a hand over his face, as if trying to rub sense into his head. "So this has something to do with Rosie's childhood?"

"I don't know. I mean, it could just be some freak. Someone who wanted to disfigure the victim and happened to pick someone who had been disfigured as a child. The killer is right-handed; hitting the left side would be natural—"

"Bullshit. Even if that were true, what's the point of taking her hair?"

Dani sighed. "Yeah. That's what I'm thinking."

He waited, narrowing his eyes on her. "Who's the blonde?"

Dani saw the light, curly hair in her mind's eye, felt an aftershock of the horror she'd felt seeing it in the envelope at her house. "I don't know," she said. "But the notes I've been getting have hair in them. The first, at the airport, had Rosie's hair. The second...had blond hair."

Mitch gaped at her. Dani could feel the shock roll off his body. "What do you mean, the second?" he asked.

"I got another one last night."

Mitch closed his eyes, then looked at her. "You okay?"

"Of course," she said. "It's just that I think there's another woman out there, and we don't even know where to start looking because we don't know who she is. Since no one's been reported missing, it's probably a hooker or addict or runaway—someone nobody keeps track of. And I should be out there. I should be looking for—"

"Stop," he said, covering her hand with his. His touch cut off the rising tide of helplessness.

They sat for a moment in silence, both staring at the rain pummeling the windshield. Finally, he said, "Do you know what OCIN is?"

She looked at him. "Yeah. Your branch that does adoptions. Overseas—"

"Children in Need," he finished for her.

"Why?"

"Brad had some OCIN forms in his apartment tonight. I saw them as I was leaving."

"And?"

He shook his head. "It shouldn't mean anything; Brad deals with forms all the time. Except that the one thing that keeps coming up whenever we talk about Rosie and Russ is a baby. And I swear, Dani, I don't think Russ fathered a child with a teenager."

"Then what *do* you think?"

"I think the only thing Rosie and Russ had in common was adoptions. She adopted out her baby, decided to find him again, and somehow connected with Russ. Maybe because of OCIN, she thought he could help. Isn't that what Brad said? *He would have helped her.*"

"That's a stretch."

"Do you have anything better?"

"Maybe," she said, but she didn't like what she had. "I'm starting to be afraid that whoever killed Rosie isn't looking much like a man worried about paternity. He's looking more like a man scarring up women."

"God help us if you're right."

Mitch turned the ignition, revved the motor like a teenager. The wipers slapped away raindrops the size of bullets. "Is your car at your house?" he asked.

Dani had to think about it. After her stitches, she'd gone back home to meet the forensics team, then Tifton had dropped her at the precinct. "Yeah," she said, then remembered what her house looked like. She wasn't ready to share that. "But you don't have to take me."

"Right. I'll just throw you out in the storm and you can walk." He pulled out. "Where do you live?"

Dani thought fast. The police were finished at her house. Mitch could drop her there and she'd grab some clothes, get her car, then go check into the Radisson like she was supposed to. Truth be told, she wasn't interested in testing her mettle tonight, sitting at her house and waiting for the killer to come back. Listening to thunder ring out like gunshots.

"West Ashe Street," she said finally. "But I'm not inviting you in."

By the time they got to Dani's street, the downpour had eased into a steady, gentle rain, but lightning flashed on the horizon. A line of full-fledged thunderstorms was coming through.

Mitch pulled into her driveway and turned off the car. Reached for his seat belt.

"I told you—"

"I'm just walking you to the door. You know, if your dates aren't even bothering to walk you to the door, you need to upgrade the caliber of men you're seeing." He arched a brow. "I would have thought I set the bar at least that high."

He'd set the bar at an impossible height, Dani admitted to herself as she climbed out of the Cuda and dodged raindrops, but she couldn't pull her mind into thinking about that just now. She looked at her house and remembered what she'd walked into last night. Automatically, her hand moved toward her gun, then she noticed a black-and-white rolling by.

Of course: They'd be keeping an eye out in case the asshole came back. Or in case Dani started engaging in nefarious activities with criminals.

No, that would be the inconspicuous gray sedan of Internal Affairs. This was your basic patrol car.

"Just a minute," she said, and left Mitch on the steps. He hunched his shoulders against the rain and she darted out to talk to the kid in the cruiser, pulling out her ID. "I live here," she told him, keeping her voice low enough that Mitch wouldn't hear. "Any activity?"

"Nope," he said. "All clear."

"Thanks."

He rolled on up the block and parked, and Dani jogged back to Mitch. Drenched, they went onto the porch where a motion-sensor light flicked on.

"Thanks for the ride," she said, digging out her key. "I'll call you in the morn—"

He wasn't listening. He reached up behind her to a piece of yellow ribbon on the top corner of the door-frame. Dani saw what it was and a lump came to her throat: police tape. They'd strung it across her door last night when they were processing the house, and some-one had just given it a yank when they were finished. A couple of inches still hung to the frame from a staple.

Mitch tugged it free and glanced at the cruiser a block away. When he looked back at Dani, his gaze was fero-cious. "What the hell happened here?"

Dani opened her mouth to push him away, and the look in his eyes stifled it. In the space of one breath, the events of two days settled on her shoulders like a lead cloud. Two people dead. No more than a few hours of sleep. Her furniture was slashed. Her dog was in a fucking coma. Someone—a killer—had watched her, followed her, taunted her, caused an accident, and then, because of Dani's father, the chief of police had pushed her off the case.

And on top of it all, here was Mitch. After eighteen years, here was Mitch.

She closed her eyes and shivered when Mitch's finger touched beneath her chin and drew her face upward. "Don't shut me out again. Tell me," he demanded, his voice like a low rumble from the storm. "What happened?"

Her resolve melted and she held out the key. "See for yourself."

He took the key from her hand and pressed the door open. Hit the light switch on the wall.

"Holy shit," he said.

CHAPTER
23

MITCH WALKED INTO DANI'S LIVING ROOM, flabbergasted. Neat rectangles were missing from almost every soft surface, chunks of foam cut out of sofa cushions and pillows, squares of fabric missing from curtains.

"What is this?" he asked.

"Whoever left a note on my car yesterday afternoon redecorated my place last night. The second note I told you about was left in a spare room." She nodded to a segment on the back of her couch that was missing a piece exactly the size of a brick. "The crime lab came in overnight and made it look neat."

It all became clear. "This is why you're off the case, isn't it? Because the bastard's onto you."

"Partly," she said. She hit one of the cushions with her fist. "The chief says he wants me out of sight."

"Good for him." Mitch was furious. "You should have told me. I would have stayed with you."

"I haven't been out of your apartment all day, except with you."

He intended to keep it that way. "What did the notes say? Did they threaten you specifically?"

"The one at the airport said, 'Not innocent,' and had Rosie's hair. In a news interview yesterday, I referred to her killer as a monster preying on an innocent woman."

"So, he saw you on the news," Mitch said, and the notion sent a chill through his blood. He hadn't considered that she might be in personal danger. "What about the note left here?"

"It said, 'Stop protecting them.' And had a swatch of blond hair."

"Ah, God." Mitch ran a hand through his hair, realized a second later the significance of that gesture. "And there's no identifying whose it is? What about DNA?"

"There's no DNA without a root; this hair was cut. Probably with the same scissors that killed Rosie and slashed my furniture."

"Scissors?" Mitch didn't know why the idea of scissors made Rosie's death any more gruesome than a knife. A murder was a murder. But something about scissors and hair elevated it beyond that. Commonplace murderers didn't carry scissors. "Why would someone cut a hank of hair?"

"I don't know. A trophy, maybe. But those pictures tonight freaked me out. The damage to Rosie's face and hair mimic the scars she had from those childhood surgeries. I'm starting to think it's got to be someone who knew her, or knew about her scars."

"In her picture, I didn't notice them."

"In real life, I didn't notice them. She looked good." Dani paced, her brow wrinkling in thought. "But something Janet said tonight got me thinking: When I asked about a girl with blond hair, she said Rosie knew a lot of girls from the other side of town. She meant Reading. She meant hookers."

"You think he's killing hookers?"

"'Not innocent. Stop protecting them.' Like it's a group, and he's passing judgment. And if it's *not* someone from the streets, someone would've noticed. We'd have a missing persons report."

"So we look for a missing hooker or runaway with blond hair."

"Christ, Mitch, girls in that world come and go like the wind." She started pacing, wringing her hands. "I keep thinking about the girls I've run into, but these girls change their color week-to-week, so it could be anyone. And I keep wondering, Is it someone I might have known and she's gone now, and she's dead and I had her hair in my hands last night? Or is she still alive and I don't have any way to search for her because I'm off the case and—"

"Easy," he said. She trembled with emotion. It wrenched his heart to think about how much she'd been through in the past two days.

Hookers, Rosie, Russell. Mitch had no idea how they were connected, but he knew one thing: A murderer knew where Dani lived.

He looked around. "Is everything ruined?"

She moved her shoulders a little; she was holding on by her nails. Mitch took it as a "Yes," then noticed the dishes on the floor. No dog had greeted them. "Where's the dog?"

Dani hugged her arms around her waist.

"Oh, Jesus."

"No, no, she's not..." A shimmer came to her eyes. "She's at the vet."

"She okay?" he asked.

"No. Whoever came in here dosed up some meat with

opioids. You know what opioids are?" Dani started to ramble. "They're narcotic painkillers, like oxycodone and methadone, and they work on the central nervous system and doctors prescribe them like morphine. But they're for humans. Dogs get loopy and drool and wander around and can't control their actions until they lose the ability to walk and—"

Mitch pulled her in. She stopped talking when her lips hit his chest, the tears rolling now, and he held her, both of them soaked to the skin by the rain, Dani's body shuddering with cold and tears. He laid his cheek against her hair and held on, wondering how long it had been since he'd wanted to hold a woman he wasn't screwing.

About eighteen years.

Her breathing smoothed out and she pushed back. "I chased him," she said, and Mitch's brow rose. Of course she did. "He broke through a window and I saw him outside and ran after him..."

She told him about the rest of the night—the accident and the vet and the hospital—

"Hospital?" he asked.

"I got cut on the window. I got a few stitches."

Mitch's chest thickened. "Your left leg."

She nodded and Mitch cursed himself. He'd known something was off but hadn't bothered to press it. His MO: see her hurting and let it go. What a bastard he was.

He drew his fingers down her cheek but got no reaction; her mind was somewhere else, her eyes staring blankly at his shirt button.

"If I hadn't been chasing him, Mrs. Gardner wou—"

"No," Mitch snapped. He cupped her shoulders. "Don't do that, Dani. It's not your fault."

She rubbed her hands over her arms—unconsciously, Mitch thought. "Go get out of those wet clothes," he said. "You're trembling."

She stepped back, seeming to notice the cold for the first time. "My chief made me a motel reservation. He doesn't want me staying here."

"Good, because there's no fucking way I'm leaving you here." He wasn't sure there was any way he was going to leave her at a motel, either, but he'd deal with that later.

"I need five minutes to pack," she said and went down the hallway.

No woman had ever packed in five minutes. Mitch watched until she disappeared then went upstairs. There was a small room being used as an office or den, a bath, and a loft area; the minimal furnishings in each were ruined, the bathroom mirror looking as if it had been struck with a hammer. He went back downstairs, into the kitchen and dining room—same treatment—into a hallway with a bath and one closed door. He pressed the door open, frowned.

This room was empty. Totally. No furniture, no wall hangings or curtains—even the carpet had been lifted, revealing rows of tacks sticking out along the edges and a bare subfloor. The only window was boarded up and the walls were bright gray-white—not paint, Mitch thought, but primer. One wall had a fresh repair in the Sheetrock, and that section was brighter than the others. A jug of bleach sat beneath it, the aroma just touching his nostrils.

He walked to the closet, pressing open the accordion doors. A man's life was crammed inside. Clothes, shoes, books, boxes.

Her father.

Mitch shut the closet doors and crossed to the freshly boarded window. *I chased him...* So this was the broken window from last night. But the rest? Her father's life hadn't been packed away overnight, the room torn apart and sterilized. That had been done before.

He felt her at the door and turned. Her expression stopped him cold.

"What the hell are you doing in here?" she said. Her face was white with fury.

Mitch stood his ground. He was finished being pushed away. "I wanted to see how much damage was done."

"Get out." Her voice vibrated. Not fury, though, he realized. Fear. "Go, damn you."

No. Not this time. "Did your father live with you?" he asked. Silence. Mitch stepped toward her. "How did he die?"

She looked him straight in the eyes. "He blew his brains out against that wall."

Mitch glanced at the bleached wall, then back at her. "Oh, Dani," he said, but she spun on him and stalked out. Mitch went after her. "Hold on. Honey, wait." He caught her arm. He could think of only one thing. "Where were you when he did it?" he asked. She stared at him, startled by the question, but he had to know. Please, God, don't let her have been here. *Press hard, kid. Stop the bleeding.* "Tell me. Where were you?"

"On the other side of that wall, sleeping. It was storming. A crack of thunder woke me." Her face was hard as stone. "Then I realized it wasn't a crack of thunder. It was my Glock."

Jesus. "You were alone? Are you the one who found him?"

"No, I was with my harem of lovers. Of course I was the one who found him. It was the middle of the night and he was ten feet away."

Mitch's heart caved in. "Did he leave you a note, anything?"

"Why should he?"

"To explain what was wrong, or why he did it." To try to soothe his child a little.

"What was wrong was he was a miserable, spiteful old man, and having to move in with the daughter he hated shamed him into killing himself. There. And I did that without even going to a shrink, how do you like that?"

Whoa. "I know he was in trouble with the law, Dani, but he was your father."

"Father?" She took a step forward, the dam cracking. "Let me tell you about my *father*. He was a filthy cop who used his badge to run with criminals on the side, then gambled and drank everything we had. When I was six and Mom was sick with cancer, I begged him to take me places and let me hang out with him. And he did—to dogfights and brawls and card games—all the things he fronted for an asshole named Ty Craig. Then Jason was born and our mom died, and I spent the rest of his childhood making sure he had lunch money and forging permission slips and driving him to baseball practice even though I didn't have a license, trying to make sure no one noticed I was the only one taking care of him."

Mitch was flabbergasted. After her dad had been busted, he'd learned that Artie Cole wasn't the airline pilot Dani had made him out to be, and that life for her and Jason hadn't been easy. But Mitch never knew she'd grown up in such fear. He'd been a hot-blooded young man, head over heels crazy about her and so hurt and angry when she betrayed him that he never looked back. All she'd had to do was plant the seeds of jealousy in his mind, and he'd walked away, too blind to see what she was doing and too bullheaded to keep up with her later, even through the grapevine.

Mitch Sheridan, revealer of tragedies around the globe. Too big a coward to look closely at things at home.

A memory climbed on top of him. Every muscle in his body turned to stone. "You didn't go four-wheeling with your dad," he said.

Dani winced, looked away. It all came back and Mitch couldn't believe it.

"The bruises," he said. "You had them all over."

She shrugged. "Sometimes."

A curse exploded from his lips and he spun away, rage curling his hands into fists. He wanted to kill the bastard, but his chance for that had passed. He'd walked away from it.

He came back to Dani. "Why didn't you tell anyone, later, when you had custody of Jason?"

She grunted. "I barely saw him then. I was a cop, and my father kept his distance. But later, he went to jail for a pretty long stint, and when he got out"—her brow wrinkled—"he'd gamble on anything. He couldn't keep any money. That's when I brought him here and tried to take care of him, but—" She stopped, but Mitch knew what she was about to say: *It wasn't enough.* Instead of loving her or thanking her, the bastard took his own life while she slept in the room next door.

Mitch closed his eyes, feeling her pain like a knife between the ribs, and stepped close to her. "I'm sorry," he said.

"For what? For getting your nose broken trying to help me?"

"For not seeing. For not making sure you were okay afterward." He studied the guarded posture, the dark shutters of lashes. She'd spent a lifetime building walls to protect herself, since no one else did. "For not taking care of you."

"I don't need for yo—"

His lips cut her off, and he cupped her face and brought her forward. The flush of her cheeks seared his palms, her breath catching in her throat, and Mitch pushed past the instant of surprise and uncertainty, roving and tasting and playing on her lips until they fell open on a sigh. He deepened the kiss, the age-old heat of young love simmering with wisdom and time, boiling into a wild, unmet need to have her again. Dani leaned into him, her hands gripping his wet shirt and breasts pressing to his chest, and they kissed and stroked and shared one another's breath, while the rest of the world faded to nothing. Mitch pressed her close against his zipper, making sure she felt what she did to him, and only when he ground her hips to his did Dani make a desperate little sound and push away.

"Wait, wait," she said, working to catch her breath. "It's too much."

Mitch nuzzled her neck. "No, it isn't."

"It's too fast."

"Eighteen years isn't too fast."

"*Mitch.*"

He stopped, tipping his forehead against hers and waiting for the blood to head back to his brain again. He took a deep breath. "Tell me there's no one else," he said against her mouth.

"It's not that." She shook her head, as if trying to

juggle things into place. "This won't undo the past. Feeling guilty for something isn't a good reason to get involved."

"We need a reason? How about the fact that we never should have been apart?"

"I don't want to be your penance, Mitch. I'm not interested in being your cause."

His muscles tightened and he looked at her. "What about being my lover?"

"Mitch—"

"Goddamn it, Dani, what do you want me to do?" He strode away, putting distance between them. "You want me to leave you again, but this time to a madman with a pair of scissors?"

"I can handle it."

"Yeah, I've heard that before."

She advanced on him. "And I did fine: I didn't need you."

"I know you didn't." Mitch looked at her. "But didn't you *want* me? Just a little, when you were lying in bed at night, being so by-god tough and holding things together all by yourself...Didn't you ever wish I'd stayed?"

She looked down, but not before Mitch caught the glitter of tears in her eyes. They spoke volumes to Mitch.

She ran her hand over a blouse now damp from their embrace. "It's getting late," she said and picked up a dry jacket. "I should get over to the Radisson."

"Fuck the Radisson." She scowled at him, but Mitch held up a hand. She might be afraid to come to his apartment and climb into bed with him, but she wouldn't pass up the chance to further the investigation. "Rosie's baby, remember? We were gonna hit the OCIN files."

"Oh. Yeah," she said, and picked up her overnight bag.

She went around hitting off lights and Mitch dropped her house key into his pocket. He opened her front door and took the overnight bag from her hands as she passed.

"I can get it," she said.

"I know. But you don't have to."

CHAPTER
24

MARSHALL KETTERING FELT A HAND on his.

"Where are you?" Mia asked, laying her napkin on the table. They'd had a late dinner at Goby's. Kobe beef and seared prawns, with sake-poached asparagus and a bottle of Cabernet Sauvignon. Marshall had tried to make it a treat, but being with Mia and thinking about Kristina was like watching a car wreck in slow motion. He couldn't stop it or change its course or even tell anyone it was going to happen. "Are you all right?" she asked.

He leaned back while the waiter took his empty glass, eyed her over a fresh one. Her hair was up tonight, caught in pins at the back of her head with a rainbow of subtle highlights and dyes threaded in. They'd probably cost him a fortune at the hairdresser, but he didn't care. She was beautiful. Sometimes he wondered how he'd gotten so lucky to have her.

And sometimes he felt the weight of the world on his shoulders in having her.

"Long week," he said, though it was only Tuesday. "The murder of that girl—uh, McNamara. Russell's suicide. The pressure of having the exhibit ready for this weekend. And"—he hesitated, but had to know—"to top it all off, I'm having problems at the office."

"The office? What do you mean?"

Marshall took a deep breath. Do it. Putting it off any longer could only lead to tragedy. He leaned forward onto his forearms. "I'm going to fire Sarah Rittenhouse tomorrow."

Mia gaped at him. Sarah had been his office manager for nine years, and he knew Mia had always liked her. "Why in the worl—"

"Keep your voice down. I don't have any choice. She's been stealing medications from the practice."

Mia stared. "*Sarah?* Marshall, there's got to be some mistake. She wouldn't do something like that."

"I didn't believe it at first, either, but it's true. Barbiturates, amphetamines, opioids... It's big, Mia."

"But why? What could she want with medicines like that?"

A stab of pain got Marshall in the chest. Dear God. She *was* hiding something. Mia would never question the value of the drugs; she'd grown up in the underworld of drugs and prostitution, forced by her own mother to service men by the time she was ten. In the privacy of his own mind, Marshall had often thought her mother's death—burned in her ratty little trailer—had been too good for her. For Mia's sake, he liked to think she'd suffered.

Mia must have read his thoughts. Two seconds later, she backpedaled. "I mean, of course I know what some people would want with medicines like that. But Sarah? I can't imagine her selling drugs on the streets."

"Maybe not on the streets," he suggested. "Maybe to

people she knows." He shook his head. "I don't know. I only know I have no choice but to let her go."

"Did you ask her, point-blank?"

"Not yet," he said. "But I'm going to confront her tomorrow. I have to."

Mia's face paled a shade, but the waiter came by, picking up a leather folder in which Marshall had stuffed three hundred dollars. "Do you need change, Dr. Kettering?"

He waved him off. "No, it's all right."

"I don't think you should confront her," Mia said after the waiter left. Her voice sounded urgent. "What if you're wrong?"

"I'm not wrong. No one but Sarah has access to the records and cabinets." *And you, perhaps.* He waited for Mia to speak and when she didn't, it was all he could do to let the conversation drop.

"Let's get going. I have another late night of work to do," he said and pushed from the table. He walked around to hold Mia's chair, unable to resist a small kiss in her hair. He pulled out the keys to the Saab and tried to look nonchalant, though his heart had gone dead inside.

He was right. It wasn't Sarah who was stealing drugs from the practice.

It was Mia.

Dani drove her own car back to the Foundation and, like a Doberman with a new job to do, Mitch followed. *Fuck the Radisson.* In one breath she cursed him for being overbearing and sexist, and in the next she wanted to dissolve into his overbearing and sexist arms. No matter how it shamed her, she had to admit there seemed nothing more lonely than the idea of sitting in a motel tonight alone, listening to thunder and worrying about Runt and some unknown blonde.

The idea of being with Mitch was only a little less disquieting.

She shivered just remembering their kiss, and cursed again. God, it was official: She was pathetic. One summer in his arms when she was seventeen had left her pining for him like some weak-kneed, hormonal girl. One moment in his arms tonight had left her longing for him like some craven, sex-starved woman.

She was a cop, and she was strong. She couldn't go weak in the knees just because some asshole had chosen her to taunt. She needed to use the asshole's own game to find him. This was a murder case and besides the obvious, OCIN was the only thing that connected Russell Sanders, Rosie, and an adopted baby. Dani wasn't going to Mitch's apartment because she was afraid of being alone. She was going because she had to find a killer.

Good story, Cole, stick with that.

He met her as she got out of her car and walked beside her, her bag slung over his shoulder and one hand on the small of her back. In the lobby, he pounded on Brad's door.

No answer.

Dani knocked, too, calling to him. "Mr. Harper. Open up. Police."

Nothing. Dani propped her hands on her hips and blew the bangs from her face. "Want me to kick the door in?"

Mitch smiled, an ounce of admiration in it. "It won't do any good. He's still slumped on the floor against the sofa. Come on, let's go upstairs." She hesitated and he smoothed the errant bangs from her forehead. "Stop analyzing it, Dani. You can trust me."

Dani wasn't so sure but went anyway. She followed him to the office of the apartment where he punched the desktop computer on and pulled up a second chair. She took it and watched while he typed in a few commands.

"Here we go," he said, and she leaned in to look at the screen. "As far as I know, Russ didn't handle any specific aspect of OCIN's work. The deputy director for that branch is a woman named Robin Hutchins, and she's been heading it up for years."

Dani jotted down the name. "I remember that name. She wasn't there this morning when we interviewed Foundation employees. I'll see if she comes up anywhere in connection to Rosie."

"How will you do that?"

She cursed. She had to keep reminding herself she wasn't an active participant in the investigation anymore. "Tifton won't shut me out," she said, hoping it was true. "When did the Foundation start doing adoptions?"

"Eight years ago. I was one of the throngs who visited Romania after the fall of Ceauşescu. By the time I went, in my mid-twenties, there'd already been so much publicity about the Romanian orphans I almost didn't do the shoot. Figured the story had already been told. Then I went into a *Cassia dei Copii*, a house of children. When I saw them..."

"I know. I have your books." That blue gaze locked on hers and she moved one shoulder. "Don't gloat. I have a lot of books I don't read."

His lips twitched, but then he was sober again. "At that point, the Foundation was a couple years old and generating money, but these kids needed more than that. They needed homes."

"Are all the adoptions from Romania?"

"None of them are anymore. The Romanian government suspended U.S. adoptions in 2004, unless it's with a close relative of the child. Now we do adoptions from something like fifteen different countries."

"But none here in the U.S."

"Like Rosie's baby, you mean?" he asked. "No. The 'O' stands for 'Overseas,' remember?"

She remembered. It was something she'd never understood. "There are kids here who need homes."

"There are, but you'll remember I had reason to get away. As far as I could."

She blushed.

"Besides, conditions here are nothing compared to the places I've been. There are literally thousands of children waiting—some in squalor you can't imagine."

"Then why do I always hear how hard it is to adopt?"

"You're hearing about the availability of infants—white male newborns, to be exact. There are waiting lists a mile long for them. But there are plenty of older kids. In fact, newborns aren't available from overseas. Different countries have different regulations, but in most places, the child has to be unclaimed for at least six months before being eligible for adoption."

"Unclaimed? I thought these were orphans."

"The legal definition of the word 'orphan' is mind-boggling. The majority of these kids are relinquished by parents who can't—or won't—take care of them. It's not unusual for a parent to drop them off when times are hard and come back when things get better. But sometimes they don't come back at all."

He leaned back in the chair, suddenly pensive, and Dani looked at the screen. PLEASE ENTER YOUR PASSWORD.

"Oh," she said. "You want me to leave?"

"No, I wasn't thinking that. I was wondering if mine would still work."

"What?"

"Russell, Brad, and I are the only ones with total access."

"Okay." Dani didn't understand. He typed in a password. ACCESS DENIED.

"That sonofabitch," he muttered. "He did change it."

"Brad changed the password?"

Mitch nodded, rubbing his chin.

"Can I kick in his door now?"

He smiled at her and pulled a set of disks from the bottom drawer. "You don't need to. I copied them last night."

Dani was impressed. "James Mitchell Sheridan with a suspicious streak."

"When it's warranted," he said, and slanted a look sideways. "That's the difference between you and me."

"Humph." She waited while he loaded the first disk, then he went and got a laptop for her and put the contents of the disk on a memory stick. He handed it over.

"We can hit twice as many files working separately. Do you get along with computers?"

"Sure," Dani said, installing the drive. "Only I don't know what I'm looking at."

"You're looking at adoption files. Private information like adoptive parents' medical records, incomes, family histories. Stories adopted children themselves aren't privy to unless their families choose to divulge it."

"Sounds like letting me do that would be a breach of ethics, maybe law."

"Yes," he said, looking her in the eyes. "Like what you did confiding in me about the blond hair and the condition of Rosie's body."

Warmth seeped into Dani's limbs. Okay. So they could trust each other that much.

Mitch reached across to her keyboard and typed in the password. The files came up on the laptop and he stuck another disk in the desktop. "The good thing is," he said, "if Brad locked me out, it means there's something here. Now it's just a matter of finding it."

CHAPTER
25

T HE PHONE VIBRATED—THE PREPAID CELL. One in the morning.

Grab it, get out of the bedroom. A call like this would be difficult to explain to one's spouse. Quick, into the hallway.

"Yes?"

"I have her," Fulton said. "We're at my cabin in Virginia."

Relief came in a flood. Nika Love. Finally. No chance now that she'd disappear with the baby. Thank God.

"Did anybody see you?"

Fulton was insulted. "I'm smarter than that. It's why you pay me so well." His tone inched toward humor. "I gave her the gift, by the way. Those stupid-ass little baby booties."

A bubble of excitement swelled. "And?"

"She threw them at my face and came at me, called me ten kinds of names. Not nice ones."

Good, then. She knows what this is about. They have to understand why they die. "Did Nika say anything about the baby?"

"I knocked her back down with chlor[ ] wanna fight her all damn night."

"Don't leave her. Whatever you do, don't leave her unattended."

"I won't be responsible for a baby," he warned.

"You won't have to be. Call when she goes into labor."

The phone closed with a snap and a surge of anticipation rose up. Nika was ready.

Go, now. Finish her portrait. Then there'll be no rush doing her hair.

The stairwell to the dormer was narrow and cool, the lock on the door an old-fashioned iron key. Inside, a string hung from the ceiling. One tug and the bulb flickered to life, but the light bathed only the entrance. The rest of the room was cast in shadows that turned the easels into dark mesas.

The Fresnels were on a single switch; all three came up together, casting a cool wash of light in the display area. Then, one by one, the six par cans flicked on—each aimed down from the ceiling at one of the portraits, like good museum lighting. *Flick*: Heather Whyte, number one on the list. *Flick*: Rolinda Sills, number two. *Flick, flick*: Jill Donnelly and Rosie McNamara, three and four. *Flick*: Alicia Woodruff—number five.

And *flick*: Nika Love. Her portrait was yet untouched. It was time.

Within minutes, the portrait was out of its frame and matting, spread out on the worktable with Nika's face staring up at the ceiling. A nice-looking girl, if you liked the porcelain-skinned, pleasantly plump sort, and there were plenty of men who did. Her file had said she was from North Carolina, eighteen years old, a runaway.

The nitric acid was in a small safe beneath the table, a silicone-tipped paintbrush, gloves, and mask all locked in together. Odd that something like nitric acid was so readily available, but a company in Denver sold it over the Internet, ostensibly to chemistry teachers and labs. They wouldn't fly it, so you couldn't be in too big a hurry when you needed it, but otherwise, getting it was no trouble at all.

And it was perfect for leaving an accurate record. Nika Love would soon look the way she deserved.

Nika looked up at the ceiling from that porcelain-skinned face, and a thin drizzle of yellowish, acrid-smelling liquid trickled onto her head. It hit the left side at her hairline and cheek, and the silicone-tipped paintbrush spread it around. In seconds, her skin bubbled up, the hair frying and cheek burning away, the left side of her face and jaw simply disintegrating beneath the acid. When it was finished, there was little left of the girl. There was only the hideous, scarred face of evil.

As it should be.

Back into the mats, the frame. And now, move her easel front and center: When the time came to add her hair to the wig, she'd have a good view.

Now, clean up, put things away, get back to bed. Tomorrow was an early morning, another busy day.

Sarah Rittenhouse rose to mind. Now *that* was an unexpected problem. Yes, get some sleep. Another busy day.

Mitch rubbed his eyes and reached for another disk, looked across the room to the deep leather sofa where Dani had settled. The laptop glowed on her face, her eyes wide with effort to keep them open. He looked at the clock. It was almost one-thirty in the morning and God knows she hadn't gotten any sleep last night. Tonight had been less dramatic but difficult nonetheless: One line of thunderstorms after another had rolled in. Dani flinched with every crack of thunder.

Thunder woke me... Then I realized it was my Glock.

Mitch's pulse grew sluggish and he tried to remember the last time his heart had factored in with a woman. He'd played around with them most of his adult life but had rarely considered one a threat to healthy indifference. A British journalist in Somalia came close once, and later a pathologist he'd met in the airport at Tel Aviv. He'd truly cared about them, had maybe even been on his way to love.

Which is why he couldn't stay. The journalist, angry, had asked why he cared more about the great masses of anonymous strangers than for her; the pathologist hadn't had to. She was just like him, hiding behind closed lab doors with her microscopes and cancer cells. When they said good-bye, she'd kissed him, saying, "Call me if you ever finish saving the world." And Mitch had said, simply, "Ditto."

Maybe she'd been more successful at it than he had.

He shut down his computer and walked over to Dani. "Sweetheart," he said, aware of the endearment only after it slipped out, "it's time to quit."

She blinked. "I haven't found anything yet. I can't stop."

"For now." He slid the computer from her lap, tried to imagine what the last two weeks had been like since finding her dad with his brains all over the wall. He knew what those weeks—months, years—had been like for him. A nightmare. "Are you afraid to go to sleep?" he asked.

Her expression frosted. "Why would I be?"

"Your dad's gunshot. You don't hear it in your sleep?" She quailed, but Mitch went on. "I do. Not a gunshot, but a chopper. The one that blew up the camp at Ar Rutbah. For months, I heard it every fucking time I closed my eyes."

She looked up at him. "Still?" she asked.

"Sometimes," he said. "Not so much. Lately, the dreams keep changing. Merging with things here at home." His sister, pulling away and running into the street...His father, bleeding. Sometimes he dreamed about his mother and the battles she later faced—alcohol, depression, financial hardship. All because Mitch had let go.

Lightning struck and Dani closed her eyes—as if not seeing would take away the sound of thunder—and a wave of helplessness washed over Mitch. J. M. Sheridan, mover of mountains for nameless strangers in far-off places. But when it came to the people he cared about right here in Lancaster, he'd always been powerless.

But not tonight. At the very least, he could get the storm out of Dani's ears. Drown it out.

Mitch found a remote and aimed it at the sound system. "What do you like to listen to?"

"What?" She saw the remote. "Oh. I don't, usually."

"Why doesn't that surprise me?" He said it lightly, but the thought sobered him: No, it wouldn't cross Dani's mind to hide inside and try to cover up the noise. She'd stalk outdoors and wave her gun at the sky, challenging God to take her on. "How 'bout this?" he asked, landing on some easy jazz. He sat down and stretched an arm behind her.

"I should go," she said.

"You should sit here with me. Preferably, like you aren't afraid of me."

"Don't be stupid. I'm not afraid of you."

"Then come here," he said, and nudged her in. She curled up against him and after a moment, Mitch felt her relax against his body. He laid his hand over the side of her face to shield her ear from the storm, gently pressing the other against the drum of his heart. Touched a kiss to her forehead.

Then another. And another on her cheek and then Dani tilted her face to him, and without hesitation, he accepted the invitation and found her lips. Gently, openmouthed, he slanted his lips across hers and slid his fingers into her hair. She kissed him back, her mouth opening and her hands climbing up his shoulders and neck, and soon Mitch bent over her and they sank together into the sofa, a flame sparking from nowhere.

And a sound. Dani heard it first and went stiff, tried to pull away.

"Stop, stop," she said against his cheek, and the sound came again. A tinkling sound, distant.

"Damn it," she said. Her arm was stuck between the cushion and the back of the sofa. Mitch lifted his weight and she came up with a cell phone. The tinkling sound came again, this time from her hand.

"Aw, Jesus," Mitch said, cursing the phone. Dani juggled it into position to answer while Mitch tried to get his brain working again.

"Check the number," he said. Too late for a social call.

She did. "Tifton."

She walked away from the sofa and from Mitch's reach. Grunted into the phone. Mitch could hear Tifton's raised voice and Dani closed her eyes. "I'm fine. I just haven't checked in to the hotel yet." She paused. "Well, you shouldn't have bothered. What are you, my babysitter?"

Mitch leaned back, stretching both arms across the back of the sofa. Liking Reginald Tifton more and more.

"Listen," Dani said into the phone, "I got a couple things for you to put into the mix on Rosie's case. Rosie McNamara had a bunch of surgeries as a kid; she was scarred right where the killer marked her. You gotta look for people who knew that about her. And do me a favor: Look up a woman named Robin Hutchins. She runs OCIN. She was on our list, but we didn't talk to her. She works for Mitch Sheridan in adoptions. See if she comes up anywhere in Rosie's life." Silence, then Mitch saw her spine stiffen. "What for?" she asked. She listened for five more seconds, then said, emphatically, "No," and hung up. She was fuming.

"No, what?" Mitch asked.

"He asked to talk to you." She snorted, but color seeped across her cheekbones. "How come he'd think we're together?"

Mitch chuckled. "Sweetheart, he knew we were together before we did."

His cell phone rang. He looked at the number, grinned, and showed it to Dani. She let out a string of curses.

"Don't answer it," she said.

"Hello?"

"Listen to me, Sheridan," Tifton started in. "Dani shouldn't be out there alone, you understand?"

"She isn't alone. She's with me." He winked at Dani. She rolled her eyes.

"Goddamn it," Tifton groused.

"Detective," Mitch said, still looking at Dani. She looked like she was ready to shoot him if he dared to give Tifton the time of day. "Have you ever tried to tell Dani Cole what she can and can't do? She's a little on the stubborn side."

"Someone's got a bead on her, man."

"I know. I saw her place."

Tifton paused. Mitch knew more than he should—clearly a breach of protocol—but Tifton was smart enough to know Dani was safer that way. "I got worried about her when she wasn't at the hotel," he said. A beat passed. "I'm not sure I feel any better now."

"You should," Mitch said. "I'll take care of her."

He hung up and dropped the phone on the table. "He was worried."

"I've lived for thirty-five years without anyone check-ing up on me, and—"

"It's high time someone did."

Dani blinked. That caught her completely off guard, and Mitch's resolve strengthened tenfold. It *was* high time someone looked out for her. And that someone shouldn't be Tifton.

He strode across the room, brushed her hair back from her face. Dani shook her head. "You're doing it again, Mitch—trying to make up for the past. You don't owe me anything. I don't need for you to take care of me."

"But I need it," he said. "So the only question left is whether you fall asleep tonight in my bed and in my arms or alone on that sofa. The choice is yours, but one thing's for sure: The Radisson is out."

CHAPTER
26

Wednesday, October 6, 7:20 a.m.

SARAH RITTENHOUSE WAS as predictable as the sunrise. She arrived at the Hillgrove Medical Practice each morning carrying a spill-proof mug of coffee with a dash of cream, wearing a long ruffled peasant skirt and low heels, and spinning her key ring on one finger. She was always the first one in, at her desk no later than seven-thirty. She'd do the office orders and paperwork, check the schedule, and make sure all was ready for the day's appointments. By the time the rest of the staff started trickling in at nine-thirty, and the doctors at ten, Sarah had already accomplished more than the others would do all week.

In the early days, when Marshall had moved from social services work to private practice, Mia had done Sarah's job. American psyches being fragile, and Lancaster being filled with the affluent overflow from old Baltimore, a psychiatric practice wasn't bound to struggle for long. Now, he had two partners, a nurse, a receptionist, an insurance specialist, and Sarah.

Today, she pulled in at seven twenty-two. Oblivious to the fact that it was the last day she would do it.

I don't think you should confront her about it...

No choice.

Wait, now. Give her a few minutes to get inside, get her coffee, and get into the day's work. Then slip in the back door with the key.

The dashboard clock seemed to trudge through molasses. Then, finally, ten minutes was up. Good enough.

Sarah's office was down the hall. Go. Quiet, now. There was no reason to think she'd balk at coming along, but it was best not to give her time to think.

"Sarah."

She jumped, whirling around at her desk. "Oh my God. You scared me to death." She sounded breathless. And a moment later, she frowned. "What are you doing here? What's the matter?"

Stay calm. It was fine to look stricken—good, in fact—but keep your head. "I had to come get you." Let the words be hard to say. "It's your sister. She's...had an accident."

"What?" She was up. "What happened?"

"A fall...I don't know exactly. I only know they said they couldn't reach you."

She glanced at her purse. "But my cell phone's right—"

"She's at the hospital. Southview Memorial."

That confused her. "Southview? That's all the way—"

"I know. We need to hurry." During the morning rush hour, Highland Bridge could serve as a back route to Southview. When something works, there's no reason to tamper with it. "Aw, God." A little sway.

"Are you all right?" Sarah asked.

"Yes, yes. I'm just not feeling well this morning. I'll be okay."

They walked down the hall, Sarah hurrying, looking back with worry in her eyes. She saw the moment of unsteadiness, the hand over the belly. Frowned.

"Maybe you shouldn't drive," she said. "Leave the Saab here. We'll take my car."

Perfect. I was just about to insist on that. "Fine. Go on and get it. I need a bathroom. I'll be right out."

Sarah scurried out the door.

Go back. Leave a trail, something at Sarah's desk to buy some time before anyone started looking for her.

Her computer was already up and running. Control-A. Delete. Whatever Sarah had been working on gave way to a blank screen.

Perfect.

Dani woke to the smell of bacon.

Bacon?

She blinked, looked around. A huge bedroom, a king-size bed. Lush pillows and a down-filled comforter.

What? She'd chosen the sofa. For good measure, she'd scolded Mitch's authoritarianism, but inside, she'd had no desire to go alone to the Radisson.

Still, she'd chosen the sofa. So how did she get in here?

She got up, piecing together the night: OCIN files, Mitch, the sofa. A storm outside, but inside, roving lips and hands. The crook of Mitch's strong shoulder and the thud of his heartbeat in one ear, gentle jazz in the other making the thunder seem inconsequential. The sensation of being safe, cared for, even cosseted.

She scanned the room for a clock: 7:45.

"Morning."

She whirled and found Mitch propped against the doorframe. He wore jeans with a loose polo shirt and moccasins, and his hair was slightly damp. The shadow of morning beard darkened his cheeks. He wielded a spatula.

"Greetings like that are generally met with something like 'Hi' or 'Good morning,'" he said.

Dani was suddenly shy. Eighteen years ago, they'd done a lot more with each other than they'd done last night, but waking together and sharing breakfast wasn't part of it. There was an intimacy to awakening in Mitch's apartment that crossed new boundaries.

"How...?" She gestured to the room.

"You made the wrong choice," he said, as if it were the simplest thing in the world. "You think I'd make you take the sofa when there's a three-thousand-dollar mattress in here? You were sleeping like a log, for the first time in three days, from what I can tell. I carried you in."

Dani glanced down at herself. Her top blouse button was open, her clothes twisted.

Mitch walked over to her, stopping a foot away. "No," he said, eyes glittering like a lake. "I didn't ravish you in your sleep."

"I didn't think that. Jeez, I'd remember something like that."

He ran a finger down her throat. "You sure as hell will," he promised, and his touch fluttered in Dani's belly. He tipped his head toward the hallway. "Bathroom's across the hall. There's a new toothbrush in the cabinet. You still like your coffee black?"

She couldn't believe he was fixing her coffee. Or

bacon, or anything else. "I have my own toothbrush. And I've been taking care of my own coffee for a long time."

"I know," Mitch said. "Now you don't have to."

She pushed past him, ignoring the shiver that brushed her skin. She had to keep cool. At his core, Mitch had always been the great fixer—perceptive and chivalrous and protective. At her core—if Dani were to combine a dose of bald honesty with all those psychology classes she'd taken—she'd probably find some tiny nugget of need that made those qualities attractive to her. But that's why he scared her: She might start getting used to being worried over or even liking it, or—heaven forbid—start to count on it.

She cleaned up and went to the kitchen, finding that Mitch had raided Sanders's fridge and pantry. In one whiff, Dani got over the fact that he was coddling her. She ate like a horse.

"I'm gonna hit the streets today," she said, finishing with a piece of toast and strawberry jam. "There are some people I need to talk to."

"I'll come with you."

"No," she said. "If you're with me, no one on the streets will tell me a damn thing. It's not like I'm running around alone and defenseless late at night. It will be broad daylight, lots of people around, and I'm both trained and armed." He peered at her, not quite buying it, she thought. She decided to add a dollop of truth. "People know you, Mitch. You'll draw attention I don't need."

"You mean, Chief Gibson could find out."

That, too. "I'll call you later." She picked up her coat, headed to the door. Mitch followed and just as she opened it, braced his arm over her head and pushed it closed again. "Check in with me every hour," he said. "An hour goes by I don't hear from you, I'll send Gibson and Tifton both after you."

"I'll be fine, Mitch. You don't have to worry about me."

He set his hands on either side of her face and kissed her, fervently and thoroughly, a little urgency behind it. Dani reeled.

"Yes," he said, and the look in his eyes ribboned all the way to her toes. "As a matter of fact, I do."

Sarah drove like a maniac, just about begging for a police car to stop her, and chattered about her sister the whole way. It was annoying as hell, but it was about to be over. She'd just pulled onto Highland Bridge.

"Oh, God."

Sarah looked over to the passenger seat. "What? Are you all right?"

"Oh." A little hiccup. "Oh, no."

"What's the matter?" Sarah asked. She kept glancing over but couldn't really look while driving. The bridge was just two narrow lanes. Fifty feet high.

"I'm...Stop the car. I'm going to be sick."

"I can't stop here—"

"*Arhnk*." It was a convincing gag, complete with hand-to-mouth as if Sarah's upholstery were about to get doused.

"Okay, okay." Sarah—simpleminded Sarah—stopped the car.

Out of the car in a rush, dash to the railing of the bridge. An Emmy award–winning fit of nausea. Sarah put on her flashers and came up beside, worry in her eyes.

"Are you all right?"

A car passed behind them. Stay bent over the railing, wait. Glance both ways. Clear now. "Y-yes. I'm just fine."

The gun wheeled toward Sarah's face and her eyes widened, noticing, but too late. She flinched back, but the gun sight smashed against her temple—her orbital bone splitting like the shell of a coconut. The impact flipped her halfway over the railing, legs crumpling, and her body twisted until her head lolled to the side and she caught the eyes of her attacker. She gasped in shock, then, one shove later, plummeted over the railing, long peasant skirt tangling up over her face and sensible white panties preserving her modesty. Fifty feet below she splashed into the Monocacy River.

Sarah Rittenhouse was predictable as the sunrise. Easy pickings.

CHAPTER
27

EVERYTHING WAS SILENT, and the air didn't stink.

That's what woke Nika Love. She'd been dead asleep—the kind of sleep that's almost unconscious—until cramps began pricking at her gut like thorns. She rolled into a ball and that's when the silence screamed in her ears. No snoring. No coughing or sniffling. None of the constant murmur of shelter life, with row after row of canvas cots lining the floor, and at least one body claiming each. No smell.

She opened her eyes and daylight lanced through her skull. She closed them and lay still, afraid to try again. She wasn't at the shelter anymore—she knew that much for certain. She was in a bed, a real bed, in a bedroom. It was comfortable, the room quiet.

One heartbeat at a time, she dared to open her eyes again. Her head ached like a bastard, but she was ready for it this time and blinked the fuzz away. Licked her lips. They were parched. The insides of her nostrils, too—as if she'd sucked in ammonia.

The memory came back in a tidal wave: the man, the truck, the damp cloth over her mouth, smelling like a chemistry lab. She'd fought—she remembered screaming and trying to twist away—and after that, there was nothing for a long time.

Then the man again, the baby booties, his brutal clamp over her mouth with the damp cloth, time and again. Some sort of chemical that parched her mouth and left her head pounding.

And the baby? She touched her belly in dread—still there. Of course he was. Otherwise, what would the thorns be? Funny how something that had been so unwanted a few months ago had now grown into something she'd do anything to protect. And keep. She couldn't tell her pimp that, of course; she'd promised him that after the baby was born, she'd come back. But Nika had changed her mind. Just yesterday, she'd told Dr. Housley: She was going to keep her baby.

She stood, a wave of dizziness pushing her back a step, then waddled to the door. She reached out to open it and the panic came in a rush.

No doorknob.

Her heart jumped to her throat and she ran her hands around the edge of the door. Nothing. She pounded, scraping with her fingernails, trying to find anything to grab hold of. She screamed and hurried across the room to another door, but it was a bathroom—no way out. Terror clawed at her, tenterhooks of fear grabbing in her gut.

Where the hell was she?

Nika forced herself to breathe and walked to the window, gasping at the sight. No city. No nothing. As far as she could see, there was nothing but forest and mountains, the sun peeking through the trees like a butterscotch candy. It looked like the mountains of North Carolina where she grew up. Dense and leafy, a little morning haze hanging in the air.

Tears sprang to her eyes: North Carolina. Her parents would still be there. Hating her? Possibly. That's what she thought, anyway, when she ran away from home. What was that argument about? Oh, yes—a boy. Nika couldn't remember his name now. Mike? Jeff? How strange that she couldn't remember.

But there had been so many since then. At seventeen years of age, there had already been been dozens of men. Hundreds, maybe.

No, not seventeen. Nika looked around, searching for a calendar. There wasn't one, but she knew it was the first week of October. So, she'd had a birthday. Nika was eighteen.

And she wasn't really Nika Love. She was Monika Wheeler. Daughter of a hardware store owner and assistant preschool teacher. Sister to an annoying little brother who used to poke her in the ribs in the pews on Sunday morning. She wondered if Loopy, the family hound, still raided her bedroom for stuffed animals whenever someone left the door open.

"Monika," she whispered, trying the name again. It felt good to hear it, like a long-lost friend. She closed her eyes and remembered where Monika had come from. She had parents. A bedroom and a dog. A family.

And a baby. She stroked her bulging belly and wondered, not for the first time, what Burt and Laura Wheeler would say about that. Would they welcome her home, even after all the screaming and harsh words, the teenage accusations that they didn't understand her or love her or care about what's-his-name? Would they want the baby in their family or be too shamed by what she'd become to accept her home again?

Monika knew the answer, but a noise snapped it away. She started, backing up against the window. Footsteps, heavy ones, climbed the stairs. She glanced around, but there was nothing that would serve as a weapon. Her gut clenched and she doubled partway over, hand at the bottom of her belly as if she could stop the pain.

The locks—plural, she realized—rattled, and a moment later the door pushed open. A man filled the doorway, the one from last night.

Every instinct tightened in Monika. After years of servicing men, she'd learned how to read them. This one was cold as ice.

"I heard you up," he said without concern for small talk. "I'm supposed to make sure you're all right."

A flicker of relief: That was a good sign. "Where am I?"

"Think of it as a resort."

"For the baby? I've changed my mind. I don't want to give up my baby, I want to go home. Tell the broker I'll pay him back. Tell him." Monika was fighting tears. "I just want to go home."

The man's features edged into a smile—the hardest, coldest smile she'd ever seen. "Stupid bitch," he said, checking the lock as he left. "You're not going home."

Dani left the Foundation apartment, hit the hotel for a shower, then headed for the streets. Kept looking over her shoulder for gray sedans, even though she knew Chief Gibson had pulled the IA surveillance; if he hadn't, there would have been a witness to the intruder at her house.

She dialed Tifton. "Gibson was gonna talk to Ty Craig about Rosie," she said. "What did he learn?"

"*Nada.* Craig's not around. One of his goons claims he's on vacation in Cancún."

Damn it. "That's bullshit; Craig hates Mexicans. He won't even eat a taco. No way he vacations in Cancún."

"I'm just saying."

"So he's holding out."

"Looks like it." He paused. "There's a rumor or two, Dani. That he might be thinking to reel you in, with your dad gone now and all."

She closed her eyes. Goddamn it. She didn't worry about what Tifton thought; he knew her. But the fact that other cops might be talking about it...Sometimes she wished she hadn't been so stubborn to have become a cop. Sometimes she wished she could go someplace where no one knew her name...

Great. Now she was a TV theme song. "Well," she said, "Gibson's already taken care of that for me, hasn't he? He's not taking any chances that I might interview Craig about Rosie."

"It wasn't a bad move," Tift said. "Protect you from rumors about Craig *and* from a murderer."

"Yeah, well, like I keep saying lately, I can take care of myself."

Dani hung up. Craig in Cancún—she didn't believe that for a minute. But even his going underground at all was out of character for him. Ty Craig kept a public profile, complete with heavy gold chains around his neck, the pair of sultry women expected of a pimp, and the pair of bodyguards expected of a loan shark. He lived in a luxury condo building where he owned three floors, one of which he'd turned into putting greens. For thirty years, he'd insulated himself from the law by having henchmen do his dirty work and by making significant donations to certain mayoral candidates and commissioners.

And by owning the occasional cop. Guys like Artie Cole, and someone up the totem pole a ways.

Dani spent the morning asking around, touching snitches and fences and hookers, hitting her sources. Everyone said the same thing: *Blond-who? Don't know. No blondes disappeared that I know of. Haven't seen Rosie in years. Cops been asking the same thing. Ain't seen Ty...*

Then, about two-thirty in the afternoon, the talk changed. There were rumors about drugs and a bust, and Ty going inside.

Dani dialed Greg Holmes, a guy she'd last seen at her dad's funeral.

"Nails," he said. "You finally change your mind about letting me show you a good time?"

"You've heard the phrase 'cold day in hell'?"

"More times than you could count."

She smiled. Greg Holmes had been a narc for twenty-five years, and he played the part with the conviction of a strict method actor: greasy strings of hair on a weather-beaten face, cigarette hanging from his mouth, tar-stained fingers. His clothes were from Goodwill, and he washed them rarely enough that anyone trying to score with him on the streets was taken in by his veracity. He had more busts than the rest of the narc unit put together, largely because he didn't get hung up following rules. To Holmes, rules were for breaking and policies were mere suggestions.

"I need some info," Dani said.

"I heard you were on vacation."

"I'm looking for Ty Craig."

"You see the Ravens game on Sunday?"

"Screw you. Where's Craig?"

Holmes paused and Dani's hackles lifted. Something was up. "Got a sting going. But you didn't hear it from me."

"With what?"

"There's a stash at the club Craig owns on Brewer Street. If he hasn't materialized by tomorrow night, narcs are gonna shake it down."

Aw, God. "You plant the stash?"

"Hey, I'm an officer of the law, sworn to uphold and—"

"Did you plant it?" Dani repeated.

"No."

She wasn't sure he'd tell her if he had. "But you've ignored it until now."

"Pick and choose your battles, baby, pick and choose. But as soon as we bust this one, we'll close down every club he owns. Flush him out and make him trade. If he knows anything about McNamara, his lawyer will make him sing like a canary."

Dani hung up, feeling the sudden need for a shower. It wasn't the same as what her dad spent his career doing—cops made choices every day about letting some things go in order to get bigger things later, and her dad had gone to play for the other side. But the setup left a bad taste in Dani's mouth.

Still, if it worked, police would make the club-bust go away in exchange for information about Rosie's murder.

Dani would like to have a crack at him first. The longer the case went on without her, the harder it would be to stay in the loop. Another woman might lose a hunk of hair, while Dani sat in a hotel room watching game shows on TV . . .

She cursed. Stop it. This was what Craig wanted—to

draw Dani into his camp. The only one who wanted it more was Dave Gibson. It would be all he needed to have her badge.

She sighed, trying not to feel sorry for herself. There were other leads she could follow.

Like Keller Brookes, Rosie's counselor.

"The police were here this morning," Keller said, folding herself crisscross into a deep sofa in her office. A Miami transplant with a weakness for chocolate, she wore jeans and a lacy tank layered under a long-sleeved shirt. On occasion, Dani helped Keller with a situation of her own: Her sister had been missing for years, believed dead, and the case was still open. Keller hadn't given up on it.

"So what did you tell my esteemed colleagues?" Dani asked.

"They said you're on vacation."

"I'm back. What did you tell them?"

"That anything Rosie and I discussed in the course of counseling is confidential."

"Death breaks the legal bounds of confidentiality. Besides, they can come back with a warrant."

"They'll have to."

Dani peered at her. "We know about the baby, Keller."

"Yes. The autopsy."

Dani nodded.

"Her mother doesn't know," Keller said. "That was important to Rosie."

"And I'll try not to let it out. But we need to know what was going on in her life that ended it. Her sister can't think of anything over the past couple years, and she was murdered just a few weeks after she came back.

So it's possible it's related to something that happened here, a long time ago."

"Like what?"

"Like the baby. What happened to it?"

Keller stood, pacing in front of wide windows. "Convince me that my divulging confidences to you about Rosie's past is going to somehow help you find out who murdered her."

"The more we can know about her, the better chance we have of—"

"Not good enough."

Dani sighed. "I have reason to believe that she had recently decided to try to find her child. I also have reason to believe Russell Sanders might have been helping her."

"How do you know these things?"

From the dead-drunk son of Russ Sanders. "I can't divulge that."

Keller closed her eyes. "Okay. She *was* looking for her baby. A boy. But she hadn't used legal avenues for the adoption."

"What avenues did she use?"

"Dani . . ."

"Christ, Keller. You're going to protect some illegal baby market?"

"I'm going to protect this center." The Target Center for Teens. Keller and her colleague had founded it. It did good work, and no doubt some of that work involved teenagers who were pregnant.

"Where did the baby go?" Dani asked.

"I don't know. That's the God's truth. Rosie didn't know, either."

"Had she ever met Russell Sanders, from the photography foundation on Franklin Avenue?"

"I know who he is. Was. She never mentioned him."

"So they weren't working together."

"Not that I know of."

"And they were never lovers."

"Lovers?" Keller asked. "Russell Sanders was sixty years old."

"And Rose McNamara was a hooker."

Keller looked at her. "You're thinking the baby belonged to Sanders?"

Dani shrugged.

Keller pressed her fingers into her eyes. "Rosie said the baby's father was one of her johns, but she didn't know which one. I can't see Russell Sanders doing that."

"You knew him?"

"A little. He was a good man."

Dani was getting tired of hearing that. *You always assume the worst...* "Okay. But Rosie *was* trying to find her baby. That much you know for sure."

"Yes." Keller took a deep breath. *This is the part she doesn't want to tell me*, Dani thought. "She had some baby things... a pacifier, a knit cap."

Dani straightened. Her sister said the same thing. "But why *baby* things? Her son would be two years old now."

"That's the point."

"That she was acting crazy?"

" 'Crazy' is a word I frown upon, Dani. But she had the baby items and a camera full of pictures of little boys his age."

"Jesus. She was stalking toddlers?"

"Not just any toddler. She had leads, some way to narrow down the choices. I don't know what it was. But over the past couple of weeks, I'd say there were three or four boys' pictures she carried in her camera who, in her mind, were possibilities."

Camera. Dani remembered searching through Rosie's cell phone, but not her camera. There hadn't been a camera. Was there one at her apartment?

First thing to check. She stood, then remembered. "Did Rosie ever talk to you about her childhood?"

"I'm a shrink, Dani. *You're* the only one who doesn't talk to me about childhood."

"She had scars, from surgeries."

"Yes," Keller said, "I did know that. Rosie was adopted by the McNamaras. She was burned in a fire when she was two, and taken from an unfit mother."

"So, her scars..."

"The physical scars were almost nonexistent. She showed them to me once, and I could hardly see them. Emotional ones are always harder. She had a lot of guilt about her adoptive family, which made her entertain the idea of meeting her birth mother."

"The one who let her get burned?"

"It's not unusual. The bond between a parent and a child is pretty tough to sever, even when it's negative." She tilted her head. "I shouldn't have to tell you that."

Dani frowned. "Nice try, Doctor," she said, but she wasn't going to fall for it. "Why the guilt?"

"Her behavior. Rosie's mother and father were strict Catholics—Rosie becoming a prostitute was the ultimate sin. It was especially hard on her sister."

"Janet?"

"Some sibling stuff there—a little rivalry and jealousy. Rosie's surgeries cost the family dearly in financial terms. Janet actually gave up going to college because her parents couldn't afford it."

Dani felt the bump of a possibility. Shamed mother? Resentful sister? She asked Keller as much.

"Her family's not dead, so I can't talk about them," Keller said but thought it through, anyway. "Pretty far-fetched, I think."

But something to keep in mind.

Dani said, "Did Rosie ever meet her birth mother?"

"Not yet, but had she lived, I think she was going to. She'd just turned eighteen, you know, so the records could be opened. She'd been contacted by the adoption agency that her birth mother wanted to meet her. Apparently, her mother had wanted to meet her for a long time."

Dani scratched her head. Rosie was trying to find her child and meet her mother. Who might not want one of those things to happen? Who would be angry enough to kill to prevent it? A blood sibling to Rosie? An adoptive parent of her son? A long-lost birth parent?

She left Keller's office with the questions swirling in her brain. She dialed Tifton again and left a message: "Tift, we need to get a warrant for Rose McNamara's adoption records. And take a look at her adoptive family. I'll explain; call me."

She mulled it over and got in her car. What Brad had said about his father made no more sense now than it had before Dani had talked to Keller. *He would've helped her.* Because Russell knew how to go about adoptions? Because he was the baby's father? Because he was just such a gosh-darn *good man*? She didn't know, but one thing was certain: They needed to get into Rosie's apartment. They needed to find the baby Rosie thought was hers.

Her phone bleeped. Mitch, checking up. He'd been buried in preparations for the exhibition this weekend but hadn't missed a phone call.

"I'm on my way over to Janet Milano's," Dani said, working to be annoyed rather than touched by the fact that he was five minutes shy of the hour mark. "I'm gonna see if Janet will let me look around Rosie's place."

"I need a break," he said. "I'll meet you at Janet's."

CHAPTER
28

MITCH BEAT HER THERE by ten minutes. When Dani pulled up, something that might have been relief touched his chest.

Christ, he'd been worried about her. Watching the minute hand inch between numbers, wondering if some bastard with a pair of shears was following her around... He'd spent half the afternoon cursing himself for letting her go. *I'm trained and armed.* So what? Training mattered when you came up against an opponent of comparable size and strength, who played by the rules of fighting. What about when the opponent was a hundred pounds heavier and came out of nowhere, armed with a pair of scissors and no rules at all?

He stalked over to the door of her car and held it open, did a quick once-over: She was okay. She got out and he blocked her with a kiss—nothing wild, but nothing chaste, either. Made sure she knew his intentions.

"How's the leg?" he asked, taking her arm. The stitches had been mean-looking, the cut an angry red line. He'd come across it last night while reacquainting himself with her body.

"It's fine," she said. All business.

"Any luck?"

"Maybe. How 'bout you? You gonna be ready for the exhibition this weekend?"

"Most of the show is up. I'm still working on one particular set of photos." Correction: He still hadn't *started* working on one particular set. The ones Neil had given to Russ after the attack, while Mitch was still half-comatose. He couldn't stand the thought of seeing them.

They followed Janet Milano to Rosie's place. It was a small, one-bedroom apartment in a building of eight apartments, on a street of apartment buildings. When they got there, Dani filled them in on her visit with Keller Brookes.

"Camera?" Janet said after hearing it. "Yeah, now that you mention it, there should be a camera here someplace. She bought it about a month ago at WalMart."

"Did the police look through her apartment?"

"Yeah, but I don't think they found a camera."

"Would you show us around?" Mitch asked.

"Sure. But it was usually in her purse. She bought a skinny one so it would fit in her purse."

"What about her car?" Mitch asked.

"It was parked at the carnival," Dani said, "so they'd still have it in Property. We got a list of everything in it, though. No camera."

"I can call Mom and see if she has it," Janet offered.

"Do that," Mitch said, and turned to Dani after Janet left the room. "Was Rosie's purse at the crime scene?"

"Yes. But there was no camera. But—"

"What?"

"I remember looking at her body, her right hand. She was all clenched up except that her hand was open, like something had been in it."

"Huh," Mitch said, imagining someone pulling a camera out of a dead woman's hand. And cutting her hair. Goddamn freak.

Janet came back. "Mom doesn't know about a camera."

"Okay," Dani said. "Does Rosie have a computer?"

"An old one. It's in her bedroom. I'm not very good with computers, though."

"I am," Dani said.

Janet gave Dani carte blanche with Rosie's computer and her belongings, showing no worry about what she might find. The momentary plot of sibling rivalry and jealousy lost a bit of its punch. Dani spent ten minutes working through Rosie's desktop and found a folder of photos almost immediately. She opened it. A chill shuddered over her skin.

Little boys.

"Dear God," she said. There was one at a preschool playground, hanging from a jungle gym. One with his mother in a mall, trying to push his own stroller full of shopping bags. One with his dog and older sister, picnicking at a park.

"Oh, no," Janet said, her fingers on her lips. "It's like she was...stalking them."

Something came to mind. "Her phone," Dani said. "I checked the numbers but not pictures. I wonder if there were any other pictures in her phone."

"There were," Janet said, a thread of shock in her voice. As far as Dani could tell, it was genuine. "At least one. She sent it to me, phone-to-phone."

"What was it?" Mitch asked.

"A little boy. Like these. I still have it." She was pushing buttons on her cell phone. "Here."

She handed her phone to Dani. Another picture of another dark-haired child, being held by his mother. Dani passed it on to Mitch.

Janet gaped at the computer photos, tiptoeing toward hysteria. "She *was* stalking them. Oh, God."

"That's not what this is," Dani said, remembering what Keller had said: Rosie had some way of narrowing down the possibilities. Russ Sanders? "There's something controlled about this. These pictures weren't taken spur of the moment, whenever she saw a two-year-old kid. She *picked* these children to photograph."

"Why?" Janet asked.

"I don't know. They're all about the right age for her son, they're all Caucasian, they're all boys." And that was the end of that list. Nothing else seemed to stand out as being common to each child.

"They're all well-off," Mitch said.

"What?" Dani looked again, starting with the boy on the playground.

"That's the Parker Preschool," Mitch said. "I haven't been by there for years, but I recognize the landscape."

The Parker school was elite—one of those that rich people signed their kids up for years in advance.

"And this"—Mitch pointed to the kid at the mall and tapped the purse hanging on the stroller—"it looks expensive."

"Gucci," Dani said. She went to the picnic photos, looking for whatever had given Mitch the impression of wealth. Touched the poodle. "That's a professional cut on Fido. You don't get that kind of grooming at Pet-Smart." She looked at Mitch, impressed. "Pretty good, Sherlock."

He shrugged. "I don't see that sort of thing in my

photos. It stood out. Janet, hand me that phone again, will you?"

He looked at that photograph. "The rings," he said, holding it out so Dani and Janet could see. "This woman's wearing a freaking sapphire mine."

Janet seemed dumbfounded. "What was Rosie doing?"

"I don't know," Dani said. "But one thing's for sure: This is the Russell Sanders crowd. Not the crowd Rosie would have known from her hooker days in Reading, or even her more recent days living here and working at Big Lots."

"Any bleached blondes?" Mitch asked.

There weren't, at least, not white-blond and curly.

"I just can't believe that if Rosie knew these people, I wouldn't have known about it," Janet said. She pointed at the phone, still in Mitch's hand. "And why isn't this boy on her computer? Why is he only on the cell phone?"

"Maybe she didn't have her camera handy for that one," Dani said. "Or maybe she just hadn't gotten them off her camera yet. It's from Sunday. The real question is, who else knew she was taking pictures? And did the photos pose some sort of threat to someone?"

"Russell?" Mitch asked, but the question seemed directed more inward than outward.

Dani looked at Janet. "Do you mind if I search through her other files? I mean, I know they're private and all, but—"

Janet's voice trembled with emotion. "Someone stabbed my sister and destroyed her face and hacked off her hair. Do anything you have to. Just find the freak who did that to her."

Brad opened the safe in his bedroom and ripped into the files. Find her: Nika Love. She hadn't been at the shelter where Housley said she was staying. She hadn't checked in at the clinic. Housley said he hadn't heard from her since yesterday, though she was already partially dilated and was supposed to check in with him every day now. She wasn't picking up the phone Brad had supplied for her or returning any messages.

He decided to check files for the birth mothers. Maybe they'd list a friend or a relative or alternate address. Brad didn't remember. He rarely looked at these files. When Housley came across a pregnant girl who was a good candidate, Brad collected minimal information—just enough to make a match for her baby to a set of adoptive parents—then locked the information in the safe. Until now, there had never been any need to consult it.

He pulled out the small stack—files on ten or twelve couples whose OCIN applications showed signs of being good prospects for an under-the-table adoption, and some scant paperwork from Housley about the six birth mothers they'd used so far. When he got to Nika Love, he sifted through the pages.

Medical information, birth certificate, financial receipts...A few tidbits in case a little blackmail ever became necessary to convince her to keep her mouth shut. Where was the biographical page? Sometimes the girls were hesitant to give that sort of information—and more often than not they probably lied. Still, it was collected to share with the adoptive parents, at least as much of it as was pertinent to the baby's health and background.

But for Nika, that page wasn't here.

A stitch of worry tightened in his chest. He went to another file—Heather Whyte. Her street name had been Silk, and she had been the first of the six girls he and Housley collaborated on. Brad remembered how nervous the whole thing had made him that first time... Going through OCIN applications to find potential clients, vetting the parents for their willingness to take part in what Brad might suggest, then awaiting the birth and getting the money and the baby and the fudged paperwork all into the right hands. Since then, it had gotten easier, of course—they had it down to a science now. The only wild card was the availability of pregnant women who walked into Housley's orbit, but lately, even that had become easier. A network had been established. Girls in the right circumstance were beginning to know where to go and what doctor to ask for. And since they were all guilty of something, no one in the network dared to speak up.

Except Rose McNamara. She'd broken the code, decided to find her baby. She'd gone to Housley then followed him to Brad and confronted him with her fists clenched and her ire up, demanding to know where her child had been placed, threatening to tell the police. Brad strong-armed her: threw his position into her face and let her know in no uncertain terms that if anyone went to jail it would be *her*, that he had means and money and know-how she couldn't even fathom. He thought she'd gone away.

But she hadn't. She'd gone to his father. Goddamn bitch. And Russell distrusted Brad just enough that he'd actually believed her.

Heather Whyte's records slid through his fingers and the stitch of worry turned to a pang of alarm. No biographical data on her, either.

Jesus. Brad checked another: Jill Donnelly's personal data was missing. Rose McNamara's. All of them.

His lungs seized. Jesus Christ. All six files were missing that page.

He could hardly think. How? Why? Had he removed

that information at some point and not put it back? Did he have another stash somewhere? No way. Brad was a lawyer. He was careful. Dotted every i and crossed every t. He'd bought this safe specifically to keep these files, and no one else had ever even seen it. The only two people who even knew the safe existed were the maid and—

Brad staggered to his feet. He stumbled across the room and rubbed his face, cursing the bruises from Mitch's temper, unable to believe he had been so stupid.

Fuck.

Mia stood at the master-bath mirror wearing a white silk robe and diamond pendant. Her arms ached from being held overhead so long, the new blond stripe in her hair giving her trouble. She'd never had to do it herself before. She always saved enough hair for the wig and took the rest to her hairdresser, Darva, who would mutter in some Slavic tongue about Mia's new penchant for hair extensions. *I never understand why you cut your hair off…And now, you want me weave this in?* Or, *Mrs. Kettering, you want more color, we use highlights instead, or I order you some extensions? This hair is not made for weaving…*

Darva got over it when the first five-hundred-dollar tip crossed her hand. Shut right up, fashioned extensions from the hair Mia brought her, and wove them in. Probably rolled her eyes and gossiped about eccentric rich people after she left, but Mia didn't care. She considered each woman's contribution her just reward and wore them like ribbons of honor: Heather Whyte's, a light brown that was barely noticeable. If Mia ran a fine-tooth comb down just the right spots, she could feel the teeth scrape over the knots that held it in, but otherwise, Heather's hair was almost no change at all. Marshall hadn't even noticed.

Rolinda Sills's hair had been harder; Rolinda was black with hair dyed an unlikely shade of orange. Darva just about had a fit. *The color won't matter, but the texture not right, Ms. Kettering. I can smooth it now, but when it gets wet*, pfft. She'd spread her fingers, trying to show Mia how the hair would behave. It was Mia who'd looked up information about permanent relaxers in black women's hair, experimented with them in the wig, and convinced Darva to do it. Mia could feel the difference in texture when she ran her fingers down just the right places, her secret pleasure.

Jill Donnelly was third—a honey gold that Darva wove in as highlights down either side of Mia's face, a touch of brightness. This time, Marshall had noticed, touching the lighter strands with a small smile. "It looks nice," he said dutifully, but Mia knew he didn't care.

Then the dark, almost black hair of Rose McNamara. Beautiful, strong locks, with a healthy shine that offset the lighter highlights. Marshall said nothing, but Mia supposed that was a matter of his preoccupation with troubles at the Foundation.

Now, Mia was working with the blond curls of Alicia. The wig sat on its wig block on the counter, for comparison, while Mia worked painstakingly to weave the same blond stripe from the wig into her own. She didn't dare take it to Darva; it was too soon after Rosie. And with McNamara's body having been discovered, Mia lived in fear that the cut hair would hit the media. If it did, would Darva start to question where Mia had gotten the hair, why it was so important to use? Would she wonder why Mia had been in such a hurry on Monday to get the latest extensions woven in? It was something to keep in mind.

Mia had spent the morning looking online, but she

couldn't fashion the extensions herself—not the way Darva or her mother might have done it. She tried to remember if her mother had ever handled extensions— she'd gone to hairdresser school for a while, and did a few shampoos and cuts in the tiny kitchen of their trailer, but she couldn't recall. Most of her mother's money came in the old-fashioned way: She was a prostitute.

And when money was extra tight, so was her daughter. A striking little girl with green eyes and thick, auburn hair. Mia's tricks paid three times what her mother's did.

Until her mother's boyfriend, Grady, started wanting her, too. He'd fawned over Mia's hair once, in front of her mother. That's when the shears came out. *Shorter*... Hack, hack. The shears pulled more than they cut. They were rusty and dull and for the next five years, until Mia ran away, she'd kept her head covered in shame, and still her mother would come at her in a fit... *You know better*. Hack, hack. *Keep it short*...

Mia gritted her teeth, biting back the memory. She'd survived. It was more than she could say for her mother or Grady.

She lowered her hands and looked at the blond stripe down the right side of her hair. She picked up a comb and went through it, carefully, making sure the knots that held it in didn't snag. Mia breathed a sigh of relief. It wasn't perfect, but when she held the wig up next to her face, studying both heads of hair in the mirror, the likeness was stunning.

Kristina would be overwhelmed. Mia almost couldn't wait until Sunday.

"*Mia.*"

She jumped, the wig slipping from her hand. Down-stairs, a door slammed and the housekeeper's voice shot off a round of protests in Spanish. A man's voice fired back.

"I want to see her, damn it," he said. "Where is she?"

The voices came closer, the housekeeper's voice chasing him up the stairs.

Mia grabbed the wig on the block and tossed a towel over the top of it. She dashed from the bathroom into the master bedroom, and just made it into the hall when the housekeeper met her.

"*Señora, señora,*" Catalina said. "*Por favor, señor,*" she said, trying to back up the intruder. And to Mia, when it didn't work, "*Lo siento, señora.*"

"Get out of my way," Brad said to the startled woman. "I need to talk to Mia."

"It's all right, Catalina. Let him come."

Mia crossed her arms, momentarily taken aback by the black eye and bruises Brad sported, and when Catalina had gotten down the stairs, she lifted her chin. "My husband wouldn't like finding you here, Brad."

"My safe. You got into it."

Mia gave her best impression of looking bored, her fingers stroking Jill's highlights down one cheek. "What are you going on about?"

"The personal data sheets for the babies' birth mothers. You took them." He seethed, spittle spraying with each word, and when she didn't protest, pure disbelief darkened his eyes. "What the hell have you done to those girls?"

CHAPTER
29

W"HAT?" MIA WAS ASTONISHED that Brad had finally figured it out, part of it anyway. She didn't let it show, though; she was too good for that. Instead, she touched the new streak of blond in her hair, spreading the rest of her hair around her shoulders in an act of seduction that men across the globe never failed to recognize. Stroking her prizes. "I don't know what you're talking about."

"You do," he said, advancing. Every word came out between gritted teeth. "Why?"

"Brad, you need to—*Ungh.*" Brad seized her by the arm, hard, and pushed her into the bedroom from the hallway. He kicked the door closed with one foot.

"Don't try to deny it. You're the only one who's been in there."

"Let go of me."

"What are you doing?" he snarled. He glanced over her loose hair, noticing the new blond stripe, but couldn't seem to make any sense of it. His eyes were like devil eyes. For half a second, Mia would have sworn they glowed red.

But he'd met his match with Mia. She remembered her mother telling her once to quit looking at her with the shark stare. At ten, Mia hadn't realized how powerful a mere look could be, but then she'd honed it on the johns who thought to get more than they paid for. And by twenty, her life cleaned up and a wedding to Marshall Kettering in the works, she'd cornered her mother in the trailer with that very same shark stare, ripped the shears from her hands, and driven the blades between her ribs. Set the place on fire and watched it burn, her mother smelling like roasted pork.

She saved the shears.

No, Mia was no wilting flower. She pulled away from him, her robe falling open in front, and met Brad's devil eyes with the shark eyes of her own. "What do you care? It can only be better for you to have them gone. Rosie would have risked your little operation with Housley."

His skin went white. Mia liked it. She had him now.

"Would you like to hear about it, Brad? How I got her address by fucking you then forced her to remember her baby? How I stabbed her in the throat so she couldn't scream then destroyed her face like she deserved?"

"Y-you're insane."

Brad was backing up, but Mia could see his brain begin to work. Remembering.

She stepped closer to him, the silk loop of her tie falling around her hips. The robe slid open, one breast showing. "You're part of it, you know," she said.

"I had nothing to do with it."

"You gave them to me."

"Them?" His head shook back and forth, as if not believing what he was hearing. He began backing up. "Jesus Christ, what have you done?"

"I've exacted justice," she said through gritted teeth. "They all deserved it. Handing their babies to a stranger for a few dollars."

"Jesus God."

"*I* would have done anything..."

Brad gaped at her. "You wanted a baby? Is that what this is about?" Brad took another step back, a crazed look in his eyes, and a thought snapped in Mia's mind like a twig: He would tell. Brad Harper might risk the brokerage to turn her in.

But no, she realized—he wouldn't. Even if his father wasn't around to shame anymore, Brad would never give up the easy money from the babies or give Mitch the satisfaction of watching him go to prison. Brad was essentially a coward. A spineless, easily manipulated coward.

She advanced on him, the loops of her robe slipping around her hips, the silk falling open and exposing her crotch as she walked. He stared at her as if she'd turned into something he'd never imagined before. "You didn't even wonder about Jill Donnelly, did you?" she asked. "The news reported her missing and you barely gave her a thought."

"I hadn't seen her in years...I never thought..." He swallowed. "Jill Donnelly is dead, too?"

She touched her hair. "They all are."

Brad groaned. "Nika? What about her?"

"Not yet. Don't worry, you'll get your baby." She leaned forward, whispering. "I don't want the babies."

"Then what do you want?"

"I want the mothers to pay," she said simply, "to give back."

Brad looked as if he might topple. "You're insane," he said. "Christ, you're a madwoman."

She let a smile grow beneath the shark eyes. "Something you would do well to remember."

"Don't threaten me."

But she could see the thoughts tripping on one another behind his eyes. The Caymans. Brazil. Europe. Where could he go and how fast could he get there, and how would he take his money?

"I need to know where Nika is," he said. Desperate.

"She's safe, for now. I have no interest in killing a baby."

"But after?"

Mia gave a little toss of her head. "I'll take what I need from her and send her to hell with the others, where she belongs."

Brad closed his eyes. "You're crazy. I'm calling the police."

Now she chuckled. "And what about those pages of personal data? You know, the pages that are missing from your safe." She crossed her arms. "Where are they?"

He only glared at her.

"I have them. All ready for the police, folded in a piece of letterhead from your office with your fingerprints all over it. All this time, you planned to blame the brokerage on your father if it ever came out, didn't you? Well, there's no doing that now."

"My fath—" He stopped, and his voice quaked. "You killed my father."

"You should thank me. He was about to turn on you, with Rosie."

"Noooo." It was the sound a wounded animal might have made and he pressed the heels of his hands against his eyes, as if trying to keep his head from exploding.

"Why?" Half groan, half whine. He lurched around the

room as if he were lost, drowning. Mia was disgusted. She saw his hands go to his pockets, feeling around, but there was nothing there. He had degenerated to a common addict over the months: no better than a street junkie, just using a higher-class drug. Mia knew he could hardly function anymore without a bloodstream full of OCs or opiates.

And she knew that as long as she provided them, he belonged to her.

"Careful, Brad. You wouldn't want to bite the hand that feeds you."

He knew what she meant, smacked his lips almost as if tasting the bite of the drugs. Glared at her. "You know Mitch is buried in the files. And that Detective Cole."

Mia frowned. "Cole isn't on the case anymore."

"You stupid whore."

Red sparks burst in Mia's eyes. "Don't call me that." She bared her teeth. Her fingers curled, as if holding the shears. "Don't ever call me that."

"Cole's still helping, going through every page with Mitch and a magnifying glass. I changed the password so it will take him some time, but with Cole's help . . . I'm not even sure she left the apartment last night. This afternoon, I heard him on the phone when he left. He said he was meeting Sergeant Cole at Rosie's apartment."

Mia's bones turned to ice. *Bitch. Damn her.*

She moved to her purse, which sat on the dresser. Brad needed her. He wouldn't forget that. She stuck her hand in and pulled out a tiny envelope, and the unmistakable rattle of pills inside caught Brad's attention. "Just imagine," she said, "prison *and* no drugs." She walked over and pressed the pills into his hand. "Sort of makes you want to play along, doesn't it?"

He closed his fingers on the pills. Mia stepped back and opened the bedroom door.

"Get out, Brad. I'll let you know when the baby is born. Be ready to take it."

And, she thought, her brain already racing, *I'll stop Dani Cole*.

Dani stood, cracked her back, and took a turn around Rosie's bedroom to get a second wind. With Janet's permission, she'd stayed all afternoon to work through Rosie's computer. Mitch had headed back to the Foundation. Made Dani promise to call before she left the apartment.

A little shiver tightened her skin. She should hate it, having him insist that she check in, having him hover over her. She ought to feel ashamed and tell him to mind his own business.

But, God help her, she liked it.

She picked up a little blue teddy bear that sat on the nightstand, remembering what Keller had said: Rosie had gotten some baby items. Did she really believe she could get her baby back? Dani looked around, opened a couple of drawers. In the third, she found more of the things Keller had referred to: a pair of knitted baby booties, a little blanket, a pacifier.

She checked her watch and decided to call it quits, called the vet before they closed. No change. Then Tifton. The jerk had promised to stay in touch, but he hadn't returned an earlier call. This time, he was rushed.

"Nails, I got no time for this," he said when she finally got through.

"What do you mean—"

"An eighteen-year-old girl was kidnapped last night;

she's pregnant. The FBI jumped on it this afternoon and I'm in."

"In? With the FBI?" Dani's heart thumped.

"There's a task force getting going. A couple of us cops and a bunch of Feds."

She swallowed. Damn Chief Gibson for pushing her away. Dani could've been in, too. "What about Rosie and Sanders?"

"Sanders isn't a case: suicide. Rosie...I'll still work it. But Christ, Dani, this girl may still be alive. What if she's still alive?"

"What if the owner of the blond hair is still alive?" she shot.

Tifton cursed. "If we had a name. The name of a blond girl someone misses. Something to chase. Jesus, Dani, you know the score. We've got nothing to go on."

"Okay," she said, still trying to swallow it. An FBI task force for a kidnapped, pregnant teenager. It didn't get much more important than that. "I need some info and I can't get it right now."

"What?"

"Adoption records for Rosie's baby."

"What agency?"

"I don't know, maybe black market. That may be how Sanders got involved."

"Involved in helping her *find* the baby last week or helping her get *rid* of it two years ago?" He sounded cynical; Dani couldn't blame him. That had been her first instinct, too.

"Hey, I know what it looks like, but I don't think that's it, Tift, not anymore. It really doesn't look like Russell Sanders was the kind of man who'd get a teenage hooker pregnant and dump her."

There was a pause, then Tifton said, "So, you're in bed with Sheridan now."

For the space of two breaths, Dani was speechless. Then she gathered her cool. "Even if I were, which I'm not—not that it's any of your business—that wouldn't be enough to change my mind about Sanders. There's something else going on, Tift."

"Okay, what?"

"Rosie was looking for her baby before she died. I'm thinking she contacted Russ Sanders for help. And it turns out Rosie herself was adopted by the McNamaras, after the fire that left her scarred. She was also thinking about meeting her own birth mother."

He drew a deep breath; Dani could almost see him rubbing a big hand over his face. "I don't get it."

"I don't either, yet. But adoptions and mangled faces and babies keep coming up, and I don't know what else to do but look at Rosie from the beginning. Her adoption was instigated by the State. There've got to be records you can get."

"That's confidential stuff, Dani. Even with her being dead, there are other parties involved."

"So make a convincing case and get a warrant."

"Geesh," Tifton said. He'd gone from sounding hyped about his new case to sounding defeated about his old. "Okay. As soon as I'm caught up on this new FBI file, I'll look at it. You're saying you think it's someone from her childhood, marking her up again?"

"I don't know. Her sister doesn't track with that, but we have to consider it."

"Rollins is heading it up now, handling the questioning; we can start adding people to the list who knew Rosie as a child."

"And what about some manpower to look at pictures? Rosie has photos of some wealthy people, the kind who attend art galleries. We need to get copies and run them around the Foundation, find out who they are."

"Send in the pictures. I'll see what I can do."

He was in a hurry—big FBI case now. No time for Rose McNamara. No time for unknown blondes or cops who weren't trusted to work because their dads were dirty. "Tift, you can't blow off Rosie."

"I won't," he said. "Honest, Nails—I'll come back to her. But, man, I'm a fucking homicide cop. They're always dead by the time I get to them. This one maybe isn't..."

CHAPTER
30

M IA STUCK HER HEAD in the den. Marshall had been on and off the phone all evening. Something wrong.

"What's the matter?" she asked when he hung up. The dutiful wife.

"I was trying to reach Sarah. She left work this morning, before anyone else even got there. Left a note on her computer saying she wasn't well."

Mia wasn't impressed. "Maybe she knew you were about to confront her about the drugs."

"I don't know how she could have."

"She probably just wasn't feeling well."

"I went by her house on the way home. Her Corolla wasn't there."

"Maybe she went to the doctor," Mia said.

"At this hour?" It was past seven. He scratched his beard but pushed the phone away. Noticed Mia's purse. "Where are you off to?"

"Libby's. She's been wanting me to see her newly decorated living room for a month and I keep putting her off. I can't come up with any more excuses."

He didn't argue: It was just the kind of thing a socialite like Mia Kettering, the lovely wife of Dr. Marshall Kettering III, was supposed to care about. *The Real Housewives of Lancaster County*, she thought, driving right past Libby's turnoff.

She headed toward the Foundation, her mind obsessed with one thought. *Stop Dani Cole.*

Halfway back to the Foundation, Dani's phone rang. She answered without looking at the number. "Mitch, for God's sake, stop calling me—"

"Danielle."

She almost crashed. "Jesus," she said. She hit the brakes, then—belatedly—glanced in the rearview mirror. She swerved off the road and stopped, heart galloping.

Ty Craig.

"How's Cancún?" she snapped.

He chuckled. "A little cooler than I expected. Almost like Maryland."

Dani wasn't amused. "Police want to talk to you."

"You're the police."

The simple sound of his voice made her bones tighten with hatred. "Not me," she said, letting the spite come through. "For some reason they don't trust me with you—imagine that. Ask for Reginald Tifton, or a guy named Rollins."

"I want you."

"I'm not even working the case."

"That's not what I hear. You spent half the day out working it."

Shit. Of course, Ty Craig had eyes and ears on the streets. "If you didn't kill Rosie, why play games with the officials?" But she knew the answer and her muscles tightened with an emotion somewhere between tears and fury. The *bastard*. "You can't buy me. I don't gamble or play cards or run dogs, so I don't need the kind of money my father did. I don't have any habits for you to support and you have nothing I need."

"Really? You don't need to know about my last conversation with Rosie?"

Dani's blood stopped moving. "Fuck you."

A smile came into his voice. "That could be arranged." He let the moment age and Dani had the ridiculous impulse to scrub her skin with lye. "I'll be in the private office above the Gemini in ten minutes," Craig said, "and for precisely ten minutes after that. I do hope you'll join me."

The line died. Dani closed her eyes, the crawling sensation coming back to life. Under her skin this time, where she couldn't get rid of it. Like her blood.

She should call Chief Gibson, let him know. There was an APB out on Craig and she was an officer of the law and—

Craig had talked to Rosie. In all probability, that part wasn't a bluff. He knew Dani wouldn't sell out for nothing.

Out of a two-week-old habit, she scanned the street for those gray sedans, then stopped herself. All she'd done was talk on the phone; there's no crime in that. No one could know who was at the other end of the line.

A thread of panic whipped through. Had the IAB tapped her lines?

God, get a grip. Dani fisted her hands on the steering wheel, trying to make sense of things. Ty's last conversation with Rosie? Was it recent, or two years ago? Her brain flew. She didn't really think Craig had killed Rosie.

He was capable, but it wasn't a good business move. If he'd been concerned about Rosie leaving his stable, he would have been more likely to have one of his goons bust her kneecap than kill her, so she'd be able to come back. He'd do it in front of the rest of the girls in order to send them a message, and he wouldn't wait two years to do it.

And what of the hair? Did Ty Craig have a hat with a tail of Rosie's hair on it, like Daniel Boone? Craig was smart and mean, but he wasn't crazy. Shears weren't his style.

Even so, a chill blew through the car. She thought about the person she'd chased from her house last night: slender, not burly like Ty, and not quite as tall. No, not Ty. Then again, Ty had plenty of people on his payroll. Was it possible this whole thing wasn't about Rosie at all, but about bullying Dani into following her father's footsteps? Would Ty Craig kill Rosie McNamara just to bring Dani to him?

She pulled out into the street, turning left on Addison and right onto Barrett. A couple of miles later, left again, two more blocks, and there to the right, a greasy little strip club at Ninth and Fisher. The Gemini.

She wasn't sure what Craig's connection was to this bar—he wasn't frequenting his usual haunts these days—but she'd been in it before. To get to any private offices upstairs, she'd have to go through the club. She looked at the clock on the dashboard: 7:20. The clientele would be thin at this point, still sober. A least one or two of them would probably recognize her. Craig would be there for precisely five more minutes.

She swallowed, scanned for black-and-whites, then IA sedans. No one had followed her; she'd made sure of that.

She could go in, look Craig in the eyes, and find out if he'd really talked to Rosie or if he was pulling Dani's chain. It would take five minutes; no one would need to kn—

Her phone bleeped. She about jumped out of her skin.

Sheridan.

"Jesus, what the hell are you doing?" she shot, when she answered.

"You're late. You didn't check in."

Her breath left her body. "Ah, man..."

"What are you doing? You sound upset."

Dani cursed, tried to slow her heart rate. She felt like she'd been caught in the midst of committing a crime. Damn it, there was nothing illegal about walking into a club. Even if her superiors found out, what could happen?

They'd feed her to the Internal Affairs Bureau, that's what. It wouldn't matter whether she made any deals with Craig or not. Carrying around Artie Cole's legacy into the same club where Ty Craig sat would be enough.

Paternal pride. The gift that keeps on giving.

"I'm coming," she said, starting her car. She shook off the cloak of insanity that had brought her here. God, what had she been thinking?

"How long?" Mitch asked.

"Fifteen minutes."

"Make it ten. I found something."

CHAPTER
31

MIA TRADED HER SAAB for Sarah's Corolla, stuck in the corner of a strip-mall parking lot ten blocks from Marshall's practice. The interior smelled of old coffee and French fries, the muffler puffing smoke and sounding as if it had indigestion. Seven-thirty now, dim and misty but not quite dark, time for the working stiffs of the world to be done for the evening. Time for Dani Cole—if Brad hadn't been blowing smoke—to be heading in.

With Mitch. Damn her. Damn them both.

Mia came around the block past the Foundation, turned, and parked in the same place she had when she shot the photos of Dani Cole. If Brad was right and Cole *was* getting hot and heavy with Mitch, she'd be here sooner or later. It was only a matter of time.

She settled in to watch. Set an old .32-caliber Remington on the front console, loaded, ready. It wasn't particularly her style, but she wasn't afraid to use it. Mia much preferred the shears—silent and brutal. A gun—*pop*—you're gone. One of the greatest regrets of Mia's life was that her mother's boyfriend Grady had never seen it coming.

So, for the girls, the shears were more to her liking. Seeing the moment of reckoning in their eyes, when their blood was already leaking from their veins, when they saw the blades and understood that part of them would be used to right their wrongs. *That* was the moment that made it all worthwhile.

Dani Cole wasn't part of that. She just needed to get the hell out of the way. The gun would be fine. Just like with Grady.

Mia reached up and ran a hand over her hair, the whole of it twisted into a smooth bun. A classic look, and the bold white-blond stripe along one side only added style. She'd worried a little that Dani Cole might recognize Alicia's color after handling her hair at her house, then remembered: Dani Cole would be dead.

She picked up the gun and pointed it toward Sheridan's apartment building, a little thrill rushing through her limbs. Sooner or later, Cole would show up here. Then, *pop*.

When Dani and Tifton had first conducted interviews of Foundation employees, Marshall Kettering gave them a tour: The offices and galleries were housed in the 1800s castle; the gigantic home beside had been built with an underground tunnel connecting the cellars of each structure. There were entrances to the cellars in the backs of each building, and while Dani knew she couldn't get in those doors without a key, she still opted to park in the back alley and take advantage of the cover of darkness to walk around the building and enter. She didn't do it because she was worried someone would think she and Mitch were involved, and she didn't do it because she was afraid of being seen working the case. She did it because she couldn't shake the sensation that someone was keeping tabs on her. A snake from Internal Affairs. A hoodlum who worked for Ty Craig. A hacker with a rusty pair of shears.

She hurried up the stairs and knocked on Mitch's door. When he answered, she said, "You found something?"

He peered at her. "Do I get a kiss first?"

"What?"

"A kiss. It's that thing we've started doing again, after way too many years—"

"Stop it," she scolded, but it lacked heat. He'd held her during the storm last night, checked up on her today, and demanded a kiss the minute they were together again. God help her, it felt nice.

She took a step forward, curling her fingers into his shirt and rising up on tiptoe. She kissed him, feeling every muscle in his body tighten with restraint as he stood and let her set the tone and intensity, gently parting his lips to invite more. Dani played there a moment then let her tongue slip along the edge and in the next breath, Mitch's fingers were in her hair and his tongue in her mouth, her body crushed against his.

Dani's lips were on fire when they finally broke apart, both of them needing air, both of them reeling from the explosion of what should have been a simple kiss. Mitch gazed down at her, and his voice came out rusty. "I don't know how I ever walked away from that," he said seriously.

Dani clung to his shirtsleeves; if she hadn't, she might have stumbled back into a wall. "As I recall," she said, her own voice thready, "I was screaming at you and you were bleeding."

"Good point."

She conquered the moment of giddiness and stepped inside, trying not to notice Mitch fondling the hair at her neck. "You said you found something?" she asked again.

He took her hand and led her to the sofa in the office, where the laptop sat out on the coffee table. Beside it lay a thin stack of pages he'd apparently printed, facedown. He sat down with her, saying, "Rosie's baby was born sometime before spring of 2008, right?"

"Right. Janet isn't sure exactly when."

He touched the computer pad and the screen lit up. "These are adoptions facilitated through OCIN, starting in January 2008." He began scrolling through the pages. "Each file includes a photo of the baby, a photo of the adoptive parents, and in rare cases—where both parties wanted the records to be open—a photo of the birth mother. Sometimes there are letters from birth mothers—"

"I know. I looked through a bunch of these last night." And didn't really want to see them again, she thought. Some of the pictures were heartbreaking...A toddler, emaciated, at an AIDS clinic in South Africa. A fifteen-month-old from Russia with fetal alcohol syndrome. A four-year-old from Latvia, with his twin sister, who didn't remember their parents. A six-month-old from Ukraine, who looked more like a newborn than a six-month-old baby. A preemie, the report said—not unusual.

But Mitch stopped on that one. "This is a boy named Sasha. He went to a couple right here in Maryland. Cheshire Heights, in fact."

"Robert and Alana Kinney," Dani said, reading the name. It didn't ring any bells. She shook her head. "I don't get it."

Mitch reached for the pages he had printed, handing them to her. "Here's their picture."

Dani took the top page—a late-thirties couple, looking stable and happy, well-off, with the shine of genuine hope in their eyes. They'd had these photos taken just to submit their application for the adoption, she thought, in their front yard, with a Christmas tree, leaning in toward one another lovingly, holding hands, and—

"Dear God," she gasped, staring at the woman's finger. The sapphire mine. She looked at Mitch, shocked, then back at the baby picture. "But..." She couldn't formulate a thought.

"Does that baby look six months old to you?"

"No, but as a preemie..."

"Or a newborn, born right here and labeled as a preemie."

Dani's pulse began to throb. "You think?"

"I don't want to, but explain the sapphires."

Dani couldn't.

She paged through the paperwork Mitch had copied, a shot of adrenaline pulsing through her limbs. The Kinneys: They'd been married for thirteen years, they were both in their mid-thirties. Robert had done postdoctoral work in chemistry at the U of Maryland and worked in research and development for a pharmaceuticals company. His wife, Alana, had a teaching certificate in early childhood education. Pictures of their home confirmed that finances were comfortable. They lived in a starter-castle, in a neighborhood of starter-castles that differed from one another only in the color of shingles, the pattern of stone, and the choice of shrubs in the requisite natural area across the front. At the door of the Kinney's three-car garage sat a Mercedes.

Dani went back to the woman's sapphire ring. "They have to be the parents of the child Rosie photographed. How many of those rings can there be?"

"This is the *last* boy that Rosie photographed. She hadn't even loaded these photos onto her computer yet."

"She got killed first." Dani stood, synapses firing in her brain. "Okay, let's go through it. Rosie McNamara had a baby boy in the spring of oh-eight, and gave him up for adoption, on the black market."

Mitch picked it up. "Around the same time, the Kinneys adopted an underweight six-month-old from Ukraine, through OCIN."

"Two years later, after Rosie's nephew was born, she started thinking about her son again, thinking about finding him. So she calls Russ Sanders for help. Why? Becau—" She stopped, looking at Mitch.

He finished for her. "Because Russ knew where her baby was. Because he did it through OCIN, pretending the baby came from overseas."

Dani's heart cracked. She could almost hear Russell Sanders tumble from his pedestal.

She walked over to Mitch. "Maybe not," she said. "There are others in the Foundation, right?"

The ghost of a smile shadowed Mitch's eyes and, belatedly, Dani realized she didn't want to believe the worst of Russ, either. "Brad's the likeliest candidate," Mitch said. "He does the legal legwork, could certainly doctor files. But the thing is, we know he didn't murder Rosie or his dad. Christ, Dani, a hundred people put him in Philadelphia last weekend. Even driving back and forth—"

"I know. You're right." Dani thought about the prowler. "And I don't think he's the man I chased from my house. The size isn't so far off, but…he doesn't feel the same."

Mitch closed the laptop. "What did you find at Rosie's after I left? Anything?"

Dani shook her head. "It's like she never had a baby. No doctor's appointments, no receipts for medical care. Nothing but a few baby toys and items. If it weren't for the autopsy, I'd be thinking she never had a baby at all."

"She was a hooker, out in the world. There's no way *no one* knew. Other girls, her johns, her pimp."

That's what Dani was thinking. *Ty.*

She closed her eyes, despair dragging at her. Ty Craig wasn't blowing smoke; he did know something. But to get it from him, Dani would have to sell her soul. Do exactly what Chief Gibson expected her to do.

She shook her head. No. There had to be other ways. Like the Kinneys.

"Do you have the Kinneys' contact information in there?"

He handed her a page. "While you're talking to them," he said, "I'm going to call Robin Hutchins—OCIN director. Find out if any of this takes her by surprise."

Two minutes later, they each hung up. "The Kinneys agreed to see me in the morning," Dani said, feeling a little pale around the gills. She'd used her detective-sergeant status to convince them. "How about you?"

"Robin's at a performance of *Don Giovanni* in Baltimore. I left a message with her daughter."

Dani looked at her watch: eight-fifteen. Still too early to track down the crowd she wanted to talk to, but—

The doorbell rang. She followed Mitch to the living room and he looked through the peephole.

"Tifton," he said. He opened the door and stepped back, a slight grin on his lips. "Honey, it's for you."

Dani rolled her eyes and Tifton came in, carrying a three-ring binder with two inches of paper in it. His face was drawn.

"You gotta tell me what you've got, Dani," he said, alarm edging his voice. "You gotta tell me about Rosie's baby."

CHAPTER
32

DANI STEPPED BACK and Tifton dropped the heavy binder on the table. "Tift?" she said. She'd never seen him so frazzled. He looked like he was riding on caffeine and adrenaline. "What's going on?"

"Just give me the highlights, Dani. It's important."

She did: Rosie's baby, the gifts, the photos. The Kinneys and their "preemie" and the theory that OCIN served as the cover for the illegal sale of Rosie's child. When Dani was finished, she said, "Okay, Tift. Your turn."

He glanced at Mitch, who crossed his arms: Not going anywhere. Tifton considered it then pushed the binder across the table to Dani. "I told you a girl went missing late last night. Hooker, just turned eighteen, pregnant. Like, *real* pregnant."

"Your FBI task force case," Dani said.

"Yeah." He swallowed. "She's one of Ty Craig's girls."

Dani flinched.

"Who's Ty Craig?" Mitch asked.

"He was Rosie's pimp when I helped her get out," Dani explained.

"And you've talked to him about Rosie?" Mitch asked.

Tifton shook his head. "He's gone underground. We don't have him by tomorrow, we're gonna smoke him out. He'll either come forward or lose half his clubs." Tift pointed at the binder in Dani's hands. "That's the file on the missing girl."

She frowned. "There's a file this thick on a girl who went missing *last night*?"

"That's the point. The FBI thinks she's Number Three."

Cold dread gripped Dani. "No way."

"It started with Jill Donnelly three months ago. Hookers disappearing. The first two had given birth and adopted out their kids. This one..." Tifton's face twisted with fear. "She's still pregnant, but barely, and her friends say she was considering the black market for her baby. Gonna pop any minute."

"Jill Donnelly. I remember that case," Dani said. "She got back in touch with her family then no one could find her. She'd had a baby?"

"Yeah, a few years ago. Her family didn't know."

"What happened to Donnelly's baby?" Mitch asked, and Dani could see the horror in his eyes. His Foundation. His best friend.

"No one knows," Tift said.

"Ah, Jesus." Mitch turned away, looking like the weight of the world had just fallen onto his shoulders.

"But she didn't work for Ty Craig," Dani recalled.

"No," Tift said. "She worked out of a stable in Baltimore. The FBI worked her pimp over during the investigation, but he gave them nothing. Today, they collared him on a drug charge, hoping to shake him up. He's in custody, but his lawyer's got him gagged."

Dani considered the thick stack of paper in the binder, then pushed it away. "Give me the highlights," she said.

Mia's heart turned over when a man swung his Chevy a block in front of her car and nosed against the curb. Cop. The one who'd been working on Rosie's case with Dani Cole.

Dear God.

She reached to the passenger seat and slid the pistol under her thigh out of sight, then held her breath until the detective had gone inside. She skimmed the block. No one else; he was alone.

But she was in a dead woman's car, carrying a loaded gun.

Mia wasn't stupid. As soon as the door closed behind the detective, she turned the ignition and pulled out. Didn't breathe again until she was a half mile away.

Lord, that was close.

Sergeant Cole would have to wait.

Dani was flabbergasted by what Tifton told them. The FBI report had Jill Donnelly, a seventeen-year-old runaway from a little town in northern Michigan, pregnant and giving her baby up for adoption three years ago. The girls who knew her said a sugar daddy had put her up until the baby was born. They didn't know who.

"Then, three months ago, Donnelly started cracking up," Tifton said. "Her friends say she was scared, having nightmares. They found baby things in her belongings."

"Baby things?"

"A pacifier, a bib, a couple of stuffed toys, things like that."

Dani's mind raced: Rosie's bedroom.

"Donnelly broke down and called her sister in Michigan—no one in her family had heard from her in years, but after the first call they never heard from her again. The girls working with her decided she'd gone home; police decided she'd run off again. There was no evidence of foul play—she just disappeared."

"And this new girl, the one from last night—similar?" Mitch asked.

Tifton leaned back, rubbed a bear paw over his scalp. "We don't know it all yet. The name she was using on the streets—Nika Love—doesn't match any girls in the missing persons data bank."

"So there's no way of knowing who she really is," Dani said. "How come they think she's in trouble, instead of just going somewhere?"

"A couple of Ty's girls called it in. Nika was scrounging on her own since she stopped working, and friends were slipping her help. She'd been offered a price for the baby but hadn't decided yet whether she'd sell. Then, last night, she didn't show to pick up some cash from her girlfriends. They went to the shelter where she'd been staying and saw some big dude wrestle her into a truck. She was screaming, fighting."

"Big dude," Mitch said. "Bigger than Brad Harper?"

"Way," Tifton said.

"Got an ID on the vehicle?" Dani asked.

"No tags, and the two girls who saw it could only say it was a dark pickup with an extended cab."

"How is Nika Love a third girl?" Dani asked. "I only count two: Jill Donnelly and her."

"Feds started pounding the pavement and turned up another name: Alicia Woodruff. Hooker, addict. Had a baby eight months ago. Lives in Reading. Except when they went to talk to her this afternoon, no one could find her."

"Oh, God."

"She work for Craig?" Mitch asked.

"No. But we can't find her in any legal adoption agency, so she didn't take her baby to any of them. The Feds got subpoenas digging from here to the moon: no baby."

"You look at hospitals? Clinics?"

Tift nodded, his eyes hard. "I'm telling you: no fucking baby."

"Okay." Dani felt as if her brain were made of Swiss cheese, possibilities slipping through the holes. She looked up just as a big one almost got away: "Do either of these girls have scars?"

"Not that we know of," Tifton said.

Huh.

Mitch said, "You said Nika had been offered a price for her baby. By whom?"

"We don't know." He held Mitch's eyes. "Do you?"

His Adam's apple bobbed, his jaw going tight. "No."

Dani stood, trying to string it all together. "So, three years ago, Jill Donnelly sells a baby and eight months ago, Alicia Woodruff does the same thing. Both of them disappear in the last three months. And now, there's one more fitting the pattern, Nika Love, whose friends think something happened to her. Except she hasn't had a baby yet." She looked at Tifton. "And you think Rosie's another?"

"She doesn't fit," Mitch said. "She didn't just disappear. She was murdered and disfigured."

"But we don't know that the same didn't happen to these others," Dani said. "We haven't found their bodies."

Tifton looked at Mitch. "We're trying to establish whether they had contact with Russ Sanders."

Mitch's voice was like chipped glass. "It may have slipped your mind, Detective, but Russell didn't kidnap a girl last night."

"Man, I know that. But OCIN's still in the middle of this; what you two just told me about Rosie and the Kinneys only confirms it. I'm gonna go back to interviews with all the employees. The Feds are coming this time."

"Good," Mitch said, a little testy. "You think I would feel otherwise?"

"Ask about prescription narcotics," Dani said to Tift. "Anyone at OCIN who uses them."

"We will, not that you need a prescription. You can buy that shit anywhere."

Dani turned to Mitch. "Last night, you said Brad was toast. Maybe more than alcohol?"

"I wouldn't be surprised."

"Find out what he's taking, Tift. If he'll submit to a blood test, then along with the Philadelphia trip, he'd be in the clear. Try that angle with him."

"Dani, he's a lawyer. He knows the angles and he knows he's in the clear already. He ain't gonna submit to a blood test."

"Ask anyway. I wanna know how he reacts."

"Fine. Meanwhile, you gotta let me see the adoption records for the Kinneys from OCIN. If what you two suspect is right and that baby belonged to Rosie, then she may well be Number Four."

"Get a subpoena," Mitch said. "I can't give them to you otherwise."

"Come on, man, by the time I can get that—"

"I've already set up an appointment with the Kinneys

in the morning, Tift," Dani said. "Nine o'clock. It's all set."

He considered it. Dani knew he couldn't arrange for anything to be done any sooner; he also knew Mitch wouldn't release adoption records without a warrant. "Okay," Tift said, "we'll jerk another judge from bed in the morning. Meanwhile, Dani, you call me as soon as you talk to the Kinneys, all right?"

"Gee," Dani said, a little snide. "It's almost like I'm working the case."

He cursed and got up to leave, taking his big-ass federal binder with him.

Dani stopped him at the door. "Tift," she said, "what made you come over here all hot to know about Rosie? This afternoon, you had no idea she might be connected to Nika Love."

He held up the binder. "You must not have seen Alicia Woodruff's picture when you were thumbing through here."

"No, I didn't."

Tifton's shoulders drooped. "Caucasian, about five-five, green eyes, nineteen years old." He paused, and the blood in Dani's veins iced over. "Curly blond hair."

CHAPTER
33

MITCH SHUT THE DOOR on Tifton and looked across the room at Dani. She looked like a statue, her face like white porcelain. She closed her eyes and he knew she was picturing a curly blonde.

"Alicia Woodruff," she murmured, almost to herself. "That's her name. She's not just missing, she's dead. Like Rosie."

"We don't know that, Dani."

"Bullshit, we don't know that. You sound like Gibson. We do know it. We just don't know where to find her."

She snapped to, suddenly moving around the room. Found her jacket, looked for her purse and snatched it up, plunging her hand inside.

"Whoa, honey," Mitch said. "What are you doing?"

"I'm finished sitting around here looking at files. I have to do something, damn it. Alicia Woodruff and Jill Donnelly worked out of Reading. You know where Reading is?"

Rich boy like you know about Reading? Mitch ignored the subtext. "I know. And I know you're not going out there."

"I have to."

"Dani, the FBI's doing that."

"But they don't know about the baby gifts. Not yet. They won't know until the task force meets in the morning, and they're Feds: They'll spend half the day analyzing the data and trying to track down what stores sell those things, chasing shadows."

"Let them," Mitch said. "You don't need to go out there."

"I do." Her fire was coming back and she walked over to him. "You know how you have to do this exhibition because it's for Russell and you owe him, even though he's dead? Well, I have to do this for Rosie. *I have to.*" She turned and Mitch reached down and snatched her keys.

"Not alone."

Monika thought she was alone, until the footsteps. The iceman was back, or maybe hadn't left. She didn't know. All she knew was that she recognized the heavy thud of footsteps coming up the stairs.

He worked the locks, and Monika held her breath as the door opened. He stepped in with a tray of food and set it on the table next to the door. "You didn't eat earlier. This is your last chance."

Monika moved to the edge of the bed, then let out a cry. Clutched her belly. "Unnh," she moaned. The iceman didn't move. "I need a doctor," she said. "It hurts. I need a doctor."

He watched her for a minute and she sat still, sobbing just a little, her dark hair falling over her face. Don't overdo it. But he seemed to be interested in taking care of her until the baby was born. If she could just get him to bring someone else in...

Then again, he was the iceman. She wasn't sure he'd bat an eye if he walked into the room and found her dead. He'd probably just step over her body and go his merry way.

"Please," she said.

He started back out of the room. "Best to eat. You'll need your strength."

The door latched behind him, the locks clicking into place.

Damn it. Monika choked on a sob, this one real, then pulled herself together. She hauled herself to the edge of the bed and waddled over to the food. Strength—he was right. Even if she wouldn't need it, the baby did.

She reached to the tray and blanched. Another baby gift sat beside the plate—a little carousel music box with a blue ribbon tied around it.

Monika hurled it against the wall and listened to it shatter.

Then she ate. *Keep up your strength…*

Mitch wanted to drive and Dani didn't fight him: That's when he knew she wasn't quite operating at full potential. They took her car—the Cuda would attract attention they didn't want—and he headed west through downtown and north on Graeter's, out to Reading Road. It entered the city as a two-lane state highway and exited about fourteen miles later. The last six or so miles skirted along the north edge of town, an untamed stretch of warehouses and abandoned buildings, and a warren of old overpasses, tunnels, and viaducts along chunks of broken-up railroad tracks.

"The Safari," Dani said, explaining to Mitch how cops referred to the area. "A haven for wild animals."

He nosed the car in just under a viaduct at the old railroad hub, where Dani told him to. "No one will bother it here," she said. "They're too afraid of the bogeyman."

She sat on the passenger seat with her feet out, switched from heeled loafers to boots that had been in the back floorwell of her car, then asked for the keys. Mitch watched as she tucked a flashlight under her chin and aimed it into the trunk. From a metal lockbox, she pulled out a .22-caliber Smith & Wesson with a four-inch barrel. She checked the rounds then tucked the small pistol into a leather strap above the left ankle of the boot. Finished by wiggling the .38 standard-issue semiautomatic in her holster.

"Are we ready, Rambo?"

"Don't be smart," she said, killing the light. "My bet is you've never been here."

Not in twenty years or so. But he wasn't easily shocked. "My bet is I've been in worse."

They turned from the car and started walking, and Mitch touched his belt through the leather bomber jacket he wore. Dani wasn't the only one who came prepared.

They inched west, away from the old railroad depot. A sickly moon gave the landscape the aura of a desolate, battle-ravaged village. A handful of buildings had lived and died along the railroad tracks—warehouses, tenements, storage units—their corpses precariously balanced on rotting frames. Tattered pieces of plastic clung to decaying wood and rain-gooey cardboard was tacked over holes in what sufficed as roofs. Shards of windows hung on for dear life.

Mitch winced: He hadn't expected this much ruin. Not in Lancaster. Of course, he'd never looked for it here. He'd purposely looked elsewhere.

About a mile in, the odors of hard living layered into the night—urine and marijuana, cold sweat and rotting garbage—and a couple of blocks later, people started to appear. Drunks dotted walls and stairwells, addicts approached hoping to score. Hookers, male and female, called out offers. The deeper into Reading they went, the more the nightlife crawled around them.

Dani spoke to anyone who would give her the time of day. *Do you know Alicia Woodruff? Light blond hair. Is she scarred up? You remember a girl named Jill Donnelly? Nika Love? Anybody got baby toys floating around?*

Mitch hung close in Dani's shadow, keeping an eye out for assholes, keeping a hand near the bulge at the side of his jacket. There was nothing for an hour or so, then a woman with snakes tattooed up both sides of her neck and around her throat had an idea. Her name was April.

"You talk to Chuckie?" she asked, puffing on a joint. "Chuck got a teddy bear he been carryin' around."

Dani straightened.

"Where did he get it?" Mitch asked.

"Don't know," April said. "Only had it a day or two. Won't put the damn thing down."

"Chuck who?" Dani asked. "Where do I find him?"

"Chuck Who-Knows? Back at the depot, usually. He's the only one crazy 'nough to stay there."

"Jesus," Dani said, and Mitch could see the hope blossom in her eyes. This was the first glimmer they'd had.

"Let's go," he said.

They worked their way back toward the viaduct, faster now, Mitch getting used to the stench and the sights, trying to meld the images with his lifelong impression of Lancaster. He was doing okay until the whine of a dog caught his ear and a scuffling sound pulled him into an alley. Then the sight stopped him cold.

A kid, eleven or twelve, with a mongrel dog. The boy leaned into a barrel of trash, feet off the ground, rooting deep. The mutt was on his hind feet with a nose in the barrel, sharing in the hunt.

"*Kûçik*," Mitch whispered, and his heart stalled.

Dani stepped up beside him. "What?"

He snapped back, surprised by her voice. The boy was surprised, too. He took off running, the dog trotting after.

"Whoa, what was that?" she asked.

Mitch shook words from his throat. His voice was a little bit stuck. "A kid, looking for food, I guess."

"Aw, jeez." She went a few yards down the alley, pushed the beam of her flashlight around a couple of corners, and came back. "He's gone." She peered up at him. "You all right? You look like you've seen a ghost."

He felt like a pillar of ice. "There was this kid in Ar Rutbah, about that age," he said, the memory gnawing at his gut. "Ran around with a dog a lot like that."

"Oh," Dani said, but seemed hesitant to let it go. "What happened?"

Mitch could almost smell the camp—the aroma of curry rising from fire pits, the smoke-tinged air from artillery practice ranges. The stray dogs and chickens. "He liked the camera," Mitch said. "He followed me around for days, and finally I let him shoot some pictures. He was good, you know, for a kid. A natural. He couldn't get enough of the camera."

"I'll bet you made quite an impact," Dani said. "He'll be the next great world-changing photojourn—"

"He won't. He's dead." Mitch nearly choked on the

words. "I let go of him during the attack and he ran. He got hit—"

"Oh, God. Mitch, I'm so sorry." She looked in the direction this kid had gone, then laid her hand on Mitch's arm. There was sadness in her touch, and comfort. "What was his name?"

Mitch winced. "I don't know. I never asked." He looked down at Dani and saw the disbelief in her eyes. Dani didn't know any anonymous strangers. The people she touched had names.

He shook it off, but the stitch of an idea took hold in his brain. Something to nurture later. "Come on," he said. "We gotta find a guy named Chuck."

CHAPTER
34

THEY LEFT THE ALLEY, passed by the viaduct where they'd left Dani's car, and headed toward the railroad depot. Dani could feel Mitch's emotions dragging on him, but this wasn't the time to slow down. If the woman with the snake tattoos knew what she was talking about, they might actually learn something.

"She could've been full of shit," Dani said, trying not to get too jazzed, "but man, a teddy bear. And just in the last couple days." Her heart was going like a piston.

They found the depot, the bones of buildings making eerie shadows in the moonlight. They crossed the train tracks and picked their steps carefully through the dark across broken concrete and years of trash. Chuck would probably spook easily; Dani didn't want to scare him into hiding by using the flashlight.

"Shh." Dani stopped, a movement catching the corner of her eye. Thirty yards in front of them, someone skulked behind a building. She picked up her pace, keeping to the shadows. The figure materialized into a person ducking into the next building. She inched closer and the stench hit: urine and feces and rotten food. Home sweet home for someone.

Chuck?

She edged sideways and caught another movement—inside the building, visible through a gap between rotten boards by the light of a candle or lantern inside. Her hand moved over her gun, lingering. Mitch stuck his hand under his jacket.

"Hey," she called out. "Police. Come out. I wanna talk to you."

The movements went still. The person froze.

"I just wanna talk, man. Is this Chuck? Come outta there."

The hairs on the back of Dani's neck prickled—more from the silence of the shadows surrounding her than from the occupant of the railroad building. She did a quick three-sixty, peering at every alley, shadow, and building she could see, then stepped closer. "Come on, man. I'm not here to make trouble. April sent me. You know April?"

A few seconds passed then the crack around the door began to widen. The sudden flare of a cigarette lighter dented the night and settled among the shadows. The door inched open and the lighter died.

Mitch moved but Dani put up a hand, stopping him. She stuck her flashlight in her belt so it aimed at the ground, casting enough light to barely see. She held out her shield. "I just need some help, man. What's your name?"

The figure in the doorway shifted, then slithered the rest of the way through the crack like a shadow. A man with ratty tufts of what might have once been dreadlocks, now so matted they looked like an old shag rug hanging off his head. He looked at Dani then his eyes darted to Mitch. Fear.

"He's cool, man," Dani said, pointing to Mitch. *Stay there. He's afraid of you.* "We just wanna talk. April said you could help us. Are you Chuck?"

"Chicka-chacka-chucka." His voice sounded like tin. In the darkness, he was little more than a silhouette. He wore a long ragged coat and his body vibrated with the tremors of a druggie. One hand was deep in a pocket and he seemed to be holding something against his body, beneath that arm. "Chuckeeeee."

Dani stepped to the side, away from the direct sight line of the partially open door. "Anyone else in there with you?" she asked.

Chuck snickered. "Puss? Nah. Chuckee ain't got no puss in there."

"Let me see."

Chuck stepped from the door and Dani brought out the flashlight, stuck her hand in, and looked. Four walls and trash. Nothing that could hide another person.

"Told ya," Chuck said when she stepped back out.

"You been around here awhile? Is this where you stay?"

"Here. There." He chuckled, pointing all around him. "There-a-Chuck, here-a-Chuck."

"Stop. What're you on, Chuck? You crankin'?"

He jerked. "Don't do no crank. I do some bennies, ice. Not crank. Crank'll fuck you up."

Drug addict logic. "I heard you found a toy, Chuck. A stuffed toy. That true?"

He pulled back, and Dani saw his arm tighten against his body. She looked closer. Something there.

"Is that it, under your arm? I need to see it, man."

Chuck backed up. "Mine, mine. Don't you touch it." He reached across his body and pulled it from under his arm with his free hand. Dani hit it with the beam of the flashlight. It *was* a bear, smudged with a dark stain. Her breath caught in her throat.

"Where'd you get that, Chuck? You get it from a blond girl? You seen Alicia?" Chuck kept backing up, closer to the entrance of the building. Dani noticed Mitch arcing quietly around to the side.

"Don't know no blond girl you talkin' about. Stay back, stay back."

Mitch eased to Chuck's left, just behind him. Dani frowned; the arm that had held the bear against his body hadn't moved, with that hand tucked in his pocket. The image of bloody shears flashed through her mind but didn't make sense: A junkie with a pair of shears at Camden Park? Leaving Dani notes?

"What's in your pocket, Chuck? Take out your hand."

He clutched the bear tighter. He was almost crying now. "Mine. No blond girl. Mine."

"Hand out of your pocket, now." Her cop voice, and she drew her gun. Mitch straightened and stepped forward, keeping left, out of range of a shot Dani might take. Chuck whimpered, the bear in his free hand, the other trying to twist from his pocket. It pulled the coat up, like something was snagged inside, and a second later, the right hand came out.

Dani gasped. At first she thought it was a dark glove, and that it had pulled partway off when he lifted his hand, but a second later she realized it was the hand itself. Mangled and withered, as if it had been slammed in a car door and nearly cut in two. The loose part hung on by a dangling snarl of flesh, and above it, the wrist was swollen like a balloon, the coat sleeve tight around it.

She lowered her gun. "God, Chuck, what happened to your hand?" He looked at the flesh as if he'd forgotten, then at the bear in his left hand. He started to hold it up, but jerked back, ducking. Looked up and ducked again, as if dodging missiles or bugs or meteors.

He was losing it.

"Jesus," Mitch said under his breath. He looked past Chuck at Dani; she could see the tension in the silhouette of his jaw. She shook her head. No way Chuck had committed Rosie's murder. That had been a right-handed killer and it was an act of focus. Chuck didn't have enough brain cells left to systematically aim for Rosie's left cheek and scalp, not to mention a right hand.

Slowly, Dani put her gun away and traded it for the flashlight, trying to catch the waving bear in the column of the light. A ribbon was tied around its neck, and what looked like a note.

"Give me the bear, Chuck. I need to see it."

Chuck sobbed but handed it to her. The stain was sticky and the note...Dani's knees went weak. Block letters in black:

RR DEPOT, 8:30. IT'S ABOUT YOUR DAUGHTER.

Mitch came to her side. He read the note, holding Dani's elbow as if to steady her. "Where did you find this?" he demanded.

Chuck stared at the bear in Dani's hand, the ring of light from her flashlight showing the whites of his eyes like moons.

"Show us," Mitch barked, and Chuck pointed to the

alley that ran behind the building he'd come from. Dani aimed the flashlight that direction and told him to go.

He stopped about ten yards in, beside the wall of the building. A heap of old wooden planks sat on the cement, rats scurrying when Dani's flashlight hit them. The concrete was broken and wet. Chuck pointed down.

Dani shot the flashlight at the ground. Mud and puddles, and she looked at the bear again in the light and ran her fingers over the stain. Then she realized. It wasn't mud on the bear: It was blood. She looked back to the ground where Chuck had pointed, but there'd been too much rain. Even if Chuck had picked up the bear from a puddle of blood, the storms had washed it away and—

"Dani."

Mitch took her wrist, guiding the flashlight to the side of the building. Dani followed the halo of light to the planks and her stomach turned over.

That was blood.

CHAPTER
35

MITCH FELT DANI GASP and his mind raced. The planks of the building were rough-hewn and weather-beaten. Rain hadn't hit beneath the overhang in years, so the stains on those planks could be anything. Old paint, mud, the splatter from a spilled drink, or—

Bullshit. It was blood.

Dani stared, her arm beneath Mitch's fingers gone to stone. "This is it," she said in a daze. "Chuck found the bear here on the concrete. Look at the blood on it, and then there on the wall..."

Mitch let her talk it through, keeping an eye on Chuck behind her while she studied the stains on the wall with the flashlight. Chuck stood ten feet back. His gaze focused on the bear with lunatic intensity, the whites of his eyes like saucers. He was trembling—half from drugs, Mitch thought, but also half from something that looked an awful lot like rage.

"Ah, God," Dani said.

Mitch glanced. Her face was inches from the wall, at shoulder height, the light a ball of white quivering on the planks. "What is it?"

"Nooo," she moaned.

"Dani." Mitch stepped over to her, moving backward to keep an eye on Chuck. For two seconds, he turned and looked at the planks. "What did you—"

Chuck lunged. An animal cry erupted from his throat and Mitch turned to see a long plank in the good hand, wheeling toward Dani. He sprang, one arm batting away the plank, the other coming from beneath his jacket with a Smith & Wesson. He slammed Chuck into the opposite wall, *unk*.

"Back off, fucker," Mitch said, the gun pushing Chuck's chin upward. The man began to whimper and slid down the wall. Mitch stood over him with the gun, looked back at Dani. "You all right?"

"Christ," she said. She was panting, her own gun in hand and the flashlight rolling across the ground. She must've pulled the gun when she whirled around, but now she stood gaping at Mitch as if not believing what she saw.

She scooped up the flashlight and found a spot on the wall again. Mitch stepped close enough to look, his gun still pointed at Chuck.

"What is it?" he asked, but no sooner were the words out than his eyes found it. Above the spray of blood on the wall, snagged on the edge of one plank: blond, curly hairs.

When the cell phone rang, Mia started. Dear God, it was late. Was it Nika?

She looked at the number. "Fulton, what do you want?" she asked.

"Get me the doctor," he said. "I think she's faking, but I won't do any goddamn baby. The girl's up there bent over with cramps, screaming. Get the doctor."

Mia closed her eyes. Thank God. It was time to finish the wig, and now she'd have Nika's hair in time. Kristina's wig would be ready for Sunday.

"I'll get him," she said. Inducing labor was an easy thing, done all the time. Even if Nika *was* faking, it was time. "I'll get him tonight."

A little after two a.m., Mitch finally escorted Dani back to her car under the viaduct. She was shaken, he could tell. She'd been professional and calm and straight-thinking, but the discovery of the blond hair on the wall with the spray of dried blood had knocked her for a loop. That, and nearly being assaulted by a madman.

No, it was Mitch who'd been shaken by that. He'd seen a lot of frightening things in his life, far more horrific than what he'd seen tonight. But none of it had ripped at his soul so much as that instant he'd realized that Dani was in the path of Chuck's rage.

"He went for you," Mitch said, climbing into the driver's seat. "The asshole came at you."

"I know," Dani said. "I felt him coming. But not until you already had him." She looked over at Mitch. "Guess it's a good thing I had you."

Mitch blew out a curse. For five seconds tonight, he'd thought she was going to get hurt—right in front of him. Five seconds of pure hell. "I don't think I could have handled it if he'd hurt you."

"I'm all right."

"That's not the point. The point is that I would've killed him. Without a second thought, if he'd laid a hand on you, Dani, I could have blown the sonofabitch away."

She cracked a smile. "You talk so purty."

Mitch laughed, and the tension broke up a little, a

glacier melting. "What's with you and Chief Gibson?" he asked. Gibson had shown up with an evidence collection team, took the bear and the note from Dani, and ordered her to get the hell off the scene. Would finish with *on-duty* cops, he'd told her. Dani made him promise to get Chuck some help, and once he had, she finally let Mitch walk her back to her car. "Why doesn't he like you? You refuse to sleep with him or something?"

She shivered. "Ick. I do have *some* standards."

"Well, thanks."

A flicker of a smile, then it disappeared. "Why do you ask?"

"He didn't want you on the scene, working the case."

"You already knew that."

"Yeah. But this wasn't because he was worried about your being targeted by the murderer... He didn't quiz you about the hotel or where you'd been tonight or whether you'd felt safe. He just didn't want you around."

"Humph," Dani said, and Mitch wondered what else was there. If Chief Gibson had put Dani in a motel because he was so worried about her safety, he sure hadn't shown any sign of it tonight. Mitch was pretty sure there was something else at play for Gibson, but decided to mull that over later. Right now he just wanted to get Dani someplace safe and warm and private. He wanted to pull her into his arms and hold her away from everything bad in the world.

Naked.

Jesus, he was a Neanderthal. But the physical was too much a part of what he and Dani were together to ignore. Trying to keep it hidden all week had taken its toll, and on top of his emotional upheaval tonight, watching as she came close to being hurt, Mitch's patience was at an end.

He turned the ignition and pulled the car around, drove a block from the viaduct and stopped. To the right was the Radisson, to the left, the Foundation. Time to make a decision.

"What's the matter?" Dani asked when she realized he wasn't going anywhere.

He wrenched the gearshift into park, looking straight ahead through the windshield. "Where am I taking you?" he asked.

At first she didn't realize the import of the question, then her frame stilled and the air stopped moving. Mitch decided to make things perfectly clear. "Be careful how you answer, Dani, because I'm not just talking about tonight. If you come with me now, I'll still be there in the morning. And tomorrow and the next day and the next. I won't let you push me away again."

Dani's gaze fell to her lap, fingers twisting together. Her voice, when it came, was barely a whisper. "I don't want to push you away."

Mitch's heart took a tumble. And his blood rushed south. "I'm gonna hold you to that," he warned.

She looked at him. "I hope so."

CHAPTER
36

THEY HELD THEMSELVES in check until they got into the apartment, then the clothes started flying. Mitch pulled Dani against his body and delved into her mouth, stroking and kissing and getting his hands up under her blouse to free her breasts. Buttons burst as he spread her blouse wide, crowding her back against the door and drawing her nipples into his mouth, bringing first one and then the other to tight peaks.

Her hands worked at his belt and when she fumbled with his zipper, Mitch said, "Not here," and scooped her up. He carried her to the bedroom, deposited her on the huge four-poster bed, and stripped the rest of both sets of clothing. "Christ, you are beautiful," he said when she was naked, and stretched out over her slim, supple body. She sighed and arched into his hands, her touch everywhere, an undercurrent of frenzy driving them as they feasted on each other's flesh. Finally, Mitch entered her, a strong, single stroke that pushed an *Ahh* from her throat. He took her sounds into his mouth, struggling for control but sinking deeper with every move. She came off the bed with him, linking her ankles behind his hips and meeting him thrust for thrust, until at last she came apart in his hands and he exploded over the edge of sanity.

Panting, the sheen of sweat between them, a tingle of consciousness touched Mitch some minutes later. Dani's cheek lay against his chest, his heartbeat still slamming against his rib cage and lungs working to recover. He felt her lips curve up in a smile.

"What?" he asked, cocking his head to look at her.

She curled up against him like a cat. "I think your heart is beating my cheek black and blue. That much exertion can't be healthy at our advanced age."

In one motion, he rolled her on top of him, seated with her thighs straddling his hips and his hands at her waist. He waited until her eyes found his, then held her down and drove upward, pushing a gasp of pleasure from her throat.

"Fuck healthy," he said. "I'll die happy."

Steven Housley worked the clinic one evening a week, and his shift ran from seven p.m. to three a.m. A simple call to the clinic gave Mia that. Mia had seen him only once, three months ago on that fateful night, though he hadn't seen her. She knew little about him, except that he had a smoking habit that required frequent attention.

She left Marshall sleeping and sneaked from the house, picking up Sarah Rittenhouse's car again. It had spent most of the day parked in the WalMart lot. By tomorrow, if someone got worried about Sarah, leaving it there might not be any good. But for tonight, as far as anyone at the medical office knew, Sarah was all tucked in bed, sick. So the Corolla was still safe to drive and the Saab would stay at WalMart overnight.

The clinic where Housley worked—where he recruited women and cultivated illegal babies—was on the outskirts of Baltimore. It catered to the poor and indigent and homeless and backed up to an alley. Mia pulled up to watch the back door, the gun in easy reach.

Nothing for twenty minutes, then the back door opened. Housley came out, tapping the cigarette carton against his leg, digging out a lighter from the pocket of his lab coat.

Mia tucked the gun into the waistband of her skirt and got out, pulling her coat around her. "That's a nasty habit, Dr. Housley," she said. Use his name, disarm any natural suspicion.

He turned, peering into the darkness. She could tell by his body language that he was confused: woman, knew his name. Middle of the night.

"Who is that?" he said, apparently deciding there was no threat. He didn't move toward the door or snuff out his cigarette.

"Mia Kettering. You don't know me."

Now the body language tightened up. "I know who you are," he answered. "I've met your husband. What the hell are you doing out here like this?"

"I'm here on behalf of Brad Harper," she said, giving him a moment to let that sink in. As it did, his entire frame straightened. He flicked away the cigarette and glanced around.

"No one else is here, Doctor, don't worry. I'm here about Nika Love. You remember her, I presume?"

He said nothing. Feeling the noose tighten around his throat, no doubt.

"You don't have to say anything," Mia said, "but it wouldn't matter. I'm not wearing a wire for the police and I'm not interested in anything you may have done that might be considered...unethical. I just want you to deliver Nika's baby."

He was still unsure but asked, "Where is she? Is she in labor, at the beach house?"

Brad used a beach house in New Jersey to house the pregnant women. "No, she's not with Brad. There's a house in northern Virginia, in the mountains. She's there."

Housley frowned. "She told me she didn't want to give the baby up."

A wave of black rage swept through Mia. "It's not a decision a woman can go back and forth on, Doctor. Surely you understand that. She made it weeks ago."

"No, no," he said, and stepped back half a pace, holding up his palms. Lowered his voice to a whisper. "I don't *steal* babies. All the girls we've done were willing. Eager, even. I'm not getting involved with one who might turn on us."

Stupid bastard. "She won't turn on you," Mia promised. She thought it through. Tomorrow—today, really—was Thursday. By evening, if Housley did his job, the baby would be with new parents and Nika dead. Everything would be ready for Sunday evening, seven o'clock. The precious moment she'd waited more than sixteen years to experience would be here.

So long as Housley did his job.

She reached into the wristband of her watch, pulling out a folded piece of paper on which she'd written directions. "Use these to get to the cabin. It's about a three-hour drive. Go first thing in the morning, and call me when you get there. I'd like to see the baby before you take him away."

Housley rubbed a hand over his narrow face. "What am I doing with the baby?" he asked, and Mia had to give him credit for the question.

"The same thing you always do."

• • •

Mia arrived home in the wee hours of the night. Marshall sat in a chair in their bedroom, listening to the garage door rise and fall, the clack of her heels on the marble floor, the soft rustle of her skirt when she climbed the stairs and walked into the bedroom. She pulled up short when she saw him.

"Dear God," she said, hand going to her throat. He'd surprised her; he was never up this late. "What are you doing up?"

Trying to save you, he thought, but he couldn't say it. He wasn't ready to lose her yet.

He rose, the light from a single bedside lamp throwing a warm glow at one end of the room, the rest of the massive bedroom plunged in shadows. "I never knew Libby was such a night owl," he said, walking over to her.

"Libby?" Then she remembered and groped to cover. "Oh, yes. Her new living room is beautiful. I told her I want her designer's name." She moved to the dresser and set down her purse, her keys, then slipped from a burgundy wool jacket, revealing the trim waist and deep cleavage men admired. Not looking at him. "I'm sorry I'm so late," she said, laying down the jacket. "You know when we girls get to talking. Time just got away from me."

Lies. Marshall's heart felt like a lump of clay. But he couldn't give her the truth any more than she could give it to him. She'd waited sixteen years to see the daughter she'd lost, convinced Kristina would come to her on her eighteenth birthday. When she didn't, that day had gone from a bad dream to an unending nightmare. First the heartbreak of Kristina not coming, then the shock of seeing photographs Marshall had kept carefully hidden for sixteen years. He would never forgive himself for that carelessness; Mia had simply broken. All the years of careful therapy and medication, all the years he'd controlled her illness—gone, in one horrible moment when Mia saw what her daughter had looked like and sanity simply disintegrated. Marshall had barely recognized her that night—in the bathroom with her mother's old shears, hacking her waist-length hair at her shoulders, hurtling full-blown hatred toward Marshall. To this day, he didn't know where she'd gone when she stumbled from the house. He was only grateful that she'd come home more calm, more rational, and more prepared to go on waiting.

But it wasn't over. During the past three months, he'd noticed the signs. The lost hours, the blackouts, the nightmares. The nights in the attic, hours on end looking at pictures of Kristina—happier pictures, happier days. There were times he suspected the horrors of her young life were haunting her again: Grady's abuse and the johns who came after. Worse, her mother's twisted hatred, keeping Mia's hair hacked at the scalp out of sick jealousy.

Finally, Marshall hadn't been able to stand it and went to Kristina himself—a breach of ethics as the court-appointed psychiatrist who had testified in the original custody hearings, but no more so, he reasoned, than having kept track of her for sixteen years. He'd pleaded with her to meet her mother and Kristina agreed. And when he'd given Mia the card that showed the date and time they would meet, it had been one of the happiest moments of his life.

Now, those happy moments were winding down. Marshall would have to savor them while he still could.

"Come to bed, love," he said, stroking her hair. "Morning will come too soon."

So would Sunday.

CHAPTER
37

Thursday, October 7, 7:40 a.m.

MONIKA WOKE SLOWLY, a distant wail dragging her to the surface. A siren, she realized. Faint, but audible.

Siren?

She hauled her bulging belly to the edge of the bed, her lower back feeling as if a truck had run over her. She hurried to the window and peeked through the slit in the curtains, but couldn't see any lights. Dawn painted the sky in faint purples and grays, daylight only a few minutes old. Yesterday, she had decided she must be facing northwest: It was nothing like the east window in her bedroom at home. There, the sun popping over the hills in the mornings could sear the cornea.

Here, she could only see past the trees to the next set of foothills, to the next and the next. A never-ending wilderness.

And yet, somewhere, there had been a siren. She held her breath and listened, then her heart sank. Nothing. No police car coming to save her or an ambulance called in to help with the baby. It might have even been a dream.

She let the curtains fall back down, turning to face her second day locked in this bedroom with the iceman as her guard. Tears threatened and she fisted her hands and smashed them into a pillow. The broker was insistent about buying her baby, and early on, she'd considered it. Then, those first few flutters inside, the kicks and squirms. A boy, Monika had decided in her own mind, though her mother always said she'd felt like she was carrying a soccer player when she'd been pregnant with Monika. By the time she'd hit five months, Monika was having second thoughts about giving the baby up.

A sound. Monika froze, the familiar footsteps trudging up the stairs. The iceman opened the locks and set down her food, picking up a little package from the tray and tossing it to her. She caught it and he left, without a word.

Hands shaking, Monika peeled off the wrapping paper and looked at the gift. A rattle, made of silver, and some letters engraved on the bulbous end.

Baby Boy Doe. Born Thursday, Oct. 7.

Monika almost collapsed. That was today.

Dani woke to tender nipples and a pleasant ache inside, an empty bed. She looked around, caught the aroma of coffee in the air, and pulled on Mitch's shirt to go into the kitchen. A note stood next to the coffeepot. *I'm still here*, it said, and was signed, simply, *M*.

Emotions collided in her throat. Relief, first, that he hadn't left, and on the heels of that, disgust. Since when was she the type of woman who worried whether or not a man would be there?

Since Mitch Sheridan was the man.

The door opened and her heart skittered. Mitch walked in, wearing jeans and a T-shirt, his cheeks rough with morning beard. He carried a large photograph, framed and in glass. He leaned it up against the wall and came straight to Dani, wasting no breath on words as he bent his head and took her lips in his, his hands sliding under the shirt and bringing every nerve to life again. He kissed her until her toes curled with pleasure then pulled back and smiled. "Not a bad way to start a day," he said.

Dani grunted. "You didn't tell me you were cheerful before eight in the morning. I think that's a deal-breaker."

"Bullshit. There are no deal-breakers now. I thought I made that clear."

He went to the cupboard and pulled two mugs down, handed one to Dani. "Because of you, I have to revamp the concept of the whole exhibit in the first ballroom."

Dani was confused. "What? Because of me?"

"You'll understand later. Right now I just need time to work and don't want to have to worry about knowing you're safe."

Her spine stiffened. "Are you telling me to go to the hotel and hide out?"

"I know better than that," he said, but he straightened, towering over her in what might have been a little play of power. "I know you need to see the Kinneys and I imagine you'll be going to Rosie's funeral today. I'm asking you to check in when you're alone—with me, with Tifton, I don't care." He stroked her jawline. "I'm asking you to make sure you come back to me in one piece. I don't think I could lose you again."

Dani's cheeks warmed. "Damn it, you're making it hard to argue."

Mitch smiled. "Good."

"What's the picture?" she asked.

He set down his coffee and walked over to it, turning it around so she could see. "It's one of the photos from Ar Rutbah. The day of the attack."

"Oh, Mitch," Dani said, amazed. It was a black-and-white image of a little boy and a patchy dog, sharing a piece of wafer in the desert, a robed man in the background holding a grenade launcher on his shoulder. It was poignant and heartbreaking and inspiring all at once. "Is that him?" Dani asked. "The boy you were talking about last night?"

He nodded, the muscles in his jaw tightening.

"What are you doing with it?" she asked.

"It needs to be re-matted. It's the dumbest thing, because Russell was a fanatic about matting."

"What do you mean?"

He tipped back the picture, holding it on the floor by its frame, and pointed to a corner. "See the cuts?" he asked, and Dani squatted down to look. There were three layers of mat—all in shades of charcoal to compliment the image. Mitch pointed at the corner of each of the three in the bottom, left-hand side of the picture. "They're overcut. See how the razor mark dips into the mat? You cut mats with an angled blade, and a good matter will have perfect corners."

"I never would have noticed."

"Maybe not, but Russell would. I'm surprised he let the shot go up like this. I'm going to recut it before the show." He moved it to a safer spot and leaned it against the wall. "But first, I have a lot to do on some other images."

Dani glanced at the boy in the photograph and remem-

bered Mitch's emotion when he told her about him. A kid
with a knack for photography. She knew one of those.

"Need some help?" she asked.

Mitch kissed her. "You're wonderful in many ways,
sweetheart, but can you crop and mat and frame, digitally
alter light sources and—"

"Not me, you idiot. But I know someone. I thought
of him last night when you told me about the boy in Ar
Rutbah, and now you're saying you need some help. I
mean, he's a kid, but he's good. I'm not the only one who
thinks so."

Mitch frowned, looking torn. Maybe not ready to get
attached to another kid with a camera.

Dani didn't care. He needed this. And it would be
good for Terence, too. "Trust me," she said, and looked at
her watch. "Come on. He shouldn't be at school yet."

Mitch followed Dani to a tiny clapboard house on
Woodland Drive. It was bright blue. It sat in a row of
tiny clapboard houses that had maybe ten feet in between
them.

He put the Cuda behind her Chevy and started to get
her door, found himself jogging across the sidewalk to
catch up with her instead. Before they got to the porch, a
tall, lanky kid popped the door open.

"Terence," Dani said. "How've you been?"

A thick-bodied woman came from behind him, wearing custodial garb. "He's been good, Sergeant," the woman
said. Her voice carried a suspicious tone.

"This is Mitch Sheridan," Dani said. "Mitch, this is Terence Bonnell and his mother"—a little girl peeked around
the doorframe—"and Shondra. Hi there, Shondra."

The little one giggled and her mother pushed her back.

Behind, Mitch noticed, there were two more kids. Dani probably knew their names, too, he thought, with a little rush of affection.

"Is Terence in trouble?" the oldest asked.

"Not that I know of," Dani said. She turned to Mitch. "I met Terence last summer, buying stolen cameras from a fence and hanging with guys he shouldn't hang with." She looked at the teenager. "I talked to the truant officer a few minutes ago. She said if you keep goin' the way you have been, you'll make the A-B honor roll this term."

"Yes, ma'am," he said.

Dani lifted a hand and Terence high-fived it. "And are you still taking pictures?"

His Adam's apple bobbed and he looked at Mitch. "All the time," he said.

Dani smiled. "Mitch wants to see them."

They threaded past an ironing board and between cramped pieces of furniture, to a bedroom where a bunk bed climbed one wall and a separate mattress lay on the floor. Terence gestured to a desk, the surface littered with used books on photography. Mitch picked them up, recognizing some, then saw his own two books on a plywood shelf above. They'd retailed for about $130 and were too trendy to make their way into used bookstores. Mitch wondered how he'd gotten them.

"Craig's List," Terence said, reading his mind.

Mitch smiled, turning his attention to a wall covered with photos. He stared. The images were remarkable— emotion so real it grabbed Mitch by the throat and technique so clean it vanished and left the viewer to simply become immersed in the essence of the portrait. Some of the better ones were expertly matted and framed...A junkie rolled up in a ball with a dozen dirty needles scattered on the cement. A woman dragging sheets of cardboard into a corner for a bed. A preschooler, watching the police arrest his mother.

Mitch looked at Terence. "These are yours?"

He nodded.

"And you took them here, in Lancaster?"

Again.

Mitch swallowed, the itch to hold his camera making his fingers rub together. It was something he hadn't felt for six months. He glanced at Dani then looked at the kid. "Terence," he said, "do you need a job?"

Ten minutes later, Mitch walked Dani to her car. He pulled her close and kissed her, doing a thorough job of it, though several pairs of eyes watched through the windows of Terence's house. Dani turned dark pink.

"What was that about?" she asked, glancing around.

"A thank you," he said. "I can't explain it now, but you have no idea what you just did for me in there."

"Oh. Well, then. You're welcome." She looked at her watch. "I told the Kinneys nine o'clock. I need to get going. We've got to know about the adoption of their little boy. If he belonged to Rosie, maybe they can lead us to whoever brokered the deal."

"Call me when you get there, and when you leave."

"Right," she said. "Where are you gonna be?"

"Telling stories," Mitch said, and thought Russ might be smiling down on him.

Dani left Mitch and drove to the Kinneys' house, arriving about ten minutes early. A woman with a toddler came down the front steps. Austin and Alana Kinney?

No, wait. That was a little girl, not a boy. And the woman didn't look anything like the picture of Alana Kinney, even given that the OCIN photo was more than two years old.

Dani got out of the car and walked up the cobblestone sidewalk, calling to the woman. She looked dazed.

"Ma'am?" Dani said, meeting her on the steps. "Are you here to see Mrs. Kinney?"

The woman looked at her. "Who are you?"

"Detective Sergeant Dani Cole," she said, but resisted showing her shield. Given that it was inactive. "Is she here?"

"Police? Oh, God, what happened?"

"Nothing's happened. I've just come to talk to Mr. and Mrs. Kinn—"

"But they're gone. They aren't in there."

"Oh," Dani said. "Well, we weren't supposed to meet until nine, so mayb—"

"No, you don't understand. I mean, they're *gone*. I have a key, I went in. Almost everything's gone. They've vanished."

CHAPTER
38

READING ROAD LOOKED EVEN WORSE by day than by night. Mitch got there a little after eight-thirty and found Chuck inside the depot building, sleeping. So much for Gibson's promise to get Chuck some help.

Jackass.

Mitch looked at him for a long moment. This was the bastard who took a wooden plank to Dani last night, a man who was certifiably crazy. He might have killed her, all for a stuffed bear.

Mitch moved the gun in his belt out a touch, just in case, then called to him. "Chuck. Chuck." Nothing. He bent and wiggled his good arm and Chuck came up like a shot.

"Stopitstopitstopit." One word.

Mitch stepped back. "Easy, man. Wake up."

Chuck blinked, daylight wreaking havoc on his pupils. He wasn't high now, but coming down, instead. Weak, shaky.

Mitch gave him a minute to come to his senses. When he seemed like he could focus, Mitch said, "Chuck, I need your help..."

• • •

Dani texted Tifton; he'd be in a task force meeting. `Kinneys gone. Call me.`

And Tifton texted her back: `Alicia W body found a.m. VA. Cut throat/hair.`

Dani stared at the letters on the screen. What? Dear God. She read it again, then closed her eyes, feeling as if she couldn't breathe. Of course she'd known Alicia was dead; she'd known that last night when she found the hairs and blood on the side of the depot building. Still, knowing they'd actually found her body...

And Dani hadn't even known. Christ, if it weren't for Tifton, she wouldn't know anything at all. She was off the case. Goddamned Gibson.

Don't think about it; there was no time for self-pity. Alicia Woodruff's body had been found, hair and throat cut. The FBI was right: They *were* looking at a series. Jill Donnelly's body was out there somewhere, too.

VA. Virginia?

Dani pulled herself together. The Kinneys. She might not be sitting in the task force meeting or out looking at crime scenes, but *this*, she could do.

She offered some empty words of comfort to the neighbor and, squelching the thought that she had no warrant, started through the house. Personal items were gone and appeared to have been packed in a hurry. Several items had been taken from the walls—meaningful pictures, Dani supposed, and one cupboard in the entertainment center in the family room had been emptied. The neighbor had known what was in there: scrapbooks.

At nine-thirty, Tifton called her back. "You're shittin' me," he said when she told him about the empty house.

"I shit you not. I already called Austin's preschool and they said he didn't come in today. But he was supposed to—it was his day to provide snacks. On the kitchen counter there's a bag of Cheez-Its and juice boxes, ready to go. And it was Alana Kinney's turn to drive the little girl next door."

"Christ," he said, and Dani could see him pacing back and forth, rubbing a hand over his scalp.

"Are you gonna tell me about Alicia?"

"Jesus, Dani, there's nothing to tell. A couple of deer hunters found her body this morning at the mouth of an old mine shaft in Virginia. They got sheriff's deputies on the scene and a team of Feds are headed over. She was stabbed in the throat and a chunk of the hair on the left side of her head was hacked off."

Dani's stomach turned. "Her face?"

"Left side is messed up."

She wanted to retch. "Did you go see the railroad depot?"

"Yeah, this morning. The lab says the blood there matches Alicia's blood type and the hair looks like hers."

Dani could hardly think. "Christ, Tift, why Virginia?"

"Wilderness, maybe. Real isolated area. A few cabins and hunting lodges spread out over hundreds of square miles. When I know anything else, I'll let you know."

Neither of them knew what to say for a minute. Finding Alicia's body rang like a death knell for Nika Love. Pregnant Nika Love.

"Dani," Tifton said, "you're a step ahead of the task force on the Kinneys. What's it look like there?"

Dani walked the empty house as she spoke. "I got two things from the neighbor: First, she says it's totally unlike Alana Kinney to pick up and leave. She was a home-body—a big trip for her was going to Baltimore or inside the Beltway." She walked through the room that had been Austin's bedroom again, back out. "And second, she said Alana had gotten very protective of Austin lately—more so than usual. She wouldn't let him go to the park with the neighbor, and they'd done that lots of times." Dani ducked her head into a hall bathroom.

"So she knew Rosie was watching her."

"Sounds like it." Dani opened the cupboards. A few cleaners and a toilet bowl brush were there, but that was it. Everything personal had been collected.

But not the trash can. Dani looked, and her breath stopped. A Curious George Band-Aid peeked out from a bed of used tissues and Clorox wipes and a gum wrapper. Her pulse jumped a beat and she pinched the Band-Aid between her thumb and forefinger. A smear of blood had soaked into the gauze.

"Oh, God," she said.

"What? What?" Tifton asked.

"I think I've got a blood sample from Austin Kinney."

"Okay," Tifton said. "Jesus, Dani, don't take it. Leave it there. You take without a warrant, it's—"

"Illegal. I know, Tift, but thanks for the reminder," she said bitterly. "You better send a unit to secure the scene here. I gotta get out."

"Will do." Then Tifton blew out a curse. "Goddamn it, Dani, I want this girl back. I want her to be alive."

"She's alive," Dani said. "They want the baby. She's alive until she has the baby. After that, she's dead."

Brad sat in the passenger seat of Stephen Housley's car, headed to some cabin in Virginia. Housley had suddenly gotten on board: Wanted to deliver Nika's baby as soon as possible.

Mia Kettering had gotten to him.

"That woman, she scares me," Housley said. "I don't trust her." He scratched at his cheek, then shook out another cigarette, one arm handling the steering wheel. "I don't see why you had to tell her about the brokerage in the first place. Just because she'd been greasing you up doesn't mean you had to cut her in."

"I didn't cut her in. She saw us, remember? She saw you handing off a baby and followed me to give it to the parents. And she was nuts that night. I remember thinking she was strung out, but she wasn't. Something had happened between her and Marshall. Her hair was even a mess, cut every which way. You've seen Mia Kettering. Her hair is never a mess."

"She scares me," Housley repeated, and there wasn't much Brad could say to that. She scared him, too.

Brad had gone through his apartment after they talked, and through his office. If there was evidence Mia had planted to implicate him in the girls' murders, he didn't know what it was. But the files were implication enough. Even if no one suspected him of murder, they could put him away for selling babies, not to mention committing fraud where the Foundation was concerned.

No matter how you sliced it, he was fucked. Time to get out, take the money, and run.

And send this last girl far away. Tell her to move as soon as she can walk and leave no forwarding address.

"Aw, shit," Housley said. He put his foot on the brake.

"What?"

"I don't know, but look up there."

Brad lifted his sunglasses. Sheriff's deputies, a whole posse of them. "What's going on?"

"I'm not sure, but I think that's our turn, isn't it? Check the directions."

Brad checked.

"Shit, look," Housley said. "They're everywhere."

Cold fingers of fear caught Brad by the throat. "Go. Turn around. Get the hell out of here."

Dani called Mitch. "I'm on my way to see Robin Hutchins," she said. At Dani's request, Tifton had vetted Hutchins, the deputy director at OCIN, and found nothing. He'd even sent his partner to talk to her. But with the Kinneys acting suspicious, it was time to talk to her again.

"Okay," Mitch said. "I want to be in on that one. I'll meet you at her office. She's on the first floor of the Foundation. Did you talk to the Kinneys?"

Dani filled him in, including finding the Band-Aid. "Why do you care about a used bandage?" he asked.

"Because it could tell us whether or not Austin Kinney was really Rose McNamara's son."

"Oh," Mitch said, and Dani could tell that he got it. They'd also be able to tell whether Austin Kinney was Russell's son. "Bring it on."

Mitch introduced Dani to Robin Hutchins, a fifty-year-old Brit with high breasts, a thick trunk, and hair pulled into a tight knot. If she wasn't running OCIN, she'd have been singing at the Met, or at least, that's what she had people believing. A recording of opera always played in her office. Today, Mitch thought it was Bizet.

"Puccini, you cretin," she corrected, and pointed them to chairs. Robin looked at Dani. "The FBI is here now. Doing private interviews with every last one of my staff, at least those who are here. I have eight people overseas."

"It will be good to rule people out," Dani said.

Robin looked at Mitch. "Brad's not here right now. Is there anything I shouldn't be sharing with the authorities?"

"No," Mitch said, lacing his fingers between his knees. "Give them anything they ask for and more." He paused; he could hardly believe he was saying it: "We think the Foundation may have facilitated illegal adoptions—here in the U.S."

Robin went white. "*You* think this?" she asked. "I can understand suspicion from the Federal government, but *you*?"

"I think it's possible, Robin."

"It's not only possible," Dani interjected, "it's likely. I can tell you about four pregnant women right now who sold their babies and then disappeared or died. At least one of those infants was almost certainly adopted through OCIN."

Robin looked at Mitch. "We don't handle domestic adoptions."

"You did this time."

Robin stood, walked to her window and looked out. "Tell me."

Mitch did, and when he was finished, Robin went to her computer and called up the files for Alana and Robert Kinney. They all reread the pages for a few minutes, then Mitch asked, "Do you remember it?"

Robin shook her head. "I don't remember any of them," she said with a certain sadness in her voice. "I am a figurehead here, you know. I raise money. I raise consciousness. Other people do the real work."

Mitch knew exactly how she felt.

Dani said, "Of all the people on your staff, who would be most likely to recognize a red flag in the files?"

Robin thought for only a second. "Gary Schmidt. He knows more of each country's laws than anyone else, and he would have made the travel arrangements and all."

"Travel arrangements?" Dani asked.

"There's always travel in adopting a child from overseas. The Kinneys' baby came from Ukraine, and Ukrainian adoption provides for the parents to come choose the child. Then, a few weeks later when the dossier is approved, they go back to take him or her home."

Dani got up without a word and went into the hallway. She was gone ten minutes, while Mitch and Robin talked through adoption policies.

"What was that about?" Mitch asked when Dani came back.

"Alana Kinney's neighbor said she didn't like to travel, so I was having Tifton check passports. Guess who's never been to Ukraine."

CHAPTER
39

MONIKA HAD A PLAN. It wasn't great, but it was the only thing she could think of.

She'd searched every drawer and nook and cranny of the room for something to use as a screwdriver or wedge. Nothing, and, eventually, she'd settled for working at the edge of the bathroom mirror with her fingernails. It hadn't taken long to see that was no good. The glass was set in a wood frame and before the wood splintered enough to dig out, her fingers would be ground beef. Monika straightened, studied it some more, and finally thought of something else. But first, she had to get it off the wall.

Quiet now. The worst thing she could do was alert the iceman. He'd been in and out today, and at the moment, she thought, was in. And Monika was no heavyweight champ. At five-four, her normal weight was something under one-thirty, and pregnancy, while adding on the pounds, did nothing to add strength. If anything, she was awkward and uncomfortable, and even late into her ninth month hadn't gotten used to the little things that made getting around clumsy. The location of her center-of-gravity, for example, or the ridiculous impulse to turn sideways to slide through narrow openings. If she were put in a position that required agility or strength, she was screwed.

Between the bathroom sink and her belly, she couldn't reach the edges of the mirror's frame. She dragged a wooden chair in and climbed on top, leaning forward, struggling to stay balanced and still get a grip. The mirror moved when she got it—a good sign—but mirrors are heavy. Holding the position and lifting at the same time was out of the question. She put one foot on the counter for leverage, but the ceiling was too low to stand. No good.

A cramp seized her belly and Monika almost cried out. She grabbed the underside of her belly and teetered, catching herself on the mirror. Labor? She didn't know. The only thing she knew about having babies was what little she remembered about her brother's birth, and stories from some of the other girls on the streets. No comfort in that. But there was some in remembering what her mom had said when Loopy had been born of a stray bitch in their barn: "Mother Nature knows what's s'posed to happen. Mama dog don't need to."

Pray her mother was right.

The cramp unknotted and Monika sat on the sink with her feet propped on the chair, craning around to look at the mirror again. Her heart leaped. *Oh, dear Lord, thank you.* The mirror was askew.

That little bit of success rallied her. She climbed back up and grasped the frame again—careful, careful—for God's sake, don't let it fall. Her lower back screamed in pain. She supported the mirror's weight, hung on through two more cramps, and hoisted it upward with all her strength.

The mirror came into her hands.

Thank you, Jesus, she whispered, wrestling it down to the sink. The frame found the counter and she stopped to catch her breath, then maneuvered herself to the floor, one hand still balancing the mirror. She hauled it down another step—to the chair—and glanced around. *God, please, don't let him have heard me*, she prayed, feeling as if her heartbeat alone was loud enough to alert Fulton. She rested for another minute, and when she'd finally caught her breath again, hoisted the frame into the bathtub, stood it on edge, and let the mirror fall back against the tile.

Nothing. Again, and a little shove this time. The frame just thumped against the tile. She pushed it again—same thing, and kept repeating it, a little harder each time. She didn't dare just let it smash. But sooner or later, it would hit just right and hard enough to—

Tink.

That was it. The smallest sound—*tink*—and the glass looked like something from a horror movie. Spider legs of cracks fanning out.

Thank you, Jesus.

Monika sank to the toilet seat, heart beating like a drum. She took a few deep breaths, walked out into the bedroom and listened, and when Fulton didn't materialize, nearly wilted to the bed with relief.

She'd done it. She was going to get the hell out of here.

She started back for the bathroom, pausing at the window. It was later than she'd hoped; the sun hovered at the edge of the trees. Not too long until it sank, and then these hills would be drenched in blackness. Still, Monika was less afraid of the mountain than she was of the iceman. And the broker. She couldn't wait for the right moment or pray an opportunity would be thrown her way. She had to make her own opportunity, and the sooner the better. She didn't know what was happening out there in the wilderness, but the first day she'd been here, there wasn't a single sound or movement outside—and the iceman hadn't gone in and out at all. Today, beginning with the sirens, things had been different. The mountains had been alive. At one point, she could have sworn she'd even heard dogs barking in the distance.

It wasn't much, but it did tell her one thing: Somewhere out there not too far away, there were people. She wasn't all alone.

She took a deep breath and yanked loose the bottom of the sheet, gnawed at the edge until she got a rip going, then tore a third of it into shreds and took them into the bathroom. The iceman was huge, built like a stone wall, and possessed of little, if any, emotion. He wouldn't be afraid of an eighteen-year-old girl who was nine months pregnant.

That would be his downfall.

Gary Schmidt knew the regulations like the back of his hand.

"You were right to question the age of the baby, Mitch," he said, looking at the Kinney file. "But you were wrong about how much. Ukrainian kids aren't available until *eighteen* months. The law there provides for a twelve-month period for parents to come reclaim them. You might be able to pass off a newborn as a six-month-old who was a preemie, but no six-month-olds leave Ukraine. And you know what else?"

"No, what?" Mitch was fascinated.

"There's another adoption here from Estonia that says

it was done in November. You can't adopt kids that late in the year."

"Why not?" Dani asked.

"Because there aren't any left. The Estonian government puts a limit on how many come to the U.S., and we've usually reached that quota by May. An Estonian baby in November? No way."

Dani looked at Mitch, then Robin. "Can you spare this guy for the day?"

Robin held out her hands. "Take him."

They did, setting him up with the OCIN files in the apartment. He would notice things no one else knew to notice.

"Flag anything weird," Dani told him, once Mitch had logged him in and left the room. Mitch disappeared into the darkroom, taking his camera. Busy.

"Okay," Gary said. He was a skinny man in his thirties, with glasses the size of movie tickets. A little excited about working with the police.

"Start with adoptions in the pipeline now—parents who applied but haven't yet adopted. There's a girl out there who fits the profile and could pop a kid about any time."

"You got it. What are you gonna do?"

Dani looked at her watch, let out a slow breath. "I've gotta go to a funeral."

Fulton's number came up on Mia's cell phone. "Is it Nika?" she asked, her heartbeat picking up. "She's in labor?"

"No. It's not good news."

She stilled. "What do you mean?"

"They must've found Alicia. Cops are all over the place, and a news chopper just started circling."

A brick fell on Mia's chest. *No, no.* Not when she was so close to finishing.

"I can't be sure yet, but I tooled down there and some county water system surveyor said they were bringing a body out from the woods. A hunter found it at a mine and he muttered something about the girl being some blonde from Maryland. Heard them calling Lancaster police."

"You stupid bastard." She wanted his throat in her hands. "I told you to be careful."

"No one except the county guy has seen me, and even if they start digging around these mountains, it'll take forever. Even knowing this cabin is here, it's hard to find. And the county sheriff's a dumb-ass homeboy. Probably never even seen a murder before."

Mia was in motion. Forget Rosie McNamara and Alicia. What about Nika? Mia combed through the hair on the wig block. She was the last one. Mia couldn't lose her. "The doctor," she said suddenly. "He's not there?"

"He might have tried. I'm telling you, he'd have to pass through half the sheriff's department to get here."

Dear God.

"Get out. Get Nika away from the cabin."

"And take her where?" Fulton asked, sounding disgusted. "It's not like I can pose as her husband and go get a room. That girl's ready to run. Want my suggestion?"

"No."

"Let her go. I don't know what your sick little fetish is for these girls and I don't care. But this one's bad news. Right now, she doesn't know who you are or where she is. She'll never see me again. Let her go and she can't tell anybody anything."

No. Mia was too close. She'd waited too long, and getting another girl could take months. As far as she knew,

Brad didn't even have one. Even if he did, she was sure he wouldn't give her the name and address—not now that he knew she'd killed the others. And Kristina was coming in two days. "No, I'm not waiting for another one. Nika is the last."

"Damn it—"

"*Do as I say*," she screeched, then stopped herself. She didn't need Fulton bailing out on her. "I don't care if you have to tie her up and gag her. Just get her out of the house and make sure there's no sign she's been there."

"I'll have to wait 'til night; there's too much activity out there right now."

"Do whatever you need to."

She hung up, and for the first time in three months, true fear nibbled at her heart. If Fulton was right and they had found Alicia and knew she was from Lancaster, the police would be quick to begin looking for Nika. And on the heels of Rose McNamara...Even if nothing else connected them, the hair would. Dani Cole would.

Mia closed her eyes, every muscle clenched. It was happening: One little thread had unraveled and now the entire tapestry was coming apart. How to stop it, how to stop it? Not even for long, but just long enough to kill Nika and finish the wig? How to keep the police from coming around to Mia?

The answer was the same answer it had been all along, and hit Mia's bloodstream like a drug: Stop Dani Cole.

Dani didn't cry at Rosie's funeral. She sat two rows behind the McNamaras, holding back a grief so tainted by rage she thought she might explode. Helplessness clawed at her soul.

When it was over, she walked down the cathedral steps

on stiff limbs. One by one she watched Rosie's family emerge through the heavily carved oak doors. Any resentment toward Rosie had melted away over time, the family now weeping and shell-shocked. Dani closed her eyes and remembered the photos of a little girl all bandaged up, the lost expression of a sixteen-year-old prostitute who needed help, the lifeless mass of bloodied flesh in the woods at Camden Park.

She moved away from the mourners and pulled out her cell phone. She called Tifton. No answer. She called Gibson. Not available. She started to call Mitch, but her phone vibrated, a text message coming in.

She held up the screen, expecting Tifton. She was wrong. Instead, a statement rolled across the screen: You can't stop me.

Every cell in her body went rigid and Dani looked around, stupidly, as if the sender might be watching her. She hit the callback number, fingers punching so hard she kept making mistakes, but no one was there. She called headquarters and got to the tech lab.

"Find out where that number came from, damn it." But she knew it would be untraceable. A prepaid cell phone, or maybe a phone that had been reported stolen. A savvy caller could make contact anonymously.

Dani clenched her fists. Damn it, there had to be something she could do.

It came to her as a bitter pill, one she should have swallowed long ago. *Fruit of the poison tree*. Chief Gibson had said.

Time to live up to it.

CHAPTER
40

THE GEMINI WASN'T OPEN for business during the day: Its clientele haunted the nights. Late in the afternoon a couple of employees would be there. And Ty, of course.

Dani climbed out of her car, went to the side door as Ty had instructed, then reached under her blazer and unsnapped the holster on her gun. Habit, she told herself. She wouldn't need it.

She knocked three times then shouldered the door open. Stepped inside.

The air smelled of smoke and stale beer and roach spray; a bare bulb hung from the ceiling in the middle of the room and slanted shadows across the stage. Three dancers' poles reflected the light. Nothing moved.

"Craig?" Dani said, the soles of her shoes sticking to the floor. The alley door shut behind her, latching with an echo. "Craig?"

A chair scraped and she drew on it. In the same second, a figure came from either side and wrenched her gun from her hand. Each held one of her arms twisted behind her back.

"Fuck you," she snarled.

"Tsk, tsk," Craig said, strolling onto the stage. "I thought you were here to negotiate, not fight."

Dani snarled at him, curling her lip. The gray light of the bulb barely reached the stage. One side of Ty's face was entirely in darkness, the other touched by shadows. He stood with his hands in his pockets, casual, a middle-aged jock gone soft.

"Call off your hounds," she ground out.

Ty studied her a moment then gave a small nod. Her arms came free, though the two henchmen stayed within reach.

She rolled her shoulders and looked up at Ty. "What do you know about Rose McNamara's murder?"

"Only that I had nothing to do with it."

She made an ugly sound. "Why should I believe that? You were livid when she left."

His silhouette gave a shrug. "I never like to lose an employee. But if I'd wanted her dead, I'd have hunted her down and taken care of it. Well, not me, personally," he said, with a smug twist to his lips, "but as you know, I have *associates* who do occasional favors." *Artie Cole.*

"Where's Alicia Woodruff?"

"I'm afraid I don't know."

"Right."

"But when I find her, she'll have some explaining to do. Seriously, Danielle, why would I want to murder girls who are making money for me hand over fist? If I didn't get rid of them back when they so irresponsibly became pregnant and had to be out of business for months on end, why do it now?"

He had a point, except for Rosie, of course. "If you're so innocent, why haven't you agreed to be interviewed by the police?"

"I'm an opportunist." Craig pushed from the dance pole he'd been leaning against and strode toward her to the edge of the stage. "And I see for us an opportunity here."

"I'm not my father."

Ty chuckled. "So you say. And yet, here you are. What is it they say about where the apple falls?"

"Go to hell." She turned, but the two guards stepped in her way, blocking her path. She pulled up short. Do it, she said to herself. You're here. Just do it.

She turned back. "What do you want?"

"You know what. Tit for tat. I paid your father well when he was on the police force. I paid him even better once he was off."

Dani wanted to take him by the throat.

Craig went on. "Now, I have a friend or two in the higher ranks of your fine organization, but eyes and ears on the streets are something else. And I'm sure you could think of *something* you want from me. A little hint on Rose McNamara's case, perhaps?"

"If you know anything at all, it's because you had something to do with it."

"You know I didn't kill her. That's why you're here."

"Then prove it. What do you know?"

"It's nothing certain. But it might lead you somewhere. What is it those TV cops always say to witnesses? 'If you think of anything, anything at all—'"

"Spit it out."

He took a deep breath and crossed his arms. "There's a clinic over on Heritage, just outside Baltimore proper. I sometimes send my girls there. I think you'll find that Rosie and Alicia both saw the same obstetrician."

Dani's skin pulled tight. Jesus. The doctor. Why hadn't they thought of that?

Because they didn't even have another girl until today, that's why. There was no pattern yet.

But she could see it forming. *A doctor.*

"When did Alicia have her baby?"

"About eight months ago, I think." Craig bent down. "Good tip?" he asked, and he was smiling.

Dani clenched her fists.

"And now, Sergeant Cole, I believe you are indebted to me. I'll look forward to the payback."

"I don't want to owe a slime bucket like you," she shot, trying not to feel the dirt caking her soul. "You have a stash of drugs at your club on Brewer Street. Narcs have it made. They're gonna bust you tonight, shut down all your clubs to get you in a position to deal."

Craig's face registered surprise for two seconds, then slid to smug. "Well, well, I'm proud of you. It looks like you'll make a fine little apple after all." He smiled. "Fruit of the poison tree."

Cold fingers brushed down Dani's spine, but she was careful not to show it. "Debt paid," she said. She held out her hand, and the goon on her right set her gun back in her palm, dropping the bullets in her other hand. She made a point to keep her shoulders back and chin high, walking straight to her car and driving away.

Three blocks out she pulled over and cried.

Dani went to the Radisson, showered and brushed her teeth, then dressed and went outside. She waited for a Corolla to pass by, got a face full of smoke from a bad muffler, then crossed the street and headed to a clinic outside Baltimore.

"Stephen Housley," the office receptionist repeated, snapping her gum. She hadn't asked for a warrant, hadn't asked why Dani wanted to know. Dani hadn't even shown her a shield, a technicality that would be moot if anyone ever chose to take up the cause against a dirty cop.

"I just want to know if he saw patients named Rose McNamara and Nika Love," Dani said.

"Yeah. Well, I mean this one, Love, she hasn't given birth yet. So he's still got her. The other...er...McNamara, let's see. That was a while ago. Yeah, here it is. Hmm. That's funny."

"What?"

"She came here, but there's no sign that she ever had the baby. We didn't see her here after the fourth month. She must've gone someplace else."

The gears in Dani's brain started moving. Did Housley stash the pregnant women somewhere? "Check two more. Alicia Woodruff, in the last year. And Jill Donnelly. Would've been about three years ago."

The gum-snapper looked. "Donnelly came in once, in July of 2007."

"Was she pregnant?" Dani asked.

"Yeah. Three months."

"And McNamara?"

She blew a bubble and popped it. "Wow. Weird. It's the same thing with her."

Adrenaline rushed in. "Is Dr. Housley here today?"

"No. He was here last night. He only works once a week. The rest of the time he's at Spring Grove Hospital. You want the number?"

Dani jumped up. "I know where it is."

Housley had taken the day off. He wasn't at the hospital and wasn't picking up his pager. The receptionist tracked down a nurse who said, "He called and said his wife was ill."

Now Dani was in a quandary. Stephen Housley had seen three of the four girls they knew of. But Dani couldn't know that, not without a tip from a gangster she was forbidden to see.

She weighed the possible outcomes of telling Tifton or reporting to Gibson. All possibilities reeked. Decided to pay a house call to the good doctor herself.

His number was listed in the directory; his address wasn't. Dani went by a florist and picked up a bouquet of roses, then put her car midway between the hospital and the clinic, hoping Housley had the good sense to keep a residence convenient to both. She dialed his number.

His wife answered.

"I have a delivery of flowers from Compton Florist, ma'am, but I think my address is wrong and I'm a little lost…"

"Flowers?" she said. "Where are you coming from?"

When Housley's wife answered the door, she was surprised to see Dani. "Oh, police. I'm sorry. I was expecting someone else."

Flowers, maybe?

"I'm looking for your husband, Mrs. Housley. We have a patient at the hospital involved in a police matter, but she left and we need to find her. Dr. Housley spoke with her last."

"He's not there, at the hospital?" His wife looked at her watch. "He left early this morning. Usually, he's home by now. I just assumed he had an emergency and was running late."

No, he took the day off because you were ill. "Do you have any idea where we might find him?"

"No, I...Oh, God. Should I be worried?"

"Probably not. But here's my number. If you hear from him, have him call me right away. It's about that patient..."

Dani pulled away. When her phone rang, she glanced at the number but didn't recognize it. Her throat closed up. The texter? Ty? She answered anyway.

It was Gary Schmidt. He was having a conniption. The OCIN files had crashed.

"I don't know what happened," he said to Dani, his alarm reaching right through the phone lines. "I was looking at a file and suddenly, boom. Nothing. I can't figure it out."

Dani could.

Gary went on. "I had a couple years already transferred. I can still look at those, but I can't get to the others anymore."

"Do what you can. I'll be by later. Is Mitch there?"

"He's at the gallery, with that kid who came over. Terence."

Okay. She glanced at her watch and decided not to call him yet; she'd been checking in all day. She dialed Tift, instead: no answer. She called the FBI field office and a receptionist confirmed he was in a meeting there. Dani decided to go stalk him.

He walked out a little before six o'clock with a middle-aged couple at his side.

"Tift," Dani said.

He looked, shot a glance to his companions, then excused himself and came over to her. "What's up?"

"What do you mean, what's up?" She poked him in the chest. "You're supposed to be keeping me in the loop."

"Jesus, Cole, give me a break. I just walked out. I would've called you."

"With what?" She peered at the couple. "Who's that?"

He looked at the man and woman and said, "Come on. I'll introduce you."

Dani tagged along.

"This is Dani Cole, my partner on the police force. Sergeant, this is Burt and Laura Wheeler, from North Carolina. They drove most of the day to get here."

Dani was perplexed but held out a hand. "Mr. Wheeler. Mrs. Wheeler." She looked back at Tifton, who added, "Nika Love's mom and dad."

"Oh, God." She looked back at them. *Wheeler.* So that's her real name. "I'm sorry. Is there any progress?"

"We just met with the man in charge—the SAC, they called him." Burt Wheeler spoke with a soft southern drawl. He was a clean-cut man wearing a flannel shirt and Dockers, with a pair of work boots. His wife had on a flowered housedress that Doris Day might have worn and twisted a handkerchief in her hand. "They said they're doing everything they can," he added, "but there's no sign of Monika yet."

Mrs. Wheeler spoke through tears in her eyes. "They said she's...my baby's pregnant. She's goin' to have a baby."

Dani asked, "How did you come to find out that Nika might be in trouble?"

"Monika," her father corrected. "Her name is Monika. Someone from the FBI called us late last night."

Tifton explained: "We went through the bag she left at the shelter and found her real name. Her friends placed her from North Carolina and authorities found a missing persons report from more than three years ago."

Mrs. Wheeler's eyes leaked. "We argued about a boy and she ran off."

"She called us a couple times," her husband added, "but that was it. We weren't sure where she was or what she was doing. Now"—he looked down—"I guess I know what she's been doing, God forgive her." He took a minute, then looked back up, determination in his eyes. "That don't matter, though. We want her back. The Lord will forgive her sins. We just need her back."

Dani swallowed. Oh, to have a father who loved like that. For a minute, she wondered if Monika would live long enough to learn how much her parents loved her.

"Now," Mrs. Wheeler said, "they're saying someone might be trying to take her baby from her. That's what her friends are saying, and the FBI—"

"But if that's the case, then it's good," Tifton said. "Like the SAC explained, Mrs. Wheeler, if Monika's been contacted by a black-market baby buyer, she's safe, at least until she has the baby."

Dani couldn't take it: The Wheelers didn't know anything, not about Nika Love. They only knew Monika Wheeler. "Could you excuse us for a minute?" she asked.

Tifton followed her.

"They don't know about Alicia?"

"Not yet. We're waiting for the autopsy." He looked at his watch. "Should come yet tonight—the SAC put a rush on it. A search team is scouring the mountains nearby, thinking they might find Jill Donnelly. But it's wilderness, you know? Miles and miles of it."

"But they're convinced now it's a black-market baby ring."

It wasn't a question, and a touch of sadness came to Tift's eyes. "With your boyfriend's Foundation at the center of it."

"What about Brad Harper?"

"Jesus, Dani, he's the one person who couldn't possibly have killed Rosie. Even if his dad was in it, it doesn't mean he was."

"But he could be in the baby market. He signs off on the paperwork."

"And we confiscated it. As of an hour ago, we have all the OCIN files in FBI custody." Ergo, Gary's computer crash. "But do you know how long it will take to confirm whether or not a baby of the right description came from Latvia or Indonesia or some fucking place three years ago? We need time."

Dani shifted. Be a good sport, now, don't be a glory-seeker. "Call Gary Schmidt," she said, feeling as if she were giving away a winning lottery number.

"Who's Gary Schmidt?"

"The guy who can tell you which babies didn't come from Latvia or Indonesia or some fucking place. He's on OCIN's payroll."

Tift jotted the name down on his hand, a tiny smile on the corners of his lips. "If he pans out, I'll owe you."

"He will and you will, so pay up now. What's the scoop on the Kinneys?"

"Three agents are assigned to do nothing but look for them, twenty-four hours a day."

"Three agents. Geesh." Another dead end. She turned to leave, but couldn't. She went back to him. "Tifton, if I give you something, do you promise not to ask where I got it?"

He frowned. "Jesus, Dani, what're you doing?"

"Look up an obstetrician named Stephen Housley.
He's had his hands on all the dead women."

Mia picked up Dani Cole outside the Radisson, purely
by chance. She'd driven by Cole's house and the Foundation, looking for the Chevy, then cruised the police
station. The hotel was just a block away. Cole's car arro-
gantly parked in a loading zone.

Of course. Her house wasn't in very good shape these
days.

After twenty minutes Cole came out, her eyes hidden
by sunglasses and hair bouncing in a fat ponytail. Mia followed, lost her once at a traffic light three blocks ahead,
but made a logical guess based on which lane she'd been
in, and found her again in a mile. Mia kept an eye on the
environments as she drove, wanting to be prepared wher-
ever Cole stopped. Total seclusion wouldn't be necessary,
but relative seclusion was. A parking garage or alley, the
rear of a gas station, a quiet residential street. Someplace
where Mia could get off a shot or maybe even two, and be
out of sight by the time people came running.

Cole moved deeper into the east quarter of town,
rolled to a stop at Gaines and Herring Street and turned
right. It was then it hit Mia: She was going toward the
clinic.

A steady drip of uneasiness became a gush of panic.
Housley. Dear God, Cole was onto him. Think, *think*, but
there was nothing she could do. Cole parked at the clinic
and talked to a gaggle of loiterers, then to a drunk curled
up outside. She went inside.

Mia's mind raced. It was Thursday. Housley worked
here only one night a week, and he'd already done this
week's stint. Otherwise, he worked at some hospital on

the outskirts of Baltimore. But if the sergeant had reason to look for him...

Cole came out, a slip of paper in hand. She drove out of Lancaster, heading toward Baltimore.

Spring Grove Hospital. Again, the bitch parked illegally right in front of God and everybody. Mia waited, her breathing shallow. Was Housley in there? But Cole was out just a few minutes later. No doctor.

Mia drove in a trance, the panic turning to rage. She watched Cole swing into a flower store, frowned, but stayed on her. All the way to a well-off neighborhood with big homes on acre lots. She stopped at one and knocked on the door, Mia drifting past to try to see.

The mailbox said *Housley*.

But she was only there a minute, and on the road again. Mia hesitated, considering a new plan, then decided to follow. She tailed Dani Cole into Baltimore, to an FBI field office.

FBI?

Fingers of true fear squeezed Mia's throat. Get the hell out of here.

She put five miles between herself and the FBI field office, leaving Cole behind. She had to think. If the FBI knew to find Housley, it was only a matter of time. And just where was he? He'd never gotten to the house in Virginia and he was a weak link. If the police cornered him, he'd break and cut a deal. He was a small enough player that with the right lawyer, he'd walk with nothing but fines, maybe ethics charges from the AMA. A weak link indeed.

Of course, thanks to Dani Cole, Mia knew where he lived.

CHAPTER
41

M ITCH CALLED AT SIX-THIRTY. Dani was drained. She was dirty. She wasn't much closer to finding the killer. And yet, when she heard Mitch's voice, she felt a little thrill. She wanted to see him, be with him. She wanted to curl up in his arms and let him keep the world at bay.

What was that about?

"Come to the Foundation," he said. "Ballroom Two."

The Foundation offices had mostly emptied out for the day, except for Kathleen, Russell's assistant.

"Mitch has been in and out all day, but now he's up in the second ballroom," she told Dani. "He won't let you in. He hasn't let anyone else."

Dani was confused. "He called me."

Kathleen's brows went up. "Well, I guess that just says you're more special than the rest of us. Go ahead."

Dani climbed the wide marble staircase and found the plaque on the door for Ballroom 2. It was locked.

She knocked. "Mitch?"

Terence opened the door. "He'll be here in a minute," he said, trying to appear casual. A twinkle in his eyes.

Mitch slid out the giant double doors a minute later. Same twinkle. Camera in hand.

"What's going on here?" Dani asked.

Mitch propped his shoulder against the doorframe. "We're working on the display, that's all."

"That's all," she echoed dubiously. "I know Terence is good, but you have a staff here. Where are they?"

"I'm doing this one myself. Along with the kid prodigy you found me." He bent a kiss to her lips then lifted a camera. "Say 'cheese.'"

Dani was so surprised, she couldn't help but laugh. "Stop it," she said as he clicked off five or six quick shots. She put her hand in front of the lens. "I didn't really even come to see you. I came here to talk to Schmidt."

"So, that's how I rate," Mitch said. He handed the camera to Terence. "Schmidt's in the office at the apartment. I'll walk you over."

Stephen Housley arrived home at seven.

Mia was waiting for him.

While she waited, she'd considered several options: Fire. Accident. Burglary. But time was of the essence. She needed to try to catch Cole and also hoped to spend some time with Marshall this evening. He was beginning to worry her. He was cryptic about his whereabouts and nosy about hers. She didn't want him starting to keep tabs too closely.

So, in the end, simple expediency won out. Mia gave the sky a few more minutes to darken, went to Housley's front door and knocked, pushed him inside and shot him in the chest. When his wife materialized, she fired again, the woman stumbling back and sprawling onto the stairs. Mia stuffed the gun under her coat and walked—careful not to run—from the house. Got in Sarah's car.

A neighbor heard something and came out to her front porch, and Mia watched in the rearview mirror as she drove away. The neighbor cocked her head, looked up and down the street once, then went back inside.

Done.

And now, for a final message to Dani Cole. She'd have to have Fulton deliver this one.

Schmidt popped up when Dani and Mitch walked in. "Man, thank heavens you're here. I was just getting ready to call you."

"What did you find?" Dani asked. Schmidt was wired.

"Three adoptions so far that don't ring true. They all have my name on them, but I swear, Sergeant—and you, too, Mitch—I didn't facilitate them."

"You remember every adoption you ever arranged?" Dani asked.

He hesitated. "Maybe not. But you told me to look for something that raises a flag. These do."

"Okay." She sat down and he pulled the files. Mitch stood behind her. "Tell us"

"First, the travel. I make travel arrangements for the parents. This one's not right." He opened one of the files. "This is a boy from Kazakhstan. According to this, the mother traveled there once, for two weeks, to meet and bring home the baby."

"So?"

"Kazakhstan requires *both* parents to come, and they're required to be there a minimum of five weeks. It can be done in two separate trips, but if the couple is married, they have to both go. And it can't be only two weeks."

"But the mother did go?"

"I don't know. There was an airline ticket purchased; here's the itinerary. But I don't have any way of knowing if the ticket was actually used."

I do, Dani thought, her mind racing. *At least, Tifton and his Fed friends do.* But it didn't really matter, not if the number of weeks wasn't right.

"And this one," Schmidt said, his voice animated, "look at this. This is a baby girl, supposedly from Kyrgyztan. But the name isn't right for the baby pictured."

"What do you mean?" Mitch asked.

"Kyrgyztan has both Caucasian and Asian babies to adopt, and it's one of the places you can get them as young as six months. This baby was Caucasian—look at the picture—but the name on the birth certificate suggests she should be of Asian origin."

"So maybe she just doesn't look it," Dani suggested.

"I thought of that. But you told me to flag anything that stands out—"

"Let him go," Mitch interrupted. Dani could sense the anger building.

"One more. This is a girl supposedly from Estonia. Remember I told you Estonia only permits twenty U.S. adoptions per year? I checked with the government agency that tracks these things. She would make twenty-one."

Dani looked at Mitch, whose face had gone to stone. "God," she breathed. Schmidt was onto something. Put these together with the six-month-old boy the Kinneys adopted—who didn't look six months at all—and that was four, without even having access to the files the FBI now had. "So you're saying there's a good chance these adoptions, which on paper, were conducted by you through the Foundation—"

"—were actually black market sales using the Foundation as a cover," Mitch finished.

Schmidt shook his head. "I guess I don't know what these adoptions *were*," he said carefully, "but I know what they weren't. They *weren't* mine." He paused, then looked at Dani with a trace of worry in his eyes. "Detective, you're right that I might not remember every single case, but I don't make mistakes like this—not knowing how long the parents have to spend in Kazakhstan or not knowing how many adoptions are permitted through Estonia. It's my job to know."

"No one's accusing you of anything," Dani said. "We just need to figure this out."

Mitch was pacing. He looked like he wanted to kill someone.

"Look," Dani said. "I want you to keep going, Gary, but you're gonna have to do it with the FBI. They'll be calling you soon—they're the ones who crashed the files and I gave them your name. Just do me a favor." She paused. Had felt subversive all damn day. "If you find anything more for the Feds, call me with it, too."

"Will do," he said.

Mitch turned to Gary. "Where are these babies now? Who's the closest adoptive family?"

He checked. "These parents were from Illinois," Gary said, tapping on the names. "And this one from Alabama. But this one—the boy from Kazakhstan"—he looked and a gust of wind seemed to lift him up—"they live in central Pennsylvania."

Dani looked at her watch. Seven-ten. "Can you mapquest this address for me?"

"Sure." He exited the pages he had up on the computer

and came up with directions a minute later. "One hour and thirty-six minutes."

She looked at Mitch. "Let's go see a little girl from Estonia."

As they were leaving, Dani's phone rang. Mitch watched her answer and his blood ran cold. She looked like she'd just lost her best friend. By the time she disconnected, there were tears in her eyes.

"What?" Mitch asked, thumbing away the tears. "Who was that?"

"It was a guy from the vet's office. He said Runt took a turn for the worse, and she isn't going to make it."

"Aw, sweetheart, I'm sorry," Mitch said. The hurt in her eyes cut right through his chest. He dropped her jacket on her shoulders. "Come on. The vet is only a few minutes out of the way. We'll stop."

"No, it's okay."

"We'll stop."

When they got there, Mitch walked her inside. He couldn't seem to keep his hands off her. Her arm, her hand, the small of her back. He wasn't letting go.

"I'm here to see Runt," Dani said, her voice breaking.

The receptionist was unreasonably cheerful. "Oh, sure. Let me get the doctor for you, too."

A minute later, the doctor peeked his head out: "Come on back, Ms. Cole. This is gonna be one happy pup."

Dani started. She looked up at Mitch then back to the vet. "I thought—"

"She's doing great. Had a meal for the first time. Now we just need to get her through a day of normal pooping, and she'll be good to go."

Dani looked dumbfounded. She couldn't seem to speak. "But—"

Mitch took over. "About fifteen minutes ago someone called and told her the dog was in trouble. Going down fast."

The doctor pulled a face. "Runt's not going anywhere but home, in a day or so. I really think she's out of the woods."

Dani touched her chest. "Oh, God."

But it was short-lived joy. Dani pulled out her cell phone, hands shaking, and punched the last number up. Mitch looked and handed the phone to the doctor.

"That's not us," the doc said. "Our numbers all start with 752."

"Then why..."

Mitch cursed. "Someone doesn't want us to go see a baby from Estonia."

"But who?" Dani asked. "Gary Schmidt. He's the only one who knows we were going to the Averys'."

Mitch pulled her back outside. "So, maybe Gary called someone," he said, but couldn't believe it. Gary? He jogged across the parking lot, pulled Dani up short to avoid a car backing up, then ran to the Cuda and threw open the driver's-side door. Dani was two strides behind him, going for the passenger door.

"Damn it, Mitch, that doesn't make any sen—"

A shot rang out.

Mitch ducked, dropping behind the steering wheel. His heart stopped.

Dani.

He looked out the side. He couldn't see her; she'd fallen down beside the car.

"Dani!" He unfolded across the seat, shoved the door wide.

"Shit," Dani said; the door thumped her. She clawed up, using the door as a shield, her gun out and searching. On the street, a set of tires squealed, a muffler growling into the night.

"Are you all right, are you all right?" he demanded. He couldn't see any blood.

"I'm fine, damn it. *Go*. There." She used her gun to point and Mitch began to breathe again. She wasn't hurt. The car that squealed had turned. Nothing but taillights and smoke. He turned the ignition and lurched back out of the parking space, but he couldn't get out. Too many cars, too little space.

"Go, go, go," Dani said. She was dialing the phone, handling the gun, too. Mitch pulled into the street, following the direction of the car. "This is Sergeant Dani Cole. Eleven-fifty-four heading east on Forsyth, shot fired. I need backup."

Mitch kept driving, but after the first turn had no idea which way to go. He went one way, did a U-turn and went the other.

Dani spoke into the phone. "Dark car, small, maybe an Accord—"

"Corolla," Mitch said.

"Cor—" Dani stopped. She lowered the phone. "God-damn it."

"What?" Mitch gunned around a corner. Taillights and headlights, streetlights. That was it. Too dark.

"A Corolla. I saw that car today."

"Jesus, what?"

"It was on the street outside the Radisson. The muffler almost choked me."

He turned again, both of them searching the streets, and Dani spoke to Dispatch: "No, I don't know.

He's gone. But run Corollas with the suspects in the McNamara case, and let Tifton know." She blew out a breath and set the gun on the seat. "Damn, that's all I remember."

Mitch slowed down, giving up. They weren't going to find it. "Now what?" he asked, and Dani got back on the phone.

"Patch me through to Gibson," she said.

She gave Gibson the bare facts.

"What the hell are you doing out there?" he complained. "You're supposed to be holed up."

"I went to the vet to see my dog," she snapped. "The car was in the street, but the driver knew I was coming. He was waiting. Hold on." She checked the phone number again that had called her and rattled it off to Gibson. "He told me to come to the vet. It was a man. I didn't recognize the voice."

Dani glanced at Mitch and mouthed, *Brad?* Mitch nodded, whispering, "Check."

"Hey, Gibson. Find out where Brad Harper is."

"I know where he is. He's up in Jersey at his beach house."

"How do you know that?"

"He called. Said he wanted to get away, but we'd told him to stay in town. I told him it was okay to go."

"Check it, will you? Make sure that's really where he is. And find out if that number belongs to him."

Gibson disappeared for a minute, giving orders to someone. Then he was back. "Doing it, and I'll run the phone number you gave me. I'm coming to the vet with the team. Maybe we'll find the bullet, find someone who got a look at the vehicle, something."

"Look for the bullet in the bricks of the building on the north side of the doors. It went right over my head, I felt it."

"Show me when I get there."

Dani took a breath. "Chief, I need you to make a call for me, to some cops in Pennsylvania."

"What?"

"Please. Just forget my fucking father for once and trust me, will you? I need the locals to stake out a house. Sandy and Richard Avery, in a town called Wooten. Just have someone keep an eye there, out of sight. Have them call me if the Averys look like they're going anywhere."

"Dani, what the hell is this about?"

"It's about Rosie McNamara, I think. If you want confirmation, call Tifton. Please. Go make the call. If nothing happens in two hours, call off the surveillance."

Gibson called back five minutes later. Mitch and Dani were headed for the interstate. "It's done, Dani, you got your fucking cops in Pennsylvania staking out a family I know nothing about. I'm on my way to the vet. When I get there, you damn well better have a good explan—"

"What? Chief, you're breaking up . . . I can't hear . . . Stupid cell phone."

She hung up.

CHAPTER
42

MITCH HEADED INTO PENNSYLVANIA, pushing the Barracuda, feeling as if a time bomb were set to go off inside. His emotions were already raw; a day in Lancaster's lesser-known neighborhoods had done that, working with a kid who already knew all about them, and changing the entire concept of a show that had already been finished. Changing the entire direction of his career. Then he'd been confronted by indisputable evidence that his own Foundation was indeed trafficking babies, someone was killing mothers, and then...

Mitch's jaw clenched. He could hardly bear to think about the rest: *Then* Dani had been shot at. Jerked around by some fucking asshole into thinking her dog was dead, and shot at in a cramped parking lot like a deer that had been baited into a corral. She could've dropped on the pavement and bled to death in his ar—

He jerked his mind from that, clenching the steering wheel.

"You might wanna ease up on the gas there, stud," Dani said, and her voice snapped him back. "Rural deputies would like nothing more than to pull over a famous photojournalist and a cop in a vintage Barracuda."

He looked at the dash: Eighty-seven. Slowed it down to seventy-five but couldn't stop seeing what might have happened.

"I thought you were hit back there," he said, his voice scraping in his chest. "It fucking scared me to death."

"It happens, you know. I'm a cop."

"I don't know if I can live every damn day of my life worried that you're in danger."

She pulled back, her brows rising. "Then you better go back to the faraway places of the earth where you won't notice."

"Yeah, well..." Mitch hesitated, then shook the words from his throat. "I don't want to do that, either."

The Averys' house was a brick mansion with a four-car garage and a mailbox that looked like a small guesthouse. Dani hadn't called first—she'd made that mistake with the Kinneys—but the lights were on. Good. And a black-and-white squatted at the curb, just out of sight of the front windows.

Two officers got out of the squad car.

"Thing One and Thing Two," Mitch muttered.

"What?" Dani asked, then realized he was talking about the two cops. They were almost identical in stature, though one walked with a heavier stride than the other.

Dani introduced herself and Mitch, showed her shield, then told them the plan: "I just want to ask them some questions about the baby they adopted three years ago. We have reason to believe the adoption might not have been conducted legally."

The two officers looked at each other.

"What's the matter?" Dani asked.

One said, "Nothing. You wouldn't be the first to wonder about that baby, that's all."

Dani's pulse danced a beat. "What do you mean?"

"The baby died about three months after they got him," Two said. "SIDS—sudden infant death syndrome."

"Was there an autopsy?"

"Sure," Two said. She was a woman with a crew cut. "That's what first raised questions. SIDS can happen at nine months, but it's more common in younger babies. They said this one had been a preemie, so the ME looked at it with the adjusted age in mind... Still, there were some eyebrows raised."

Dani looked at Mitch, whose face was wooden. A chill ran down her spine.

"Come on," Mitch said.

"Hold it," Two said, and they stopped. She shifted on her feet, avoiding her partner's focus.

"Fisher," her partner warned.

"No, Weelkes. Man, we gotta tell them."

Mitch stiffened. "Tell us what?"

Fisher considered it for three more seconds, then said: "The ME at the time was Sandy Avery's uncle. A lotta folks around here think there might have been an investigation if that hadn't been the case, but..."

"Aw, jeez," Dani said. So no problem covering up the baby's real age. She threw a glare at Thing One, Weelkes. "Thanks a lot, man. You've been real helpful."

"Hey," he said, "these are good people. They lost their baby, and even if it wasn't quite a legal adoption, that sucks, you know what I mean?"

"Yeah, it sucks," Mitch said. He took a step closer to Weelkes, drilled those eyes into him. "You know what else sucks? That the birth mother might've been hacked up by a serial freak. *That* sucks."

It was time. Monika breathed deep, praying the baby held on. He was lower now. She felt as if the floor of her belly was going to give out and splat, the baby would land on the floor.

Don't be ridiculous, she told herself, that couldn't happen. There'd be a lot of pushing and shoving; she knew that much.

And it was time. The iceman had been in and out a lot today, and he had just come back in. She'd wanted to make her break before dark, but day or night, she was going. It wasn't like she'd be wandering through the wilderness on foot. The iceman had a car here—a truck, rather. Monika couldn't drive—she'd left home at fourteen and never gotten her license—but it couldn't be that much harder than driving the old tractor, or the riding mower. Of all the things she had to fear right now, handling a truck wasn't high on the list. It was nothing compared to facing the iceman. And the broker.

She went into the bathroom, where mirror shards were corralled in the bathtub. Two of the sharpest pieces sat on the counter—one only a few inches long, and the other the size of her mother's largest butcher knife. She'd measured the small one to be sure it fit in her pocket, and wrapped it in strips of sheet to keep it from slicing through her pants or skin. The large one she'd wrapped as well, but only the bottom third. Now, she picked it up, turning the padded handle in her hand, deciding which angle felt right. She opted for her right fist closing around the base with the sharp segment pointing behind her. Then, when the iceman came close...

She closed her eyes and envisioned it, playing through every conceivable action he could take—and her reaction—and when she'd gone through them all a third time, she took a deep breath and asked Jesus to guide her hand.

Monika pressed the bathroom door open so the iceman would be sure to hear her. She lifted the loose hem of her shirt and reached into the elastic waistband of her pants with a sliver of extra glass. She held her breath, worried about going too deep. She'd need to be able to move, maybe even run.

She almost chuckled at that. Run, with twenty pounds of belly and her feet swollen to the size of canoes.

She stopped, suddenly frightened. What was she thinking, trying to take on the iceman? What would happen if she failed?

What would happen if she didn't even try? That answer was all the motivation she needed.

Reaching around her belly, she maneuvered the glass shard against the bare skin of her thigh. She closed her eyes and pressed, drawing on the shard until she felt the bite of her skin splitting. She cringed and withdrew her hand, breathing like a freight train, then sat down and let herself bleed. Within a minute, the inside of her tan knit pants grew damp with blood, the stain creeping quickly through the weave. She pressed her legs together, spreading the stain to both her inner thighs. Then she picked up the glass butcher knife, folded to the floor, and palmed the butt of the makeshift knife in her hand.

She closed her eyes and murmured one last prayer: It was time.

Monika screamed.

• • •

Fisher and Weelkes introduced Dani and Mitch to the Averys: That first moment of greeting iced over the instant they were told it was about their baby. A pair of meaningful glances tossed between husband and wife, their responses carefully cryptic, and then—just five minutes into the conversation, though it was ten o'clock at night— Richard Avery said, "I'm going to call our lawyer."

And that was it, until the lawyer arrived. Thirty minutes, on hold. Nothing to do but stare at each other and wonder if Nika—Monika Wheeler—was still alive.

When the lawyer finally walked in, Dani stood. "You aren't a cousin or anything, are you?"

"Huh?" the lawyer said. Dani let it go, then laid out the reason they were there: "Here's what I think," she said to the lawyer, as if the Averys weren't sitting in the same room. "I think your clients bought their baby illegally. He wasn't from Estonia and they knew it. I think they lied about his age to cover that he was born here. Furthermore, when he died, the ME, being *close* to the Averys, might have covered suspicious evidence."

"Evidence of what? Are you accusing my clients of murdering their baby?" the attorney asked.

"Not at all." She looked at the Averys, softened a touch. "I'm terribly sorry about the loss of the baby, really I am."

"Aw, shit," Mitch said. Dani looked up, realized what he was doing, and shot, "Shut up, Sheridan." She turned back to the Averys. "My investigation has nothing to do with the baby *after* he came to live with you. I'm looking for the person who brokered the deal for you."

The lawyer: "They adopted through OCIN at the Foundation for—"

"Bullshit," Mitch said. "They *applied* to adopt through the Foundation, but someone else took over. Was it Brad Harper?"

The Averys went visibly white. Mitch turned up the heat. Stepped closer.

"There's an FBI task force working on it," he said. "In a matter of hours, they'll be all over you, and everybody in the town will kn—"

"Sheridan," Dani warned. He was actually pretty good. Dani spared a thought to acknowledge that even she might have been daunted by him in his current state: exhausted, suspicious, angry. She took the cue and tried to play nice.

"He's right about the FBI, but you can talk to me. I'll try to keep them off your backs."

Sandy Avery teared up, her husband covering her hand with his. The lawyer stiffened.

"Take it easy, Sandy," the lawyer said, but he looked worried. There was a leak in the hull and he knew it. This ship was going down.

"Don't take it easy, Sandy," Mitch said. "Forget that you opted to forgo legal channels in order to get an infant. Forget that you *bought* a baby on the black market. Think about the fact that you could be an accessory to whatever happened to the birth mother. All we need you to do is tell us who handed you the bab—"

"That's enough." The lawyer again, and Dani wanted to choke him. If the Averys hadn't called this bastard in, she would've had the story from Sandy Avery by now. She softened a little more. "Mrs. Avery, you didn't do anything so terrible, even if it wasn't lawful. I saw the files. I know the heartache you went through to have a child, the miscarriages, the fertility treatments. I can't imagine. All you wanted was a chil—"

"He was mine." Sandy Avery broke. Her lawyer came to the edge of his chair. "The birth mother didn't want him. She was unfit. She was a drug addict and a prostitute. She couldn't have taken care of him. He was *ours*."

She broke down, sobbing. Dani stood, but predictably, the lawyer stepped between her and his clients.

"This interview is over, Sergeant. If you want to talk to my clients any further, you'll need either an arrest warrant or a subpoena. Either way, you're finished here this evening."

"Al, wait—"

It was Richard Avery, but the lawyer, damn him, held up a quick hand. "Dick, don't say another word. I'm counseling you to keep silent until we've talked." And to Dani: "I'm going to confer with my clients, Detective. If we find there's anything to tell police—"

"Or the FBI," she reminded them.

"—or the FBI," he conceded, "I'll see to it that you're notified. Meanwhile, Detective, we're done."

The iceman was coming, just as Monika had planned. She could hear his heavy steps on the stairs, hear him enter the bedroom door and say, "Nika?" and then hurry toward the partially closed bathroom door. He pushed it open and saw her sprawled on the floor, her crotch bleeding, and he came over and bent down and Monika swung with all her might. The blade sank into the hollow beneath his jaw, hit something, and she pulled it out and shoved again. It went in hard, the sound like gristle tearing from chicken bones, until her hand hit his neck and she let go and the sheet-wrapped handle stuck out one side of his throat and the bloody mirror blade stuck out the other, like a Halloween costume her brother had once had. Monika stared and his hands fumbled at his throat, and then he gurgled and collapsed on her legs.

She squirmed and screamed, wriggling from beneath his weight. She got free and clambered to her feet, her clothes drenched with his blood. Her chest pumped like a bellows and she could hear small cries that must have been hers. The iceman was still alive: His legs bucked and his mouth gaped and the whites of his eyes lolled, and she started to run as far and as fast as she could, then remembered. He had a gun. And a phone. And keys.

The gun was right there at the side of his belt. She tugged on it, her breath coming out in a *whoosh* when it came into her hands. She looked for the phone and keys. Nothing. She worked hard turning him enough to reach his other pocket, but there was nothing there, either.

The baby kicked and she groaned, one hand finding her belly. The phone wasn't in his pockets; she had to get out of here. Taking the gun, the extra blade of mirror safely tucked in her pocket, she hobbled down the stairs. A couple of jackets hung by the door and she took one— the heaviest, in case she got stranded outdoors. She stuck her arms through and tucked the pistol in the big pocket, then her eyes landed on her salvation: keys, hanging on a hook right beside the door.

She grabbed them; they had the emblem of a Texas steer on the fob. A big truck, she imagined, remembering almost nothing about the trip here, but it didn't matter. Whatever it was, she was going to take it.

She stroked her belly. *It's okay, little guy*, she said. *We'll get home.*

She walked around the foyer—there *must* be a phone here somewhere—then heard a thump upstairs. She froze. No, it couldn't be. She clutched the jacket tight and sneaked back into foyer, peering up the stairwell. The thump came again and again, and she began backing away, praying, her lips moving on the words she repeated by rote, until suddenly he was there, on his feet and coming toward her.

It was a horror movie. It couldn't be real. But it was. Monika backed away, the sight stalling her brain. Her hips bumped into the door and she turned, grabbing at the handle, but her hands were slick with blood. It wouldn't turn, it wouldn't turn, and she whirled back around and the iceman was partway down the stairs, his legs like lumber and one hand clasped to his throat while the other reached out for Monika.

Her gut wrenched; the baby moved and her lower back seized with pain. Her knees buckled and she sank to the floor, and the iceman came closer. Monika doubled over in pain, then recognized the steel-hard shape pressed between belly and thigh.

The gun.

She stopped crying and groped in the pocket, her hand shaking as if she were palsied. The iceman stumbled but stayed on his feet, coming, coming, and Monika finally got her hand on the gun and stuck her finger on the trigger.

She pulled it from the pocket and pointed. Squeezed and squeezed and squeezed.

CHAPTER
43

THERE WAS NOTHING MORE from the Averys, at least not tonight.

"Let them stew, Mitch," Dani said. "Give their lawyer a chance to talk to them about the penalties for buying a child, and get them thinking about an investigation into the SIDS death."

"It *was* SIDS," Mitch said. "Or at least, probably, if the baby was as young as we think."

"Probably. But they won't want the investigation." She thought for a minute. "For such a humanitarian artist-type, you were pretty good back there at being the bad cop. Downright scary."

"I'm fucking *pissed*."

He wasn't the only one. Gibson had left a series of irate messages on her phone. Dani skipped over them and listened to the others. One was a report that Brad Harper was indeed at a beach house in New Jersey, and he was confirmed to have been there at the time of the shooting. One was Greg Holmes, reporting that the bust on Ty Craig hadn't happened. Instead, he had come into the station and was cooperating fully in the questioning, but didn't seem to know a thing...

The last one was from Tifton. Dani returned that one.

"Jesus, Nails, you ain't gonna believe it…Stephen Housley was shot dead. And his wife. Right in their foyer."

Dani's skin went cold.

"We started looking at him, just like you told us to—"

"Ah, Jesus," Dani said, her heart in her throat. "You think I fingered him?"

"I don't know how. Not unless you talked to someone other than me about it. Here's the other piece: The bullets look like .38s. So's the one they found outside the vet clinic."

Dani could hardly process it. The killer had been following her. She hadn't seen it. Been too busy on the lookout for the gray Fords of IA. "It's gotta be whoever called me about Runt."

"Probably. We checked the call. It was made on a prepaid cell phone. But it wasn't Harper."

"Why not Harper? Anybody can buy those."

"Because the cell towers that bounced the signal for that call weren't in Jersey. They were in northern Virginia."

"Virgi—" She stopped. Where Alicia was found.

"It's a big wilderness, Dani," Tift said, knowing what she was thinking. "Cell service towers are pretty spread out."

But her blood had turned to ice. "He was dumping Nika."

"We don't know that."

"Why else would he call me from the same vicinity where he dumped Alicia? Jesus, it's his dumping ground." Then she thought of something. "But if he was there, then who was following me?"

"That's the next thing. We found a Corolla dumped in a WalMart parking lot. Security says it's been there on and off for a couple days. The WalMart manager was getting ready to have it towed."

"And?"

"That car is owned by a woman named Sarah Rittenhouse."

Sarah Rittenhouse. Sarah Rittenhouse. The name didn't ring any bells. "Who is she?"

"I don't know, but I don't think she's the one who was driving."

"Why not?"

"Her body washed up on the bank of the Monocacy River this afternoon. She's in the morgue."

Dani felt as if she'd been hit in the head with a bat. Another woman dead—what did she have to do with any of this? It was getting too complicated, too spread out, and for the first time, true fear crawled down her spine. Not only for her life, but for her career. Gibson would want to know: *Why does Mrs. Housley's phone show a call from you?*

She tried to rally the anger. She hadn't done anything wrong. Off duty or not, she was just following leads, and giving them to Tifton almost as fast as she got them. The fact that she'd gotten the Housley connection through Ty Craig may have been a violation of Gibson's orders, but not of law. Talking to Ty Craig wasn't a crime.

Tipping him off about the raid was. How long did she have until Gibson hooked her for that?

Fruit of the poison tree.

"Nails," Tifton said, and sounded like he'd said it two or three times. "Your moving around has been a big help. But Gibson put an officer at the Radisson to watch your back." *I'll just bet he did*, Dani thought. "Maybe now would be a good time to let him."

Monika was out—driving the iceman's truck on a tiny, one-lane road, her eyes plastered to the short distance the headlights hit in front of her. She drove and drove, the pitch darkness and narrow hairpin curves making it impossible to know where she was headed. She struggled to reach the foot pedals and still see—her belly rubbing against the steering wheel—and held her breath through pains that came and went, came and went. These were different from the pains she'd been having. This, she knew without a shadow of a doubt, was labor.

The clock on the dashboard said 12:06. She'd driven for more than an hour until direction no longer made sense. For a while there had only been one road, so she knew she wasn't going in circles. She should have stayed on it; sooner or later it would have had to lead to somewhere, but no, she'd gotten impatient and turned, then turned again and again. After a while, she couldn't tell if she was headed toward the house or away from it, if she was going nearer or farther, up the mountain or down. There hadn't been a single other car in sight.

And then the rain had started. She was on a mountain in the forest in God-knows-where, it was raining, her baby was coming, and she had murdered a man. Maybe this was the punishment for her sins, her own private circle of hell. Heaven knows, she'd earned it. She deserved whatever she got.

But her baby didn't. That thought spurred her on. One thing was lucky; she had plenty of gas. And the pains, though almost unbearable when they happened, came with space in between. She still had time to find help. To get *somewhere*.

The tires ground and she gripped the wheel, trying to keep control of the huge truck. It dipped and jerked, and the noise of the road told her she'd hit gravel—the pavement, rough as it had been, had ended.

She stopped, breathing hard. This wasn't good. A gravel road late at night, in the middle of nowhere—she'd *never* pass another car if she stayed on this. She had to turn around, get back on something more traveled.

She put the truck in reverse and cranked the wheel. She had no idea how wide the road was, how much space she could use to turn. She opened the driver's-side door and looked down, but it was pouring now; she couldn't even see directly beneath her, let alone around the perimeter of the truck.

Still, she had to try. She gunned the gas a little, felt the tires spin in the mud and stopped, her heart jumping in her chest. Oh, God, please. She tried again and the tires spun more and she took her foot off the gas, found the overhead light in the cab, and turned it on. Think, think. What did her dad always do on those rare days when they had snow, or when he was climbing a steep or slippery hill? She took the gear shift and moved it two notches—to the L—then pressed, gently, on the gas. This time, the truck lurched back and she slammed on the brakes.

Okay. At least she wasn't stuck. Baby steps, now. Don't be impatient.

A spasm hit and she gritted her teeth, fingers clamped on the steering wheel. "Not now, not now," she said to the baby, and he seemed to hear her, the cramp fading away. She blew out a breath and shifted in the driver's seat, then went back to the business of turning—a few feet forward, a few feet backward with the steering wheel cranked as far as she could and still get some traction under the tires. Rain pounded like it must have on Old Man Noah, but she stuck with it, forward-turn and back-turn, forward-turn and back-turn, until once, she gunned it too hard and the back wheels dropped.

Monika froze. OhGodOhGodOhGod. She tried to stand on the brake, but she was tilted backward couldn't pull up from the back of the seat, the truck at an angle, lurching. It bumped backward. She knew it was getting away from her and tried to jump out but she was buckled—stupid habit—and she was trying to hang on to the wheel and jam the brakes at the same time, and suddenly, a warm gush flooded the seat beneath her, a faintly sweet smell rising to her nostrils.

"No, no, no," she cried. It couldn't be, not now. Monika shifted against the seat—yes, the seat was soaked, and she started in praying, in earnest now, repeating every set of words she could remember from her childhood, which wasn't, she thought illogically, so long ago. The truck bounced and lurched again, backward, barreling through the spindly trees and over rocks and underbrush, until it smashed into something hard and Monika's neck seemed to snap and the last thing she thought when the horn started blasting was, *Jesus, please, save my baby*.

At the Radisson, Mitch scouted the room as if the bogeyman might be waiting. Dani watched, her skin feeling cold. It wasn't a big deal, a cop getting shot at. That was what she'd told Mitch and she'd even believed it herself—at first. But now, knowing Housley and his wife had been shot dead within hours of Dani's visit, knowing some woman named Sarah Rittenhouse was dead and that

the person driving her car had an accomplice in the wilds
of northern Virginia, knowing Monika Wheeler was still
out there somewhere—it all added up to something that
made Dani feel true fear.

Mitch finished his inspection of the room and came up
behind her, his arms closing around her waist. He kissed
her temple. "You okay?" he asked, and Dani sank back
against him. Without warning, tears came.

He turned her around, wrapping her up. "Shh," he said,
"I've got you. I'm right here."

Dani sank against him, burying her face in his chest
and letting his body support her weight. Mitch stroked
her and held her and let her cry, and when the storm
had passed and she was breathing more easily again,
he smoothed the hair from her face and kissed her
forehead.

"I'm sorry," she said, struggling to get hold of herself
again.

"I'm not," Mitch said. "I waited eighteen years for you
to lean on me. I like it."

Dani laid her head back on his chest and closed her
eyes. *So do I.*

CHAPTER
44

Northern Virginia
Friday, October 8, 7:38 a.m.

FINGERS OF SUNLIGHT slipped between the trees, mist hovering on the mountain. Deputy Frank Goody hiked along a gravel road, worried, talking to himself... *There? No, no, that's nothing. Phew. Keep going...*

Frank was part of a hundred-yard-wide line of deputies armed with archaic maps of mine shafts and the knowledge that the FBI suspected another body. They'd started just before dawn and, at this time of year, would have about twelve hours of daylight. Frank was counting... *Two hours, then a break...*

He wasn't lazy; Frank was a wimp. He had no stomach for the more gruesome parts of a deputy's job, yet he always seemed to find himself the unlucky one, getting called to the worst accidents and nastiest crimes. He'd hurled his cookies more than once, gotten a reputation for it.

So he whacked through briars and stepped over puddles and muddy ridges hoping, if there *was* a dead girl to be found, *he* wouldn't be the one to find her. He clung to that hope until he saw a streak of underbrush unnaturally packed down in a wide line. Heart picking up speed, he climbed to the edge and looked through the foliage into the gully.

Frank was always the unlucky one.

Mitch rolled from bed and saw the motel's clock radio blinking at him. Morning.

He pushed back a pang of regret and woke Dani. "When this is over," he promised, nuzzling the side of her neck, "I'm going to take you someplace elegant. Make love to you all night and let you sleep in as late as you want. Do whatever you want during the day."

"Drive your Barracuda?" Dani muttered, eyes closed.

"Don't be insane." He ran his hands down the gentle curves of her body. "I have to get going," he said.

"Have fun."

"Uh-huh." He yanked the covers down. "You're coming, too. There's no way you're running around alone as long as the driver of the Corolla is still out there."

They hit the Foundation first so Mitch could change clothes and handle a couple of details for the exhibition. With the preview opening tonight, the place was buzzing. Dani was surprised by the hum of excitement in the air, thought she could almost get caught up in it herself if it weren't for the fact that an eighteen-year-old girl was in danger and her kidnapper taunting Dani. While Mitch spoke to Terence and his exhibit coordinator, Dani walked through some of the displays.

Mitch's work tore at the soul, but something else

struck Dani even harder. She stopped at one alcove and stared, unable to fathom the half dozen photographs there. They were labeled "premiere artist." They belonged to Terence.

Her eyes grew misty. A fifteen-year-old boy with a display in a J. M. Sheridan exhibition. Mitch had no idea what something like that would mean to a kid like Terence.

Yes, he did.

"Dani." His voice caught her by surprise. She spun. "Sorry," he said, "I didn't mean to scare you."

"I can't believe you did this for him," Dani said, her voice a little choked up.

Mitch scanned the photos. "He deserves it. He's good. And it will help make up for another kid who never got to display his." He took a deep breath, seeming to need to shake off a memory. "Besides, this exhibition is a departure for me, too."

"What do you mean?"

He held out a hand and Dani took it, following him to Gallery Two. Mitch went to an electrical cupboard and flipped some switches. A series of lights came up. "Have a look," he said. "See what you've done to me."

"What I've done t—" Dani stopped, looking around. Mitch's photographs stared back at her. All of them displayed in pairs.

"Oh, God," she said, disbelieving. She walked up to one. It was Chuck. He squatted in front of a wall at the railroad depot, his shadow broken up by chunks of cement. One hand, gray and dead, peeked from beneath the cuff of his coat.

Dani swallowed and looked at a photo beside Chuck's. This, too, was a grizzled man, but draped in robes instead of a coat and crouched in sand rather than on concrete. The sun threw his shadow out behind him, an elongated, bizarre shape with only one arm.

She moved to another pair of photos. A boy and girl, filthy and barefoot, playing a game with a die in front of a half-lit neon sign on Reading Road, a pair of discarded hypodermic needles on the concrete at their feet. Dani cringed and looked at the mate to that picture: a girl sitting cross-legged in the sand, her arms cradling a torn-up doll baby, an assault rifle leaning against a storage bin at her back.

Dani couldn't breathe. Every shot from Iraq had a twin from right here in Lancaster. A mother thousands of miles away, brown-skinned and veiled, crouching over a baby in front of a baked-clay home that had crumbled to the ground…A mother ten miles from Dani's house, white-skinned and bareheaded, crouching over her baby in the stairwell of a condemned apartment complex. A family, in loose clothing and sandals, carrying everything they owned away from their shot-out home…A family, in tattered overcoats, pushing a grocery cart piled with their belongings. A village of abandoned, burned-out buildings silhouetted against the desolate desert…A street of abandoned, neglected tenements rising against a panorama of McMansions in the distance.

And a boy and his dog. One pair in Iraq. Another in Reading. The one Mitch had seen on Wednesday night.

Tears clogged Dani's throat. This wasn't a show about Ar Rutbah. It was a show about Mitch's own backyard. It was a show about everywhere.

She turned, and her gaze snagged on one more thing. Just beneath the photograph of the local boy hung a label. *Gabriel.*

She blinked and backtracked to the previous display. Beneath the two American kids: *Nicki and Adam*. She turned back to the first set, saw the tag, and didn't need to cross back to the portrait in order to know what it read. *Chuck*.

"They have names," she murmured.

"Not all," Mitch said quietly. "Just the ones from here. And the ones I do in the future."

Dani looked at him, her heart swollen with emotion. "I don't know what to say."

"Say, 'You're welcome,'" he said. "You opened my eyes."

A smile grew from the inside out and Dani walked over to him. She stood up on tiptoe and kissed him with all her heart. "You're welcome."

Mitch wanted to keep her there, in his arms, in the safety of the gallery and the people and the cameras he knew would be everywhere, but he couldn't. A pregnant girl was still out there. A gunman with a thing for Dani.

"I need fifteen minutes," he said, crossing to one of the photos Russ had already had finished. "Remember I showed you these mat cuts on this picture?"

Dani looked. "Yes. You were going to redo it."

"I cut the mats yesterday, but then we had to put this photo back up here to check space and lighting. It'll only take a few minutes."

They took the photograph back to the workroom at the apartment and Mitch went to work disassembling the frame. Dani fingered the mats.

"Careful," he said, "you'll get prints on them."

She humphed. "Is that any way to treat the woman who inspired the exhibit?"

Mitch leaned over and kissed her. "Hands off."

He slid the first layer of mat from the frame and turned it over to look at it. The cut edged a full quarter inch into the mat board. "This is so unlike Russell," he said. "He must have already been worried about the Foundation when he cut these. Either that or he hired some help I'm gonna need to fire." He took out the second layer and it was almost as bad. And when he lifted the third, exposing the back of the image itself, he froze.

"Christ," he said, and in one fleeting instant, everything became clear. *Promise me you'll do the show…This one matters more than the others…* "He knew," Mitch said. "Jesus fucking Christ, Russell knew I wouldn't hang the photo this way."

"What?" Dani came over. "What are you talking about?

He reached to the back of the mat. A folded piece of paper was taped there.

"What's that?" Dani asked, then Mitch felt her recoil.

"There's no hair," Mitch said, reading her mind. He felt it with his fingers. "It's empty." He unfolded it, held it down for Dani to read: *Baby Boy Doe, b. February 12, 2008. Mother: Rose McNamara, age 16.* And a picture. A picture of the same infant who had been in the OCIN files as having come from Ukraine.

Mitch reeled. "'*You have to do the show, Mitch,*' Russ said. He made me promise. Because he knew I'd take it apart." Then the rest hit him: "'*If something happens…*'" Mitch looked at Dani. "He knew he was in danger."

He could hardly breathe. Russ had been worried, in danger. And Mitch had been on the other side of the planet.

"What does that say?" Dani asked, and Mitch looked

down. There was more. "'*Make SURE*,'" and the "sure" was in capital letters. Mitch couldn't make sense of it. "Make sure? Make sure of what?"

Dani read, "'*2793 A-H.*' What do those numbers mean?"

"It's pictures. Christ, Dani, he left me pictures." Mitch got up, heart racing, and went to the computer. "Twenty-seven—"

"—ninety-three, A-H," Dani finished. Mitch scrolled through files. Flying through them. They were all in order.

"Here."

He came to the file and thumbnails of a hundred shots dotted the screen. He held his breath and clicked on A, and the thumbnails reduced to a dozen. People, mostly. He peered at them but couldn't make out who they were.

"Go ahead," Dani said.

He was almost afraid to learn whatever Russ had known. He held his breath and clicked on a thumbnail.

And there it was.

"Oh, God," Dani said.

CHAPTER
45

"BRAD HARPER." Dani called Tifton with the news.

"Jeez, Dani, get off it. I told you, we have nothing on him."

"*We* do." She could feel Tifton's antennae go up. "Mitch just found a note Russell left behind. It documents Rosie's baby as the same baby that went to the Kinneys. It also pointed to some photos."

"What photos?"

"Brad Harper and Stephen Housley."

"Together?"

"Yes. They're meeting in a parking lot of some sort, I can't tell where."

"Hell, Dani. That's not exactly illegal."

"But it puts him with Housley, who was the doctor for four girls, all of whom are dead or missing."

"Yeah, okay. It's grounds for more questioning, but all he has to do is clam up. He knows it."

"There's one more thing. Russell knew Brad was involved. Or at least, he thought so. He stashed these pictures and the note about Rosie in a place he knew Mitch would find it. He also wrote, 'Make sure.'"

"Make sure of what?"

"That it was Brad. Don't you see? He was just starting to realize what Brad was into, but he wasn't willing to turn him in yet. It was his son, for God's sake. He didn't want Mitch to jump to conclusions, either. *Make sure.* 'Sure' is in capitals."

"Yeah, yeah, fine. Bring the evidence in, we'll put it in the hat with everything else. But just in case Monika Wheeler is still alive, we gotta keep moving. Which brings me to the owner of the Corolla. Single woman, thirty-six years old, worked as an office manager at some medical practice. She took a hit to the back of the head and drowned."

"A hit with what?"

"Something hard. Christ, I don't know."

"So what does she have to do with OCIN or babies or the other girls?" Dani asked. "Is she an ex-hooker? Adopted? Scarred? Patient of Housley? What?"

"None of the above. She's not connected, as far as anyone can tell. The task force isn't looking at her as someone involved with the baby ring. Rodgers and Flint caught her murder." Rodgers and Flint were two night-shift homicide dicks in the police department.

"You're not even going to look at her?"

"She has nothing to do with the shot fired at you last night. Only her *car* does. And her car, it turns out, was wiped down."

Damn it. "What about other employees of OCIN?"

"There's nothing there, Dani. I mean, I'm sure there is, but we can't find it. We conducted in-depth interviews with everyone. We got exactly *zero*. As far as we can tell, there's no one handling babies outside the traditional routes. Or if they are, they're lying so well we'll never catch them."

"Harper still signed off on the adoptions."

"But that's all: *signed off*. A formality. He uses a freaking stamp."

"Someone had to know."

"Like Gary Schmidt, you mean? Prove it. He looks at the papers, says, 'My name's there but it wasn't me,' and how're we supposed to argue with that? Harper says the same thing, if he says anything at all. But so far, he just says the babies came from where they came from and it's gonna take time to prove they didn't. You been in a Kazakhstanian orphanage lately?"

Dani cursed. "Did you look at bank accounts?"

"You mean, has Harper put any baby money away over the past few years?"

"Yes."

"No. At least not here." He paused. "Where're you gonna be today?"

Dani wanted to groan. "You mean, who's watching me?"

"Something like that."

"Don't worry. Mitch is playing nanny. But he has things to do here, and I'm gonna give Rodgers and Flint a call, follow up on Sarah Rittenhouse."

"Go for it. Flint's been hot for you for ten years; he'd probably love to have you along. And hanging with two other cops—that's a good thing."

Rodgers and Flint were only a mile away. They came by the Foundation and met Dani in the apartment. Flint carried a bag of donuts.

"Perpetuating the image," Dani said.

"Screw you. Man, this place is somethin'." He leaned in to Dani. "Where's the famous picture-dude?"

She whispered, a big secret. "He's in the workroom, looking at pictures."

"Ah." Flint nodded. An artist at work. It seemed to fit his image of Mitch.

"We just finished interviewing Rittenhouse's coworkers at the medical practice," Rodgers said. "No one knows a thing. The doc she worked for doesn't keep Friday hours. He has some big shindig to go to tonight so we wanna catch him early in case we need to come back to him."

"She have any connection to any pimps? Hookers?" Dani asked.

"Not that we've seen, but we aren't very far into it yet."

The unspoken expectation: Dig around enough and you can find dirt on a nun. "When was the last time she drove her car?"

Rodgers popped the end of a cruller into his mouth and spoke around it. "She disappeared right from the medical practice, over on Lynsdale Avenue. Drove there Wednesday morning then left. Left a note on her computer saying she didn't feel good, but we don't know if she went straight home or what. Doesn't look like she went to a doctor or hospital."

"Okay," Dani said, but it wasn't. Tifton and his Fed friends were right: Sarah Rittenhouse didn't fit. Dani shook her head, the words to a little kids' song floating through her mind... *One of these things is not like the other, one of these things just doesn't belong...* She picked up her purse. "I wanna ride along with you to the doctor. Tifton's feeding me task force stuff. Maybe I can put something together."

"I thought you were on vacation."

"Someone driving that woman's car tried to kill me last night. It put a little damper on my vacation plans," Dani groused. But she thought of Mitch, the worry in his eyes. "Hold on, I gotta go tell Mitch I'm with two heavily armed and highly trained professionals."

Flint puffed up a little, said, "Yeah, you do that."

Mia dialed Fulton again. Come on, come on, answer the damn phone. She let it ring to the voice mail and left yet another message—the third or fourth this morning. She hadn't heard from him since yesterday, when he promised to get Nika out of there.

"Damn it, Fulton, where are you? I need to talk to you," she said into the phone. "There's a story in this morning's paper about a manhunt for Nika, and police think it could be connected to Rosie and Alicia, maybe even Jill Donnelly. The FBI is in it, so it's not just some bumpkin county sheriff like you thought." She clenched her teeth. "*Call me.*"

She disconnected. Fulton had either taken Monika underground or decided to defy Mia and stay put, try to handle the sheriff's deputies with an innocence he would be hard-pressed to pull off. The helpful resident: *No, Sheriff…I haven't seen anyone around here dumping bodies in mine shafts…*

She checked the clock. It was nearly nine-thirty in the morning; she should be weaving in Nika's hair by now. With the preview tonight and Marshall's weekend obligations at the Foundation, she needed the day to work on Kristina's wig and finish her own hair to match.

She took a deep breath, feeling control slipping away. Little things were spinning from her grasp, like Fulton having disappeared and Brad getting spooked by the killings and Dani Cole tearing apart OCIN. Okay, not little things—big things.

And Marshall. He was distraught about something, but she wasn't sure what. The Foundation's future? Sarah Rittenhouse? It wasn't like Marshall to fret. He was calm and Socratic, ever solving other people's problems. Yet this week, things seemed to be spinning out of control for him, too. She'd never seen him so preoccupied.

She dressed for comfort, for a drive to Virginia, and slipped up to the workroom in the dormer to gather a few things. Her camera, the gloves, the pistol. The bottle of nitric acid. Her mother's shears. Everything into a Louis Vuitton handbag. She might not need them yet, but then again, Nika Love had been showing signs of early labor for a couple of days. Depending on where she was now and how much excitement Fulton had created, she could go at any time even without Dr. Housley's help. Best to be ready.

Now, for Marshall—he always took Fridays off. Mia thought about it, then decided she'd tell him she was going shopping for a new gown for the preview tonight. He wouldn't mind. He liked showing her off.

She added a pair of simple pearls to her ears, put on a hat that matched her coat, and headed downstairs. At the bottom, Marshall was just opening the front door.

"Dr. Marshall Kettering?" a strange voice asked, and Mia's nerves got a jolt. She inched a couple of steps closer. "I'm Detective Hal Flint and this is Detective Bill Rodgers and Sergeant Dani Cole. We'd like to talk to you about Sarah Rittenhouse."

CHAPTER
46

DANI FROZE. MARSHALL KETTERING? she stared as the doctor came forward, his wife, Mia, just coming down the stairs behind him. A striking woman. Tifton had referred to her as "the hottie."

"Sergeant Cole," Kettering said. "What a surprise."

Flint's brows went up. "You've met?"

"Yes," Dani said. "Just the other day, in fact."

So much for Sarah Rittenhouse having no connection to the baby ring. *One of these things is not like the others... Yes, it is.*

"You're the doctor Sarah Rittenhouse worked for?" Dani asked, but it wasn't a question.

Marshall Kettering gave a heavy nod. "Yes. Please, come in. I'm so shocked I don't know what to do. I thought it was strange that she just left a note on her computer, but to think she's dead... It's unreal."

Mia Kettering came forward and took her husband's arm, a possessive gesture Dani had seen when women were the jealous type. "Sarah had worked in Marshall's office for nine years," she said. "We just can't believe someone would kill her."

"Yeah," Dani said. "There's a lot of that going around."

Twenty minutes later, they had learned precisely nothing. Marshall Kettering seemed genuinely stricken by the idea that someone could want to hurt Sarah Rittenhouse, and further aghast that someone had later used her car to try to hurt Dani. He said he could think of no reason for anyone to want to hurt Sarah, that there was nothing about her life that could even raise an eyebrow.

But he was lying.

Dani studied him as Flint and Rodgers handled the interview. He was good, except for that involuntary dart of his pupils to the left, the fingers of one hand rubbing together deep in his pocket. Marshall Kettering—JMS Foundation board president—had something to hide.

Dani listened until there was nothing new, then excused herself while Flint and Rodgers hung behind with Dr. Kettering. They knew the drill.

"I'll walk you out," Mia said and followed Dani into the hall. She cradled her designer handbag against her body, as if fearful of losing it.

"So, I suppose I'll see you at the Exhibition tonight?" In other words, *Since you're sleeping with Mitch, you'll be on his arm this evening?*

"Probably," Dani said, then couldn't help herself, "unless I catch a break and solve this case instead."

Mia went a little pale. So, Mia knew her husband was lying, too.

"Well, not that I don't want to see you there," Mia said, "but I hope you get that break. These murdered girls, right here in Lancaster—it's frightening. And now Sarah and you're telling us there was an attack on you, too. I just don't know what the world is coming to." She rubbed her hands together, the right one striped with little red scrapes on the knuckles and down the backs of her fingertips.

"What did you do to your hand?"

"Oh, I scratched it on some cement when I stumbled. Clumsy of me." Then she swallowed, glanced to the closed door of the study. Nervous.

"Mrs. Kettering," Dani began.

"Call me Mia."

"Mia." Buddies now. "If there's something you think you know about Sarah Rittenhouse's disappearance, you can tell me. I can see there's something bothering you."

"Why would you say that?"

Dani stepped closed, pushed another inch. "Your husband is lying, Mia, I already know that. Flint and Rodgers know it. That's the reason I left those two in there, to work him over without you." Mia straightened, aiming for the study door, but Dani put out a hand to stop her. "It's a little game we play and, well, my partners in there are gonna break him down and I guarantee he'll crack. Those guys are good." Bullshit on top of bullshit. Dani deserved an Academy award.

Mia closed her eyes, then opened them again. Tears. "He didn't kill her, I know he didn't."

"Okay..." Keep her rolling.

"But you're right, he *is* covering something. Marsh was... He told you he didn't know about anything going on with Sarah, but he did. He'd just found out..."

"Found out what?"

"That she was stealing from him—drugs. Sergeant Cole, we were at dinner Tuesday night and he told me he was going to fire her. Marshall said she'd been tampering with pharmaceutical orders for months. He was furious. He could lose his practice over it."

Dani was leery. "Toxicology didn't find any drugs in her system."

Mia looked at her as if she were an idiot. "They weren't for her. She was selling them."

Huh. "Mia, where was your husband on Wednesday morning?"

Mia shook her head, the tears beginning to fall. "At work, I thought."

"Okay, jeez." Dani wasn't good with crying women. Especially when it was over a man. "And where was he last night, around seven forty-five?"

Now Mia looked at her, and dawning seeped into her eyes. "Oh, dear God," she said on a hush. "He was out. I don't know where."

Rodgers and Flint came out a minute later. The three of them said their good-byes and piled into Flint's car.

"Anything?" Dani asked.

"He's lying about something," Rodgers said, "but he didn't crack. He's a tough old bird. What about the wife?"

Dani said, "I let her think you two were putting the thumbscrews to the doc. She told me Marshall Kettering was planning to fire Sarah Rittenhouse. She'd been stealing medications from the practice."

The two detectives exchanged a look. "That fits," Flint said. "A receptionist at the practice said they'd been having some trouble with the inventory, and Kettering's partner confirmed that the doc seemed on edge lately."

Dani felt the kick of adrenaline. Marshall Kettering was tied up in this somehow. "I'd like to know where Kettering was when someone was shooting at me last night from Rittenhouse's car."

"He says he was at the club."

"His wife said she didn't know where he was."

Flint and Rodgers looked at each other, sighed. They were used to it. Everyone lied to cops, sometimes even the innocent ones.

"Okay," Rodgers said. "So we'll let them talk it over and come back and ask again. Five bucks says one of their stories will change. But let's go to Sarah Rittenhouse's apartment first. See if we find any pills with Kettering's name on them."

They started out and a phone bleeped. All three of them reached for their waists. It was Dani's.

"What?" she asked, expecting it to be Mitch, hovering, even though he knew she was with two other cops. But it was Tift. He was wired.

"Dani, I'm in Virginia. They found Monika Wheeler. She's alive."

Dani's breath stopped. "Oh, God."

"And the baby's alive, at least so far. She's at a hospital—we just got here. They're doing surgery for the baby. A deputy found her at the bottom of a gully in a truck..."

He spent all of thirty seconds on the details, breathless, moving fast. Dani jotted down each point, wishing she were in the thick of the case. This was the biggest break an investigation could get: a victim who survived.

"Who owns the truck?" Dani asked.

She heard papers juggling as he walked. "His name is Ronald Fulton. Long rap sheet. No job, no address. But drives a brand-new Dodge Ram. We're putting together a file on him."

"Did he ever do time?"

"Yeah. Eight months for robbery in Texas and three years for attempted murder. The gun misfired, so instead of killing the guy at the other end, the victim lost the hearing in one ear."

"What kind of gun was it?"

"I don't know, I'd have to check. Why? You're thinking he got it fixed and fired it at the vet's last night?"

"It's a thought."

"I'll look for a phone call to you. But seems odd he'd be in Virginia. Still, the fact that he did hard time means we have DNA," Tift continued. "If it's his blood all over Monika Wheeler, we'll find out."

"And she hasn't said anything about the broker or selling the baby?"

"It's all rambling. *Don't take my baby, Jesus, forgive me*—stuff like that. But I'll tell you what, Dani, this kid planned for a fight. She had a shard of mirror wrapped up as a weapon in one pocket, a recently fired pistol in the truck."

"Oh, God."

"A couple of us from the task force are joining up with the field office here and a half dozen sheriff's departments. They're getting cadaver dogs and using radar on any old mine shafts they find. The search team's like an army now. Interviews have turned up two more girls who moved or left lately, whose friends say they once had babies."

"There's gonna be more," Dani said.

"Yeah." Tift went quiet. "But at least we've got this one."

One victim, still alive. That was huge. "Okay," she said, genuinely relieved for him. "Go do your thing, buddy."

CHAPTER
47

Panic pulsed through Mia's veins, all the way to Virginia. Sergeant Dani Cole, still kicking, still digging, and getting far too close. Brad was nervous, Marshall distrusting, and Nika and Fulton had dropped out of sight.

Threads unraveling.

She'd left the house the minute the police were gone, turning on the radar detector and blowing past traffic, through small towns and out into the narrow mountain roads, until suddenly, no more than two miles mile from the cabin, she saw the commotion.

Mia frowned. She went no farther, edging to the side of the road to watch, the roadblock a good ways down the road—at the cabin's gate? Two black-and-white police cars, and a brown county sheriff's vehicle. She lowered the window and looked up. A chopper orbited in the sky.

"Dear God," she said. Her heart hammered. Her cabin? It must be. There was nothing else within miles. Unless...another body? Had Fulton really been fool enough to dispose of another body so close to the cabin?

And where the hell was he?

She sat at the side of the road for a good five minutes. Think, think. She turned on the radio and tried to catch some news. Nothing. She closed her eyes, trying to imagine what could be happening.

Finally, she couldn't stand it anymore. She checked her face in the rearview mirror and smoothed back her hair. County sheriffs and state patrol officers were mostly men, and men always talked to Mia.

She pulled up in the Saab and slowed when a deputy stepped into the road and flagged her down. Closer now, she could see that a number of other emergency response vehicles lined the long drive, as well. The area was teeming with law enforcement.

Her fingers clenched on the steering wheel and she lowered her window. Put on her innocent housewife demeanor. "Deputy?" she asked. "My goodness, what's going on? I need to get through."

"Sorry, ma'am, not now. We're blocking this off for a little while, to let the crews get in and out."

"But my mother lives in Addison, a few miles west of here. She's waiting for me to take her to the doctor."

"You'll have to call her and tell her you'll be late. We can figure out a detour for you—"

"No, no. I'm afraid I'd get lost." She looked at the drive that disappeared into the woods toward her cabin. "What's happening up there?"

The deputy looked down, took off his hat, and scratched at a spot above his ear. "I can't really talk about it."

Mia laid her hand on her breastbone. "Oh, dear, oh, dear," she said, letting a thread of panic fray. "It's not...Oh, no, Mother will be heartbroken. Deputy, I think my mother knows the person who lives back there...Is there a cabin?"

He nodded, interested now.

"Oh my, tell me no one is hurt in there," she said, pointing at an ambulance waiting on the road.

The deputy bent down to her window. "You say your mother knows who lives there?" he asked, concern on his face.

"Oh, no, someone *is* hurt. What happened?"

"I'm afraid someone has died there, ma'am. We don't know who it is. Do you know who lives here?"

Oh, God. *Nika.* Stay calm. Play it out. "Well, I don't know...Was it a young girl, with dark hair?"

He let out a breath. "No," he said. "It was a man. Big dude."

Mia gawked. "What happened?"

"Someone stabbed him through the throat then shot him five times."

Mia was speechless. *Fulton?* But that means Nika...No, no. Where was Nika? "No girl?" she asked, and now her shock was real.

"No, ma'am. Could you have the wrong house?"

"You know," she said, "yes. I must have been thinking about another cabin. Thank you, though. I think I'll take that detour now."

On the way to Rittenhouse's apartment, Dani got another call from Tifton. He was running at the other end of the phone.

"Monika's hanging on, but not coherent. We can't get anything out of her."

"What about the baby?"

"They think he's okay. They're getting ready to take him. Her parents are here."

Okay. Dani closed her eyes on something that might

have been a prayer. "You gotta find the owner of the truck she was driving, Tifton. That Fulton guy."

"That's what I called to tell you. We did find him. He's dead."

"What?"

"We're keeping it out of the news until we get a handle on things. He was in a cabin deep in the mountains—the dogs and scouts finally found it. Looks like Monika was here. She broke a mirror and stabbed him through the throat with it, then shot him five times."

Dani was flabbergasted.

"They're trying to find out who owns the cabin now..."

Dani couldn't hear him. Her blood drummed in her temples. That poor girl. The images of this night would stay with her forever. She'd spend the rest of her life trying to put them from her mind.

How dare someone put her through something like this? Why couldn't someone have spared her some of this? Why couldn't someone stop the madness now?

The rage climbed on top of her. Someone could. If they only would. "The other adoptive parents," Dani said. "The ones Gary Schmidt flagged—"

"Field offices all over the country are talking to them— Schmidt flagged ten. But you're talking about parents and their *kids*, Dani. Which one of them is gonna come forward and say, 'Oh, you're right, she's not really ours...' They put some warrants in front of judges this morning, asking to force some DNA. But these parents aren't just afraid of jail. They're afraid of losing their *child*."

Except one family, Dani thought. They'd already lost theirs.

She said, "I need the pictures—of the crime scene and

of Monika, the way she was when she came in to the hospital. E-mail them to me."

"Jesus, it's gruesome, Dani. Why do you want them?"

"Just trust me, Tift, okay? What have you got to lose?"

He thought about it for a moment, but Dani knew he'd do it. Tifton did trust her. And this case had just about done him in.

"Okay," he said. "It'll take me awhile to get them together. Give me an e-mail address..."

Dani asked Flint to drop her at the Foundation, at Mitch's apartment: She needed a computer.

The photos arrived forty minutes later. Dani looked at them and nausea seized her gut. The man, Fulton, lay pulverized at the bottom of the stairs, a spear of mirror through his throat and several bullet holes in his body. Blood everywhere.

Dani called Thing One and Thing Two, in Pennsylvania. Shot the whole collection of pictures to the PA computers and got a call back within ten minutes.

"Holy Christ," Two said. It was the woman named Fisher and her voice had the thready quality of someone in shock. "And you want me to show these to the Averys?"

"Take their lawyer with you," Dani reminded her, hearing someone knock at the apartment door out in the living room. Mitch answered it. Angry words. "Shock them into agreeing to a DNA test for their baby. Cross every i and dot every t—don't get anything that could be thrown out of court later."

"I'll do my best."

Dani hung up and went out to the living room. She saw the look on Mitch's face first—unadulterated fury—then the two uniforms in the doorway.

And then, Chief Gibson.

CHAPTER
48

MIA DRESSED FOR THE EXHIBITION preview in a daze. She didn't want to go, she wasn't even sure she could think. How could she arrive at the Foundation on Marshall's arm, making small talk when Fulton was dead and Nika Love was out there somewhere?

Tomorrow was Saturday. If she didn't have Nika's hair by morning, there would be no way to finish the wig in time to meet Kristina.

She went upstairs, all the way to the dormer, and turned on the lights. Perhaps, if things didn't turn out right, she could bring Kristina here, *show* her everything she'd done. The women's portraits scarred for life. Their hair on the wig block, woven one fine strand at a time into the wig that would make Kristina as beautiful as she deserved to be, as beautiful as her mother. Were there still facial scars, as well? Probably, but Mia knew people. She'd get Kristina the best cosmetic surgeon there was and restore Kristina to the beautiful child she once was.

Mia opened a cupboard and pulled out a scrapbook. Marshall thought she kept photos of Kristina as a baby in here, pictures that preceded the fire. But that's not what it was. It was copies of the court transcripts and evidence photos, the file she'd come across on Marshall's desk the night Kristina turned eighteen. The night Mia had learned the truth.

Her fingers trembled as she opened the book and touched each little black-and-white photograph. Kristina, ruined. Kristina, in pain. Kristina, on display for the courts so they could take her away. Mia had never been allowed to see her or hold her or touch her again after the fire. She was an unfit mother...

And Marshall. There was no picture of him here, but there were his words to the court. He'd taken her side and tried to make them understand.

Dear, dear Marshall, Mia thought. He'd been enamored with her way back then. Yet the court was unimpressed. Kristina had been taken into the State's custody. Mia had battled for two years, fallen for Marshall and his pledges to someday help her get Kristina back. Mia hadn't understood the move to Maryland until later, but when she learned that Kristina was here, and her adoption records would be unsealed on Kristina's eighteenth birthday, it all became clear. Marshall had brought her to be near her daughter.

Mia lived for that day. But when the day came, instead of seeing Kristina, she'd seen this file on Marshall's desk. A two-year-old, brutally burned, the left side of her face and scalp ruined...

That was three months ago, the beginning of the carnage. She learned about Brad's girls, selling their babies when Mia had lived her entire adult life without hers. One girl was still at Brad's beach house—had given birth only hours before. Mia went there, shears in hand, her own locks still scattered on the floor of her bathroom.

She might not have known what she was going to do when she left, but she'd known an hour later, when Heather Whyte's scalp looked like baby Kristina's and a shock of long brown hair was in Mia's hand. The shears dripping...

And the plan took shape, a way to make Kristina whole and beautiful again, to give back her hair and her life and her mother. A beautiful wig, made of Mia's gorgeous locks, infused with reminders that proved Mia's love.

A clock chimed and Mia looked up. *Time, time.* Marshall had finally accomplished the goal. He'd spoken to Kristina and set the date and time. And last week he'd handed Mia the beautiful note that was the most precious gift he could have ever presented: *Next Sunday, 7:00 p.m.*

Worry prickled Mia's skin. What if she couldn't find Nika in time? What if Nika had decided to keep her baby, what if she wasn't one of them? What if Fulton had panicked and told someone where Nika was?

She walked into the display of photographs in her own personal museum, touching each ruined face. When she got to Nika, something inside her dissolved. Nika was gone. Mia wasn't going to be able to get her back. Police were too close and Fulton was dead. The FBI was in full swing.

She turned to the image of Dani Cole. A feather of a thought touched her mind and she walked over to that photo.

Dark hair, thick, and smooth, porcelain skin.

Nika was gone. Dani Cole wasn't.

"Mia?"

She jumped. She shoved the photos into the scrapbook and hid it away, hurried from fixture to fixture killing the lights.

"Mia, are you up there?"

She opened the door. Marshall stopped halfway up the stairs.

"Darling," he said, looking worried. "I've been looking for you. It's almost time to go."

Be calm now. A fancy social occasion; Mia was good at those, and Marshall would be even more suspicious if she showed any signs of distraction. "I'm almost ready," she said, stepping down the narrow staircase. When she reached the step with Marshall, he didn't turn to go back down, but peered at the door at the top. "Pictures again?" he asked.

She swallowed. "I just thought, maybe, she'd want to learn about us, me. I want to be able to help her know us—"

"Stop," Marshall said, and Mia blinked. It was uncharacteristic for Marshall to be sharp.

"What's the matter?"

He seemed at a loss for something to say. "What if Kristina's not…the way you think?" Mia frowned. He'd never been anything but encouraging before. "I just mean, maybe you need to prepare yourself…Even though she agreed to come, she may not be what you hope."

Mia laid her hand on his cheek, the beard prickly against her hand. "You've met her, Marshall. You said she was looking forward to meeting."

"She was, yes, but…" he stammered.

"I think you have too much going on right now to enjoy the excitement. You need to get Sarah out of your mind for tonight and stop worrying about Kristina. This is our special weekend—you with the exhibition and me with Kristina."

She wasn't sure she was being very convincing but

gave her hair a toss and started down the stairs. Marshall stopped her. "Mia. You aren't keeping up with your medications." He held out two of the little pills he'd used to help keep her sane all these years. "Take them. You know how important they are."

Stay calm. Don't give him cause for worry. "Of course," she said, and popped them into her mouth. "Let's get going. You don't want to be late."

Marshall held her hand down the rest of the stairs and to the bedroom. As soon as he wasn't looking, she spit out the pills.

Tonight she'd get Dani Cole *and* her hair. It wasn't a night to be sane.

Dave Gibson stood at the Foundation apartment door with two officers in tow.

"What the hell are you doing here?" Dani said, coming to the door.

As if she didn't know.

Gibson shot a glance to Mitch. "Is there somewhere we could talk? This would be better handled in private."

Mitch looked down at Dani. "Do you want to handle this in private, sweetheart?"

Dani cringed, her hands tightening into fists. "Oh, I don't think that's necessary. You have something to say, Chief? Oh, wait, I'll save you the trouble and say it for you." She lifted her chin. "I tipped Ty Craig about the raid."

Gibson's face tightened. "Sergeant, let's go someplace."

He was worried; she could almost smell him start to sweat.

"I don't want to *go someplace*," Dani said.

"This is grounds for dismissal, Sergeant." Gibson's teeth clenched. "You don't think I'll fire you, but I will."

"You're wrong, Chief, I know you will," Dani said. And she had a pretty good idea why, something that had been niggling at the back of her brain ever since she'd spoken with Ty Craig. *Fruit of the poison tree.* Strange colloquialism to be used by both of them.

A vein throbbed to life on Gibson's forehead. "I'll take your service weapon and your badge, Cole. And I'll have your locker emptied out. Come by tomorrow and get your things."

She slammed the door behind him and stood for a moment, breathing hard, afraid to turn around and face Mitch. She could feel him standing there, felt the sear of his gaze and the weight of his silence. Thinking she was just like her father, no doubt.

Finally, she turned. "Well?" she said. "Is there something you'd like to say?"

Mitch nodded. "You're beautiful when you're angry. But remind me not to piss you off."

Mitch left Dani locked in the apartment to dress for the preview. He'd sent Russell's assistant shopping for something—he didn't want Dani going back to her house. Two hours later, while Dani had been out with Flint and Rodgers, several hangers and bags from a couple of the nicer stores in town had arrived. Mitch offered to stay and watch Dani try things on, but she threw him out.

By six o'clock, the hype had started: VIPs and media, tuxedoed men and bejeweled women, board members and critics all milling and sipping champagne. Cameras were running, reporters standing in front of picturesque portions of the property, talking in excited voices to the little green light flashing at the cameraman's forehead. It was a spectacle—all because Mitch had been caught in a terrorist attack and lived to show pictures of it. It made him sick to think he'd almost given them exactly that.

Mitch used the back entrances, avoiding the lower-level circus, and did one last walk-through of the exhibition, carrying an extra print with him: Brad and Housley. It was clear that the FBI wouldn't get back around to Brad for a while, and what better place than in the middle of two hundred important guests to solicit Brad's reaction? Mitch went to a portrait right in the middle of the new display he and Terence had set up, replaced his photo with one Russell had taken. Slipped his behind the door in an alcove, to switch them out again after Brad got a peek.

He exited the back door of the ballroom and down a narrow stairwell, moving through the dark tunnel with the ease of a man who'd done it hundreds of times. He didn't think of anything but getting back to Dani—getting her dressed up and showing her off tonight, keeping her safe and close—until a figure stepped out and slid an arm around his throat.

CHAPTER
49

MITCH TURNED TO STEEL, the man's breath right in his ear.

"You know what to say," he demanded. The stance, the voice, the words were all familiar.

"Fuck you," Mitch said, and broke free. They both staggered a step, then straightened. Mitch looked at his brother in the dimness of the tunnel.

"I could've had you," Neil groused, making Mitch wonder how many times they'd done this as kids. In the drainpipes under the park, with bricklike walkie-talkies and imaginary foes. In those days, the good guys always won.

"You were about to get thrown on your ass," Mitch said. "Except I heard a rumor that you've turned soft lately, so I didn't want to hurt you."

Neil scoffed, and the ritual of their meeting melted away. Tension rolled in, filling the space between words. Even in the shadows, Mitch noticed the ragged scar that ran along Neil's jaw and crooked beneath his chin, and winced. He'd never really gotten used to seeing it—testimony as to how much time they'd spent together in the past decade.

"What's her name?" Mitch asked.

"Beth. We're getting married next month."

"Rumor says you saved her from a madman."

"She pretty much saved herself; I was just there."

Mitch studied him. *I was just there.* Simple words, but big ones. Neil had never been there—not for Dad's death or the aftermath, not for his daughter and wife later on. It was Neil's MO not to be there.

Until Beth, apparently. Scary what a woman could do to a man.

"You know I came to Switzerland," Neil said. "A couple times."

"Or five," Mitch said. He knew. "I was a little fucked up."

"Russell told me about the kid. Is he the one up there in the gallery? All the pictures?"

Mitch closed his eyes, nodded.

"It's not your fault he died." Neil paused. "It's not your fault Dad died, either."

Mitch couldn't speak but looked at him. The brother who'd gone away because Mitch let go.

"I've been wondering," Neil said. "Is there a number?"

"Excuse me?"

"A number. How many people do you have to save before you let Dad go?"

Mitch's heart took a tumble, and pure truth poured out. "One," he said. "Come on. I think you should come meet her."

Dani couldn't get the zipper up. It was a sleeveless silver dress that hugged too low on the chest, too high on the leg, and too close all over. No wonder she couldn't get the thing zipped.

She heard the door and went to the living room, cursing the spiky heels. Her hands clasped the dress together in the back. "Mitch?"

She blinked. A second man came in beside him. The man's gaze dropped to her shoes and back, blue eyes glittering and an appreciative half-smile growing on his lips. He looked just like Mitch, except for the scar twisting along the stranger's jaw.

He held out a hand. "I'm—"

"Special Agent Neil Sheridan, FBI," Dani said. He was a legend in law enforcement circles. She looked at his extended hand and her cheeks warmed. "I can't exactly let go to shake hands."

Mitch cursed and moved behind her, tugging the zipper up.

"Now," Neil Sheridan said, and offered his hand again. "You're—"

"Dani Cole. Detective Sergeant, Lancaster P—" Not anymore. Well, shit. "Dani Cole." She pulled herself together, glanced at Mitch and then peered up at Neil. "So," she said, "do all you FBI types know what the other FBI types are doing?"

"You mean did I know about the task force that's trying to bust up a baby ring? No. I was lent out to a case in Santa Fe until this afternoon. But I asked around when I found out Russ and the Foundation were involved. I'm caught up except for the latest."

Dani gave him the latest, trying to ignore Mitch, who paced back and forth in his tuxedo, chomping at the bit to move. "I gotta go," he finally said. "It's past seven and the upstairs galleries open at eight. I want time with Brad first, and before he's stoned out of his mind."

Neil frowned. "You both said Brad is using. But you don't think he's the one who broke into your place and poisoned your dog?"

Dani closed her eyes. "He didn't run like Brad. Brad's an athlete, like a tennis player. This guy ran like...he had a blister or something."

"Or was stoned?"

She thought about it. "Could be."

"Maybe that's where Sarah Rittenhouse fits in," Mitch said. "Stealing drugs from Kettering and selling to Brad."

Dani shook her head. "She's clean as a whistle and the closest she's ever come to a museum is at the movies."

"But Marshall said he suspected it for months," Mitch said. "You told me he was going to fire her over it."

"*Marshall* didn't say that," Dani corrected. "Marshall's *wife* did—" She stopped and stood up, her own words pricking her brain. Her words and the image of the prowler running in the night, an awkward gait that had made her think the perpetrator had a blister or something. They'd found a boot print near Rosie—a man's boot, size eleven. But what if a woman had been wearing them? Running in too-big boots would look much the same. "Jesus, we're not doing this right," Dani said. "All along we've been thinking about a man killing hookers, keeping trophies. Like some religious freak cleaning up the world or having some sort of hatred toward women, or something. But what if it's a woman?"

"A profiler wouldn't go for that," Neil said. "Female serial killers are rare. And when they do kill, they kill children, not other women. Occasionally a string of husbands."

"But there are plenty of cases out there where a woman

has done something incredible to get a child. Why not kill a child's mother?"

"This killer isn't getting the children," Mitch reminded her. "That logic doesn't follow. Besides, it was a man who lured you to the vet's office and took a shot at you."

But Dani couldn't let go of the notion. "What if it's something else motivating the killer? A lost child or something." She looked at Mitch. "Does Sarah Rittenhouse have children? Did she ever want them, maybe give one up?" Then she thought of Mia, pointing a finger at her husband. "What about Mia Kettering?"

"Hell if I know," Mitch said. "Marshall has some kids, grown. I think they were grown before he married Mia."

It was a long shot, but she couldn't get the idea out of her brain. She picked up her cell phone and dialed Flint.

"Aw, Dani, I can't work with you. Jesus, Gibson is all over us. What happened?"

"You can read about it in tomorrow's paper," she predicted. DIRTY COP TURNS CRIMINAL; DAUGHTER FOLLOWS FOOTSTEPS. "Meanwhile, I don't want to go anywhere with you, I just need to know one thing," she said. "When you went back and quizzed Marshall Kettering about his whereabouts last night, what did he say?"

"He was at the golf club, having dinner."

"Did you check that?"

"Yup. Two dozen people confirmed it. A couple of them had asked where his wife was because they usually go there together, and he told them he'd asked her along but that she didn't want to come."

"So Mia knew where he was that evening?"

"That's what I gather."

Dani hung up. "Mia Kettering is lying. I wonder what she's covering." She turned to Neil. "Police say the only thing the FBI is good at is looking up old paper. Can you look up old paper?"

Neil smiled. "It's what we do best."

Watching Mia Kettering grow up in the documents Neil found was like watching someone go down in quicksand. She never had a chance.

She began life as Mia Dixon, daughter of a prostitute and drug addict named Liza. There was no mention of a father. Liza had multiple arrests and never held a job, though she once attended cosmetology school for a few weeks and later cut hair for money. Mia grew up in the lowlife, a street kid, and by the time she was ten her mother had taken to sharing her with johns for extra income.

Mia was beautiful, even as a child. Hair like a fountain and skin perfect.

Until another photo, when she was a little older. Short, hacked hair, a look in her eyes of utter despair. She could have hung in any one of Mitch's exhibitions over the years.

Mitch frowned. "Why is there so much information about her?"

"There's a court case here," Neil said, "and they dug into her background. It looks like there were criminal charges that were dropped, and later a custody hearing of some sort."

"Custody?" Dani asked.

Neil pulled pages off the printer, handing them to Dani. She summarized as she read, and her heart stood still. "Oh, God. At fifteen, Mia became pregnant. The baby's name was Kristina. Then, when the baby was two, there was a fire—" Her voice broke. She wasn't even sure why, except that her eyes had darted ahead. She kept going, more slowly now. "The State took her to court and took away the child, whose hair and face were— Oh, dear God."

"Dani?" Mitch was at her side a second later. Finger shaking, Dani pointed at a picture of the two-year-old.

"Jesus Christ," Mitch said. He bent down, looking hard. "That looks like—"

"Rosie."

CHAPTER
50

THE VALET ROLLED OFF with the Saab and Marshall held out his arm. Mia summoned a smile for him. She'd pulled out a gown she bought years ago but had never worn—a deep blue couture affair with a neckline that plunged almost to her navel. A handbag was a little more challenging—it wasn't very fashionable to carry something much larger than a credit card—but she found one that would do. So long as she didn't need lipstick or money or a mirror, she was set. She'd removed all the standards to make room for what she really needed: the list and the shears and a little .22, just in case.

They walked in, the crowd nodding and talking, drinking champagne and nibbling caviar, anticipation in the air. Mia portrayed a Kettering with aplomb, but her gaze never stopped searching. The shears seemed to vibrate in her bag, the need to finish with Cole and complete the wig like a current running through her limbs.

No one had been admitted to the galleries upstairs yet—they'd wait for the star of the show for that.

God willing, Dani Cole would be on his arm.

• • •

"She killed her own daughter," Dani said. She still couldn't believe it. "She killed Rosie. She let her burn up first and then she killed her and all those others."

"You can't be sure of that, Dani," Neil said. "Neither one of you is a hundred percent sure that's Rosie in the pictures."

"It's got to be," Dani said, but inside, she knew Neil was right. She and Mitch had only seen photos of Rosie a little older, when Janet was going through them. And these pictures weren't good.

"Let's confront her." Mitch's voice came out like chipped glass. His fingers twitched, as if he wanted Mia Kettering's throat in his hands.

"We can't," Dani said, "we need proof. Jesus, if we tip her off before we have her, there's no telling what she could do." She was getting her cop-head screwed back on now, feeling sanity creep back in. "Besides, I still want Brad and you've already got the photo set up to do that. I say we still go for it. Put him in front of that photo Russell took and see if he caves."

Mitch blew out a breath, standing with his hands on his hips. In his tux, he looked like the star of an action film, just before the star takes an M16 to a bunch of bad guys. "I'm running out of time," he said.

"Go," Dani said. "Keep an eye on Mia, but don't tip her off. Leave her to Brad. Keep everything looking normal."

"Sure. Normal." He walked over to Dani and kissed her hard, then squeezed her as if he might never hold her again. "Hurry up and get over there. I want you where I can see you."

Mitch was late to the VIP reception. For God's sake, his own opening for the biggest show in years and he decided to show up late. Mia was fit to be tied.

"Slow down, darling," Marshall murmured, laying his fingers across the top of her champagne glass. "As I recall, you didn't have any dinner. I don't want to have to carry you home."

"I'm just excited," she said. *Keep your head, keep your head.* "You know I've always been a fan of Mitch's work."

Marshall stroked her arm. "Did I tell you how beautiful you look in that dress?"

She managed a smile. "You can tell me again."

He smiled and asked, "Where did you say you got it?" A casual question.

Too casual.

A shiver tightened Mia's skin. Marshall never gave a damn where she shopped.

Then she got it: the mileage. Of course, he'd seen the mileage on the Saab from the drive to Virginia. She'd told him she was going shopping.

Easy now. "I got it at Phipps, but not today," she said. Thrust and parry. "I went all over and couldn't find a thing. I've actually had this dress a long time, you've just never seen it."

"Ah. Well, I approve."

Pointe. But Mia went on the offensive. "I know you're bucking to figure out what I have planned for your birthday. You're not subtle, Marshall, and I have no intention of telling you where I went today. So stop it. You'll just have to wait until your birthday." *Feinte* and retreat.

Marshall tipped his glass to hers, a touch of relief in his eyes. "Something to look forward to, then," he said.

Win.

Suddenly, the crowd moved in a wave. Mitch stepped in the front door of the lobby, cameras flashing like strobes, the audience erupting in applause. Finally, *finally*. Mia moved, trying to see through the heads in her path.

When she did, rage seized her: no Dani Cole.

Mitch suffered through a few minutes of the preview—the media, the smiles, the kudos for surviving something others hadn't. Normal. Keep everything normal.

The Ketterings ricocheted from guest to guest. Mia looked perfectly coiffed, as always; Marshall looked worn and worried behind his smile. Mitch was taller than most guests, able to keep his eye on them most of the time. Not always, though—there were two hundred people here and they all wanted to talk to Mitch.

He found Brad and approached with two glasses of champagne, making a show of delivering one to Brad.

"You're looking a little green around the gills," he said. "I think you should see doctor, man."

Brad sneered at him. "What are you talking about?"

"I've heard a guy named Housley is pretty good— Oh, wait. But he's an obstetrician." Mitch chuckled. "Guess you'd have no reason to see him. And, well, Christ. There's also the fact that he's dead. No, he wouldn't be of any interest to you."

Brad blanched. The tendons on the sides of his neck stood out. He spoke without moving his mouth. "I don't know what you think you're doing, but I think your public is waiting."

"Yeah, the public." Mitch glanced around, giving the impression of being pleased by so many people. "There are a lot of people here, aren't there? And all of them will see the photos upstairs tonight."

"What are you rambling about?"

"Nothing," Mitch said. "I just thought you might want

to see what everyone else is going to—maybe you'd like a sneak preview."

"I saw it."

"Oh, but I made a last-minute change. I'm sure you *haven't* seen that one. Be my guest, though. The second ballroom." He started to walk away, and added, "Oh, and pass the word to anyone else who might be interested."

In the apartment, with Neil's access to the FBI, information flooded in and none of it mattered. Austin Kinney's DNA came back from the Band-Aid: He was the biological child of Rose McNamara. The Averys came around and consented to DNA tests; chances were good that when their baby's DNA was located and tested— even if they had to exhume the body to do it—it would show that the mother was a girl name Heather Whyte. Sooner or later, her body would probably turn up in a mine shaft, with a hank of hair missing.

And at the cabin, the scene was more gruesome than anyone had even imagined. Monika's hair and fibers from her clothing had been found in the back of the truck, along with bindings that matched marks on her wrists and rags soaked in chloroform. The upstairs bedroom door had locks on the outside. The phone lines were disconnected.

The bathroom mirror had been turned into a weapon.

"The deed to the property is in Ronald Fulton's name," Tifton said. He was on speaker phone, had seemed a little excited to be chatting with Neil Sheridan. "His cell phone was in a jacket hanging by the door; if Monika had grabbed that jacket instead of the heavier one, she would have had a phone. It only has two numbers on it that Fulton called. One is a cell phone we can't identify—

probably another prepaid cell; they're a dime a dozen. And one is to Dani, last night."

"Telling me to come to the vet," Dani said.

"Right."

"Bastard," she said. "How is Ronald Fulton connected to Mia Kettering?"

"Huh? Kettering? Well," Tift said, "funny you should ask. Years ago, Marshall Kettering was his shrink."

Brad walked into the ballroom with his mind in a daze, stuck his hand in his pocket and popped a couple of blue pills. Focus. That's what he needed tonight, but he'd already taken a handful of OCs and drunk plenty of champagne. The Adderall was necessary now—to focus.

He walked upstairs right in front of everybody, not caring that everyone in the lobby was chomping at the bit to see the exhibit. He slipped into Ballroom Two and strolled the perimeter first, not knowing what he was looking for. He'd seen the exhibit earlier and had to admit, it was extraordinary. This might not be the J. M. Sheridan fans or critics expected, but it was still J. M. Sheridan. No doubt it would be touted as an inspiring new phase of his career, another facet of the man who—

Brad stopped, stumbled back a step. He was staring at himself. Himself and Stephen Housley. A two-by-three framed image, shadowy but identifiable, right in the middle of the room.

He panicked. *Where* had this come from? Were there more? There must be. Brad knew enough about photographers to know that for every shot that got framed, there were twenty or more on the cutting-room floor. He grabbed hold of his dancing brain and studied the picture more closely, trying to remember...This wasn't taken by Mitch. But who else?

The answer hit him like a brick in the chest. For a moment, Brad wanted to sob.

He heard noises, people coming, the guests coming up the stairs. Oh, Jesus, the gallery had opened. Get this down. He looked around and saw the other, right behind the door, then made the exchange and knew everything had changed. There was nothing left to do, no way he could come out of this unscathed. His father had known—taken pictures—and now Mitch, and of course, there was Mia, with her sick fetish and that damned Dani Cole.

And Brad thought, *I'll take them all with me. And Mia's going to help.*

CHAPTER
51

DANI PRODUCED A GLOCK, checked the chamber and clip.

"I thought you were off the force," Neil said.

"I am. This one's *mine*. Gotta love the carry laws in Maryland." She looked down at her gown. No place to put it. No belt, no pocket, no boot. "This is why I don't dress like this."

"Purse?" Neil asked. He was half into his tuxedo, fastening his cuffs.

"I guess." She'd probably show up as a "Don't" with a black bar across her face in some fashion magazine, but she shoved it in anyway and looped the purse over her shoulder. "Okay," she said. "I'm going over."

Neil stood.

"You stay here and do show-and-tell with Flint. I know my way through the tunnel—I won't go out in the street," Dani said.

"You sure you trust this Flint guy, and Rodgers?" Neil asked. "I could get the Burea—"

"Nah, they're good, and they know the people involved, know which judge to use." Flint and Rodgers were coming to get the information they'd need for a warrant to search the Ketterings' house. A touchy thing when everything was still speculation, but she was hopeful. "Just come get me as soon as they call with it. I want to be there."

"Dani," Neil said, as she turned and headed for the door. He looked so much like Mitch, her heart skipped a beat. "I'm glad Mitch has you."

Her cheeks warmed. "Yeah, well...Same to ya."

Brad made an excuse to take Mia from Marshall's arm, walked her to a corner, and said, "Mitch has photos of Housley and me."

"What?"

He dug his fingers into her arm. "Just listen. I took care of it for now, no one will see them. But we need them."

"How did he get them, what are they?"

"*He* didn't take them." Brad swallowed, then tamped down the sensation of a spear in his gut and said, "My father took them. He left them for Mitch."

She began to panic. Brad could feel it in every fiber of her being, the heightened sensation coiling, ready to explode. He'd taken her there many times, he thought, illogically. Only not in fear or anger.

"Relax. The photos aren't enough to put us away; if they were, we wouldn't be standing here right now. They don't know about you yet, or precisely about me. But given some time, they will."

"So we need the pictures. Where are they?"

"Mitch has them. We just have to have something he'll be willing to trade for."

Dani Cole.

• • •

Dani skirted down the back steps and into the cellar, dialing Mitch to say she was on her way. Her phone rang in her hand.

"Sergeant, it's me. I'm sorry."

She frowned. Who?

"It's me, Ter—" He got cut off. Dani stopped and strained to listen.

"Terence, where are you? What's the mat—"

A gun stabbed into the hollow beneath her ear, the phone bouncing to the floor. "You won't be needing that anymore," said the voice. A woman, her voice sultry and low. Her hair smelling of coconut.

Mia.

Careful now. Play her game. "You can't get away with this," Dani said. "Mitch is waiting for me."

"He'll wait awhile longer."

"Listen to me. We know that Brad Harper is selling babies. We know he has an accomplice—maybe you can tell us who—"

The gun nudged deeper. "Shut up, Detec—"

Dani jerked and got a step away, but a hand clamped over her mouth. Another person, a man. She fought, but he dragged her into the tunnel while Mia followed with the gun. It was Brad, she was pretty sure, and she twisted against him and took a swing. The heel of her hand caught him under the nose and he reeled back and for one split she was free and then the gun went *fwp*.

Dani froze. A silencer. Mia had fired.

"That's enough," Mia warned. She was panting, the gun aimed into the dimness of the basement, small sounds coming from somewhere among the storage items. Dani searched, her eyes taking time to focus in the darkness, and when they did, her heart nearly burst.

"Terence," she breathed. He was bound and gagged, seated on the floor. His eyes looked like moons.

"That one didn't touch him, but the next one will go right through his stomach and the one after that into his throat," Mia warned. "And thanks to Ron Fulton," she said, showing off the silencer, "no one will hear a thing."

Oh, God, Terence, I'm sorry. Dani stared, willing him to look at her. That's where Brad had come from. He'd forced Terence to call her, just enough distraction that Mia could get close with a gun, then he'd left him on the floor and dragged Dani in.

And now he was at her back. Zip-ties going on her wrists, duct tape over her mouth and around her head, two, three times around. Mia held the derringer on Terence the whole time, and a moment later, Brad had Dani's gun and phone out of her purse.

"Any memory cards in there?" Mia asked, and Brad dug a minute more, then said, "No."

Dani listened, trying not to react. Memory cards? So they *did* know about the pictures. Mitch had gotten that much done.

"Go get my car," Mia said.

"Mine's easier," Brad said. "I put it on the other side of the garage. No press back there."

"Fine. I don't care."

They started to herd Dani back through the basement and she screeched beneath the duct tape, twisting from Brad. Mia stopped and looked at her, then lifted the gun toward Terence again. "Do you want to see this boy die right now, Sergeant Cole?"

No, no, no, no. Dani closed her eyes, shaking her head. *God, don't do it.*

"Then walk with me. Calmly and quietly." She stroked Dani's hair. "There's something I need from you tonight."

The Ketterings' neighborhood—Mitch had grown up here, too. With the happy golf course and the sparkling lake and the park studded with big, peaceful homes. It was dark now, but no less happy. Quaint wrought-iron streetlamps and the low honks of geese settling in along the bank of a lake that glistened in the moonlight. The kind of neighborhood Dani had always dreamed of.

Now it was her nightmare.

Mia let Brad pull into the garage and they herded Dani into the house. Through a mudroom and kitchen, then down the hall. Dani spent the time thinking—about Mitch and Neil finding her gone, about Mia and her mother and Kristina, trying to weave something that made sense from the pieces she knew. Trying *not* to think about Terence. She knew Mitch would be expecting her at the gallery soon. When she didn't come...

Please, Mitch, sneak back over to the apartment... Take the tunnel... Find Terence.

"Go." It was Mia, her silenced little derringer poking into Dani's back. Brad walked in front of her, but he didn't seem to know where they were going. Mia gave the orders.

She ordered Dani to climb another staircase. A third story in this big mansion of a house. A giant dormer or attic.

Brad tried the door at the top, saying, "It's locked."

"Here," Mia said, passing up a key.

He worked the key and pressed the door open. Mia prodded Dani to follow, then pulled on a string from the ceiling.

A meager light fell into the room, but the space was so large Dani couldn't see much. Furniture, boxes, typical house storage. Her skin lifted into goose bumps in the chill and she wished she could rub her hands over her arms. She couldn't—her hands were bound with the zip-ties. Standard office equipment for an art museum; a suitable substitute for handcuffs. Dani had tugged and pulled all the way here, and done nothing but get her wrists bleeding.

She stretched her neck, trying to loosen the duct tape. Condensation from her breath had loosened it some, and she wriggled her lips and cheeks. They itched.

"What is this place?" Brad asked.

"Nothing that concerns you," Mia said. "Bring her through here."

Brad hauled Dani through a space in the stored items. Darker here, and cold. Mia pulled out a chair and tossed a length of cord to Brad. "Tie her up. I don't want to have to worry about her."

No. God, no. Dani wrenched from Brad's arms—she couldn't let them tie her to a chair—but he tripped her and she fell, *thnk*, onto the floor, her head smacking the wood planks. She army-crawled as fast as she could without hands, feeling her dress hike over her hips and splinters slide into her legs, but Brad was right on top of her and hauled her to the chair. He backhanded her hard, and while Mia held the gun and a wave of disorientation washed over Dani, Brad tied her ankles to the legs of the chair and wrapped her chest and shoulders with rope around the back.

For the first time, Dani felt sheer terror.

Brad straightened, wiping off his hands. He looked around again, started into the deeper shadows of the room. "What the hell?" Dani heard him say, but her vision was blurry. Her forehead bled into her eye and she thought her nose was bleeding over the duct tape. Brad walked the space and came slowly back to Mia, his eyes looking ghastly in the gray shadows from the distant lightbulb. He looked at her in something that might have been horror. "You're fucking cra—"

Fwp, said the gun.

Brad dropped.

CHAPTER
52

MITCH TOLERATED THE DOG and pony show for as long as he could. *Keep everything normal, don't tip her off.* Bullshit. Mia Kettering had sidled around the lobby with her champagne, in her designer gown and designer hairstyle, portraying the concerned charity donor. The Foundation does such good work, OCIN saves so many children, and it's all because of Mitch...

He'd tried to keep her in his peripheral vision, but it became impossible once the upstairs opened; he needed Dani and Neil. And Terence—where was he? The last he'd seen Terence, he was talking to a Channel 3 reporter.

He wandered through the ballroom, putting up a hand to ward off the people who tried to intercept him, and slid into an alcove off the back hallway. Called the apartment. "I've lost Mia again, but she's here someplace," he said to Neil. "Did you manage a warrant?"

"Two cops just left. They're on their way to get it now."

"Okay. When's Dani coming over?"

"What?"

Fingers of panic tapped at Mitch's chest. "Neil. Where's Dani?"

"Uh, she left twenty minutes ago. She should've been there…"

No. Mitch's heart began to thunder. *Dani*.

Dani closed her eyes, a moan filling her throat. Brad's chest poured blood. By small degrees, the air began to smell of blood and urine and feces.

Oh, God.

A full minute passed as Mia waited for Brad to move, and when he didn't she lowered the gun.

"He was getting to be a nuisance," Mia said, and Dani wilted inside. Mia Kettering had nothing left to lose. All she cared about was whatever twisted plan she had.

She crossed the room to large structures that looked like mesas. Dani shook her head to clear the tears and blood from her eyes and tried to see into the dark end of the room. A flood of white lights hit her eyes like bleach. She squinted and looked away, and heard two more sets of lights come on, buzzing overhead like bees. She took refuge in looking at the floor, eyes burning.

And in the growing warmth of the room, came Mia's soft voice: "What's the matter, Detective? Don't you want to see my collection?"

Collection?

Dani blinked, looking across the room.

And gagged. Horror wrapped its hands around her and she stared at the easels, her nose clogging and breath catching in her throat. It was incredible, so surreal she could hardly believe she was conscious…It must be a dream, the knock on her head…

"Do you like it?"

Mia's voice again. Not a dream. Oh, dear God.

Dani swallowed, nearly choking on bile, and Mia came

over to the chair. She looked almost serene, dressed in her bejeweled gown with her perfect face and expensive makeup—her classy derringer in hand. She looked proud. As if she were the star of her own exhibition, right here in her attic. Dani counted the easels—six of them. In each portrait, the head and left cheek had been disintegrated by some heat or chemical Dani couldn't even fathom. Rosie, Alicia, and four others. The last was Monika Wheeler.

"Why?" Dani asked. Through the duct tape, it was only a grunt, but Mia understood. She picked up a book that looked like a scrapbook. She opened it and Dani gasped. Inside were the same pages Dani had been reading tonight—court documents and the photographs showing baby Kristina's wounds.

"My baby," Mia said. "They took her from me. I fought and I fought and Marshall fought for me, too, but they took her."

Dani looked again at the photographs surrounding her. She'd made the women all look like Kristina, and yet killed Kristina, too? It made no sense.

Dani growled from the bottom of her throat. Mia ignored her, moving to the farthest easel on the right and taking down the picture of Nika. In its place, she put up a picture of Dani.

Dani stopped breathing. She tried to close her eyes, but they wouldn't obey. She stared at her own future. In the picture, the left side of her face and scalp were fried.

She swallowed, trying to think, then went wild in the chair. She flailed and tried to crash it and suddenly something hard smashed across her temple. Dani stopped, panting, and looking at Mia with wild eyes, and Mia reached down and yanked off the tape. Dani sucked in air.

"Mitch knows about you," she said, lungs working hard. "The FBI knows."

Mia was undaunted. "Well, then," she said. "Let's give him a call."

Mitch hit the back door of the Foundation at a dead run, meeting Neil in the alley outside the apartment building thirty seconds later. Neil said, "Are you sure she isn't there? A lot of people. You might have missed her."

"She never made it," Mitch told him. "She would've found me, I would've seen her."

"Okay, okay. Let's walk it. The back way?"

Mitch hesitated. Yes, she would have taken the tunnel, to avoid the media.

They jogged to the back entrance of the apartment building, down the steps to the basement door, inside—

Mitch pulled up short. "Jesus."

Terence.

Mitch yanked him up, working the bindings; Neil went around to the back of his head and ripped off the duct tape. Terence took one breath and started talking. "It was Brad Harper, and that pretty woman—I don't know her name. They took Dani."

"Was she okay?" Mitch asked and Terence gave a shaky nod.

"Okay, only they tied her up like me."

They started out and then Mitch heard a sound and his eyes snagged on something on the floor. Ten feet away against the wall: Dani's phone.

It was ringing.

Mitch stared. He knew, he *knew*. Yet when he answered, Mia's voice took him by the throat.

"I have your little whore," she said. "If you call the

police, I'll kill her. If I see one single police car pass by my street, she's dead. Do you understand?"

My street. Over by Sedalia Lake somewhere. He'd never been to their house but knew the area. His stomping grounds as a kid.

"I understand," Mitch said. "What do you want with her? She isn't a mother. She isn't a whore."

"No, but she's helping me with my gift. And with you. I want the photographs," she said. "All of them."

Mitch reeled. The fucking photographs. Christ, this wasn't supposed to happen. "I don't have photographs of you. Only Brad. You aren't in them."

"I don't believe you. I want them *all*. Once I get them, you can have your little whore back. Of course, I make no guarantees what shape she'll be in."

"How will I know which photos you want?"

"I want them all, every copy, every negative, every memory card."

"Okay." Mitch closed his eyes. Don't question her. Don't try to figure out her mind. Just do whatever she wants and get Dani back. "Where? When?"

"Thirty minutes. Sedalia Park. You remember where that is, don't you?" she quipped, then answered for herself. "Of course you do, how silly of me. It's practically your own backyard."

"Let me talk to Dani."

"How romantic," Mia said, then, away from the phone she said, "Mitch wants to talk to you." He heard a bit of a shuffle. Reminded him of being on the phone with Russell, the unthinkable happening, and Mitch helpless to stop it. "Talk to him, bitch."

"Mitch, don't come…"

His heart stopped.

"Call the police. Call Flin—*Uhnk.*"

"Dani. *Dani.*"

Mia came back. "She's brave, but stupid. And, oh, my, bleeding rather badly now."

"I need to talk to her again. What did you do to her?"

"Why, Mitch, I wouldn't hurt a hair on her head. Oh. Well, maybe I would."

Mitch squeezed his hands into fists, helplessness washing over him like a wave. "I'll kill you—"

"Don't be dramatic. Meet me beside the playground structure on the south bank of the lake."

Mitch closed his eyes. The lake. No one would be there at night, and with the water behind and the park in front, there was no place for any cops to be waiting. "The police already know it's you, Mia. There's no sense in going any further. They're getting a warrant to search your house now."

Her voice turned to ice. "Well, if you want to see Dani alive again, you'd better stop them. No police, Mitch, no FBI. Come alone. I'm in the third story of my house, I can see. If I see one single person besides you, I'll know it's over for me. And I'll make sure Dani dies first."

Mia disconnected, looked at Dani. Dani wanted to wail. Hold on, hold on.

Mia tipped her head to the side and looked at her. "There's not much time," she said. "You have to help me finish."

"Finish what?" Dani croaked.

Mia went to the table. A cloth lay draped over something the size of a basketball, and she lifted the fabric. Dani gasped. A wig. She squinted at it, not understanding. Mia pulled the wig closer and into the light, then reached up and took the pins from her hair, letting it fall around her shoulders.

Dani nearly choked. Mia's hair looked just like the wig.

"It's for Kristina," she said. "I'm making it."

Kristina? Kristina was dead. She'd been adopted by the McNamaras and named Rosie and then—

Oh, God. Mia didn't know. She didn't know Rosie *was* Kristina. Dani opened her mouth to taunt her with the fact then stopped. *A gift for Kristina... You'll help me finish...*

Don't tell her. Whatever she expected from Dani, it was to help with Kristina's gift. If she found out Kristina was dead—by her own hand—she would have nothing left to lose. Dani would be of no importance.

"Show me," Dani said, and even that bit of feigned interest nearly made her retch.

Mia carried the wig closer. "Most of it's mine," she said, touching her own hair with one hand, then stroking each color of hair on the wig. "This is Heather Whyte." She moved to a thicker strand, a burnt orange color when held up by itself. "Rolinda Sills." She went on. "Jill Donnelly. Rose McNamara. Alicia Woodruff." Then she stopped, fingering a place on the wig where the hair was still thin. She stepped to Dani and ran her fingers through Dani's hair, weighing it, measuring.

"And Dani Cole," she said.

Mitch hung up and Neil was in his face.

"What did she say?" Neil asked. "What does she want?"

Mitch turned and started up to the apartment. Neil was right behind him, Terence quietly keeping up. "She wants no police."

"I'm not police."

"She wants me, *just* me, and if she sees anyone else, Dani's dead."

Neil grabbed him by the lapels. "That's just blowing smoke. There's something she wants. Dani doesn't fit the pattern. Mia won't do her like she did the others, you've got to believe that."

Mitch broke from Neil's grasp and took the stairs, three at a time. "Cancel the warrant. Stop the police from going to her house."

"No way. We'll flood the area."

"Damn it, Neil, no. She'll make a trade. She wants the pictures. The fucking pictures I made her believe I have." He started grabbing at photo backups. Negatives and memory cards and film, into a black case. Terence grabbed some, too, and threw them in. They didn't even know what they were. "She'll trade me the pictures for Dani, but I have to go alone," Mitch said. "Sedalia Park, on the south bank, in thirty minutes. Twenty-five, now."

"Sedalia Park," Neil said, and Mitch knew he was remembering the times they'd played there. Smoked there. Taken girls there.

"It's her neighborhood," Mitch explained. "Convenient, wide open—she's probably been watching it from her house. Even in the dark, there are plenty of park lights. She'll see if there's more than one person."

"Smart woman," Neil said, looked at Mitch hard. "Smart enough that she knows there's no way in hell she can let Dani go. She won't, Mitch, with or without the pictures. The only chance we have is to take her."

Mitch closed his eyes, feeling as if the whole world was crumbling. All the places he'd been and things he'd seen, and nothing had ever prepared him for this.

He turned and paced a few steps, rubbing a hand over his face as if making the brain inside work better. Suddenly, from the edge of the room, Terence spoke.

"You two ever play in the drainage pipes down there?"

Mitch spun and looked at him. Neil did, too, and a moment later, Neil said, "Terence, you're brilliant."

Mitch thought for a minute then looked at Neil. "We still look a good bit alike, don't we?"

"Not really. I'm better-looking. The scar makes me mysterious."

"Sure," Mitch said. Brothers again. "Stick with that."

Dani sat perfectly still. The shears came out, shears that had killed Rosie and five other women. Shears that sawed at Dani's hair until Mia held two thick clumps in hand.

Tears stung. Don't fight her, not when she's holding the shears. That was no better than the gun. Besides, it's stupid to be upset over cut hair. Hair grew back. Get a grip.

Mia was making a wig for Kristina. Dear God, she didn't know. She didn't know one of the girls she'd killed was the daughter she thought she was meeting. Dani closed her eyes and thought again about telling her, but decided not to. This was Mia's goal, her entire mission. To learn it was all for naught...No. Keep your mouth shut. There was one thing Dani knew for sure, with all her heart and soul: Mitch was coming.

CHAPTER
53

MIA WAS NEARLY FINISHED: the endgame had come.

Cleanup took only a few minutes. She collected her mother's shears, the bottle of nitric acid, and her camera, putting them all in a soft leather bag. She didn't think she would need them anymore, but she might want to show Kristina how she'd done it, prove the lengths she'd gone to. As for the wig, it went into a hatbox, wrapped in tissue paper and sealed with a lid, the locks of Dani Cole's hair inside. Tomorrow was Saturday. Still time enough to finish.

Brad. Mia stuck a handful of amphetamines in his pocket, along with a little piece of label that identified them as having come from Marshall's office. She wiped down the gun she'd borrowed from Marshall, the one she'd used at the vet's office. It would go back in his drawer, along with the hair she'd already put in some of his clothes. A little wisp from Rosie and Alicia, each. One or two strands from Jill, stuck to an old jacket he hadn't worn in years. Just enough to incriminate him. Handsome man. Devoted man.

Foolish man.

And now, Dani Cole. The detective had been watching Mia's every move, cataloging each detail for court later on, no doubt, and Mia smiled at the thought. It didn't matter. Dani Cole wouldn't live to talk about what she'd seen here tonight. Mitch wouldn't, either.

Now *that* was a shame, but some things couldn't be helped.

She picked up the derringer and checked the chamber. Gave one last look to the exhibit she had to leave behind. It didn't matter—now that the wig was almost finished, the girls had no importance. All that mattered now was getting the pictures from Mitch, and silencing the one person left who knew the whole story: Dani Cole.

Mitch and Neil hiked to Neil's SUV, cutting through hedge-lined backyards, like teenagers sneaking out of the house after dark. On the way, they trashed the bow ties and cuff links but not the black jackets.

And they talked guns.

"I have some firepower under the floor in the back of the SUV," Neil said, popping open the gate of the vehicle as they got within a few feet. "Is it still against your religion to handle something? I can give you a .38—something small."

Mitch reached to the small of his back and pulled out a .500 Smith & Wesson Magnum, a gun touted as having the highest muzzle velocity on earth and being strong enough to take down the biggest game out there. Mia Kettering, Mitch decided, without a shred of compassion, qualified as big game.

"Christ," Neil said, backing up a step. "You know how to use it? You're not going to blow your own foot off or take out your big brother?"

Mitch checked the chamber with practiced hands and stuck the gun back in his belt—at his side this time, now that he didn't have to worry about his jacket revealing it. "I've probably shot as many times as you have, Neil. Almost every group I've been with in the last five years lived on high alert."

Neil smiled; he was impressed. "Let's go, then." Neil helped himself to two guns of his choice and they piled into the SUV. "You've been in Lancaster more recently than I have. Remind me of the lay of the land."

"Sedalia Park hasn't changed," Mitch said. "It's still covered with golf balls and goose shit."

Sedalia Park was an enormous spread: a five-hundred-acre lake, eighteen-hole golf course, five or six playgrounds, a sanded beach, multiple picnic areas, and wide green spaces for Frisbees and kites. The entire west edge of the lake was bordered by private residences like the Ketterings'. Until she became a cop, Dani had never set foot in the area and even then, it made her uncomfortable. She always had the feeling residents thought she was there to mow the lawn or scoop goose shit or sell ice cream on a stick out of a little truck.

Now, she walked onto the sloped bank of the lake in front of Mia and skimmed the western shore's evening lights. Which house had Mitch grown up in? she wondered, but it didn't matter. And where was he now? Certainly Neil would have backup on hand.

Unless Mia's threats had hit their mark. Dani had heard her tell Mitch to come alone. *No police, no FBI. If I see even one person besides you, Dani is dead.* Dear God, please, *please*, don't let Mitch fall for that. Please let him be sensible enough to call the police. Dani was in danger tonight no matter who came to the park to meet Mia. She couldn't stand the thought that Mitch might die, too.

Dani closed her eyes, slowing her steps through the deep Bermuda grass.

"Move," Mia said, and Dani felt the gun touch her back. Mia had picked up a coat and put it on over her gown, and draped a blanket over Dani, and it wasn't until they'd been walking through the Kettering's back lawn and into the park that Dani realized why. She was nuts, but she was still smart enough to know that the silhouette of a woman holding a gun to someone's back might draw the attention of a neighbor, not to mention a woman in a silver dress. The silhouettes of two women simply walking down to the lake, however, even with the back woman's hand stuck into her pocket, would draw no attention at all. Even on the off-chance that someone saw them.

"To where?" Dani asked. "Where are we going?"

"To a place we won't be bothered when Mitch comes with the photographs."

She nudged Dani across a wide, paved walkway, toward a set of playground equipment that looked like some giant futuristic monster sleeping in the darkness. Beyond that, another thirty yards of grass stretched out, and then the lake. It glistened in the moonlight, and a few of the homes nearest to the shore had lights that reflected on the water. But none were nearer than two hundred yards away. Too far for anyone looking out to notice anything unusual. Too dark. All Dani could see nearer by was the playground, the water, and a drainage culvert cut beneath the pavement. She could hear the trickle of water from the pipes, spilling out into a tiny bay of the lake.

They passed the playground equipment and walked a few steps farther, onto the wide slope of the bank surrounding the culvert. Dani squinted at the dark lumps that speckled the shore like giant mushrooms, then realized what they were: geese. There were always Canada geese at Sedalia Park.

But there was nothing else. Dani skimmed the area. Nothing. No one. Just a flock of sleeping geese.

"Stop here," Mia said, and Dani did. "Sit down."

Dani didn't want to be off her feet. It was bad enough that her hands were still bound. "No."

Fwp.

Dani jumped as a bullet passed her ear. Jesus, she'd forgotten about the silencer. Mia could empty her pistol out here and no one would hear a thing.

"I said, sit down."

Dani sat. Mia put down her bag and laid the hatbox gingerly in the grass. The derringer dangled from her fingers. She paced.

"So, what do we do now?" Dani asked. "Are you going to kill me and throw me into the lake?"

Mia turned, and even in the darkness, Dani could see a glint in her eyes. "No. Mitch is."

CHAPTER
54

G IBBS STREET," Mitch said, and Neil wheeled around the corner.

"I thought it was Bells Ferry. Are you sure?"

They were on Gibbs Street, and Neil slowed the SUV to a snail's pace. They'd left Terence behind—against his wishes—and impatience nearly ate Mitch alive. "Yes. There."

He pointed and Neil stopped. Sure enough, there it was. A storm-sewer grate tucked along the concrete ledge in the curb.

"I'll be damned," Neil said.

He pulled in at an angle, shedding his headlights on the curb, and they hauled ass out of the car: two men in monkey suits, wearing guns underneath their jackets. One of them about to go down into a storm sewer.

"When was the last rain?" Neil asked as Mitch worked to free the grate.

"Wednesday night. A big storm, but it should be pretty shallow by now."

"And you remember the way? It's a fucking maze down there."

"I remember. Christ, Neil, we only spent half our childhoods down there."

"Here. I don't have a flashlight, but there was a lighter in the car. Take it."

Mitch did, then patted his gun and dropped onto the ground, gripping the cement ledge with his fingers and sliding down into the cave. It was easier when he was ten, but it worked. A second later he dropped—*splash*—to the bottom.

"You all right?" Neil asked, his voice coming from the street.

"Yeah. Just a couple inches of water, not even to my ankles. Go, damn it. Go get Dani."

Dani blanched but lifted her chin. Mia was going to try to blame Dani's murder on Mitch? She was crazy. "You'll never get Mitch to obey you," she spat.

"Oh, really?" Mia reached to the bag and pulled out a pair of shears and a small bottle. "Do you know what this is?"

Don't answer. Let her go.

"Nitric acid." She lifted her brows. "You saw what it does to photography paper, but have you ever seen what it does to organic material?"

Dani hadn't, but she could imagine.

"I'll show you," Mia said and stood up. She looked around for something to use as an example, peering at the ground through the darkness. Finally, she settled for a maple leaf. "Watch." She removed the lid and shifted to find as much light as possible. Slowly, she drizzled a few drops from the bottle on the leaf.

It sizzled, the center of the leaf burning away in seconds.

Mia held it up to the moonlight. "That's what it does. Of course, I haven't actually used it on human flesh, but I've looked at pictures online. I had to know what I was ordering. Nitric acid burns are ugly. Permanent, painful, and ugly."

"Like the burns Kristina got when you were in a drunken stupor and the place caught on fire."

Mia froze, staring with the eyes of a shark. Her body was rigid with tension. "I've fixed it now. I've made it right."

"You're insane. There's no way Kristina will accept you."

Mia charged, advancing on Dani with the bottle of acid lifted high. Dani started to roll, trying to get away, but it was no good and when she looked up, Mia was there, tipping the bottle—

"Back off!"

Mia stopped and Dani looked up. A figure on the other side of the playground equipment. Mitch. Oh, God.

He strode across the lawn, keeping his distance. In one hand, he held up a satchel. In the other, he carried a gun.

"I have your pictures, Mia. Now, back away from Dani."

His voice was a growl, and Dani winced. And there was something not right about his gait. Or voice.

"Let her go," he demanded, "or you'll never get these photos."

Dani swallowed. Mitch sounded—off. And the shape of the gun in his hand...He moved a hair to the left, to peer at her through the rails of the monkey bars, and Dani's blood stopped moving.

Not Mitch. Neil.

Dear God. What had happened to Mitch? For a minute, Dani's heart couldn't seem to pump. Was he all right?

She cursed herself. Of course he was. She'd just talked to him on the phone a little while ago. She glanced around, looking for him. Nothing. But it was too dark to see beyond a few yards. Neil was mostly a silhouette.

Mia had stepped behind Dani, the gun in one hand and acid in the other. "Toss the gun to the ground," she said. Neil did; he would have expected that. "Now stay where you are and throw me the pictures."

"No," Neil said. And it *was* Neil. Dani was certain of it. "Untie Dani and let her come to me. You're going to let her go anyway. That was the deal. The pictures for the woman."

The woman. Dani cringed. He sounded like a hostage negotiator, not a lover. Pray Mia didn't notice.

"Give me the photos," Mia said.

"Let Dani go first. No deal until she's free, do you understand?"

Mia stiffened—Dani could feel it—but the gun never lifted from her back. She bent to the bag at her feet and Dani heard her rustle in it. She felt something cold and hard probe in between her wrists—the shears—and suddenly, the zip-tie gave.

Her hands were free. Hope washed through Dani in a tidal wave and she brought her hands around to the front, her muscles groaning with relief. But where was the bottle of acid? Mia must have set it down to get the scissors. Dani climbed to her feet, risking a look—there it was, tilting in the grass—but Mia poked the derringer into her ribs, pushing her closer to Neil.

"Toss the bag over here," she said to Neil, and he hurled it past the play area. Mia herded Dani to where it landed. "Open it," she told Dani. "Dump the disks onto the grass."

Neil said, "You got what you wanted. Now take them and get the hell out of Lancaster. I'm sick of walking through goose shi—"

Behind them, the ground erupted. Geese took to the air like giant bats, honking in the night, fifty pairs of wings thundering overhead. Something had startled them. Dani ducked, saw Neil's dark form running toward them, and she lunged for Mia. She stumbled, and Mia's arm swerved toward Neil. *Fwp.* He staggered and dropped.

Oh no, oh no, oh no. She hadn't heard the gun through all the noise of the geese, but Neil was on the ground and Mia's arm veered back, pointing the gun back in Dani's face. The smell of fire singed the air.

The bottle of acid was right there.

Dani grabbed it and fell across the hatbox on the ground. She wrestled the lid from the box, even as the sky cleared of birds, and a deafening silence rolled in after. She could hardly breathe. Her fingers curled around the bottle.

"Get up!" Mia snarled to Neil. Her gun poked Dani's face. "On your knees, or the next bullet will go right through her eye."

Something moved in the culvert behind Mia, a shadow rising on the bank where the geese had vanished.

Mitch, with a big-ass pistol. "Drop the gun, Mia," he said.

Mia heard his voice from behind her, looked at Neil in a split second of horror, and realized she'd been duped. Her entire body began to vibrate.

"I'll kill her," she ground out, but she had to take a step back in order to keep both Neil and Mitch in her sight. She was still barely more than an arm's length from Dani, the derringer inches from her nose. Dani shifted almost imperceptibly, freeing the box beneath her. "Stay back," Mia said, "both of you, or I'll kill her right now."

Mitch's voice came out like steel. "I said, drop the fucking gun. It's over."

No one moved. Neil stayed on his knees with his hands in the air—if he budged, Mia would shoot Dani. Mitch stood with his giant pistol aimed at Mia, but still thirty feet away. Mia's hand trembled on her derringer.

And Dani's curled tighter around the bottle. By infinitesimal degrees, she inched the bottle into the air, until it hung a foot above the wig. Quietly, she said, "Mia, look."

CHAPTER
55

MIA'S EYES HOMED IN. In two seconds, she realized what Dani was holding.

"No," she said, the breath coming out of her. "No."

Dani tilted the bottle. Twenty degrees, thirty. She didn't know how full it was. Didn't know when the acid would begin to dribble onto the hair. She saw Mia's fingers tighten on the pistol.

"If you fire at me," Dani warned, "it will spill. Drop the gun."

Tension seized the air—Mitch and Neil afraid to move, Dani afraid not to. She kept tipping the bottle. Mia's eyes went from the beady stare of a lizard to horrified full moons, and then, with one fractional tilt, a thin liquid streamed over the lip of the bottle.

The hair sizzled. Mia screamed, lunging for the bottle, and Mitch was on her in the next second, kicking away the gun she'd dropped and hauling her out of the way, shoving her to Neil. Neil gathered her arms behind her back, seeming to not notice the blood on his own shoulder. A flesh wound, Dani thought. He was okay.

Mitch bent to Dani.

"Don't touch," she said, panicked. She tipped up the bottle slowly, careful that the drip over the lip didn't touch her fingers.

"Here," Mitch said, and held up the box. The wig inside had virtually disintegrated.

Dani dropped the bottle on top of the mess and Mitch set it down, then yanked her against his body and wrapped her up so tight she couldn't breathe. Planted kisses over her face like a crazy man.

"I'm okay," she said, stopping him. She took his face between her hands and said it again. "I'm okay, Mitch. You can let go now."

He gripped her hard. "Never."

Police streamed in. They came from the direction of Mia's house, where lights suddenly came on in every room. Mitch turned to Neil. "I thought you canceled the police," he said.

Neil shrugged. "Oops. Forgot."

In ten more minutes, half the police force and a fair number of FBI agents had descended. Floodlight poured in, and Neil sat on the back gate of an ambulance while paramedics worked on the scrape on his shoulder. An agent wearing gloves and a mask replaced the lid on the nitric acid and bagged it, and they all stood around the wig for a few minutes staring in wonder.

Mia sat handcuffed on a swing in the playground. No fewer than four officers guarded her. Dani heard her say, "Marshall," and she looked up to the house.

Marshall Kettering was jogging down the hill.

"Where's my wife? Where's Mia?" Kettering asked, in the sort of daze that comes with shock.

"We have her in custody, Dr. Kettering," Tift said. "She's right over there, but we need to talk to you first."

Dani's heart iced over. She walked over to Mia.

"You tried to frame your husband," she said, still disbelieving the extent of Mia's evil. "Look at the way that man loves you, and you would have had him take the blame for killing those women." Dani looked at her. She couldn't stand it anymore. She leaned down close, speaking right in her ear. "Kristina would have never forgiven you. She would have never worn the wig. Do you know why? Let me tell you. The fourth girl you killed, Rosie McNamara, she—"

"*Mia.*" It was Marshall, coming toward them. He staggered to Dani with Flint at his side, looking like a man who had just been knifed through the heart. "I need to see her. Just for one minute before you take her away. I need to see her."

Flint glanced at Dani, who shrugged and walked back to Mitch. They watched as Kettering went to his wife. Mia looked up at him with nothing in her eyes. They'd gone hollow when the wig burned.

"Darling," Marshall said, and the pain in his voice speared through Dani. "Come on."

He pulled Mia up by the elbow. Hands cuffed behind her back, she leaned into his arms, and for a long, long moment, Marshall Kettering held her, sobbing silent tears into her hair.

Flint came over.

"Honest to God, I don't think he knew," he whispered to Dani as they watched Marshall hold his wife. "He said she was planning to meet her daughter and had a spectacular gift for her. He'd arranged the meeting. Then, he saw that Rose McNamara was dead. But he says he didn't know she had done it."

"Do you believe him?" Mitch asked.

Flint sighed. "I kinda do. Christ, he's so broken up. But I guess we'll have to wait and see what his wife says."

Dani shook her head. Noticed one of Marshall's hands in his pocket. She watched, something tugging at her nerves, and Marshall pushed the pocket between his body and Mia's.

"No!" Dani shouted and ran, but the gun went off. Mia Kettering jerked, her spine arching back. A second later, she slid to the ground.

Police descended on Marshall. He dropped the gun while on the ground, a red stain blossoming on Mia's breast. "I couldn't let her know," he sobbed. "I couldn't let her know she'd killed Kristina."

CHAPTER
56

M ITCH USED THE KEY to get into Dani's house, carrying a large portrait inside. The room was empty—the ruined furniture gone and Dani starting to think about buying new. She wasn't quite ready to move back in yet, but it wouldn't be long. Mitch had mixed feelings about the whole thing. Wanted to make sure she expected him to come with her.

He found an empty picture hook on the living room wall and hung the photo, leaving the paper wrapped on it. Then he went searching for Dani.

She sat on the floor in her dad's bedroom, Runt lolling at her side and her father's belongings spread all around her. His photograph lay beside her, an envelope in her lap.

Mitch folded down to a hassock, planting a kiss on her head. Her hair curled against his lips in a way it hadn't when it was longer. Now, only an inch or two in length, it whipped around her head in soft waves and curls. She looked like a delicate nymph or fairy, he'd told her— which royally pissed her off.

"What happened at the board meeting?" she asked.

"The expected," Mitch said, sighing. It would be a long time before the Foundation would be running at full speed again. "I'll spearhead things until we find a new director, and until we get the new domestic branch going. Then I want to mentor, like Russell did me. We've got a dozen applicants already and just announced the program yesterday. Terence is first."

Dani looked up at him, looking dubious. "Just how long do you think you'll be able to stay at home? A man like you is pretty used to adventure."

"There's plenty of adventure here," he said meaningfully. "The kind that never gets old."

Dani made a dismissive sound; he knew she still didn't believe he was in it for the long haul. He supposed he'd spend the next fifty years or so proving it to her. But she was trying. Trying to assume the best of him. Trying to be finished with her father's legacy.

She looked down, fingers on the yellow envelope in her lap. It was old and dirty and the flap worn; someone had been in and out of it a lot of times over the years. "What's that?" he asked.

Dani fingered the flap, as if still trying to figure something out. "My dad's stash," she said, and made a sound that landed somewhere between admiration and disgust. "All sorts of things that would send Ty Craig to prison."

Mitch was taken aback. "You've got to be kidding."

She snorted. "My dad may have been dirty, but he wasn't stupid. Only I didn't expect to see this name on the list." She opened a folded scrap of paper listing dates and scrawled notes. And a name: D. Gibson.

"Jesus," Mitch said. "You mean—"

"I thought so—after I talked to Craig. They used the

same turn of phrase. Gibson is the high-placed cop deal-
ing with Craig. That's why he was afraid I'd go see him.
That's also where IA was coming from. He needed me
out of the department, or at least discredited."

"That's good, then," Mitch said, his heart lightening.
"This means you could go back. Turn this stuff over to
Tifton or IA and Gibson will have to go. You'll get your
job back."

She closed her eyes. "I will—I mean, I'll turn these
things in. But I don't want to go back."

Mitch cocked his head. *I want to be your "little wife,"
barefoot and pregnant...* He caught himself. Neanderthal. "Then, what?"

"I've been thinking...You know, I was taking classes—
got my bachelor's and started some grad work. I never
told my dad...But I was talking to Keller Brookes a
couple days ago. I think I want to be a social worker, you
know? So when I take people off the streets it's not just
to take them to jail."

Mitch looked at her for such a long moment, her
cheeks colored. She stiffened.

"What?" she snapped. "You don't think I can be fucking soft and sensitive when I need to?"

Mitch took her face in his hands and kissed her
with everything he was, pulling her breath into his. His
heart and body both swelled; it happened every time he
touched her. "I think you can be anything you want," he
said. "There's only one thing I want you to be."

"What's that?"

He took her hand and pulled her up, led her to the
empty living room where he'd hung the picture. He
pointed at it. "Go ahead, take off the paper. This is the
only thing I want you to be."

Dani frowned, but her eyes glittered with curiosity. She ripped a strip of the paper down the middle.

It was a photograph of her. Mitch had snapped it in the gallery when she first came in to see his work. It was a candid and had caught her looking surprised and natural and beautiful.

She pulled back a little, looked at Mitch. She was confused. "You want me to be me?"

"Rip off the rest of the paper," he said. "At the bottom."

She did and touched the nameplate. She blinked, her eyes glistening as she realized what it said: Dani *Sheridan*.

Mitch watched, his heart at a standstill. "What do you think? You think you might come around to it someday?"

Her cheeks colored. Mitch thought he'd never seen anything so beautiful. "I might," she said. "But I may not want to change my name, you know? I have a little something to prove as a Cole. Besides," she said, coming into his arms, "it depends on whether you can come around to something."

"What's that?" Mitch asked.

"I get to drive the Cuda."

THE DISH

Where authors give you the inside scoop!

♥ ♥ ♥ ♥ ♥ ♥ ♥ ♥ ♥ ♥ ♥ ♥ ♥ ♥ ♥ ♥

From the desk of Kate Brady

Dear Reader,

I first met the hero in LAST TO DIE (on sale now) several years ago. His name was Mitch Sheridan, and I got to know him long before his brother, Neil, came around and launched the Sheridan series. Mitch was the hero of my first foray into contemporary stories and toward the end of that manuscript, I learned he had a brother and a sister. I knew nothing about either one, but became fascinated by all three Sheridans. I went on to write Neil's story and later to sell it.

That's when I came full circle back to Mitch. His original story didn't involve the maniacal murder plot expected in romantic thrillers, but Mitch himself was a character I'd always loved. Gorgeous, famous, sexy, and driven by a deep-seated need to save the world in order to redeem his own failures, Mitch required a heroine who would take the blinders from his eyes and make him face the truth instead of running from it. Someone undaunted by his fortune and fame.

Dani Cole seemed right for the job. A cop with a hard life, Dani emerged in the story as tough as the pit bull she'd once rescued. She was stubborn, independent, resilient. And she made it clear to Mitch when they were just teenagers that she could manage life's challenges without him. In fact, she preferred it that way.

Eighteen years later, when their story opens, sexual sparks fly, but Dani still refuses to let herself lean on Mitch. Now, here's where I—as a modern female author— encounter a dichotomy that's always hard to handle. I'm an educated and progressive woman perfectly capable of taking care of myself. But I'm also sucker for a man who knows what he wants. And when what he wants is a specific woman—whom he's wanted for eighteen years—I have to admit I find that pretty darn sexy. I'm not talking about anything brutish, mind you. But watching Mitch charm his way back into Dani's life and then seeing him fear she was in danger, reminded me of why I fell in love with him and his brother in the first place. It may not be very liberated of me, but there it is.

Of course, before they come around to bliss, they'll have to track down a diabolical murderer and unravel a hair-raising plot that's motivated by far more than money or vengeance.

People continually ask how I come up with such warped psyches. I can only say that somewhere between grading papers and conducting church choirs and doing laundry and running kids around and cooking meals and cleaning up after pets—twisted little thoughts sometimes niggle. It's great fun to put pen to paper (or finger to keyboard) and flesh them out!

I hope you enjoy going along with Mitch and Dani to conquer that evil killer and find true love.

Happy Reading!

Kate Brady

♥ ♥ ♥ ♥ ♥ ♥ ♥ ♥ ♥ ♥ ♥ ♥ ♥ ♥ ♥ ♥ ♥ ♥ ♥

From the desk of Paula Quinn

Dear Reader,

When I was given the opportunity to write "The Children of the Mist" series, I was overjoyed. I couldn't wait to begin and to be reunited with my two favorite characters, Kate and Callum MacGregor, from LAIRD OF THE MIST. How exciting to meet their sons and their daughter, to fill over twenty years of time in my head discovering who my new heroes and heroines were, and who they were to become. You already met the devoted, uncompromisingly stubborn firstborn, Rob MacGregor, in the first book in the series, RAVISHED BY A HIGHLANDER. His brother Tristan, the hero (and I breathe a little sigh as I type that particular word for this particular man) in my brand new book SEDUCED BY A HIGHLANDER, is nothing at all like him. In fact, Tristan is nothing like anyone in his family. Or so everyone, including him, believes. Up until my revisions for this book, even I didn't know who Tristan truly was.

He had us all fooled.

Like every other woman who meets him, I quickly fell in love with his natural charm and vibrant smiles. But it was a façade and it took me some time before I realized it. Me, his author. Even after I did, breaking through the barrier he'd built between himself and the rest of the world made him the most challenging and ultimately gratifying hero I've ever written.

You see, Tristan had been wounded as a boy. Not physically, but it's the scars on one's heart that take the longest to heal...so they say. Being privy to his entire life, I knew the event that had changed him, but I didn't want to go back and examine how it had. Honestly, it was too painful for me. Thank God my editor is brilliant and told me I needed to go back and see the event through my young hero's eyes and then write it into the Prologue.

If you've read it, then some of you might already hate me for the death of Robert Campbell, beloved Galahad in A HIGHLANDER NEVER SURRENDERS. It's okay; I hated myself for a while for writing it. But it was in the moment of the earl's death that I finally saw who Tristan truly was—the man he had wanted to become. My carefree, reckless rogue was really a knight in shin...ok, well, rusty armor. But as the fair, feisty damsel Isobel Fergusson assures him, armor can be polished.

Pick up a copy of SEDUCED BY A HIGHLANDER and follow a knight's quest for honor as it leads him to the arms of his ladylove...even if she does hate him.

Enjoy!

Paula Quinn